W9-BBR-957

Daneclere

PAMELA HILL

Daneclere

St. Martin's Press,
New York

c 1

Library of Congress Cataloging in Publication Data

Hill, Pamela.
   Daneclere.

   I.   Title.
PZ4.H648Dan   1978   [PR6058.I446]   823'.9'14
ISBN 0-312-18215-5   78-3969

One

I

HONOR SAWTREY, her abundant auburn hair spread about the pillows, lay in the great carved bed which as a rule she shared with her husband, but now for her lying-in they had taken him elsewhere. She stared at the twisted oaken poles and carved fruit on finials at the top, and then at the curtains, embroidered on heavy linen, drawn back now to let the midwife in. Between pains Honor found her cool mind assessing the quality of the linen. She should know of such things, having brought in her dower-chest a quantity of the famous Thwaite fine-spun, fashioned by her own hand into shifts and sheets. There were other things which had come with her as a bride from Thwaite; fifty head of good cattle, four mares and a gelding, gowns and caps and a great box of gold and silver coin of which she herself was to have some say in the spending. Old Hawkin Thwaite, her father, had insisted in that.

The corners of Honor's mouth turned up in a little closed smile, making the strained face comely. "Mrs. Anna will not get her hands on the coin," she thought. The box lay under her bed. Anna Sawtrey, Richard's mother, still ruled openly in most matters of the household, but since Honor had come she had begun to make her own mark, quietly. The servants respected her. Nor was it so great a thing to be Mrs. Sawtrey of Daneclere as to cause her to give herself airs that did not come by nature, and would make her look a fool.

Sawtrey of Daneclere. The name, pronounced with some awe, took her back to the day last year when she had been riding about the farm with her father and he had told her that she was to be married. The news had surprised Honor, for she was by then twenty years old and it had been assumed by everyone that old Hawkin would never part with her. She had been his trusted companion and help since her mother, who had been beautiful, had died. Both her younger sisters were wedded by then, one to a landowner in the north-east and the other to one of the Protector's major-generals in York. Neither had ever come back to visit Thwaite. Honor's brother David, who helped to run the farm, was already married to a young woman from the adjoining shire and had children, red-haired like all the Thwaites. Robin, the other brother, would marry in time. So it should have been no great matter whether Honor did so or not. She had been happy at home and had never set eyes on a man she fancied, though she had much of her mother's looks and her father's strength and had had plenty of offers.

She had not greatly like Richard Sawtrey, whom she had often seen in church.

"He is neither for King nor Commonwealth; he does not know what to believe or how to act," she thought now. Sawtrey had kept lukewarm affinities with both sides, it was true; but she would have preferred a man who knew his own mind and was not ruled by his mother.

She shut her eyes for a moment as the pains tore at her again. They did not make her afraid; nothing ever had, and she knew her strong wide-hipped body would send the child forth readily enough when the time came. From her experience, helping with the farm-women's labours as she had, let alone the foaling of mares and the calving of cattle and farrowing of sows—from all she knew it should take maybe another hour, and during that time she could have peace to think, reflect, remember.

But it was of little profit to recall days at Thwaite; those were over. Hawkin himself had said to her that only in the gravest trouble or danger should she again cross the ford.

"Sawtreys think themselves gentlefolk, like Farmiloe of Biding before he fled abroad," he had said. "Let them learn to think of ye as gentle also. Never have that madam of a Mrs. Anna, and others, say that ye are naught but a farm-wench and cannot keep away from Thwaite yard."

"But, father, you will be lonely." It distressed her to leave him, old as he was, to the farm-men and to David and his wife, with whom he had little in common. His great grizzled head with the thick brows had turned to her, and his eyes were not faded blue, like those of other old men, but bright as the sea on a clear day.

"A man is never lonely with himself and God. When none other is by me I talk to the Almighty, and He answers me. He it is who has let me send ye dowered like a princess to Daneclere, where Danes lived once, ay, our own folk, long ago. It is right that a Thwaite should return."

"Then will you visit me, father?"

"Never. They would mock ye by reason of me; I'm a plain man with plain ways. And I doubt me Mrs. Anna had traffickings with the Court, before the godly time came. She knows me for what I am, Cromwell's man till I die. No, I will never come."

He had placed a hand under her chin and made her look at him squarely. "Ye are our guerdon in the place that should be ours. Ye are the lady of Daneclere. Thwaite is naught, except to me. I will fare well enough and when the time comes, they can bury me here."

"Father, you have many a year yet." Honor had tried to stop the tears from pricking her eyes; old Hawkin despised such women's folly. He had brought her up to be hardy, like a boy. He had waited until, by a curious chain of circumstances, Richard Sawtrey was free to wed; and then he had made his offer "as though I were an animal," she had thought, resentful that all their years together, of friendship and companionship, had meant less than this; to have her the lady of Daneclere.

Richard Sawtrey should have married Meg Stillington, but for his mother.

There was no doubt that he had loved Meg and she him; she had borne him twelve bastards. She was the tavern-maid at the local inn. Even by the time she was ageing and stoutening—she grew very stout by the end—there was no question of any other woman, despite Mrs. Anna's pleas that her son should marry well. It was the one thing on which Richard proved obstinate. He thought of no one else until Meg's death. By then, there were few wives and daughters of the nobility and gentry left in England; they had all fled abroad after Naseby and, later, the death of the King. So Hawkin Thwaite's proposal had been less unwelcome than it would have been at other times, in spite of the money. A farmer's daughter was not a noble wife, but she was better than a tavern-maid. So Mrs. Anna—which meant Richard also—had agreed; and the marriage-plans proceeded, after bargaining on both sides.

Shortly before the wedding Honor's favourite brother Robin had come home and they had gone out together for a gallop. Once away from the farm, Robin had reined in his horse and she hers and they had stared across at Daneclere, its jumble of grey wings and towers with the river winding clear below. Robin was rebellious, which Honor was not. The wind blew his red hair back from his face, and he said "Can you not refuse, Honor? It will not be the same to come home, and find you gone." Robin was at Cambridge; the fact that he had been sent there, even though it was a Commonwealth community, showed the difference in Hawkin's treatment of his sons from that of his daughters. Long ago Honor's beautiful mother had pled with him to send the girls to one of the new schools the King had founded. "They will learn accomplishments, so that they may marry well," she had suggested timidly. Hawkin had turned on her with the blazing eyes of an Old Testament prophet. "Accomplishments! Ungodly music, idle songs and dancing, lace on their shifts and I know not what else! A man needs a wife who can mind his house and keep his children from unruliness, not chatter in foreign tongues and play the lute." So that had been the end of that matter, and now she was giving birth to Richard Sawtrey's child in a godly shift without lace. Her mind sped swiftly back to the ride with Robin. They had often laughed together at the old man's notions, but Robin respected his father and Honor loved him. It had not occurred to her to question or rebel against his decision that she must become Sawtrey's wife.

"I will come and visit you, then, by God, and none shall prevent me; not chicken-hearted Sawtrey or his mother either. What a bitch that is! They say—"

Honor would not listen and spurred her horse. Robin followed, his ill mood gone—he would change it three times in an hour—and they had galloped again and wheeled past Daneclere and almost to Biding and then about, so that presently Thwaite lay once more in sight, with its familiar outbuildings neatly thatched, the cottages, the house, the poultry-yard. Then they paused again; Honor raised a hand to brush the long hair back from where it had escaped under her hat, and found Robin regarding her with a deep look, one that gave her discomfort. He was generally such a rapscallion that to find him serious, even for moments, was unusual. He said in a low voice "If that fellow makes you unhappy, Honor—if anyone does, or anything—remember I'm your friend. I would not have you fill second place to Sawtrey's fat concubine."

"Poor Meg is dead. And they kept faith for many a year."

"Ay, but her sons live. There is only one Sawtrey keeps by him, they tell me; Ned, as he's called. He is a good fellow enough, but—"

" 'But' matters naught. It is my sons who will inherit Daneclere."

"You might be the old man talking," muttered Robin. "Have a care, though, Honor. You know well they say Mrs. Anna killed her husband's son, by his first marriage, when this Richard was a boy, and she'd resolved that *he* should inherit Daneclere."

"Do not gossip of that, Robin. It is nothing more than a tale; I have heard it, but there is no proof. My sons will be safe."

"May Sawtrey not be too frail to get them on you, sister."

"Now you are mocking me."

"No. I am mocking *him*."

But it had all gone as it should, in the end; after all she was with child, in the first year of marriage. She longed for the child with fierce intensity. It would be something at Daneclere that was partly her own, like the box of gold and silver.

The pains came again.

"How is it with you?" enquired a woman's voice coldly.

Honor opened her eyes and replied "Well enough, madam." There was no love lost between Richard Sawtrey's wife and his mother, Mrs. Anna, who stood now with the flicker of firelight from the hearth behind her so that it should not show up the wrinkles on her face. She had till a late age been beautiful, a living embodiment of the legend of her youth. Now both beauty and youth had gone, and truth had begun to show in the blurring of the jawline and sagging of the fine-boned cheeks. The high collar of fashion suited Anna's purpose as it disguised her neck; contrary to practice in Cromwell's England she still wore a deep lace edge to it, and kept her fair greying hair curled with a fringe as the Queen had been used to do when she was still at Court. Her gown could not have been questioned by any major-general as it was of a quiet, lavender colour; but it was made of French satin, and jewels glistened on Mrs. Anna's fingers that she herself had brought to Daneclere as a bride. She had been a Mountchurch, and in their day that family had had lands and money and the men had gambled and the ladies danced. Even yet Mrs. Anna stinted herself of little, though in effect she had handed over the Daneclere estate to her son on his coming-of-age, and to the bailiff, who lived in the house. That last was of no account, but Richard would never deny his mother anything.

Anna stared with her china-blue glaze at her son's wife, lying in the bed where she herself had been married and had given birth. It had been a bitter humiliation that at last, when death had broken his strange attachment to the Stillington woman, Richard should have had to marry a farm-wench, for so she still thought of Honor Thwaite. That riches had come with the bride meant little. But at least the heir soon to be born was Richard's first conceived in wedlock, and that was some matter for rejoicing. Measures could be taken to see that the child did not grow up a boor.

She smiled with closed lips—her teeth were beginning to decay—and murmured words of traditional comfort over Honor's state, bade her have a care to herself and the child, and moved away, spreading her beringed hands to the fire to catch its warmth. Honor's eyes, opaque with contempt, followed the doll-like figure in its finery. There was much evil in so small a body.

Had she known, Mrs. Anna's mind was troubled. She had tried to banish the trouble by thinking first of the coming child, then of her niece, Barbary Mountchurch, who lived with them and would have to be dissuaded from an unbecoming passion for Ned Sawtrey, Richard's eldest bastard, who lived here also. But her mind had gone far, far back, to the time of her own early marriage; her husband had never loved her, nor the son she bore him; his elder son by his first wife was everything. While Edwin Sawtrey lived—how everyone had doted on him, from his father down, the servants, the very horses in the stable!—her son Richard would inherit nothing, not a penny-piece; he must live in the end as a nobody, dependent on the charity of his half-brother, no doubt. Mrs. Anna had seen to it that matters fell out otherwise. One day Edwin—they called him Ned—rode off to Court to greet the new King Charles the First, whose slobbering old Scots father had lately died; and he wore a suit of red velvet with a sword-belt braided in gold, and his lace very fine at neck and wrists. When they carried him home within the hour, the lace was all dabbled in blood and dust, and he was dead. The battered, broken body had been dragged by the lurching stirrup across stony ground, for there had been a loose girth and the servants had been unable to reach him in time. Which of the grooms could have been so careless, knowing Mr Ned's headlong starts and reckless riding?

Anna knew it was no groom. None—she could swear there had been none—had seen her hooded figure slip into the stables in the flurry of coming departure, and loose the girth. But gossip and whispering had started, after the death. Was Ned so poor a rider, men said, that he would slide out of the saddle like a child learning to handle a rein? They looked about them for who it could have been, and Anna's name—she felt much injured—had been bandied about the shire and beyond.

She'd lived it down; she had kept smiling, courageous, gracious, the lady of Daneclere. But her lord had never lain with her again. Even on his deathbed—they said he'd died of a broken heart over Ned—he had not sent for her to say farewell. He'd sent for Richard, told him to fear God and mind his ways, and keep an eye on his bailiff. Maybe—the thought came to Anna now, as so often—maybe if grief had not killed his father in his boyhood Richard would have grown up a different man. As it was, she alone had had the moulding of him. Even he, who was to benefit, had wept at first for Ned, and for his father. But by degrees Anna had made him obey her. He loved her less, she knew, than she loved him; surely the Stillington woman had been proof of that? During eighteen years, despite all she could say to him, Richard had gone again and again to that blowsy bright-haired wench, and would not be parted from her to view such heiresses as Anna put in his way. Meg Stillington must have held him by magic. Now she was dead, things were better, except that the eldest bastard, called Edwin and Ned for his father's dead brother, had been brought to Daneclere to be reared as a gentleman. The rest had been put out to service or apprenticed to trades; but there was always Ned, Ned, Ned about Daneclere, as there had been when she was a bride. He even resembled the former Edwin, with his candid red-brown gaze and shock of light-brown hair, and his impulsive ways with folk and horses.

It had been a relief to her when Richard had agreed to marry, even if it were only to a farm-wench. And the young woman's manners were quiet and presentable enough. Now there was an heir coming—it must not be a girl—the farming blood might not show. Anna prayed that it might not; she still said her prayers.

How quiet the farm-wench lay! Anyone would take it for a sleep, not labour, which, as Anna well remembered, gave atrocious pain for its reward. Honor's eyes, with their curious colour like sullen storm-clouds, were closed, and her long red lashes lay on her cheeks. Her hair was dulled with sweat; she lay still.

Suddenly she gave a great cry, as if it were wrung from her unwillingly. The women about the fire, whom Anna had neither heeded nor spoken to, hurried to the bed. Within minutes the child was born. It was a son—Honor had done her duty—and Anna's eyes shone with triumph, as if the pains had been her own. She already had her hand on the door to go and tell Richard that he had a son born in wedlock, and that it was alive, for she had heard it cry.

Honor herself saw the child as the midwife grasped it by the feet, shaking and slapping it to make it breathe. She was glad when Anna went out. The pain of the final birth-stages had been worse than she had foreseen and she had only kept herself from crying out because Richard's mother was in the room. She turned her eyes back to the child, whom one woman dried while the rest ministered to Honor. How like a little, wizened old man it was, with a fuzz of light-brown hair on its scalp, looking like Richard's! Suddenly she knew that she had no love for it, any more than she had ever had for its father. Next time—there was already, in her strong mind, the thought of next time—there should come a boy who looked like her own folk, a child of Thwaite, sturdy and merry and with red hair. This changeling Sawtrey had begotten on her was no fit heir for Daneclere, any more than his father.

2

ANNA had made haste downstairs to the bailiff's office, where she knew her son waited for news: she always knew where Richard was. She found him there with the bailiff and the accounts and, seated over by the small window, the eldest bastard, Ned Sawtrey as he was called by custom: he had returned after sone days' absence. A brief, spiteful pleasure came to Anna that there was one now at Daneclere who could use that name by right. "You have a son," she said to Richard, "and he lives."

For an instant she saw the three men before her as if painted in one of the small bright intimate pictures the Dutch made and liked to have in their houses. the long-haired heads—contrary to belief a man did not cut short his hair if he were not a Royalist—and the gleaming pale linen collars, coats of dark stuff, high boots of soft leather turned over at the top of the calf. Otherwise, the three were all different. Richard Sawtrey rose to his feet, his weak pleasant face animated more than was usual. "How fares my wife?" he said.

"Well enough." It was the answer Honor herself had given Anna.

"I should go to her," said Richard, and turned and went towards the door. After he had gone, Anna was left staring at the bastard and the bailiff. Both caused her discomfort. Ned Sawtrey—he might be eighteen or more, she had forgotten—looked, her mind told her again, like his dead uncle. She turned her eyes on the bailiff, not because the sight of him was pleasant to her but because at least, in looking at him, she had not that constant reminder of the wrong she had once done. Francis Wolffe was younger than herself, perhaps not quite young enough to have been her son; once, when he had first come to Daneclere two years ago, seeking to improve his position, he had made overtures to become Anna's lover. The Mountchurch in her had rebelled at this, even while it flattered her flesh; one could not bed with a servant. Moreover, it was her mind rather than her body nowadays that desired ascendancy. She still kept it over Richard and, she persuaded herself, over the bailiff also; if he were caught cheating or wrong-doing she could have him dismissed at once. So far, she had not. The man himself did not look trustworthy, and had had to work hard to prove himself to be so. He had a great jutting nose, a thin mouth, dark lank hair not yet showing grey, and peaked brows over eyes black and watchful as a vizier's. That they could gleam with lust Anna already knew. She ignored the remembrance and said coldly "You will inform the tenants of the birth; there should be healths drunk," and then turned and went out, without having addressed Ned. She mounted the stairs again swiftly, glancing at her reflection in the half-storey window as she always did, for a dark wall beyond turned it into a mirror. She was still slender, she saw; she'd kept her figure. If it were not that she had devoted her life to Richard, she might still have lovers at Court if there were a King.

After she had left them the two in the office waited for some moments, saying nothing to one another; then with a murmured excuse Ned Sawtrey went out. Wolffe sat on for some time, his dark eyes narrow with calculation. Then he rose and, moving carefully, replaced his chair and followed the younger man, closing the door after him as he went.

The way Ned Sawtrey went led across the courtyard and round a trodden path to the side of the house, where a turret, older than most of Daneclere, loomed above its containing wall of stone.

Above, in her room which grew very cold in winter (but she would not ask her aunt Anna for a better), Barbary Mountchurch sat at her mirror, while her young Welsh maid Gwenllian combed her hair for her. Barbary's hair was very long, dark, and lustrous with health; the little maid heard the heavy tresses crackle as she pulled the comb through. Barbary sat with her eyes half closed, savouring the luxury of being ministered to. It should have been a pleasure. Her face was oval and lovely, the great eyes dark and creamy-lidded, the mouth like a ripe cherry hiding pearly teeth. The gown she wore showed as much of her bosom as she dared, and pert white breasts swelled enticingly above the lacing. By contrast, the little maid, at fourteen, was plain. She was very small, smaller than Barbary, almost as small as a child, and with no graceful languid airs about her. Instead she was deft and quick, darting about with small precise movements like a bird's. Her tiny hands were red with work—she helped about the house and in the kitchen, for Anna would not permit her sole occupation to be that of Barbary's maid—and such times, such tasks as combing Barbary's hair, were a luxury for Gwenllian also. Her face showed nothing of her thoughts; her eyes had the secret look of the old race that cannot be wiped out, though it has been driven long since into the far hills. When Gwenllian sang, her voice was sweet; nowadays one might sing only psalms, and on Sundays she led the household in its pew. Otherwise she was humble and nobody noticed her. She loved two persons at Daneclere, Mrs. Barbary and Mr. Ned. Regarding the latter, she had a woman's full passion and he was a part of her dreams, but she knew well enough he had no eyes for her. She finished combing Barbary's hair and cleaned the comb.

"That was comforting," said Barbary. She raised her arms above her head and began to twist the hair in a great knot, but in the midst of it stopped and gave a little cry. The door had swung open and Ned stood there. Barbary left her chair and ran to him, hair loose again and swinging to her waist: in moments they were in one another's arms, kissing as lovers do who have been parted long, far longer than the few days Ned had been away.

"I had not heard you were home," said Barbary when she could. "I feared you would not return. How fared you?" For she knew where he had been; it was a secret, and not everyone must know it. He had told her, and his father; that was all.

"Well enough to ride home, as you see; many can say less." His eyes, with caution in them, rested on the little maid, and Barbary turned to her and said "No more now; do not come till I send." She smiled at the girl as she went out. "That is a sweet child," she said as the door closed. "I love her dearly; I like her to come to me."

"And meant her to hear you say so, doubtless. You are a glutton for love, Barbary." He took her face between his hands, saying in a low voice "I too am besotted."

"Lie with me; there's time; they are all busied in the house by reason of this birth. Gwenllian says she hears he is a boy like my uncle Richard. That should please everyone."

His face had taken on a tender expression, more like that of an elder brother than a lover. "Nay, Bab, I'd not hurt you again as I did that day under the whins." That had been on parting; he could not help himself.

"Fool, it only hurts once."

"It is wrong when we are not wed," he said. A shadow crossed his face as he remembered his mother, and how all her days she was spoken of as a whore because Richard Sawtrey loved her and got children on her, but did not marry her. For beautiful Bab, with whom he had lain in an ecstasy unforeseen but for her pleadings, to know a like fate was unthinkable. His young body longed to take her again now as she had asked, and it warred with the prudence in his mind. He made an excuse. "There would be trouble for us both if I'd even been seen to come up here," he said. "I evaded Wolffe, I think; he made as if to follow me."

Barbary shuddered. "I mislike that man; it is like a goose over my grave, and I think he sends reports to the major-general," she said. "Ned, Ned—"

"Do you not want to hear the news?" he asked, to divert her.

"You were with the young K—"

He laid a finger on her lips. "Do not say it. But I saw him, indeed; he was close to me; after the fight—you will have heard how they lost—I guided him seven miles by the light of a lantern, and left him in safe hands."

"The K—he was by you so long?" she said, and this time he kissed her to quiet her. "Never say his name," he told her. "If you must, speak of the Black Boy, but only in certain company. The name fits him; he is tall and swarthy, taller than I, and has a wry bitterness beyond his years. One can hardly wonder at it, remembering the manner of the death of his father."

He released her and turned away, still thinking of Charles Stuart. "Despite it, he is of such a humour that it is a delight to be with him," he said. "If I never see him again, I shall cherish that night-time journey of ours all my life."

"Where is he now?" asked Barbary.

"If I knew I would not tell you, for your own safety. As few as possible know."

"But those few are loyal, as you are."

"Ay, and count their lives' risk worth the while," said Ned quietly.

"It will surely be worth it when he rides to Westminster to get his father's crown, for he will remember those who helped him in his trouble. What of all the rest?"

"Bab, keep a curb on your tongue! I doubt me that will never be for many a year; ten thousand rode with him to Worcester fight, and now there is no army. Noll Cromwell is a fine general, firm in the saddle, and behind that homely, pimpled face there is a mind worth ten of any. I do not think we will see other government in our time."

"You sound as though you would as soon Cromwell ruled us," she pouted.

"No; perhaps I am like your uncle Richard, and can see good in both sides, which makes me weak." He moved away to the small window, taking care not to be seen from below; but nothing showed except thorns and briers, and the wall. "My father sent me with money for the Black Boy, though he'd not ride to fight," he said. "When I returned today I was agog to give him the news, but dared not speak while that bailiff sat there. I shall see my father later tonight."

"I do not think my uncle Sawtrey cares for news of the war," said Barbary. "He would as soon be left in peace to play chess."

Her lover frowned; he was fond of his father. "Many gentlemen the length and breadth of England are in like state; those who are not are like Sir Ralph Farmiloe and his sons, and must leave their homes and live abroad. Most folk welcome peace, though they may not relish the manner of it, with major-generals prying into our affairs and how we control our houses and servants, and what we say. Yet in the late King's time there was little save unrest and war. Which would you have? When it comes to the root of it, all a man wants is his own fireside and some fields where he can graze his cattle. It has always been so."

"You speak like a man of forty. And *you* rode out to fight, though you told no one."

"And did little good there, for I arrived too late, and only saw the dead on the field. Bab, I have a feeling we are listened to." He strode to the door, flung it open, and could see nothing but the draughty stones of the winding staircase. But he was still uneasy.

"I must go," he told her. "I have been here overlong."

Barbary cast her arms about his neck. "Come to me again soon, I beseech you. It is lonely here. My aunt scorns me because I have no money, and the rest are taken up with their own affairs."

"Your aunt scorns most folk," said the young man grimly. He had suffered much from Mrs. Anna. "But she is pleased now about the birth of the heir, I wager, and so—'

"I am glad for Honor, but sad for you. This child will take your place here."

"I have no place, save in my father's affection. But I had it in my mind, Bab, that as he and your aunt will be pleased now about the birth, they might look kindly on our betrothal, though I'm naught but a bastard, as your aunt keeps saying,

and you a haughty Mountchurch who should be at Court."
He put a finger under her chin, raised her face, and kissed it.

"I am haughty with most folk except you," she said against
him. It was true, he knew; orphan as Barbary might be,
living on her aunt's charity and Richard's, she used high-and-
mighty manners with most of the servants except the Welsh
girl, and the bailiff in particular caused Barbary to be at her
most ungracious: she would sweep past Wolffe with her nose
in the air and answer coldly when he addressed her, if at all.

"I doubt they will never let us marry," said Barbary,
trembling.

Richard Sawtrey had gone to his wife. He greeted her with a
quick dry kiss on the cheek, and went to look at his child. For
him, this was no new occasion; but different from the many
times he had gone to Meg, with yet another baby lying
against her ample breast. In a way, he himself had always
been her child and she his mother: in their times together, she
comforted him. He missed her badly. The wife whom his
mother had made him take had relieved his debt, which had
begun to cause him to live in discomfort. But had Meg lived
he would never have wedded Honor. Or would it have been
impossible to stand out against his mother's strong will in the
end? He knew all she had done for him, even the
story—which he could hardly doubt—about the death of his
brother. He knew his own weaknesses, shown up by her
strength; he knew himself apt to be now cozened, now bullied
into submission. Honor he was certain knew of this already
and though she did not either cozen or bully, he was aware
that she despised him. He and she were not at home with one
another: each used the other with civility, but he could not
read her mind and he did not love her; she made him
uncomfortable, and he told himself that it was by reason of
their different upbringing and that she was not of his way of
life, nor could he speak to her as readily as he might have
done to a woman of equal rank. Rank! How his thoughts still
ran in the old familiar ways of the time when the dead King
reigned! Now, there was no rank except a man's ability.
Richard knew himself to be past change. He would live out
his life as he was bid. He had never had ambition to be
known either as King's or Protector's man, or to have a seat
in Parliament or even a place in county affairs. He knew that
he had disappointed his mother in such ways; she would have

liked him to be of importance. There was nothing to be done or said about it. He stared down at his newborn son, and found a thing to say to his wife.

"What would you that we call him?" She turned her head on the pillow; they had already dressed her hair and washed her and put on a clean shift, and the colour in her cheeks was even and natural. A fine strong woman, such as Meg had been, capable of bearing many sons. This he knew, but could take no heed of it.

She answered him, in the cool voice she always used to him. "It is for you to say."

"Had you no notions?" He would be as good to her as he could, would try to atone for his lack of love by giving way to her in such things. Yet she would not love him in return for it, but on the contrary would continue, he knew, to despise him.

Honor smiled a little. "Call him Richard, if you will. He resembles you."

He nodded. There was already a Richard among his bastards; that lad had been apprenticed to a miller eight or nine miles off. All of his children by Meg were grown now, the girls married or in service in other great houses, the boys well placed: only Ned he kept about him, because he loved Ned best. Ned, he was thinking now, would always mean more to him than this little creature in the cradle, hardly yet human, able only to suck and excrete and sleep. He rose; it was time to get back to Ned, to find out how the boy had fared on the brief swift journey to Worcester, made in secret for fear of the bailiff and Anna.

"Richard it shall be," he said pleasantly. "Have a care to yourself; do not rise from bed before you need."

He left her with relief. She would recover; she had no fever, and in due course he must resume his nights beside her, the ordinary relations of a man with his wife. In the dark it was easier. He would not admit even yet to himself that she frightened him; had she been less comely and assured he could perhaps have pitied her.

3

FRANCIS WOLFFE the Daneclere bailiff sat once more by his accounts-table, with a quill in his hand which travelled assiduously over the paper. To any idle observer he would have been seen to be engaged in the occupation for which Richard Sawtrey paid him. However both mind and pen were elsewhere.

The letter he was writing would be directed to the county town eleven miles distant, and ran thus. *My Dear Sir, I commend me to you and trust you are in Health. I shall send young S. from home on Tuesday with a Message by Word of Mouth that a Certain Dark Young Gentleman is in Difficulties, and needs his Help. When he shall come to the Place Arranged, there you may lay hands on him and, I trust, keep him in Prison till his Fate be clear. Certainly he helped the Young Gentleman away from Worcester, as I have Witness from his own mouth, and he may likewise be induced to part with Other Information when once he is in Custody.*

Other Matters proceed the same. There is nothing in the house to report.

I am, Sir, your Humble Servant at all times, F.W.

This done, Wolffe laid aside his quill and began to rub absently at the ink-stain on his middle finger. His thoughts were already far from the letter and its destined recipient, Cromwell's officer for the district. They ran, as they commonly did nowadays, on Mistress Barbary Mountchurch and the great desire he had that that haughty young bitch should lie naked under him upon a bed. This desire had grown with the months, often assisted by the sight of Barbary at household prayers with her bent white neck above the collar or, if he placed himself advantageously, the sight of the cleft between her pert breasts, which young madam made more visible than was seemly by drawing down her bodice and lacing it tight. So greatly did Wolffe itch to undo the lacing and have his will that he was fain by now to quell it by any means, even one as risky as he was now undertaking. Francis Wolffe was not a foolhardy man.

He had risen from low origins by a stroke of luck. Although a parson had taught him his letters, he knew what it meant to have an empty belly and no means of filling it other than to steal a loaf and risk the hangman's rope. The Civil War saved him. As it happened, the fortune of war itself had seen to it that he was deployed behind the lines as a despatch-writer, never coming face to face with the enemy; he ended nevertheless in the company of Captain John Cromwell, the General's son, with whom he struck up a close acquaintance. After young Cromwell's untimely death the father, having risen to greatness, put certain opportunities in Wolffe's way. Being eager to better himself he had neither disappointed the Protector nor, careful in his dealings, betrayed himself or any of those to whom he sent confidential reports. He developed a high regard for himself, which ended in vicious rage if any put him down, as Barbary had done. Otherwise he progressed; he, as much as anyone, had had a hand in ensuring that the young King, Charles II, crowned after his father's death by the Scots at Scone, should meet with defeat instead of victory when he marched into England. Now Charles Stuart was a fugitive, Wolffe could turn to his own concerns, and these included the ridding of Ned Sawtrey from Daneclere. Wolffe knew, as he knew most things that happened, that the young man had deflowered Mistress Barbary already in a field of whins; despite his envy the fact suited him well enough. His plans were laid well ahead; he was already in touch with a certain shabby gentleman named Jeremy Whyteleaf. Whyteleaf had drunk all of his patrimony, and was drinking still. He would have sold his soul, even given away his flagons, to marry Barbary, but had even less chance of doing so than Ned Sawtrey; neither Anna nor Richard liked him. He should however have Barbary, Wolffe had resolved; but not yet awhile. Wolffe himself should enjoy her first, and when he was sated would bring Whyteleaf into the plan. Whyteleaf had, he knew, the mating habits of a tomcat, but none of the tavern-maids with whom he lay had ever been got with child. For this reason Wolffe had selected him from among the many who would have been glad to take Barbary on any terms: he himself could amend the lack which had proved itself in Whyteleaf.

He brought his mind back from future to present, sealed the letter and sent it off by one of the grooms. The address was to a tavern, and innocent enough.

Barbary was at her window, pensive because Ned had ridden off of a sudden and there had been no time for a kiss, for her aunt was watching. Clearly Ned had not yet made the request that they be betrothed; other matters claimed his attention. Where had he gone and why? Would he be away long? Could he write to her, and if so would the letters reach her without her aunt's scrutiny? When, above all, would Ned return? Her heart ached with love for him. She had watched the erect, gallant figure, in its brown stuff coat and wide hat, canter out of the yard on the grey horse Ned like to ride, and then turn and wave, before vanishing in a cloud of dust. Barbary had returned drooping to her tower, where she passed much of the day as a rule unless Anna required her, which was not often. That lady, as Barbary was aware, must often forget that she sheltered her dead younger brother's child at Daneclere. Barbary's mother had died at her birth. Harry Mountchurch had fallen at Edgehill, in the same flank as young Nigel Farmiloe, Sir Ralph's son from Biding. It all seemed very long ago.

To turn her sad thoughts from Ned, Barbary thought instead about her aunt, whom she disliked, and from there, unwillingly, to Wolffe the bailiff, who as she knew had tried to become Anna's lover. One noticed many things by saying nothing "but I do not think he ever lay with her," Barbary concluded. A shudder escaped her; what was the power in Wolffe that made her feel at once haughty and weak? It was safest to do as she did, and despise him publicly, for instance when he ate at the dinner table with them and was not out at the farms. Once on such an occasion she had raised her eyes from her plate to find his dark, narrow gaze full on her. She had drawn herself up and ignored his gaze and the rising colour in her own cheeks, and made a point of talking with animation to old Sir Nicholas Brockbank of Favourhall, who was a guest that night and nearly eighty. Old Sir Nick had overcome his deafness, and his age, to convince himself that he was the object of close attention of a beautiful young lady, and shed thirty years in a moment. He had—Barbary giggled despite her sadness—made an offer for her next day, but cousin Sawtrey had refused, saying the difference in their years was too great. It would have been otherwise had Sir Nick had a great deal of money. "I have received many offers, but all from penniless gentlemen," she told herself thoughtfully. Indeed, in England now there were few who could call themselves gentlefolk and prosper. Most were either in Holland with the late King's sister, or else in Paris with his widow.

Be as it might, she was alone, and afraid for Ned and for herself. It would be better to go and find some occupation than sit here idle; she could go and see the baby, visit Honor—Honor was always kind, though one could not help remembering that her family were farmers and that cousin Richard was afraid of her. In the end, Barbary did not go. She fetched some embroidery, set a few stitches, then cast it down; she would have liked to talk to Gwenllian, but the girl was at other duties. It was as if nothing signified any more now Ned had left Daneclere. If he never came back, what would she do with the rest of her life? He had not told his errand, and she guessed from that very silence that it must be some matter, again, of the Black Boy.

She would pray for Ned's safety.

4

HONOR and her mother-in-law sat together in the upstairs room where the child had been born. Honor had left her bed and its curtains were now drawn close, showing the embroidered design of flowers, pomegranates and monkeys worked by a Sawtrey ancestress in the later reign of Elizabeth. The women sat now on newly carved chairs, for not every household yet had these, and for Richard, who lounged nearby, there was only the bed-step. From an adjoining closet came the fretful wailing of baby Dick, who was troubled with wind today and refused his nurse's nipple.

Honor was sewing framed work, for she disliked sitting idle. Anna and her son, on the other hand, were drinking hippocras. Anna wore a gown of palest blue, the colour of her eyes, with a deep collar of lace and a tiny apron. Her hair had been freshly curled, and she sat, as always, with her back to the light. From time to time she would survey the stump-work Honor was fashioning, with an interest not entirely feigned; when it was finished it would be a firescreen, portraying a Court lady and gentleman at their loves, surrounded by flowers. Whatever would enrich and embellish Daneclere had Anna's approval. She was almost reconciled by now to her son's marriage, which she had resented even while mooting it for the sake of the money. No one, as Anna thought now, who did not know of Honor's origins would suspect her of being anything but a lady, and her present occupation was both gentle and suitable. She even looked the part of Sawtrey's wife; the shining hair was twisted high behind her head in a great knot, and she wore earrings; her gown, while plain enough, showed the mature, graceful curves of a body which had tautened again after childbirth. Neither woman wore a cap. They might have seemed, to any stranger intruding upon them, a household group from the days when the late King still reigned.

"Where is Barbary?" asked Honor, finishing a knot. Anna drained her tankard and set it aside, shrugging a little.

"About her own concerns, no doubt," she said. "She seldom troubles us with her company." Honor fell silent and wondered, as she had done several times, if Anna herself discouraged her beautiful niece's presence at her side. There could not fail to be unfavourable comparisons made between youth and age, and Anna liked to be the centre of admiration. "She is lonely, I think," Honor put it presently. "I would gladly see her more often."

Richard himself spoke then, strolling over to where the hippocras stood and pouring himself and his mother fresh tankards of the sweet, heady stuff. "You will not drink, wife?" he asked Honor, who shook her head. Richard raised his own, and drank a health to the two women with something of defiance. He was a handsome figure today in a suit of new-cut Dutch grey cloth, and wore his sword-belt. "I had speech with Ned before he rode off," he blurted out. "He wants my permission to marry Barbary. I said that I would speak of it with you, mother."

His pale eyes slewed from side to side, watching the response of the two women. It was a tribute to Honor's strength of mind that he already included her, in looks if not in words, concerning such a matter.

Anna herself gave a shriek. "A Mountchurch marry a bastard? And what, pray, was the business on which he rode off a second time in a month? Tumbling trulls in an ale-house, like as not." Her voice rose shrewishly.

Her son looked down at his shoe-thongs, and said no more.

It was of no avail to remind Anna that young Ned was no womaniser. He was embarrassed that she should have used the word bastard in front of his wife.

"You think, then, that it would be a bad marriage?" said Honor. Anna burst in; the Thwaite woman should keep out of this talk, which did not concern her. "You have spoiled Ned, my son; he should have been put to a trade, with his brothers. Now he is getting notions above his station as I knew he would do. They have neither of them a pennyworth of fortune; the impudence of it!"

Her daughter-in-law fixed the needle safe in the silk and spoke again, hands folded in her lap.

"Then as neither has fortune, and they love each other, why should they not marry? It will not harm anyone. They are young, and we can well house them here until they find a home of their own. Ned is a willing and pleasant lad, and Barbary lacks company."

"Company! To have a love-child in her bed! No. I'll not hear of it."

"As you will, mother," said Richard weakly.

Honor rose and went into the next room where the baby was still crying. After some talk with the nurse she returned with him in her arms, set him in his cradle and began to rock it with her foot. She might not love her son, but nobody should say she did not do her duty by him. Soon his clamour quietened and he fell asleep, a dribble of spewed milk at the corner of his mouth. Honor took up her sewing again, still rocking. She had long learned to school her feeling on any matter—she had learned that at Thwaite—and the refusal of permission for Ned and Barbary's happiness, while it angered her, did not make her betray herself. "It is a pity," she thought. Then she put it from her mind, and instead thought of housekeeping.

Downstairs there was a clatter in the yard. A horseman had ridden in.

"Maybe it is the hopeful bridegroom, back from his errand," sneered Anna. "It has not taken him long."

But it was not Ned. Richard went to the window, shook his head, and turned to his wife. "I think it is your brother, Honor."

"David? Why, there must be something amiss at the farm; I will go down."

She rose to her feet, while Mrs. Anna frowned at the

mention of farms, but Richard said "No, it is the other; the younger." He could never disentangle Honor's family, though he had watched them grow up in Thwaite pew; they all seemed to him alike, a vociferous hardy, red-headed race of men and women, never weary, never defeated. He gave Honor his arm, out of courtesy, to take her downstairs; she was smiling with delight at the thought of seeing Robin. Mrs. Anna flounced out angrily. To have Thwaites come and go about Daneclere was an impossible situation, which should have been foreseen and dealt with at the time of the marriage contract. If she had known, old Hawkin was equally adamant that there should be no comings and goings. But Robin Thwaite obeyed nobody, not even his father.

"Robin!"

"Honor, my dear!"

He had bounded up the stairs before Honor and Richard descended, and brother and sister embraced warmly and then drew apart. Once back in the room, Robert Thwaite took his sister by the upper arms and held her away from him, scanning her face.

"How is it with you?" he said. "I was glad to hear the birth went well; father wrote to me at Cambridge. Where is your young rascal?" And he was led to the cradle, with a brief nod to Richard in passing, for although the latter might be master of the house everyone knew he had not had the fortune to mend its roof till Honor came.

Robin stared down at the baby, shrugged, smiled and turned away so that the sunlight blazed full on his carroty hair and the beard he affected, though the latter was short. He had his father's eyes, but with a sparkle on the sea; not very tall, he had a breadth of shoulder seldom seen even in Thwaite men. Since he had gone to Cambridge folk down here saw him seldom; but he would return.

Honor led him over to sit by her on the bed-step. Richard murmured an excuse and went to seek his mother. When the two were left alone, Robin's blue eyes, serious for once, searched Honor's grey ones.

"Does that fool treat you well?" he asked as soon as Richard was beyond the door. Honor frowned.

"Do not speak of him so. He is as good to me as he can be, and—and he is likeable enough."

"He should be faithful, at any rate, now, with the finest woman in all England in his bed, save one."

She laughed heartily. "Robin, never say you are in love again?"

"Tush, I have never been in love before! The rest were calf-moonings, but this—"

"Tell me of her," said Honor.

"Words would not describe her very well. She is small, like a wren, with brown eyes and hair. No, she is not beautiful. Our son—"

"Your son?"

"Ay, he was got at Michaelmas. He resembles Alice in colouring, but myself, I swear, in strength; he could knock your Sawtrey suckling out of his cradle. One day he will carve a name in the world, bastard though he be."

"You have wasted no time, it seems," said Honor, ignoring the slur on her son. "How long have you known this girl?"

"Ten months," said Robin impudently.

"Where did you meet?"

"Why, if you must know, I first saw her in her father's ale-house off Jesus Lane. She—"

"An alehouse-keeper's daughter?" She thought of the sour comment Mrs. Anna would make. "You will not marry her, Robin? That would be to kill our father."

Her eyes were wide with anxiety, thinking of old Hawkin alone at the farm, but Robin shook his red head.

"Never fear, neither Alice nor I would do any such thing, and her father is well enough found with the Commission to save her from being branded a wanton. In any case, I'll take the boy when he is weaned; it's all provided for."

"I will wager that it is not. You have run mad again, that's all."

"No, I love my boy."

"Yet you were uncivil about mine."

"I cry pardon, but he's a pale wretch, a Sawtrey. Next time get a Thwaite. Maybe your son and mine could wrestle together when they can crawl; it would put hardihood into your young Dick. I fear me he pines."

"He does not, and feeds well enough, but today he had wind, and so at times will your—what have you called him?"

"Hawkin, after our father. It used to be Haakon in old time, as you know. By God, I will do all I can for that boy; the best night's work I ever did was to beget him. Do you know that he can grasp my finger and not let go?"

"And what of your studies?"

"They take their place."

Honor shook her head. "You know our father looks to you to do well, and maybe get a parson's living. How will it look to have a parson with a bastard got before he even took orders?"

"There's a-plenty has 'em after. That is the more so now Noll Cromwell has turned 'em all to cant, and black clothes and shaven faces long as the devil's arm. Truth to tell I do not think I will ever make a parson, sister."

"Neither do I."

Robin's eyes grew dreamy. "My great desire is to travel and see strange lands, as Rupert of the Rhine is doing now there are no cavaliers to lead. Maybe Hawkin will sail along with me."

"Best have a degree to take along with you also, then you can earn your bread."

"There speaks the cautious Thwaite! You were never prodigal, as I am. I doubt me not this great warren is at your finger-ends, and all the servants go on tiptoe for fear."

Honor glanced carefully over her shoulder. "It is not me they fear, but my mother-in-law."

"Ah, there goes a devil's bitch. Any other woman who did what she has done 'ud have been hanged long since, but because she was a Mountchurch—"

"Quietly," said Honor.

"How is the beautiful niece? If any but Alice could cause my breeches' strain—"

"Well, you must not strain them tonight; stay and dine." A strong desire had come to her that he must meet Barbary; the pair might deal well. Robin laughed.

"Gladly, for I'm damned hungry. There was naught but cold mutton at Thwaite."

She nodded. "Give me a moment to call the nurse, and then we will go to Richard—be civil—and I will tell the servants to lay another place."

Meantime, Barbary had been surprised to receive a summons from her aunt. Might it concern Ned? Had he spoken after all? What would the answer be? Surely if it were nay, nothing would have been said; it might be, it might, that they had considered and agreed, and then—She flew to her mirror, tidied her hair—Gwenllian was elsewhere—bit her lips to make them redder, smoothed her gown, and went. Aunt

desired to see her in the dais-chamber, which seemed an odd
place to choose; no one used it now, and she could only think
that what aunt might have to say was not, or not yet, for all to
hear. Barbary went swiftly, hurrying along the flagged
passage and down the further stairs and in behind the dais in
the hall. She lifted the door-latch and went in; and there,
waiting for her, was the bailiff.

5

HE WAS before her at the door, which she would have opened
again to escape. He put his finger against his own lips when
she would have called for help, and somehow silenced her.
She was faint with the shock of finding him here; how had it
happened that she had believed such a tale?

"You must hear what I have to say," he told her. "It
concerns Ned Sawtrey." He did not say Mr. Ned. Barbary
stared at him.

"You ... know of it?" Relief flooded her; it was not so bad.
But why had he made up the elaborate tale about her aunt,
and chosen this room? Why had he not sent Gwenllian to tell
her that he wanted to have speech with her in his office? It
was true that someone might have seen her going in.

"Sawtrey is in gaol," he said, and the words were like a
chilly hand suddenly laid on her heart. She gasped: he
silenced her. His next words were deadly and cold, cold as the
tomb. "It is for you to decide whether or not he shall hang."

She would have screamed; he laid hold of her and shook
her. "Quiet, you fool; cannot you see that there is danger in
this matter for yourself also? Listen to me, and I will tell you
the part you must play." He was smiling, and his hands
released her shoulders. It was the first time he had ever
touched her.

"I ... play a part? Anything, anything. ..." It was bad
after all. It was as bad as it could be. She should have done
more to warn Ned, to dissuade him from risking his life by
any dealings with the Black Boy. It had brought him near to
death as surely as if he had been captured with those who had
fought at Worcester. Someone must have betrayed him: who?

Suddenly she was aware that it was the man in front of her. She could not have told how she knew.

"You had him taken," she said.

He was silent; he had no need to do aught now but bide his time. He was playing her, like playing a beautiful fish. The hook had bitten and she was struggling hard and gracefully, but she would never win free. He waited, and smiled. "I have always thought you had the looks of a traitorous knave," said Barbary. "Let me once tell my cousin Sawtrey of this and you shall be dismissed, flogged out of Daneclere."

All the time she was keeping her voice low: as he had said, it was a matter of great danger. For Ned to hang ... it could happen for far less than aiding the Black Boy along a midnight road. It could happen for stealing a hare.

Wolffe laughed aloud. "Have done with such stuff," he told her "If you go to your cousin, I go to the sheriff. I have enough evidence to hang Ned Sawtrey, and enough friends to set him free. I can have him put on board a boat for Holland, or else into the gallows-cart." He still spoke as if it were, all of it, some quiet jest. She felt the room whirl about her; none of this was real. Then there came reality; his hands upon her. She jerked away.

"You are boasting," she said bravely. "You have no such evidence, and I swear you have no friends."

He leaned closer to her till she smelt his flesh; he whispered in the ear. " '*I saw him; he was close to me; I guided him seven miles by the light of a lantern and left him in safe hands.*' Would not that alone hang a man? And, sweetheart, there was the rest. He praised the Black Boy, spoke of the delight he took in his company, refused to let you, his leman, know where Charles Stuart rode next, lest it harm the cause."

"So you were eavesdropping," she said hotly, and he laughed again. "You have admitted it, you little fool! I swear you and your lover have small wit between the pair of you. Why, when he said you were overheard, and opened the door to look for me, I had plenty of warning to step behind it; all he did was glance downstairs. Such a fellow will not live overlong in these times, unless others with a better brain than he defend him."

"Had he found you, it would have been yourself who had need of wit, and a strong arm." Her mind was fencing, delaying the outcome. She continued to look at Wolffe boldly, hiding her fear. He had called her sweetheart, leman, names

that were over familiar from any man to any woman, let
alone servant to mistress, or mistress's niece ... her own place
at Daneclere was not as high as she'd made play it was, that
was true. She had scorned this man openly too often. She saw
the truth now. She must act humbly in future, let him confer
with her when he would, anything, anything ... if it would
save Ned. The bailiff was answering her now; she must
listen.

"Had he found me I should have had some answer, such as
that his father had sent me to find him; it was improper for
him to be in your bedchamber, and Richard Sawtrey would
not have questioned my bringing him away. But we speak
idleness; there is more to be said."

His eyes surveyed her. She asked breathlessly "What do
you want of me? What must I do to save Ned?" Yet, already,
she knew.

He did not put it into words. His hand reached out, thrust
its way down her bodice, and felt her breast. She dared not
draw away. "Tonight," he said.

Her knees were weak, her face afire; the blood had crept
over cheeks and bosom so that all of her was rose-colour, and
she felt it and knew her helplessness. Her mind still struggled
to be cool. Unless she gave this man his will—face it, think of
it—Ned would die horribly. But had she any assurance that,
in any event, Ned would live?

"How do I know you will save him if. ..." She bit her lip;
to what had she committed herself? To lie with a servant, a
traitor, a. ...

He had stopped smiling. "I care not if he live," he said
drily. "His soul may stay in his body for all of me,
provided—" he fondled her—"my own body enters yours,
sweetheart, and soon."

How dared he, how dared he? She felt the tears course
down her face. If he had—as evidently he had—heard their
talk in the turret room, Wolffe must know that she was no
longer virgin. That was why he used her with scant respect.
Poor Barbary comforted herself as best she could. What was
she to do? But there was only one answer.

He spoke softly now, as if he had read her thoughts. "And
mark well, Mistress Barbary Mountchurch; if any should
denounce you for lacking a maidenhead, it can earn you a
whipping at the stocks for a wanton, naked to the waist in

sight of all. Would you like that? Would you not as soon bed with me?"

"You are a devil," she said slowly. She put her hands over her face. Her voice came faintly, muffled by her hands. "I do not believe that you are Satan himself; you are one of his minions, as you are a minion here."

"For every word of that you shall pay." '

"No. ..."

"Leave your door unlatched tonight. If I can come I will; if not, tomorrow. There is a moon; we will have no need of any candle."

So she was to await his pleasure. She felt her blood pounding at the insult. "It will not do yet," she said sullenly. "I have my courses." Perhaps if she delayed, there would come some plan. Cousin Sawtrey would do something for Ned; she could ask old Sir Nick, a Justice of the Peace. She could ask others; the Bryssons at Newhall, poor Lady Farmiloe at Biding, anyone, anyone.

"You are lying, Barbary. Do not play false with me, or you will regret it, as I have made clear."

"How can you know whether or not I am lying?" she asked; she seemed to have drifted far away from this room, this complacent terrible demand. Her breast felt marked by his hand. She loathed his touch, loathed him. Yet she must submit; from the beginning she had known it; the Bryssons, Sir Nick could do nothing, in these days. Gentlefolk were powerless.

"I know from the washerwomen," he said coarsely. "Now heed me. I will come when I can, and if I find your door latched, that same hour word will be sent to the sheriff's officer that evidence is available which will hang Ned Sawtrey. At present they do but distrust him, which is why they took him to gaol." There was no need to endanger himself by making clear·the part he had played in Ned's arrest. The fish was almost landed; soon she would lie gasping on the bank. The analogy pleased him. The prospect of the nights to come made his tongue pass over his lips; his mouth was dry with desire.

"It is time for you to go now, mistress," he said softly. "Before you do, kiss me."

He seized her then, pressing his body hard against hers and his lips against her own; these parted and he thrust his tongue into her mouth. He would have much to teach her, he knew, that she would never have learned from callow Ned Sawtrey under the whins or elsewhere. He was self-confident. No more nose-in-the-air manners from madam, or sweeping past him with her skirts drawn aside as though he were a leper! He himself would draw her shift off tonight: that it would be tonight he knew.

She had sagged against him, almost as though she were fainting. He gave her face a little slap. "Go now," he commanded her. She turned and stumbled out. Wolffe was not troubled about whether or not she might meet anyone; if they saw her pallid tear-stained face, it would be put down to the decision, which had circled the household by now, that she was not to be permitted to marry young Sawtrey.

He allowed himself to smile. The tale of a ship to Holland had been a lie. The fate of Ned Sawtrey, if he did not hang, would be banishment to Virginia or elsewhere so that he would work under the whip of a taskmaster for as many years as it seemed good to the judge to inflict. Sawtrey would not trouble Daneclere again yet awhile. The news would soon spread all through the house, for nothing here was ever kept secret for long. The exception was Wolffe's own secret; what would happen tonight, and the next night and the next, at leisure ... until it was time to hand the wench, well got with child, to Jeremy Whyteleaf.

"When does Ned return?" Honor asked her husband, deliberately because she did not desire constraint on the subject of the young man at Daneclere after the day's refusing him permission to marry Barbary. They were all of them seated at supper except Mrs. Anna, who had withdrawn rather than sit at table with such as Robin Thwaite; and Barbary herself, who had sent the little maid Gwenllian to say that she felt too unwell to come down to supper, and would keep her room. There were reasons enough, but Honor thought of the business of the marriage-proposal again, and was sad that Barbary should take it so hard. Otherwise all was merry. Gwenllian had come in when Honor, in company with Richard and Robin in the solar, listened as they made music together on a lute. It was a happy hour, and Honor felt the better for the absence of her mother-in-law. A motion came of how much easier life at Daneclere would be if Anna's presence were altogether lacking. Honor drove it from her mind; of no use to wish for the unlikely unless by good fortune it came about.

She surveyed her table, which as usual was a good one. The bailiff took the best part of a fowl, while Robin himself made inroads on a raised hare pie and a dish of eggs, a roast of veal and part of a sucking-pig. By the time the oranges and raisins had been put down he punished these also, like a true Dane. He had noted little Gwenllian when she came in with the message from Barbary. "Taking wench you have there," he said to Richard, who only smiled his closed smile, but Honor put in, her grey eyes merry, "Oh Robin, and what of the ale-house in the lane?" Richard noted her dancing eyes and reflected that it was by far more comfortable to be with his wife alone with her kin. That his own mother's absence contributed to the success of the evening he would not have admitted to himself. In fact, so swiftly did the time go by in music and feasting that for one of the few times in his life, he forgot Anna.

Afterwards Robin talked of Cambridge, and how the Protector, though greatly hated in royalist Oxford, was loved in his own university town. Cromwell had once been a student—a wild one, they said—at Sidney Sussex, but had settled down after his marriage. "They blame Mistress Cromwell in Whitehall for feeding 'em blood-puddings and offal, but to my mind there are worse things than a good blood-pudding. What say you, Sawtrey? And his daughters are said to be pretty wenches, going as fine in silk, lace and pearls as the Queen in her day."

"The Queen is not in silk now, poor soul," said Richard. "They say that in Paris they have not enough to feed and clothe her and her youngest child. Say what you will, it was a cruel thing to widow her and leave her dowerless."

"What else could they ha' done with such a King but cut off his head?" demanded Robin, who had drunk too much wine to stay within the limits of caution, though he knew that bailiff fellow had listening ears. "The next cry will be Noll for king, though they say he was offered the crown before and refused it."

"Now that he has beaten young Charles Stuart it matters little whether or not he wears the crown; he is king in truth. None in this country or abroad can prevent his doing as he will. Rupert of the Rhine is aground off Ireland, and they say grass grows between his deck-planks. Nobody save Rupert

could match now with Noll, and Rupert has neither the
weapons nor the men, though his spirit is still unbroken."

"There are many, many broken spirits and broken hearts
in this war. Lady Farmiloe for one will never forget Naseby."

But the men were not disposed to discuss sad matters, and
Honor rose soon and said she would go to visit Barbary. She
was sorry Robin had not had the chance to see her tonight;
there would have been less talk then of the little Welsh maid.
Surely no man could sit close to Barbary in a room and have
eyes for any other? "It is like enough he saw her gallop her
pony, when she was a child," Honor thought, "but now—"

She found the girl face down on her bed, and did not chide
her, as Anna would have done, for spoiling the counterpane.
Had Anna had any heart, she thought, she would have
broken the news of the refusal of the marriage gently,
explaining why it was unsuitable. Barbary turned a white
face to her when she called her name.

Honor sat down by her, on the bed. "It is nothing, I shall
be better in the morning," said the girl, as if she had said she
would be dead. Honor laid a hand on her forehead, to feel for
sweating. There was none, and she said "Would it not be
better if you ate some food, child? I can have them send up
perhaps the leg of a fowl, and a cup of wine."

But Barbary shook her head and then burst out weeping.
So bitterly did she continue in it that Honor in the end took
her in her arms, forgetting the difference in rank there had
always been between them. She, the farmer's daughter, knew
how to comfort. "It is not an illness," she whispered, "is it,
Barbary? Is it because of Ned, and the marriage? Believe me,
you will make a fine marriage yet; but without money it
cannot be as it should, and you—"

Barbary sat up. "Honor, never say I said it, tell no one,
promise you will not tell."

"I promise, if it will serve."

"Ned is in prison, and like to hang. If you say a word of it
he will hang indeed. Never say I told you, never."

"How did you hear of this? It is but a short time since he
rode off."

"I cannot say. If I tell you, he will hang. But I cannot stay
here alone any longer with no one knowing, no one. ..."

Honor knew it had been better not to ask concerning Ned's
latest errand. Least said, soonest mended; it occurred to her,
for the first time, that perhaps Richard already knew what

had befallen his son; but if so, could he have been so gay tonight? Loving Ned as she knew he did, he could not have been both anxious and merry.

Nevertheless she said to Barbary, to comfort her, "It may be your cousin already knows of this. Would you not have me speak to him, privately?"

"No—no—he can do no good at all."

"He is of some standing in the shire." Honor herself was not sure of this. Richard Sawtrey's politics were now here, now there; he had no standing either with the erstwhile royalists or with the Cromwellians. "A word from him, perhaps a guinea or two, might ease matters. Permit me to speak of it."

When she left Barbary the girl seemed cheered a little, though still quieter than her wont. She had not told Honor how she had found out the news. She could never tell anyone that.

Two things were to prevent Richard's learning of his son's fate in time to avert it. Robin Thwaite was to sleep at Daneclere, and late into the night they played at cards and chess, and the men drank together while Honor waited for her chance to speak. She did not want to do so in the hearing of the bailiff, nor would it have been wise to draw Richard apart from the others lest they guess something was amiss. When the drinking and playing went on late into the night she pleaded weariness and went to bed; when Richard came up, she had decided, she would acquaint him with the news. In any case there was nothing to be done till morning.

But a rider came. It chanced that Wolffe was the one who heard him, and went out. A letter was handed over superscribed with Richard Sawtrey's name, The bailiff took it, gave the man a coin, sent him for ale, and put the letter in his pocket. Tomorrow would be time enough to give it to Sawtrey. He knew the writing.

Afterwards he opened it. He could always plead the excuse that in the poor light he had thought it was for himself. It ran *My Father, for God His Sake get me out of the Place I am now in. They took me yesterday and since then, I have been Chained in a Foul Cell, with Others it is true, but who they be or what they have done matter nothing in this, that I think they will Hang me or send me to the Plantations if they are suffered soe to do. If you will come to me, and it is said I am*

*your Sonne, there may be some Good come out of this matter.
I have no Hope otherwise, as Few know of the Affair or why
I rode out. I pray this reaches you. I have Paid the Gaoler to
find a Messenger.*

    Your sonne, E. Sawtrey.

Wolffe had lit a candle. On reflection he decided it would
be best to know nothing of the letter. He held it to the flame
and watched it burn. Outside the window the moon had risen
and he bided his time till the house should be quiet and he
could go to Barbary: he cursed the card-playing to which he
must return. He went back, and they played for a further
hour. Richard Sawtrey had lost money and wanted to win it
back, and ended by losing more; by the finish, he said with
the smile which could charm men, "I have pockets for sale;
Robin, you have cleaned them out. Will you to bed?" Robin,
yawning, said that he would go. He was lighted to his room
despite the moon, and Richard went to join Honor. Presently
the bailiff crept upstairs to the tower.

Honor was awake. She found Richard cheerful, and ready
to lie with her. She let him do so; it was rare to see this sad
man happy. Later, he fell asleep in her arms, and she thought
"I have not told him of Ned yet; but what can be done till the
morning?"

Between them they had conceived a second child, who
would take Ned's place if anyone could do so.

6

RICHARD was awakened by Honor shaking his shoulder; the
light of early morning was grey in the room. He blinked up at
her, resentful at having his sleep disturbed; the heavy plait of
her hair swung between them. Swiftly and quietly she told
him of Ned. At once he was awake. "Why did you not tell me
before?" he said. He was less angry than despondent.

"I would have given you the word last night, and had
meant to do so when you came up. But there was nothing to
be done till day." She blamed herself now, and in some way
shifted the blame to him, this thin-faced man with mouth
agape and light greying heir tousled above pouched eyes still

half-filled with sleep. She knew he was prodding himself into action he could scarcely deal with; in such situations Richard was lost. When he spoke at last, it was what she had expected to hear.

"Does my mother know?"

"Why should she? You are Ned's father, and can surely aid him." The sharpness of her reply was unlike her habitual courtesy to him, and she heard her own words with a kind of disbelief. She watched him leave their bed and struggle into his gown, and go, with bowed shoulders like an old man's, to his mother. Honor was filled with scorn; any man who called himself a man, any man of Thwaite, would have been down at the stables in instants, saddling his horse. But Richard must confer and delay. Well, it was partly her own fault; she should have told him the sooner.

Richard found Anna breakfasting early; a half-eaten manchet of bread and a mutton-chop, already picked clean, were by her. She still lay abed, as she liked to do till the household tasks were finished. If questioned, she might have admitted that at her age she felt disinclined to exert herself except by her tongue, and disliked being seen in morning light. But no one would question her.

She received his kiss and put a hand to her hair, which straggled beneath a night-cap and showed many strands of grey. "You come at an ungallant hour." she said. Disregarding this, he blurted out the news of Ned. "What am I to do?" he said. "Should I ride over to see the lawyer, visit Ned?" But she put out a hand and he felt its sudden small dry strength, detaining him.

"You must not show yourself in this; it will only harm you," she said. "Already there are those who point at you for a secret royalist who aids the King; whatever coil Ned has got himself into, he must rely on himself to undo. Young men are rash, and the punishment will be a lesson to him."

"The punishment may be death, mother."

"Do not speak so. They will keep him cooling his heels for a while, that is all."

"But, mother—" She neither knew of the day's harsh times nor had ever sympathised with his feeling for Meg's son, dearer by far to him than his other children or the baby in the cradle upstairs. Suddenly he thought of the bailiff. Wolffe was discreet; he should be sent to look into the matter, bribe

officials if needed, offer to pay a fine. Being Richard, he told
his mother, who shrugged.

"Do as you will, for I am weary of it," she said. "Your
bastards ate up all your youth."

She watched him go, not in contempt as Honor had done,
but with the possessive affection she felt for him at all times
and despite everything. She hoped the plan for freeing Ned
would not succeed. It would be unsuitable to have him in the
house again after refusing him Barbary's hand.

Richard found Wolffe already in his office, busied over
accounts. The man had an air of sleek well-being, and
Richard envied him his lack of care. He himself felt weighed
down with it, and to have displeased his mother made him
miserable. Wolffe set down his quill in its stand, and rose to
wish his employer a good morning. His face lacked all
expression as to why Richard Sawtrey should have visited
him in a bedgown. Richard told his tale, and was relieved to
hear the bailiff offer to do all he asked, without queries or
trouble; a good, obliging fellow! He would see the lawyer,
and the major-general and the commissioners; if possible, he
would enter the gaol itself, see Mr. Ned, and bring him
comfort, money and messages from his father. "I would not
write, sir; one never knows what harm a letter can do,"
Wolffe said.

Richard agreed and bade the man take enough money for
his needs. "You will hardly ride there and back in a day," he
said. "Stay overnight at some inn, for your refreshment."

But Wolffe seemed anxious to be back that night. The
news would come the sooner, he said.

All of that day they waited, or rather busied themselves to
make the time pass. Honor ordered the maids to brush the
curtains, wash sheets, take down all the jars of pickles and
preserved fruit and dust the shelves on which they stood, and
replace them; she herself went to the dairy and grimly
churned butter. This, she well knew, was a day on which it
might turn, for a disordered humour was not the best in
which to do it. Yet it came out sweet and full by the end, and
she plastered it down in the great crock cooled in water,
sealing it at last with salt dripping. She felt no weariness; it
was as if a demon drove her, and she did not even take time to
go up to see Barbary, who still kept her room. To bring her

no news of Ned would be cruel, and there was none yet to bring.

Barbary crouched in her room. Her body was filled with languor and her mind with shame. She did not understand what had happened to her; loathing, still felt for the man Wolffe, was strong in her, yet when he had entered her body it had ended in a kind of madness, a wanting, a sweet flood she had never felt with Ned. He had handled her, stripped her, as Ned had never done, and had shown neither respect nor pity; yet she had clung to him, by the end, and would have cried out with deep pleasure had his mouth not stopped hers, and it had happened like that twice ... was she a wanton? She did not forget Ned. Yet if Ned had come upon her now, she could not have looked into his eyes. How was she to face them all—she must go down—at supper? Wolffe would be there, no doubt. She could not look over at him lest her face show what lay between them. Tonight he would perhaps come again, perhaps not. She tried to will herself that he might not, but knew in her heart that she wished he would.

At supper, he was not there. No one mentioned where he had gone. Barbary felt a sense of loss, of injury. She would not lie awake tonight waiting for him, for he might not come. He might not come.

It was market-day in the county town when Wolffe rode through. He felt impatience at the busy scene, the throngs of folk and the stalls of cabbages, eggs and bales of cloth and cheeses. Laden carts and full booths impeded his progress and made it difficult to find a place to leave his horse, for the inn-yards were full. In the end he found a place, promising a coin to the ostler's boy for minding his beast.

He found the lawyer's house easily, for he knew him of old through estate business for Sawtrey. A clerk admitted him and took him to his master. The latter made him welcome and they sat down. Wolffe told his tale.

The lawyer placed his fingertips together in a way he had. "What we must establish is the source of the information," he said, speaking carefully; care was necessary, more so than ever, in the present state and practice of the law. He stroked his shaven chin with his hand. "Whence came the evidence, if such it is, that the young man had treasonable activities with

Charles Stuart? Such rumour, not cut and dried by the
presence of witnesses, could free him for very lack of
substance, and for this we must play."

Wolffe replied—he had concoted this story as he rode in,
foreseeing the lawyer's doubts—that the young man had
himself spread the tale, when in his cups, about the ale-house.
"He is rash and forthright, and many persons have heard it
from his own lips," he said The lawyer looked grave.

"That was great folly, and makes our position the harder
to sustain," he said. He was distressed; he had served Richard
Sawtrey for many years. "A pity, a pity!" was all he could
say.

Wolffe passed the prison, but did not go in. Instead he
hurried up a further rise in the steep cobbled street to where a
half-timbered building reared, at the door of which he
entered. Here he knew his way inside and was known. Before
long he was seated opposite a dark-clad individual, whose
shoulder-length hair brushed a linen collar of no great
cleanliness. The Protector was not given to it and others
copied him. The table was cluttered, as the lawyer's had
been, with scrolls and quills.

Wolffe stated his errand. Edmund Cheveley and he had
been comrades together in John Cromwell's force. They were
not close friends, for Wolffe had never made any. However he
murmured about old times' sake.

Cheveley said "It could be a hanging matter," coldly, as
one accustomed to both words and fact.

Wolffe began to argue with the preparedness he had
fostered on the way here. "Richard Sawtrey is known for a
waverer," he said, "and this young man took money—"

"Sawtrey's bastard, you say. I hear he has several."

"This is a favourite with him. A hanging sentence would
be likely to turn the father from us, no doubt leading him to
send larger sums of money to Charles Stuart and his friends."

" 'Tis a simple matter to stop that, Frank."

"Maybe not so simple. Richard Sawtrey is not disliked; he
is a weak, amiable man. Where one leads, others may follow.
There are many, as you well know, who say that to have
made a martyr of the late King was to increase our enemies a
thousand-fold."

"We can deal with our enemies," said Cheveley quietly. "I
cannot alter the course of justice for a supposition, Frank."

"Nor should you. What I would suggest, if you will hear me, is that there be no hanging. That would make a martyr of the boy also. A place below decks in a ship bound for, say, the New World is better. On the plantations he may sweat out his rights and wrongs till men at home forget him."

He smiled. A sudden look of dislike showed in the other's gaze, but Wolffe ignored it. Cromwell the Lord Protector was an honest man; but honesty made poor servants. "I will do what I may, but can promise nothing," Cheveley told him.

With this hope Francis Wolffe rode away. If she were to ask, he could at least tell Barbary with truth that he had done his utmost to prevent them from hanging her lover. As for the prison, he had not been able to gain admission. He occupied the remainder of his ride with lascivious thoughts of Barbary, remembering how the moonlight had shone on her white naked body as he forced his way into it. He had warmed her well by the end: he doubted if such as Ned Sawtrey would ever satisfy Barbary again. Tonight, once more, when he had seen Sawtrey and the rest were all abed, he would return to the turret and continue his pleasurable teachings.

His mood was cheerful; so much so that he tossed an extra coin to the boy who had held the horse, to that urchin's astonished delight; and rode off.

7

IN THE low-built farmhouse at Thwaite, old Hawkin stumped between fire and candle, alternately re-reading and thinking about a letter which had come earlier in the day. It was from a near kinsman, the son of Hawkin's own uncle, his mother's brother; she herself had been an east-coast woman and for generations her family had owned trading-vessels that ran between Veere, Genoa and Scotland. So long had they followed their trade, handed down from the Scandinavian pirates in the long ships, that it saddened Hawkin to read his kinsman's news. For Arnulf Jansen was sick. Hawkin remembered him as a tall broad fellow with bristling blue-black hair and brows, unlike the greater number of the east-coast folk, who took after the blond Danish and Norwegian ancestors settled in the ports after long-sea-roving. Now Arnulf's hair would be grey, but still had the spirit of the sea-rovers.

I have a Growth in me, the letter read, *and the Physicians say I cannot last the year. My Thoughts are for my Sole Surviving Son, whose Brother as you will know was drowned two year since off Heiligen Land. The Younger Boy is Sickly, and although he hath a Brave Spirit and would goe to Sea, I do not think that that Lyfe would prolong his. I have therefore kept an Interest for him in the Trading Vessels soe that he will not Lack for Fortune, and I greatly desire that he shall be about some Occupation which is not of the Sea, say a Farmer, once he had bought a Piece of Land. He is young yet, but Sixteen Years Old, and his Mother being dead I would that Uthred might be with some one of his Kin, who would have an eye to him until he be Perfected in Wisdom. It would please me greatly if Uthred may come to you, and I will tell him to Obey you in all things as he would myself. He is a good Lad. If you will not take him, I know not where he may Goe, for all about here are Seafaring Folk, and I would have his Mind Turned from this.*

The letter finished with some enquiry about Hawkin's own affairs and health, for the sick man had employed a notary to write for him at length. Hawkin wished his eldest son David were in the house, that he might discuss the whole question with him, but David had ridden to market and would not be back till late. Of David's wife Joan, who would have the care of the boy, Hawkin reckoned little; she was a fool, fit for nothing but the bearing of children, which she did copiously. But there was still room for Arnulf's son at Thwaite. Hawkin wished, not for the first time, a thing he would never have admitted aloud; that his daughter Honor were home again, with her quiet wisdom. But his pride would not let him ride to Daneclere, and he had told Honor not to come here. It went without saying, in any case, that he would take the lad. Loving the land as he did it would be a pleasure to instruct Arnulf's boy in the use of a plough and harrow, the feeding of the beasts and care of calves and foals; it would do his health good. "Also, if he hath the wit, he shall follow Robin, and go to Cambridge," the old man thought, for he had a respect for education although he himself could do little more than read and write.

He sat down and, laboriously in the light of the candle,

with his tongue protruding between his lips like a
schoolboy's, wrote to Arnulf Jansen, saying he would gladly
shelter his son. The boy would be no charge on him, he knew;
it was evident he had been left well provided for. Altogether
there was nothing against the matter, and it would comfort
Arnulf to have the news before he died.

Barbary solaced her body's need by means of the hard thrust
of the saddle against her thighs, and her mind's pain—no
news had come of Ned, she might never see him, or hear of
him, again, for how could they meet and love now, when she
was soiled?—by touching the mare to a gallop. Fields, fences
and steadings flew past, and the wind tore at Barbary's hair,
tugging ebony strands from under her hat. At such a speed
the fact of Ned's fate, of her own, seemed as nothing. She
must put the past from her; and yet, loyalty itself bade her
remember. She was near the place where she and Ned had
lain in a time that seemed long, long ago; she would say a
prayer there for Ned, that he might come out of prison; and
for herself, that she might not lose her soul.

She had begun to cry, and the wind made the tears stream
across her face. The quickset hedge, blurred with tears, lay
before her. She mopped at her eyes with her sleeve and
guided the mare through the gate, dismounting for this, then
put the gate back on its latch and regained the saddle.

The knoll where they had lain stood up with others against
the flat landscape, guarded by the whins from being overlooked by Daneclere. Barbary scanned the field about her.
The distance from here to the knoll seemed less than it was;
to reach it took her several minutes. There seemed no one
about. She let the mare canter gently across the intervening
grass.

Suddenly—it was as though he had been an apparition, not
flesh and blood—that other was there, emerging from the
whins. He hadn't come now for four nights. She had wanted
to forget him, but now. ... the sight of him made her
remember, made her forget, blurred her mind as though tears
fell there, made of her a wanton uncertain thing. ...

She drew a breath, and tried to turn the mare's head. It
was as though she had no strength. "When he comes to me by
night I am bewitched, and now by day," she told herself. She
watched him come, with long confident strides as though he
were sure of her, knowing she would not gallop the mare

away. Why could she not turn and leave here? Why not
fasten the latch on her door in the tower of nights? He had
done less than he promised for Ned. There was no more talk
of a boat to Holland, nothing to force her now.

He was beside her. He had taken the mare's reins and said
evenly "We will tie her to a branch. She is a docile beast, and
will not escape." He looked up and gave his narrow smile at
Barbary in the saddle; then lifted her down in his arms. At
his touch, she knew that she would not resist. She could no
longer think of anyone or anything, or remember why she
had come.

"How did you know I was here?" Her tongue was dry in
her mouth; but at his touch her knees had turned to water.
She heard him laugh.

"There are not so many ways to ride," he said. "I saw you
go, and walked to meet you here across the fields."

So he had known, from the beginning, where she would
come. She was aware of a sense of futility, yet at the same
time an intense and burning excitement. She felt him lay her
down in the green secluded place. She closed her eyes in order
not to see the very branch, silver-white and ancient and
twisted, which had borne green shoots and yellow blossoms
while she lay with Ned. Then it has been Ned's hands which
gently removed her hat, loosening her hair and running his
fingers through it. It had been Ned who—

Wolffe took her swiftly, riding her at last with strong,
certain thrusts till she cried out in ecstasy. Later he made
desultory love to her as if her conquest, once again, had been
made certain, as with a lawyer's seal. She could not resist
now, had no wish to; she let him open her bodice, fondle and
kiss her breasts, slide his hands round to her waist and back,
ease her skirts up over her loins and handle her. Soon we will
all of us be dead, she thought; what does it matter with whom
I lie? But she was avid soon that Frank should enter her
again, and raised her body and urged him until he satisfied
her. It was she who spoke, afterwards.

"Tonight you will come again?"

"I do not know," he said idly. "I have to meet an
acquaintance at the tavern. We may part company late."

He turned away to fasten up his breeches and Barbary
became aware of her own state, lying before him tousled and
half naked. She pulled down her skirts and sat up and began
to lace her bodice. "Then you will not come?" she said, trying

not to give voice to the pique she felt: he had used her, and now would do as he chose. "Perhaps I should latch my door," she thought again, but knew she would not.

Ned. She had meant to come here and think of him, pray for him. She had not even asked Wolffe if he had news. This place would never again be the same; they had fouled it. The faded whins had no more blossom, and the twigs lay pale and broken upon the ground.

The inn Wolffe had mentioned had in times past been called the Salutation, but the orders of the commissioners had caused it to be renamed. Wolffe's acquaintance was already seated at the fireside table, swilling ale. He wiped his sleeve across his mouth and rose to greet the bailiff, with gait already a trifle unsure. He was a short, plump fellow, with a red face and hair and moustaches of so light a yellow that they seemed pale by comparison with his countenance. He might have been thirty-five. He had the defensive bluster of one who is shunned by his neighbours, and this was the case; in the first place his father, who belonged to a shire family, had disgraced himself by marrying a citizen's daughter because he must. He had been ostracised by his kin although not, in the end, cut off; but his son's way of living kept him constantly in debt. However Whyteleaf's open-handed manners were those of a rich man. He beckoned the inn-maid imperiously with one stubby hand.

"Ale for m'friend here, d'you hear me? And more ale for m'self."

It was brought, but before that Whyteleaf had turned eagerly to the bailiff. "Well? How fares it? Did ye commend me to Master Richard Sawtrey? How fares Mistress Barbary? Why, I cannot sleep at nights for thinking on her." He fingered his moustache lovingly. Wolffe frowned a little.

"Do not bandy names in a tavern," he said in a low voice. Whyteleaf beamed, and obeyed; it was difficult to offend him. " 'Tis not my tongue I would employ, and that ye know well. Such a wench would cause a man's member to rise on his very deathbed. Lack of a dowry? I'd repair that state, as well as her other."

He drained more ale and said "Ye spoke to Sawtrey?"

"It is of little use to speak. He will not hear of you or the marriage."

Whyteleaf's jaw dropped, though he had been told the

truth often enough. "I cannot bear any such answer," he said. "What's to be done, Frank? Ye've a good head; use it for me, I beg. I'll make it worth while to ye, as well ye know."

"The plan I have in mind will cost you a purse of silver."

"That is nothing, nothing at all. What must I do? Tell me of't."

"Hold your tongue meantime. That is the most difficult part."

Whyteleaf roared with laughter. "Forsooth, ye are an insolent scoundrel. If 'twere not that none other can do me the favour I seek, I'd have ye out, gentleman or not, blade to blade. Tell me what is to be done; but first let us drink the health of a certain fair young wench in ale. I spoke no name; I mark my lesson."

"That is well. I will tell you some of it, but not all; that way it will be easier for you to keep silent." He lowered his voice again. "The matter is that with the wench's maidenhead gone—"

"Who says 'tis so? Has some blackguard—"

"Not yet. It is for yourself to take it. With that done, and if you can contrive to get the girl in the family way—"Wolffe smiled to himself; that would not happen"—they will be more than willing to take the first offer, for they will be in haste to see her wed. Even Sawtrey of Daneclere can ill afford to risk his women's good name, though the men do what they may. Young Ned, the bastard whom you know, is still in gaol, awaiting a ship to the Americas; all the lawyers his father employed, and all the silver he spent, did not avail him. He will be gone soon, but not before we have put him to some use."

Whyteleaf dragged at his moustache with one hand. "What has all of this to do with me, if her mind is still set—I've heard 'tis so—on young Sawtrey?" They had begun to bandy names again, but there was no one else in the room; the fire flickered, casting wayward shadows.

"Listen. I shall send her a message to say he has escaped, and would have a word with her; and when she comes, there you yourself will be standing, with a dark cloak wrapped about you. It will be night. Need I tell you what to do? We will choose a sheltered place, among the trees; the moon now is thin and will scarce light the way."

"And I am to—" Whyteleaf's colour deepened; the stare he turned on Wolffe made the other, for the first time, apprehen-

sive. If this plan failed, he had no other; and Barbary showed
more signs of cleaving to himself nowadays than to Ned
Sawtrey. It would reassure him to see her wed.

"Was that not what you wanted?" he said to Whyteleaf.
"Once she is yours for the first time, other times will follow
in the marriage bed. Within a month, or at the most two, you
should have your reward. I swear Ned himself shall never
come nigh her, for he will soon be gone."

"They were ever close," grumbled Whyteleaf.

"A youth's and maiden's fancy, holding hands and riding
out side by side! They have known one another from
childhood. Have no fear; when you try her, you will find
Barbary virgin. I swear it by all I hold dear." That was true
enough, he was aware; there was nothing he held so, except
himself. He smiled, and savoured his ale, turning the flagon
in his fingers. The other's bloodshot eyes stared at him, as if
even a fool's caution bade him hold back.

"You are over certain of yourself. You speak with too great
a familiar—a familiar—Mistress Barbary, Mistress it should
be to you; what are you but a servant?"

Wolffe said nothing. Whyteleaf grumbled and fidgeted for
a time, then suddenly burst out with "What if—what if she is
not willing, and I—"

"Then you must ravish her. Do not let her know you. That
will be easy with the cloak and the dark. She will blame
young Sawtrey, thinking he hath learned rough manners in
prison. By the time it is proved he did not win out, you and
she will be wed; have no fear."

"You are over certain with your prophecies." Whyteleaf
was sulking still. The bailiff smiled on.

"If I were not, how could I put such a proposal to you?
Would I dare do it?" That should flatter the fellow, make him
puff out his chest. Half-men were given to boasting of their
prowess with women. If he did as he was bidden, Wolffe had
the plan ready; some of it depended on Barbary, and her
unquestioning obedience to his will. He thought of her,
fleetingly; he was not yet weary of her, and looked to enjoy
her often after she was married to Whyteleaf. That fool
would never know of it.

He put up a hand to hide the broadening smile he could
not control. On the crucial night, when Whyteleaf thought he
was piercing Barbary's maidenhead, Barbary herself would

be safe beneath Wolffe in her own bed. Of that part he could make certain, without aid.

At Daneclere, supper was laid and the family sat about the table. They were silent, even with Robin again as a guest; there was some matter on his mind and he did not banter as usual, but kept his eyes on his plate. Honor, preoccupied with her pregnancy, ate little, for as always when there was leisure she was thinking of the coming child and praying that he might not be like his brother. Young Dick was upstairs with his nurse, hardly fit even yet to take other than pap; he had been slow in learning to speak and to crawl. This other child must be different, her own, a Thwaite; how often had she said it to herself? She raised her eyes for an instant and cast a glance along the table to where her husband sat brooding. he would be thinking, she knew, of Ned, and of the fact that he could do nothing to save him. But Robin should not be silent; what in the world ailed him?

Barbary sat nearby, sunk in her own thoughts. She and Robin had paid scant heed to one another. Mrs. Anna, nearby, was tight-lipped with anger; the upstart, Whyteleaf, had approached Richard again for Barbary's hand, as if a Mountchurch could ally herself with a vulgarian; and when turned away yet once more, had shown an unbecoming resilience. "I shall return, and maybe then you will be glad to see me," the little man had said. What would befall at Daneclere when she herself was no longer here to guide her son? There was some evil in her side; she often felt it nagging, and at times had to bite her lips when the pain, sharp as labour, would come. It was not so bad tonight; maybe her anger had changed its humour. But Barbary should as soon never marry at all as take such as Whyteleaf; she still bore her name.

Richard Sawtrey picked at his food, trying to conquer the easy tears that rose to his eyes at thought of Ned. He had gone to see the lad in prison, and had had more luck than Wolffe said he had in being allowed in; he had found the lad in a filthy cell, and had given the turnkeys money to find him better quarters and better food. He had tried to cheer the young man with promises, but those he could never fulfil; there was no averting the sentence of banishment. Honor had said—he was coming to rely on Honor more and more, she had sense and foresight—that it was fortunate they had not hanged the boy, and that they could at least make unceasing efforts for his return. Even in the Americas Ned would still live, could perhaps in the end be released to come home ... and meantime one must not think of the fever-stricken voyage, the overseer's whip, the heat and slavery. "In the King's day it would have been different, and I could have saved my son," Richard thought. But the King's day was over.

"Time may reverse fortune," Richard found himself murmuring aloud, and looked about the table to see if any had heard him and thought him foolish. Try to think of other things ... but what? The boy's face, white against filthy straw, could not be put to the back of one's mind or forgotten. It came between Sawtrey and his thoughts now, and he had no appetite.

The bailiff ate in his own place and said nothing, as was proper.

Nearby, Robin Thwaite brooded over his pasty. Before leaving on this vacation he had had news that angered him. Alice had been married to a haberdasher. Her lover felt a personal sense of insult. At the least, though, they would give him the child; he'd bring up young Hawkin at Thwaite, give him everything his heart might desire, and still make a man of him. Hawkin should grow up in his father's close shadow. The child's grandfather and namesake had raised no objection. The old man, Robin knew, would be glad of more company. Only ... to have arranged such a marriage without telling him, so that when he had come to the ale-house and asked for Alice they had said she was gone, and left him looking a fool! Women. ... He had no desire for any other. He was restless for new experience, some matter far removed from the softness of girls' flesh and the easy slaking of his desires. Young Uthred Jansen, now at the farm, was such a one as himself, eager for far places, some enterprise which called to the blood and guts in a man, without thought of reward beyond the ordinary. Perhaps now Robin had obtained his degree his father would let him travel a while, see strange lands and places. Meantime his boy would be growing out of babyhood, and when Robin returned young Hawkin would be old enough to put astride a pony. Joan, David's wife, could look after him with her own brood, though his very eyes were different from theirs, being dark and fierce. All his life those eyes would remind Robin of

Alice, wed now to her haberdasher, her pliant body in another's bed.

They finished their meal and rose, for the women no longer withdrew as had once been the custom. As they went out Wolffe murmured to Barbary "I would have a word with you; be at the office in a few moments." He saw her toss her head and grinned to himself; the old Mistress Barbary Mountchurch, who had swept past him time and again, had shown for that moment. If she altogether lost her haughty quality, and clung to him like any other snivelling wench, he would cease to desire her, he thought; it was the earlier hard conquest that fired him. And in the office, at least, they would not make love.

He went there. After a quarter-hour she came, her cheeks flushed. "I do not want any to see me here," she told him. "They will know we have some matter between us that should not be, and they—"

Wolffe swung her about the shoulders and kissed her, then set her back against the door. His hands dropped. "What I have to say must be brief, and you must hear it now," he said. "Listen to me carefully; this must be passed on to no one, not Richard Sawtrey nor any other; you hear?"

"How can I promise when I do not know what it is you would say?" she replied sullenly. She stood there before him, her bosom heaving; the nearness of his body made her breathing short and quick. He told her, swiftly, what he had planned to tell her. "A message has come from Ned Sawtrey. He has escaped from prison." He saw her eyes dilate. "He would speak with you tonight, in the near wood, and asks you to bring money."

Her mouth had dropped open, showing the gleam of teeth. "Ned free?" she said stupidly, as if he had struck her. "Ned?" She buried her face in her hands, and fell to weeping. Wolffe took her and shook her roughly.

"Plague take you for a little fool!" he hissed. "What will they say indeed if you leave here with your face all blubbered with tears? Dry them, for both our sakes."

"I dare not go to him as I am—I—"

"That is as well, for I would not permit you to do so."

"Not see Ned?" she said then, like a child. "But he has sent for me, he needs me, and I—"

"He does not need you; what he needs is money," Wolffe

told her brutally. "Send it by a messenger, someone you may trust; your maid."

"Gwenllian? But she would be afraid, and he would think—"

"Suffer him to think what he pleases. I tell you this, Barbary: if you go out to meet Ned Sawtrey this night I will never come to your bed again. He may take you if he will, or go alone to foreign parts. For you to accompany him would put him in double danger; you must know it. A woman would be a burden to him in escaping."

She thought of the King, whose escape last year had been made easier by a young woman, Jane Lane; why could she not help Ned so? But, as always, Frank's presence made her less than herself. She could not flout him; if she lost him she would yearn bodily in a way she had never done for Ned, had never known she could do. She could not bear to lose Frank now.

"I will send Gwenllian," she said submissively. "Tell me when and where in the wood she must go, and what she is to say."

"Why," he mocked, "you must send him your love and a purse of silver." He turned to his table. "I have the last here, at any rate," he told her.

"You—you are sending him money?" She regarded him with eyes like stars, brimming with late tears. "Why should you do so, Frank? You are kinder than you would have me know."

"I do it for you," he lied, and showed her the purse she must give to Gwenllian. The girl was to wait at a certain tree. "Tell her to draw her hood well over her face," he said. "She must not be known by anyone till Ned comes."

"Yes, I will tell her—and, oh, Frank—"

"What would you? he asked, although he knew.

"Will you come tonight? I do not think I could lie alone in the dark, wondering—"

"You shall not lie alone," he said smoothly. He was jubilant that all of the plan had fallen into its place so far. He must see to it that Jeremy Whyteleaf should be full of ale when he came, and the less liable to notice the Welsh girl's lack of height, her absence of long rich hair. And if the silver purse was indeed given to Whyteleaf, he would return it with more, much more, full of boasting as he would be on the morrow, at the inn.

A sliver of moon had newly climbed the sky: it would give a faint light, enough to see by when one dare not take a lantern. Gwenllian shivered; she was afraid of the dark. "Folly to fear a wood you know well enough by day," said Barbary. She was torn between anxiety and envy of the girl. If she herself could only have set eyes on Ned once, only once! But she was not as she had been, Barbary whom he had loved and known. She did not know who she was; it was as though a mirror would reflect only dark shadows. It was better that Gwenllian should go.

"It is the great birch, with drooping branches, where the bracken is," she reminded the girl. The bracken would crackle underfoot where it was brown from last winter. "Put on my cloak," she told the maid, "and draw the hood well forward; 'tis better than your own, and hides the face." There must not be trouble for Gwenllian over this. "Do not stay long," she said. "Only give him—give him my love and—and this."

She thrust the purse into the girl's hand and watched as she crept out and downstairs. Then she closed her door. Beyond the transom she could hear Frank breathe; he waited for her. Perhaps he would be angered that she had sent her love to Ned. Defiance claimed her and she did not care.

He came to her quietly. The light outside changed and wavered as clouds drifted over the moon. "I wonder how they are faring," she breathed. There was at least no wind tonight, and little cold. Ned waiting in the bracken would be safe … safe. …

She forgot him then; she was turned first to water, then to fire, by the new magic. She could think of nothing but being here on the bed, naked, with Frank. The lost moon no longer showed at the window. Barbary moaned in ecstasy, and Wolffe prolonged it, as was now his purpose. There was no sound from outside, from the wood, at all.

Later there came a whimpering at the door, as though a puppy wandered in the dark. Barbary flung on a bedgown and went out. The girl was lying on the steps, her face in shadow, sobbing. Barbary's heart stopped beating. "Did they come and take him?" she said. "Tell me, tell me—" She should not have trusted anyone but herself; should have let Frank go from her if he chose. It was only while he was within her that he could charm her. Ned—

Gwenllian raised a face that was swollen with crying. "He—he took me. He did not say a word. It might have been anyone. He threw me down on the bracken, and—and did it there. Then he went away."

"Child—"

She sat down by Gwenllian on the step; if only Frank were not still behind them in the room! She put her arms about the stricken girl and tried to comfort her. All the time the thought nagged at her: this is what Ned wanted me for, to be his whore again. After the time in prison he will have needed a woman. Prison changes men. It was only for that, and the money.

The poor child. Thrown down on the bracken, not a word spoken. He must have altered greatly. There was blood slippery on the step, blood sticky on her own gown. If I had gone, she thought, it would have happened to me.

"Let me sleep in your chamber tonight. I am afraid to be alone." The voice, dry with sobs, held Welsh lilting; the hood had fallen back from the child's head, showing hair still smooth. He could not even have looked at her face, or touched the hair.

Gwenllian must not come into the room, to find Frank there. Barbary remembered the fact almost idly. "Go to your own room," she said, gently.

"But I am afraid."

"Do not be so. It is over now. You are safe in Daneclere."

After the maid had gone she returned inside the room, her gown wrapped close about her. A distaste for Frank had entered her; he must go, she must have time to think, and plan ... what? Ned had gone by now, having done what he had, and she—

"You must go," she said aloud. She heard him laugh. He came over and deftly stripped her of the bedgown. "Are you afraid I will follow Gwenllian?" he said.

He bit her flesh. It was as though triumph made him mad. He took her with a force he had never used before, thrusting apart her thighs and holding her down, entering her not as a lover but as an enemy, a victorious foe after long battle. His mouth crushed hers and she could neither sob nor breathe; half-fainting, defeated, she felt her womb yield. Now again he possessed the core of her, she was nothing and no one, time was nothing, nor the world outside, with Ned making off to some other hiding-place with his money, sated. Sated ... she herself, like a wrung rag, must endure to the end what lay within her; the man had no pity, he would not leave her though she cried aloud as the sky paled towards morning.

She did not remember his going. She awoke to broad day, finding the bed empty except for herself, and dried blood on her bedgown to show that the night's horror had not been a dream. Her body ached in every bone and fibre; her flesh was bruised.

It was on that night, or on the one following, that Wolffe, of set purpose, caused Barbary to conceive.

"The poor wench cried piteously; 'sblood, had I not steeled m'slef with good ale, I had not the heart to break so tight a virginity. But the thing is done, by God, and done well."

Whyteleaf caressed his moustaches. Wolffe, smiling, turned his flagon in his fingers. "You will be able to torment her with the lack of it on your marriage-bed," he said.

"A good jest," said Whyteleaf, wiping his mouth with his sleeve. It was stained with wine and blood and ale.

8

AT THWAITE, a young man knelt in the shadowed steading, greasing a harrow. He was not tall, and had dark hair and very blue eyes which gave a direct, impersonal stare at what he first saw until he decided whether or not he liked it. If he did, the glance would soften. His mouth was broad and generous and his hands, the bones of their wrists outshooting his sleeves with growth, were large and reddened with the weather. He continued the job with the harrow conscientiously, but not as though his heart were in it. In his mind there lay not the green fields of Thwaite, the lowing of beasts brought from pasture, the neat rows of turnip-tops thrusting up through the ploughed soil, but the sea; a great eternal vista, in all its moods and colours; grey-green with lashed white, foamy crests of waves; prickled sparkling blue beneath the sparse east-coast sun, running silver currents in the morning, broken by the black shapes of trading-vessels or inshore fishermen. This was his love and had his heart, and when he had a moment to himself on the busy farm it was to dream of the wharves again, with their living silver catch emptied from the nets still writhing on the stones, while fish-wives argued, in a dialect unlike any other, a price to fill their baskets for sale in the streets. Their tongue was part Danish, like himself, and held words and intonations that the English did not, and the folk there were his own folk and his father lay buried among them. Here at Thwaite, though they had tried to make him feel at home, Uthred Jansen was a stranger. But he would work. There was no self-pity in him; he already thought with affection of old Hawkin, who was teaching him all he knew about the land, and he was fond also of dame Joan, who spared time from her growing brood to launder his shirts—not mend his hose, for that he did himself, and could knit also—and feed him with good farmhouse fare.

And he loved Robin Thwaite, and Robin's son. The last was a little devil now, already stumbling about the steadings; he feared nothing, neither man nor beast. Uthred would have liked such a son of his own; perhaps one day he would father one, but at present he was shy of women.

He finished the greasing and wiped his hands on a rag, saw a stray chick which had lost its way, for its mother nested in the back straw beyond the outer draughts; deftly caught the tiny fluffy creature, stroked its back with a finger, then went and replaced it carefully under the black hen's wing. Already she knew and trusted him, and made no fuss.

He straightened and went out. Beyond, the sky was dappled with cloud; a good sailing day. The blue gaze stared for instants at Daneclere on its rise, while Uthred recalled that Hawkin Thwaite had a daughter there he never saw. In time he would learn why; patient waiting to learn such things would have made a sailor of him, and now would make a farmer.

He turned towards the farmhouse, and went in. Hawkin, whose bones ached nowadays, sat in his place by the fire. Joan Thwaite was nearby, smoothing linen with a flat-iron. She was a fair-skinned woman of thirty, whose hair straggled constantly from beneath her cap because she was always too harassed to replace it, and her face was flushed with the heat and the ironing. She was the heiress of Bents, a farm in the next shire, which would go to David on her father's death.

Uthred nodded to her and went over to Hawkin, who looked up from beneath his bushy brows.

"Well?" he said. "Is all done as I told ye?"

"It is done. What would you have me do now?" He waited for instruction, as a servant might have done; but he had dignity. In a few months even Hawkin would trust him enough to leave him to his own devices about the farm. Now the old man mumbled that it was nearby time for their dinner, and Uthred might as well stay and warm himself before the fire. As he said it, two young men opened the door and came in. One was David, the elder Thwaite son, stocky and taciturn, whose interests were all in farming and who, for recreation, begot children on his wife. These would soon begin to assemble from their various tasks about the house and farm, wary eyes fixed on their grandfather. A smell of cooking had begun to come from the hearth, where a great cauldron steamed.

The other arrival was Robin, newly back from travels to London and France. it had been an aimless journey; as his father had said, all he had done was spend good money. Robin went at once to where Uthred stood and when the other turned and saw him, a smile spread over his features and his eyes shone. There was a strong bond between Robin and Uthred. Many a night since the wanderer had ridden home the two young men had sat up till the fire dropped to ash, exchanging tales of Cambridge and the fisher-port and Cheapside and Paris. It had been agreed already by them that, when it might be done, they would take a far journey together. Whither it was to be was not yet decided, but Uthred saw in his mind leagues of sea, and a ship ploughing through it as Hawkin's well-greased harrow ploughed the soil. They would find some matter at the journey's end to make them rich, or at least to cover the cost of the voyage. Such had always been the way with their roving ancestors, both Robin's and Uthred's. They shared the dream.

Two of the children had appeared and were shyly clinging to their mother's skirts. "Find the bowls, and lay table," said Joan. "The men are hungry."

"We are as hungry as they," said the elder, who could be pert. "Do as you're bid, and then we will eat the sooner," replied her mother. Joan shook her skirts free; she was carrying yet another child in her belly, and her temper today was uncertain. A fine lady such as Honor Thwaite had become would lie abed late if she were pregnant. Here, men took their pleasure and the women bore the pain, and did a day's work as well; mending, washing, ironing, baking, cooking, brewing, nursing babes and sick folk, salting meat, emptying chamber-pots, sewing clothes and curtains, all that and more. Joan said nothing aloud, but put the iron back in its place by the fire and folded away her linen. They did not trouble with anything on the table but platters, knives and bare wood, except at feastings, and these nowadays were rarer, for one could not keep even Christmas any more for fear of a fine. At a wedding, perhaps, or a funeral it might be allowed to folk to be merry; even the Lord Protector did so at Whitehall, when his daughters were wed. But there would be none of that at Thwaite for a while: all Hawkin's own daughters were married and the young wenches had not yet grown. "And pray the Lord we have no funerals," thought Joan, thinking of her own father at Bents; he was good for many years yet, but when he died there would be Bents to see to as well as Thwaite. As for old Hawkin, he would live for ever.

Joan overlooked the table, to see that her daughters had done their duty; then she herself went to the fire, and began ladling stew into the platters from the great pot, while the men sat down at the long benches. Hawkin said a grace, and they began to eat, with no sound breaking the silence except the supping of stew and the munching of bread Joan had baked that morning, and which was fresh and good.

9

"I—I THINK I am with child."

She stood with her body flat against the closed door of the office, palms laid flat against the wood. Wolffe paused, quill in hand, and scanned her. "It would not surprise me," he said smoothly.

He did not look at the flush which spread over Barbary's neck and face, but returned to his accounts. Yet he did not truly see the columns he was apparently adding; he saw Barbary's body as he knew it well enough, and the thought of it caused, even now, a stirring in his loins to which he must not give way. He waited for some moments in silence; if any came in, they would find no more than a house-servant with his mistress's niece. "You should not be here," he reminded her. She drew a sharp breath.

"That you should speak so to me! I do not know what I am to do and I—"

"You must marry."

The cold, brutal words might have come from a stranger. Barbary clenched her hands till the nails marked the palms; her bosom heaved as if she would cry out, but when she spoke it was with calm, even scorn. "How can I marry you—a servant?"

"You cannot. I already have a wife."

"You—"

The hands flew to her mouth, as if to stifle a scream. Wolffe laid down his quill. He was smiling good-naturedly. "If you had asked me, I would have told you," he said. "We were married when we were children. We have never dealt well together, and she lives with her kin in Somerset." He stared boldly now, having himself well in hand; the lie had bolstered his self-esteem. There was no wife in Somerset.

"You have lost nothing," he said. "Had you been forced to make such a proposal to your aunt and her son, we would both of us have been turned out of Daneclere without a penny." He lowered his head again, and made as if to scan his papers, adding a figure here, a note there. "You will find a bridgegroom readily enough," he told her. "But it should be done with speed, before you begin to thicken."

"How greatly I loathe you, " she replied. She had turned to go, her hand on the latch, and Wolffe exerted his will to bring her back; presently her fingers fell. "Then you will not have me in your bed again, my pretty?" he asked her, and laughed. Suddenly she covered her face with her hands again and began to weep, with great sobs that shook her body. "Be quiet," said Wolffe sharply. "They may hear, and come in. What would they say if you were found in tears before—a servant? Never fear, I have a plan."

"You are a devil. You planned it all from the beginning. What is to become of me? If you know, then tell me. It is your fault I am as I am. You forced me to yield to you over Ned, and now—"

"Thoughts of Ned will not avail you. How fares the Welsh

maid? Had you gone to meet him that night, you would weep
now for his cause, not mine."

"How did you know—how do you find out everything—"

"Nothing stays secret in a house such as this."

"I have had no more news of Ned," she said sullenly. "As
you know so much of matters, tell me where he is."

"Why, would you follow him, after the way he served
Gwenllian?" He lowered his eyes for instants, to hide the
amusement in them; the little fool did not yet know Ned
Sawtrey was still in prison and had never left it, nor would so
do, as far as anyone knew, till a ship waited to carry him to
the Indies. He himself must set events on foot briskly, or the
sum Whyteleaf had promised him on the consummation of
the marriage would elude him. So far, he had been fortunate;
Barbary had even aided him unwittingly by lending the
Welsh maid her own cloak. Gwenllian—he remembered the
name as useful to him—had gone about her duties since that
night quietly as was her wont, with reddened eyes downcast
like a nun's. He doubted if Whyteleaf could have made her
pregnant. "The best you can do," he said to Barbary, "is to
go to Mrs. Honor with your tale. She may make matters
easier for you when your aunt hears of is, as she is bound to
do."

"My aunt will kill me. I cannot tell anyone. I should be too
greatly ashamed."

"Your shame will make itself manifest soon enough. If you
will not to go Sawtrey's wife, then go to Sawtrey. Either way,
you must find a bridegroom." His voice dropped. "If you will
do as I say, you may escape your aunt's rod."

"I did as you said before, and what has it led me to but this
pass?" She wept still, but more quietly, and he knew she was
weakening. He remained as he was, seated; he had neither
risen at her entry nor bidden her sit down, and it had diverted
him to speak to her of Sawtrey shorn of his prefix.

"Go to Mrs. Honor," he said again. "She will handle you
with kindness. Tell her—does anyone of the household know
your maid was ravished?"

"You yourself knew. I cannot tell who else knows," she
said, and stared at him as if she would read his mind. "Why
ask of it?"

"Because you may use the tale to account for your state.
Say to Mrs. Honor that you were ravished in the wood, by I

know not whom—say by Jeremy Whyteleaf, who would
marry you."

"Whyteleaf? That creature?" She burst into tears again.
Wolffe began to see that he must woo her, not scorn her, if he
were to gain aught in the matter. Barbary was thinking of
Whyteleaf with revulsion. He ogled her in church, and had
more than once, she knew, asked Richard for her hand. To
have such as Whyteleaf in her bed!

The bailiff sat smiling and still. All her life she would
remember him as a triumphant, smiling devil. She would
never, never again—

Wolffe rose. He came to her and laid his fingers on her
wrist. At his touch Barbary flushed more deeply, and her
breathing grew faster. She did not draw away.

"I can be your lover again," he said, "if you will marry
Whyteleaf. The man will do you little harm; his boasts are
greater than his prowess."

"You—you have not come to me for long—"

"I will come, be sure."

"How can I endure to bed with Whyteleaf? He stinks of
ale."

"He is so drunk on it, sweetheart, that we can lie three in a
bed, and he will never heed it. After he is asleep I will come
to you. I will come often."

"I do not believe you. You are weary of me, and—and
would be rid of me in this vile fashion."

He caressed her. "Do you think I could lose my sweetheart
so easily? Have I no heart? As you need me, mistress, so do I
need you."

"But you do me harm—you get me with child, and then
say I must marry Whyteleaf." The cry held obedience. He
had won her, he knew.

Barbary sobbed aloud, knowing herself lost. Presently he
began to stroke her breasts, assessing, as he did so, the slight
turgid swelling of the ripe flesh. She must be wed soon. "I
promise I will come," he said, and then repeated the saying,
as if it were a charm with which to win her. He talked on
about Whyteleaf, the man's weakness, Barbary's own plight,
the only way out of it. "I must not come yet; you will be
watched after it is known," he told her.

"But soon?"

"As soon as possible, after you are wed. You must know

that it could not be sooner; they would find it out, and send me from Daneclere."

"Frank, ah sweet Frank, never leave me, never leave me." She began again to sob and cry, and he ended by taking her on his knees and comforting her, trusting that no one would open the door and find them so, to his certain undoing. He must tread warily after this till the marriage-night. Whyteleaf, as his bride had foretold too well, would be drunk, and moreover would not expect to find his bride virgin. It must all of it work out as he himself had planned; the flaw was Ned Sawtrey's continuance in prison, and the possibility that Barbary would hear of it.

She heard.

That afternoon two of Meg Sawtrey's own brothers, younger sons by Meg Stillington, rode over. One, James, apprenticed to a miller, had his mother's golden hair and fleshy body; the other, Jonas, a brewer, looked like Sawtrey. They had not been reared by their father as Ned had been; nevertheless there was strong family loyalty among all the brothers, if only in memory of Meg. They had mourned her death together, and now they likewise mourned their brother's imprisonment and sentence, and carried loving messages from their sisters who had married near at hand. It was concerning all this that they wished to speak today with Richard Sawtrey. He greeted them in his diffident way, and offered them ale.

"Jonas rode to see Ned in prison," said James, who as the elder of the two spoke first. His blue eyes stared at his father and his father's new wife, the latter not yer showing her pregnancy by reason of a lace apron she wore. She was a handsome woman, almost as much so as their mother, James decided. He made her a slight, awkward bow, then said "Tell father, Jonas, how our brother did. Tell him how Ned fares."

Jonas said he had found Ned comfortable enough in the quarters their father had paid for. "But he's to be taken Tuesday, or maybe Wednesday, to the port to meet the ship."

Richard shook his head sadly; it showed more grey than formerly. "I will go to him first. I have done everything I may to obtain his release," he said. "I have offered fines; I have even written to the Lord Protector in London to beg for clemency. But they seem determined to make an example of Ned because he helped the King."

"And who was't informed on Ned? Who told 'em he helped the Black Boy? It was never known except by those as should know. Who betrayed our brother?"

A sound made them turn. No one had noticed Barbary, who had entered the hall from the small twisting staircase which ran up to the gallery, and thence by a passage to her chamber. She still stood halfway down the stairs; it was as if she were frozen, with her hand raised to her breast.

"Ned is not free?" she said, and her lips parted, leaving her mouth agape. Her face was paper-white.

"Free?" said Jonas. "That would warm our hearts, to be sure, but they've kept firm hold on him."

Barbary stared at him without expression. Then she crumpled where she stood, falling with skirts outspread and dark hair trailing, her arm thrust out, as if to ward off darkness: and there she lay.

She awoke in Honor's chamber. For moments she did not know where she was, or remember what had happened, except that her mind was heavy with grief. Honor was beside her, seated on the bed.

"You are safe, Barbary." The voice was gentle. In her tortured mind the girl took leisure to reflect that her cousin Richard was fortunate in his wife. Then she began to cry. The tears ran down her cheeks without ceasing, and soaked the pillow.

"You are full of sorrow for Ned, and so are we all. Perhaps one day if the King comes back, he will remember his friends who aided him, and bring Ned home."

"If that were all! If that were all!"

"What, then?" Honor stroked the arm. The look of horror in Barbary's dark eyes was one she could not understand. Perhaps the thought of the overseer's whip, on the plantations—

"I am with child. Tell no one."

"With child? By Ned? But—" It was many months since Ned had been taken to prison.

"It is not Ned's child, Honor. I would it were."

"Then who—"

Barbary said, desperately, "I do not know. A—a man came at me in the wood." She remembered what had befallen Gwenllian; it would do as well as any other tale. She must never, never let Honor know, let any of them know, that she had lain with the bailiff, hungrily, incessantly, beneath the roof of Daneclere, out among the whins, anywhere. She must never speak of it. She must not—the thought came to her queerly, in the midst of certainty as to his treachery in some manner—she must never lose Frank. That was all that remained to her now: to continue as his whore.

Honor had tears in her eyes. "So pretty a creature as you should have only joy, not woe. We must tell your aunt of it. No, Barbary; she will have to be told."

"She will beat me."

"I will not let her."

Barbary gazed in astonishment at this woman, whom she had been taught to despise. If she had had Honor's strength she would not be in this pass, she knew.

"Will you tell her, then?"

"If you wish it, Barbary, what must we do with you? The child will be born, will it not?"

"I have dosed myself with herbs, but they did not avail me."

"Promise me never to do so again; you might kill yourself as well as your child."

"I do not greatly care."

"Promise me, Barbary. I will do what I may with Mrs. Anna."

"Very well, I promise," said Barbary listlessly. Presently she sat up in the bed.

"I should marry, I think. Jeremy Whyteleaf has asked Richard more than once. He would take me, even though I am as I am." Her mouth twisted bitterly. Honor's eyes widened in pity.

"Whyteleaf—but he—he is a drunkard, and—"

"And so is fit for a spoiled maid, such as I have become. Speak to my cousin of it. Honor, you are doing much for me; I thank you."

"I would I could save you, Barbary."

"You cannot. I have no dowry and I have made my bed, as aunt Sawtrey will say; now I must lie on it."

Barbary and Whyteleaf were married within the month. The bride had a scar on her lip, which folk whispered had been caused when her aunt, Mrs. Anna, heard of the reason for marrying so soon; she had struck the girl's face with the back of her hand, which bore many rings. Barbary would bear the mark till she died. Otherwise, all appeared well. The marriage feast was held at Daneclere, modestly because of the bride's state and also by reason of the fact that Ned Sawtrey had at last sailed for the Indies; it was like a household in mourning when the news came.

The new-wedded couple would live at Daneclere. Barbary had pleaded with her husband for this, and Whyteleaf would oblige anybody with anything in his new state of bliss; moreover, his own house was eaten away by rats, mice and damp, and no place to take a delicate bride. So they were bedded in the tower room where Barbary had slept before, and where—but the wedding-guests knew nothing of this—Wolffe the bailiff, who had made himself scarce till the nuptials should be over, had often visited her, and would do so again.

So time went on; and whether Honor Sawtrey or Barbary Whyteleaf would be the first to give their lords a love-pledge was the occasion of discreet wagers among the servants, except for the little wench Gwenllian, who continued to serve Barbary and to comb her hair.

Far away, Ned Sawtrey cursed his lot and struggled from his place in the jostled crowd below decks to try and reach his ration of brackish water. Events had stood still while he was in prison, and now moved too fast; all he knew was that he might never see Daneclere again, or Barbary. Already her image had faded in his mind; he remembered only a pale gown, soft lips, a cloud of dark hair. The present was about him more strongly, with its stench of excrement and sweat, the filth of that and the language the other men used, the foul air below hatches with, running past above their heads outside, the everlasting sea. After Ned had drunk the unclean water he sat in his place with his head on his arms and thought of the future, which he could not foresee. Perhaps it was as well if one could not picture what was to happen. At least he could live from day to day; many had died on the voyage. Soon—it could not be too soon to be out of here, yet he loathed and feared the thought—soon he would disembark and be obliged to find work of some kind, to support himself in a strange country. But when he tried to imagine that, his mind grew confused, and would not accept reality.

Two

I

THE MANOR of Biding lay a few miles from Daneclere on the Thwaite side of the river. One day in 1658 a plain-clad rider galloped towards it from the London road. He had come far and his clothes were dusty, his face and hair streaked with sweat. At last the brick chimneys, with their varied twists and chevrons, jutted across his line of vision out of the hollow in which the great house lay. Once it had been a Cistercian monastery, and later an Elizabethan nonesuch, with a stocked park and herb-garden. Now it was forlorn.

In the upper room which looked across to the river, Lady Farmiloe sat sewing, with eyes narrowed behind her taffeta mask the better to see. The fair, greying curls fell forward and disguised the fact that she had a missing right ear; the mask hid other mutilation inflicted on her after Naseby, together with other officers' wives and doxies in the royalist camp. Her hands were unharmed, long, well-kept and beautiful.

Her younger sons, who had not fought in the war, were with their tutor, all except Gregory, the last, who would never learn to read or write. He sat by her, playing with a little dog which was his companion. Gregory had been born four months after Naseby, by which time his father and brother Lionel had fled to France; the eldest boy of all, Nigel, had fallen long ago, a mere child, at Edgehill. It added to Maud Farmiloe's bitterness that the treatment to which she had been subjected led at last to the birth of a feeble-witted boy, who would not take Nigel's place. The only one not strong and whole among her sons, Gregory was given to fits; his head jerked constantly and his eyes turned up to show the whites. His brothers avoided him.

Maud Farmiloe was thinking, as she frequently did, of her absent lord, Sir Ralph, and of the news she had had of him lately in a letter smuggled to her at Biding. Such means were necessary, for the man who stayed in the house as tutor was, they were all aware, a spy for the Parliamentarians such as had been placed in every great house in England where the

King had had support in the fight. It was needful meantime to endure Master Matthew Pollock's thin-lipped countenance and his undoubted scholarship—he dinned, by many beatings, enough Latin into the heads of Ralph and Edgar to enable them to hold up their heads in company when the good times came again—but it was unpleasant to have to endure him at the dinner-table, with his lengthy grace and sour presence. One could only pray that a miracle might happen soon; but Cromwell in London—my lady's hands paused over her needle, and it might have been that she saw, heard, and felt again the thing Cromwell's soldiery had done to her and to others eight years since—Cromwell seemed firm in the saddle still, was well thought of abroad, had made peace everywhere save in royalist hearts, and was almost thought of as wearing the crown he had refused. "Yet they say he is having as much ado in extracting money from Parliament as the late King. Those gentlemen are close," thought Maud Farmiloe. She sighed: while Cromwell ruled, Sir Ralph and his heir must stay abroad. She tried not to let her mind dwell on the wantons at the French Court, for her lord was susceptible and Lionel twenty-four. Scarcely more than a boy, he had been, when he rode off to join his father's troop of horse before Naseby; and soon enough that bloody field had turned him from boy to man. "I would not know him now, my own son," she thought, seeing again the slender body and girlish face, with the sun shining on pale-gold hair; all the boys had had her hair. Lionel had been dear to her, almost as dear as Nigel, and she had even known guilt when she heard Nigel was dead, because her first thought had been "Thank God Lionel at least is safe."

The room was bare. The soldiery had come and pillaged here as everywhere, leaving not so much as a mirror to—But what need now had such as she of mirrors? When Ralph came home—

She faced the truth of it, shuddering. When Ralph came home he might not endure to look at her, his disfigured wife. They had left her her eyes and mouth.

In the schoolroom, the two boys, fourteen and sixteen, listened, or made pretence to do so, to Master Pollock's history lesson. It differed from other lessons in that when Master Pollock spoke of events, he would burn inwardly with the same fire which consumed him in his extempore prayers.

Now, his god was Cromwell, his devil the King; and liberty
for all men his watchword despite the fact that nobody
wanted him in Biding. "Never before hath a time been when
merit alone can raise one man above another regardless of
rank; never a time when truth may be valued above riches
and a man may speak to God without priest or bishop to aid
him. The poorest now may attain scholarship by labour—"

"Master Pollock," put in Edgar, who despite many canings
had never been cured of the habit of asking awkward
questions, "did not the monks in their day give education to
the poor, and did not the late King spare money for the
establishment of schools for young women, and did not—"

"Be silent," roared Master Pollock, "and do not give the
Man of Blood a title better men than he took from him. There
is no king now save in the Scriptures, as the Lord Protector
himself knew when he refused the crown and threw away the
mace as a bauble. Mind your tongue, boy, or you shall smart
for it, and maybe worse than that if any should hear, beyond
these walls, that you have spoken in such a way."

"There is someone riding up the drive," put in Ralph, who
spoke seldom.

"Never heed; attend your work. There is not a country
now which doth not acknowledge the coming of a new age in
this once stricken land, or faileth to honour the man who
achieved it despite the Adversary and his minion, furious
Rupert. Even France, a papist country which harboureth the
wife and brood of Charles Stuart, hath sent an ambassador to
our country, and the Dutch—"

"Our mother has gone down," murmured Ralph, hearing
her light tread on the stairs. He kept it low enough for his
brother but not the tutor to hear him, for the latter, launched
on his diatribe, went on until Lady Farmiloe herself, mouth
smiling, eyes bright beneath the mask, entered the room. All
three rose, and saw that in her hand was a letter.

"I think that this news will soon be common knowledge,
sirs," she said. "Cromwell is dead."

"What, old Noll?" roared Edgar. He cheered, heedless of
the tutor.

"What will happen now?" asked Ralph. Master Pollock
was silent, his head bowed. If the news were true, it was the
passing of a great man.

"No one seems to know; can you hazard a guess, Master

Pollock?" asked my lady. She could not forbear; they had suffered so much, and now there was—hope, if nothing more.

Pollock groaned. "Of what did he die?" he asked. It seemed as if iron had melted in the sun: no one could think of Cromwell as other than alive, boisterous, direct and powerful. "Of a festering spleen," said my lady.

There would be no more lessons today; Master Pollock was not in a state of mind to continue them, and the boys chattered together. Who would succeed Noll? (It was a question all England was asking.) Two of his sons were dead, and one was in Ireland; the only one left was Dick, a ladylike fellow, they said. How long would he rule?

Matthew Pollock turned to go. He knew a moment's dignity. He looked back at them, the maimed woman and her two sons, into whose minds he had been able to graft little of his philosophy. "We will not again have so great a man to lead us," he said. "He is gone to God."

He did not come in to supper, at which Ralph, Edgar and my lady were free to agree that Noll Cromwell had, on the contrary, gone to the devil. "Pollock will go now too," said Ralph with satisfaction; he felt himself beyond the need of tutoring, and resented having been kept in the schoolroom. Perhaps soon they would call the King home and a fellow could go abroad, and see the French Court freely, not as a fugitive; and there were other places, and it would be pleasant to ride home. The past years had been narrow enough.

The news of Cromwell's death came to Daneclere. Richard Sawtrey received it idly, as though he realised the truth of the matter, which was that it would make little or no difference to him. Honor, who adored her second-born, was drying Edwin, who had fallen into the river while fishing with Uncle Jeremy Whyteleaf. Young Dick had been there also and had not even wet his feet. He watched gravely as Honor dried the red-gold Thwaite head and put fresh clothes on Edwin. He knew, had known from as far back as he could remember, that his mother loved Edwin best and had named him to please their father, who had another son—Dick did not think from where—who was in America. His younger brother had a pink sturdy body, while his own was pale and wan; Edwin, although the younger, would do things Dick never dared do, like climbing the high ruined wall at Daneclere that lay beneath cousin Barbary Whyteleaf's tower. Edwin was always ready for sport or fun, and loved his cousin Jeremy, who was always drunk, almost as much as he loved his mother. His father did not matter at all.

Daneclere was full of children. Barbary had by now borne four to the bailiff, three of whom had lived; a daughter, Sophia, and two sons, Jeremy and Lewis. The dark-haired, sharp-nosed brood were cheerfully acknowledged by Whyteleaf as his own; what he knew, and what Mrs. Honor by now suspected, was not permitted to trouble anyone. When Wolffe came to Barbary in Whyteleaf's bed, Whyteleaf himself was too drunk to heed them and what they did.

Barbary had coarsened with child-bearing, by contrast with Honor who was in the full glory of her mature beauty. Barbary despised her husband. He could not leave her alone; he was like a tomcat, she thought contemptuously. The dark tide of her passion for Wolffe had changed but not abated; she was certain by now that he was unfaithful to her with other women. That their couplings could result in the queasy mornings of pregnancy, the pain of childbirth, she knew. By now it was part of her life.

Honor mothered Barbary's children more than she did. Barbary gave birth to them, like an animal, then forgot them for their father.

"They say they made a likeness in wax of the Lord Protector, and laid it on a catafalque at Westminster, and after three days raised it to its feet, to signify that man's entry into heaven. We see nothing of such things here."

Richard Sawtrey heard his wife with weariness. His thoughts, as always nowadays, were with Ned; Ned in the grilling heat of a far sun, bending his body to the orders of a taskmaster. Was Cromwell dead? It did not matter. Yet soon there was talk of young Richard Cromwell's weak rule, and later still of a man named Monk, who swore he would bring back King Charles II. It signified little at Daneclere. Life went on as it had always done, and Honor had not yet crossed the ford. At Thwaite, there was mourning for the Lord Protector. Old Hawkin called his grandson who had been named after him, and David and Robin and young Uthred also, to witness that there would never again be such a man as Oliver Cromwell, and that God's word would no longer be heard in the land.

Wolffe the bailiff was in a restless state. Since the death of Mrs. Anna four months since, his profitable altering of the books had had to be modified. A sum here, a sum there, had not been obvious to the eyes of the gently bred widow nor to the idle glance of Sawtrey. But now Mrs. Honor—the bailiff uttered a curse—inspected them. Under that level grey gaze any deceit would be detected; she had already pointed out what might have been an error. Wolffe was determined not to wait for worse to happen. Times were changing, and with young Cromwell's weak hands still on the reins there was opportunity in London. The wheel might come full circle; already there were whispers that the King might return. "Any man who values his own talents must be at the heart of change," Wolffe told himself. Whatever befell, it would do so first in London. He would go there as soon as he might, and offer his services discreetly where he saw prospect of advancement. He already had some acquaintance in the capital from old days; in the innermost circles he would still be known as a man who had sent information when it was needed. He had played for safety; afterwards, the record could be wiped clean. It was because of his disclaimers that Richard Sawtrey of Daneclere himself had been recognised as no more than a lukewarm supporter of the late King Charles the First, one who had not come out to fight, and would do no harm save perhaps, now and again, to send a little money to the Stuart cause; he would not spare much. Accordingly he had not been attainted like the absent owner of Biding.

But matters pressed apace; perhaps my lady Farmiloe's lord and son would soon come riding home. Wolffe did not want to be at Daneclere when they came. One could never be certain how much exiled royalists had learned of those who had informed on them, and altogether it was best to go. Moreover, Wolffe was weary of trudging and riding the damp acres of Sawtrey's estate, stooping to enter squalid tenants' cottages and later spending hours bent over his books by candlelight, making them balance.

He was weary also of Barbary. For some years she had continued to excite him, the triumph of his conquest aiding, in his mind, the challenge of her spirited young body. Now she was the mother of his children, docile, receptive, her flesh almost flaccid beneath his fingers. There would be younger women in London.

He made his preparations and, in due course, his excuses to

Richard when that gentleman was alone, brooding over his wine after dinner. "I shall be sorry to lose you, Frank," Sawtrey said.

"Alas, sir, I shall be as sorry to go. But I am no longer so young a man that I can spend all day in the saddle without an ache in my bones. I am for town."

"I would willingly take some of the work from your shoulders, if you would stay," offered Richard, and named one of his bastards who would serve in the capacity of under-bailiff. Wolffe laughed sourly to himself afterwards. "He is rough yet, it is true, but I have no doubt he would contrive, given time and patience, to aid you," his employer had said. To be tutor to Sawtrey's by-blow! No, he would go.

Richard had sighed and had gone to discuss the matter with Honor. He was surprised that she kept her eyes lowered over her needle and made no suggestions to persuade the bailiff to stay. "I had thought you would be loath to lose him," he said. "It will add to our tasks."

"Another man can be found, surely."

"But not so honest or discreet as Frank."

Honor said nothing. Richard wondered at it, but not for long; he was leaving more and more tasks to Honor, burdened as she already was with the household and the children, both her own and Barbary's. Sawtrey knew that a languor had come upon him since his mother's death; it was as though her going had taken away his strength. Thinking now of her death-bed, he recalled how as he sat by her at the last she had babbled of a loose girth. It was the fever which accompanied her state, no doubt; in the old days a confessor would have been brought to her to ease her mind. Richard could make no sense of it, and had merely sat with her hand in his until she died. He missed her.

He poured himself more wine after Wolffe had left. More and more he ached for Ned's company now old friends were going away. It had never been the same at Daneclere without the lad by him. In disloyal moments he might have said that the house was Honor's now, not his, though she made no attempt to dominate him. How did Ned fare? They had had one letter, years ago, to say he had won safe across the ocean when so many had died. How did he fare in the new land? Did he long for home?

Sawtrey tried to turn his mind back to the present. He should be content; Honor had given him two fine sons. The

inheritance was secure. He need no longer remember, beyond
all thought of Ned, Meg's face as it had been in the days
when he first loved her, bright and fair, her belly already
thickened with the first child she was ever to bear him: Ned
himself. Why must he always return to Ned? If the King
came back— if that befell—maybe then Ned could be
pardoned and brought home.

Wolffe took his leave not as he would have preferred, at
daybreak with most folk abed, but in full view of the
assembled household, who stood on the steps of Daneclere to
bid him farewell. It was not their liking for him that made
them do this, but Sawtrey's order. Wolffe had never been
popular with the servants.

Dinner, an especial one, had been long, generous and with
overmuch wine. Frank himself had a hard head, but
Whyteleaf, as usual, lurched by now in his stained clothes
and could scarcely keep his feet. He lamented the bailiff's
departure. "Ah, Frank, many's the good night we've had! I
shall miss your ugly face." Wolffe grinned to himself; ay,
better nights than Jeremy would ever reckon, with his
drunken snores on one side of the bed and Barbary's ploys
and his own on the other! Wolffe suspected, and had done for
some time, that if Whyteleaf cared to find out about the state
of matters he could; but it was no doubt an advantage to such
a man to be able to boast of having fathered Jem, Lewis and
Sophy. The girl and the elder boy were here now, with the
baby still upstairs at the nurse's breast. The boys had dark
hair, and were noisy yet sly; Wolffe resented them faintly.
His mind was already set on the future, and it would be a
relief when all farewells were said. There was no sign of
Barbary.

He bowed over Honor's hand. Thank God for no trouble
in the women's quarter! He had half expected Bab to come
and make a tantrum, to beg to be allowed to follow him, some
such thing. But she was not present. He straightened, and
looked into Honor's eyes. The contempt there shocked him;
why, the woman knew!

Afterwards he realised that he, who so despised fools, had
made one of himself in being taken at a loss. How could he
have expected such an affair as his own with Barbary to have
continued under Honor Sawtrey's roof for years without her
guessing at it? As it was, he admired her discretion. Maybe

she had suspicions about the accounts as well. It was more than time for him to be gone.

He rode off, not once glancing back at the great house on its rise, and taking pleasure at the firm hold his horse's galloping hooves had of the ground. There had been no rain for a fortnight and the going was easy. Soon he would be in town, with its lures and opportunities. "Maybe by the time I reach London, Queen Dick will have been ousted," he thought. No one could foretell; but Wolfe congratulated himself that he could sit on the fence as well as any man until matters had cleared, settled, and declared themselves. Then he would find a protector.

The thin mouth curled at the corners as he went; any other man would have hummed a tune, for now with great Cromwell dead there was little danger in singing other than psalms. But Wolffe was not a joyous man. He calculated again, as he had already done, the probable costs of the journey, including the necessity of having to spend one night at an inn. It was a tiresome expense, but as he had not yet found lodgings in London he must submit to necessity.

Honor, her household tasks done, allowed herself a few moments' pleasure in watching, from an upstairs window, Edwin mount his new pony. He had no fear, unlike Dick, who still needed a leading-rein; Edwin would learn to ride with ease and joy, as he did most things. Honor looked forward to the day when she could show old Hawkin his younger grandchild, his true heir, far more than David would ever be. But the old man still refused to come to Daneclere, or to invite her to Thwaite. Honor understood her father better than he knew; she did not waste time brooding on her hurt, but endeavoured, as he wished it, to forget her farmhouse upbringing, to become a fine lady, and make a place for herself in the county. Truth to tell there was scant leisure in which to do it. Even now—she realised it as Edwin and the groom rode off—she had let a good part of the morning pass without going to comfort Barbary.

She did not remember when it had become clear to her that Barbary was the bailiff's mistress and bore him children, none of Whyteleaf's getting. Was it the dark sly look of the two boys that had decided her? "But Barbary also has dark hair," she reminded herself. Perhaps it had been the spectacle of Whyteleaf drunk, at supper, boasting of his prowess with

women. A true stallion—she could thank her farmyard youth
for knowing of that—did not boast, but did his duty. It was
perhaps both of these things, added to her own sixth sense.
Too late to mend such a marriage for Barbary—the girl
needed pity and love, not lust—she had tried to ease the poor
creature's days, without letting her feel looked down upon:
but Barbary was still proud, and it was difficult not to cross
the line between kindness and patronage. It had been easier
after Mrs. Anna had died and could no longer question the
young woman's frequent absences at meals because she felt
sick or in despair, or blame her for not paying heed to her
children.

Honor had seldom visited the tower itself of late years: she
preferred Barbary and Whyteleaf to think of that part of the
house as their own. If Barbary desired a servant, there was
Gwenllian to send; Honor guessed the Welsh girl to be a
comfort to her, for she was deft and willing, and not stupid.
But no servant could cheer Barbary now her lover had gone;
she would be, perhaps, sullen and defiant, or else in tears. "If
Richard, my children's father, rode off never to return, how
could I feel?" Honor asked herself. It was not easy to
imagine, for she had never had need of Richard in the way
Barbary must have needed Wolffe; yet no doubt she would be
hurt if he left her. That Barbary had loved Wolffe with a
passion she herself would never now feel for any man Honor
was certain. "I am a staid matron, and happy enough," she
thought. She had her joy, who was Edwin; and at least she
was not like poor Maud Farmiloe, obliged to live out her
lonely days behind a mask of taffety.

She unlatched the door which led to the part where the
Whyteleaf couple lived, and felt the chill strike her from the
stone stairs. The place had a forsaken air, almost as if
Wolffe's going had taken all life from it. Honor climbed the
stairs and went and knocked at Barbary's door, calling out
softly "It is Honor, Barbary."

No answer came. Was Barbary perhaps lying on her bed
silent after weeping, and would she resent another woman's
entry and witness of it? There was only one way of telling.
Honor went in, and found what she had not expected; the
room was empty. The bed had been made and the curtains
drawn back. Barbary's cloak was missing, and other gear.
"She did not ride out," thought Honor, "or I would have
heard her go." In any case her riding-clothes were among

those things not taken: they lay across a chest. A man's bedgown, reminder that Whyteleaf slept here also when he chose, was cast down by them. The sunlight struck through the casement in pencilled rays, catching at the dust.

Barbary had gone, then. She must have been gone many hours; perhaps she had left while they all stood out on the steps this morning, to bid Wolffe farewell. "She must have walked to the coach road, four miles off towards Biding," Honor thought. Barbary had left her children, like a cat abandoning its litter; and her husband, for what he was worth.

This was never her home despite all we tried to do, thought Honor sadly. Within herself she admitted to a lack of surprise. It was as if, before opening the door, hearing the silence, hearing no answer, she had known that Barbary was already far from Daneclere.

She closed the door behind her and went back to the main part of the house thoughtfully wondering how much she must say and how soon. She must not start a hue and cry; why drag Barbary back to the drunkard, and then be content? He had not even been near when she left; he had his own concerns, and would console himself. She thought she would not even tell Richard; he would be bound to fuss, send a search out for Barbary, perhaps even send for Wolffe to answer a reckoning. It was better to keep silent until Barbary's absence intruded itself on Richard's notice; and he was so sunk nowadays in gloom about Ned that that might take some time. The wry certainty came to Honor that she herself was the one in need of comfort now, and did not know where to turn for it, except to little Edwin.

The inn where Wolffe had halted for the night was the only one on the road, and his horse had made good speed. He was able to eat a leisurely supper, for once under no obligation to use courtesy to his employer and his employer's wife, and later endure the importunities of Barbary. "Tonight?" she would murmur as they left the hall, hot lustful creature as he had made of her now; sometimes he would go to her and sometimes not, as the humour took him. She waited, in any case; and next day would have red eyes. He was tired of her. On the nights Wolffe did go, Whyteleaf, who as a rule lay with her—he was always at her, like a rabbit—before he slept, would have dropped off, leaving Barbary warm; then it was Wolffe's turn. Blind man's buff would be as diverting. Wolffe leaned back in his chair after the meal was over. "I shall not break my solitude again," he said aloud.

He took out his toothpick, for the dish he had lately eaten had contained succulent strands of meat: and was interrupted in his task by the maidservant of the inn, who said he was enquired for below.

Wolffe frowned; who would know for certain that he was here? "Send him up," he commanded, but the girl giggled, overt curiosity in her eyes. "Sir, 'tis a lady who waits, not a gentleman ... "

She was not given the opportunity for more; behind her, through the open door, he saw Barbary, her hood slipping back from her face. She brushed past the maid and into his room. The door closed, and she tried to take him in her arms; he sat still.

"Frank, Frank, you are not wroth with me?"

When he spoke his voice was icy. "It makes no odds. I should have known you would come. There is no other inn for miles; it did not need much wit to find me."

"I chanced the coach," said Barbary. Her eyes fell on his plate of picked bones. "Lord, how hungry I am! If the wench could bring—"

"Is it your purpose that I take you with me? Is that why you have come? I may have Sawtrey's men after me with swords, but it does not trouble you."

She was accustomed to insult, almost too dulled to resent it; she reached in her cloak's lining and found a purse of money. "See, I can buy my own meat," she said. She had the look of a dog which will fawn on its master no matter how hard he kicks it.

"Do you propose to pay for my favours?"

"How cruel you are!"

"You knew that well enough before you followed me. Am I never to be rid of you? You are like a curse, that disturbs a man forever."

She had begun to cry. "Sweet Frank, be not angry; be kind to me. I will do anything to please you, anything in the world." She had left home, husband, children to follow him; it did not occur to either of them that she had made sacrifices. Slowly he gained control of his anger, and looked at her. It was not a lover's look; it was a dealer's.

The project was already formed in his mind. She was a

handsome woman still; in the soft light of candles it would be possible not to see the signs of coarsening and ageing, the used look, the tiny broken veins in her cheeks. Selected clients—his mind formed a vision of them, men who sought pleasure in underhand ways and would pay for it while it was still beyond the law—such would pay well enough for her favours, he was certain. A slow, cruel smile transformed his mouth.

"If I agree to take you with me, Bab, I will put you to work, you understand?"

"To work?" Her lips fell apart as they had done when she was a girl. Would he make a servant out of her? She would do that, even that; he might degrade her, but she would not leave him. She would wash his clothing, keep his house. But he was speaking still, and she listened.

"Such work as you know well already. And if you do less for others than you do for me, I shall beat you. If you are afraid, or disgusted, return to your half-man and your home. I did not ask you to leave it."

"I will come with you," she said, trembling. He could beat her if he must.

They lay together on the inn-bed after Barbary had eaten. Wolffe took her leisurely, savouring his possession of what he now realised to be an asset. He was careful not to get her pregnant again; from now on there would be no Whyteleaf. Now that the notion of using her had come he confessed that it had spice in it, as well as profit. A source of income would be welcome, for a time, in London; it would be certain whoever ruled at Whitehall, for men everywhere knew lust. He patted Barbary's bare flesh contentedly. She was his now, to do with as he pleased; and he would see that she obeyed him.

2

"THE KING is bidden home!"

Robin had hardly taken time to slide from the saddle at Daneclere; he tossed young Hawkin, who sat pillion, in his arms and set him on the ground, and made his way, followed by the little boy with his sturdy trot, into the hall, leaving his horse to be rubbed down; it was splashed, like its riders, with mud from the ford.

Sawtrey was by his fire, turning a flagon in his fingers; at the news he set it down, sought vainly for words and then found none. He knew that he was not one of those who, like Farmiloe, had fought valiantly for the King's father, or aided Charles II in his wanderings and exile, like young Ned. He had in fact done nothing except to send small sums of money, and he felt it now; also that there would be those who, like Farmiloe, would openly despise the owner of Daneclere on his return. Yet what would have been the purpose in opposing Cromwell's rule after the victory? Daneclere ruined, like half the great houses of England which had been looted and burned by the soldiery; perhaps his wife, like poor Lady Farmiloe, mutilated or raped, though the maiming of women seemed only to have happened after Naseby: all their lives ordered and spied on, these many years.

His eyes sought Honor now, as they had used to seek his mother. She had risen and gone to her brother, Edwin running by her, and he and young Hawkin fell at once to tussling together near the door; it was not the news that excited them, but one another's company. The Whyteleaf children were upstairs with their tutor; Whyteleaf himself had ridden to the inn, where he would no doubt hear of the King's return and come home having drunk twenty healths. Young Dick alone, who had been standing by his father, remained hangdog and silent in a hall filled with joy. He was a solitary child who did not make friends, and did not seem to need them. He regarded the great, vital form of his uncle Robin doubtfully, and when Robin started to sing he cast his eyes down.

> *And he that will not drink his health*
> *I wish him neither wit nor wealth,*
> *But a good stout rope to hang himself,*

carolled Robin's light voice. "They will be singing that song even in miserly Cambridge, I doubt not, and maybe poor Uthred may hear it there. It will cheer him to hear of the King, for he hates book-learning and would fain be back on the farm. Poor fellow! When he would go to sea they made him till the soil, and no sooner does he grow fond of that than my father, being a man of notions, packs him off to Sidney Sussex, saying they must make a gentleman and scholar of him. Gentleman he is now; scholar he never will be. As for me, what am I but part lawyer? You shall not defeat me with words, sister, and I will see the King ride to claim his own." Robin was putting in his terms at the Inns of Court, and had only ridden down, taking time off from his tasks, to convey the news. He would return that night.

Honor smiled. "I could never defeat you with words in any case: they do not have to teach you those,' she said. "Who called the King home? When does he land, or has he already landed?"

"Not yet. A general from Scotland none had heard of heretofore; his name is George Monk, and no doubt Charles will give him a title so that he need be monk no longer. The landing? 'Twill be as soon as may be, I daresay; they are making ready fountains of wine in the Strand, and all the city is in a bustle. Anyone would think Noll Cromwell had never been heard of, so forgotten is he; and as for his son Dick, they say he hath crept quietly away to the country. Had he had a head for government, there'd be none of this joy. But now there will be a place at Court for whoever goes, provided he hath been a King's man." Robin stared openly with his blue eyes at Sawtrey, seated round-shouldered by his fire. What had possessed their father to wed glorious Honor to so dried-up a creature? "There is the house and all it means, but she would be worthy of a better man," he told himself. Yet Honor seemed content enough, and in any case this was no time for regret. "Fill me a bumper of ale, to drink His Majesty's health in Daneclere," demanded the guest. At once Sawtrey sent for a man to do so, and even made show of pleasure at the drinking, while Honor sipped from her brother's flagon once, raised it, and returned it. The two little boys were still shouting and tumbling. "Hear me, you rascals, do you know your King is to come home? You must remember this day," shouted Robin, boisterous with ale. Honor looked only to see that her darling was unhurt; he was younger than Hawkin, but gave as good as he got. Honor went and put her arm round Dick, as she would often do when her heart was in truth with the younger son, in order that the other might not feel left out of her affections. Dick was too much like his father to respond, and she was left somewhat awkwardly holding his shoulder and watching the men drink ale. The house buzzed already with news of the King; one could hear the servants' chatter and cheering through the muffling hangings and shut doors.

Later, after Robin and young Hawkin had gone, Richard said to Honor, diffidently as though he feared a rebuff, "Would it please you to go to London to see the King pass by? I doubt inn-room will not be had, but I know of a silversmith who will give us a place on his balcony, I believe, above the procession."

"It would please me indeed," said Honor. "I have never seen the capital, let alone the King. But can affairs here go on for a little while, lacking me? Perhaps Gwenllian— "

"They may surely do so," said Sawtrey gently. "It is time you had a holiday."

She was pleased; and she knew he was trying to please her, in his diffident way. Her mind ran already on what she should wear; she already had a fine black beaver hat with a wide brim, and it would furbish with a plume; and there was a gown of velvet which she had worn twice to church, but London had not seen it. Fashions, she knew, would change rapidly with the King's coming home; there would be fewer covered bosoms and high collars, fewer Puritan caps. But it could not all happen overnight, and she would see to it that Sawtery did not feel ashamed of her before all the great folk in London. Perhaps—she did not voice this, recalling Sawtrey's grief at the time of Barbary's disappearance with the bailiff, and how he had needed strong pleading not to follow her and try to bring her back—perhaps there would even be some sight, or news, of Barbary.

"The King is called home!"

Maud Farmiloe looked up from her needle, and stayed with a hand held for the next stitch, as though she had been turned to stone where she sat. In her bodice was a letter, which had reached her some days since. She had told no one of its contents, wanting to keep them secret to herself for a little while. Now, all knew.

Edgar, who had brought the news, was gleeful. "It means, does it not, that father and Lionel can come home? I scarcely knew Lionel, for he rode off to the war when we were boys. But father I remember well." He raced off to spread the news, which had come by word of mouth from the village, and Maud was left alone with her thoughts.

She tried to put these in order. She should be glad—of course she should—that the good days were come again for England. She should rejoice that her lord and eldest son were on their way home. She must show nothing of the fear she felt, and yet—

She pulled out the letter, every phrase of which she knew by heart already; but the joy of seeing his handwriting again stayed with her; nothing should take away that joy. *Dear Harte*, it ran.

He would remember her as she had been, though he knew of her wounding. He had not seen her since the time before Naseby, when, it was true, she had been heavy with his child, but even so like other women. Now—

"Ah, my love, my love, it is not that I would not have you home!"

She felt the tears trickle down behind her mask, and dried them fastidiously. What could not be cured must be endured; she heard her mother's voice saying it to her, far, far back in her childhood. She must endure this, even though it broke her heart, this certainty that her beloved husband could no longer return her love.

She rose and went to the window, looking out over the neglected park. Her own dark shape against the glass was all she could see, all she dared see. It must be lived through, this homecoming. As Edgar had tried to say, the boys would be glad to know their father. That must be her comfort.

The news of the King's homecoming had not been received with joy at Thwaite. After Robin had ridden off to Daneclere trolling his song, old Hawkin sat on in his place in the great flagged kitchen, his dog by him, and brooded over the fire. The door stood open to let in the summer sunlight, and yet the flags were still cold; the old man felt his age. David came in just then, stocky shape dark against the sun outside. Hawkin stared at him below jutting brows.

"Hast heard?" he said, in the old speech.

"Ay." David Thwaite never talked much, nor did most folk know what he was thinking. He knew, moreover, that the old man was ill-pleased and would vent his spleen on somebody, and that that might as well be himself. He sat down on one of the benches that ran along by the scrubbed table, and waited for his father to speak. Hawkin began at once, his lined face sour with disapproval. "All the fools are rejoicing; Robin says the capital is like a fairground with the shows and gewgaws there are for the return of Charles Stuart, and folk throng in from all parts. They had better be mourning still for great Oliver. Few this day think of him, except maybe his widow; yet he was the man who made the country greater than it has been since the days of Queen Bess. Respected we are abroad; may we continue so under this young man, but I doubt it."

"Charles may do well enough," murmured David, but his father was not listening.

"I knew him well once," he murmured, and he still spoke of Oliver and not Charles. "A noisy red-faced fellow he was; he cared naught for dress, never so much as troubled to put a band on his hat, and wore that till 'twas in holes, and his linen was soiled. Yet he was great in himself: he was all for truth; can we say the same for the Stuarts? I think not. The first king they sent us was a slobbering buffoon with unnatural vices; his son was a hypocrite, who destroyed himself—never say we destroyed him—with taking his popish wife's advice and breaking his word."

"He died bravely," muttered David, who had been too young to feel strongly about the Civil Wars. His father went on as if he had not spoken. Upstairs they could hear Joan moving about directing the girls to turn the mattresses and shake their feathers full, and brush the curtains, as was done weekly.

"They say this new King is a womaniser," Hawkin went on. "Soon we will have whores at Court, and they will have the power the popish queen had in her day. How may God save England then? No, it is no time to rejoice that Charles Stuart is to come home; rather should men put on mourning."

David said nothing. His father stared at him for some instants, then looked away. He would sooner it was young Uthred who sat there, listening, discussing, from time to time putting in a reasonable surmise. Uthred was a good lad; in the short years he had been at Thwaite Hawkin had grown as fond of him as of any of his own children except Honor. It was as though Uthred were the son of his old age. Proud as he was to have the young man at Cambridge, he missed his company. It would be good to have him down soon for the summer vacation, and he could help with the harvest as he had done last year, his first at Sidney Sussex. Uthred did nothing half-heartedly, unlike Robin who grudged manual work, or David who was capable of nothing else. If only—

"I grow foolish," Hawkin growled to his own mind. His silence at last caused David to look up, his unremarkable thoughts disturbed. But his father said nothing more.

3

HONOR and her husband stood on the balcony of the house belonging to Master John Spence, silversmith in the Strand, closely hemmed in by their host's family and neighbours. Opposite, very close, and alongside, were other balconies likewise crowded with richly-dressed men and women, and decked with tapestries and carpets which hung down almost to the street. Below, all the shops had locked and shuttered doors, for this was a holiday; a boisterous, glad, colourful holiday to the sounds of trumpets and bells, for Charles II, after eleven years' exile, was come home. Already the sounds of triumphant greeting could be heard, and the crowd below, common folk with no place on any balcony, murmured and swayed and sucked oranges while waiting to see their King, and drank the free wine.

To Honor the scene itself was like a great bright-threaded tapestry, the sound of joy deafening to her ears. She had never before been in a city. How could folk live here so close-packed, make themselves heard above the daily din, and sleep of nights?

She turned to smile at Richard, who had been at some trouble to procure them places; he had been, he told her, a good customer to the silversmith in days gone by. Had it been to buy rings and lockets for Meg Stillington? She did not ask. Master Spence himself had welcomed them when they came, and his fat, painted wife had bobbed a curtsy, showing her great breasts which now, as Honor had prophesied would happen once Cromwell was dead, were almost bare, and set off by loose linen rolled above the bodice. Many women were already dressed so; ringlets hung on either side of their cheeks, and there was much red-leading of cheeks and lips. It seemed as though the whole of London smiled, eyed its dressed-up neighbours, and waited for its King.

"They are coming," said the silversmith's wife, nudging

her sister-in-law who had come over today from Hackney,
bringing her large family. A sound of music carried down the
street, up from the river. First came the cavalry and infantry,
swords raised and shouting so loudly that the din they made
drowned even the clangour of the bells. The horses trod on
flowers strewn ready in the way so that the crushed scent
wafted up to the balconies, driving out for moments the smells
of sweat and horse-manure and offal from the gutters, and
reviving such ladies as were well-nigh fainting from the heat
of the day, and the closeness to others. Soon the foot-soldiers
had gone by and on came the Mayor and livery companies,
faces shining beneath the weight and warmth of furred robes
and great gilded chains glinting in the sun. Banners waved;
now there came noblemen, some of whom were known and
some not, for they had mostly come over from Breda with the
King. All wore perruques of the new fashion, said to have
been made to disguise one's politics, for a Roundhead could
wear one of the great frizzed creations as well as a Royalist,
and no one the wiser: but they had already worn them in
Paris.

The afternoon heat grilled down. Honor watched with a
feeling of unreality, her velvet gown heavy upon her. Soon the
grand horse and foot, the merchants and companies and
sounds of triumph, would pass away, leaving only a gleaming
memory. But now there came the King himself, and at sight
of him there was a great roaring from the crowd, the like of
which had not been heard all day. The tall dark well-set man
on his fine horse smiled and saluted to left and right, and
acknowledged favours thrown from the windows, without
ever losing the cynical good-natured smile on his swarthy face
or the guarded expression of his eyes. The latter raked the
balconies and found Honor among others. She felt her glance
hold that of Charles Stuart for a moment, and he smiled and
was borne on.

There was a disturbance about then in the crowd below;
from under the balconies a woman in gaudy unclean clothing
struggled to the front of the crowd, and made as if to clutch
His Majesty's bridle; but they would not let her get to him
and she was borne along perforce by the press in the street. In
an instant's silence between the clangour of bells and more
bells, her voice sounded, high and harsh as a sea-bird's, the
words clear.

"Sire, remember Ned Sawtrey, who is in the Americas for your sake!"

The bells began again, the King passed on, the crowd jeered. Charles might or might not have heard the woman. She had been knocked down in the struggle by one of the noblemen's horses close to the King, folk later said the Earl of Southampton's. It did not signify; everyone was drunk with wine and joyful at sight of the King, glad also that the times of prayer and fasting were at an end and that a man might take a woman tonight for his comfort without having to stand on a penance-stool next Sabbath. Ay, it was overlong since joy had entered London! The fountains ran to overflowing with wine.

Honor had shouldered her way out from among the women on the balcony, Richard following perforce. His expression was irritable; why must she feel faint in the good place he had secured for them with Master Spence? But he soon found that was not the cause.

She turned to look back at him on the stairs and her face was white. "Richard, 'tis Barbary, 'tis Barbary!"

"That whore? It cannot be— "

"Ah, she is changed, but I knew her—we must save her—make haste!"

Sawtrey was still incredulous; but when Honor was convinced there was no gainsaying her. Mouth pinched with uncertainty, he followed his wife down into the street, seeing the great beaver hat at last, with its brave plume, bend over the poor drab lying in the street. Few else heeded her; some turned their heads now that the procession had gone by.

"She is hurt," said Honor. Richard accustomed his eyes to the sunlight after having come through the dim and shuttered shop. The harlot lay there at their feet, with blood oozing from her mouth and a great sore, which showed she had the pox, on her right cheek, and her clothes stank; the stench came up to him from where she lay. That this could be Barbary or any woman they had ever had to do with at Daneclere, seemed impossible; and yet—

Honor meantime, in her fine velvet, had knelt down on the ground among the crowd and had lifted the creature's head on to her lap. The blood stained her skirts.

"Barbary darling, it is Honor. You are coming home to Daneclere to be made well."

Her grey eyes raised themselves, agonised, to Richard where he stood still uncertain; they were telling him to find room in the shuttered shop, to help carry in the defiled creature, lay her down in the quiet, fetch a physician. How could one be found on such a day?

He obeyed, however; so only Honor heard the words that came from the fevered lips.

"Honor."

"I am here, dearest. We will not leave you. You are coming home with us to Daneclere." By repeating the name she hoped to give Barbary hope; but she was beyond it.

"Ned." She could only say the name, no more; her mouth bubbled blood; the hooves had crushed her.

"Ned shall come home, I swear. If the King should forget, Richard and I will go to him, and remind him. Do not fret for Ned. But you must get well."

"Honor, he—Frank Wolffe— "

"Yes, my dear; I know of it."

"He made me be a whore. Then when I caught the pox he turned me out. I used to bring money to him, and if not— "

Her head had rolled sideways. The blood from her mouth ran out thickly, making a scarlet pool on Honor's skirts. They carried the body into the silversmith's shop; by the time they laid her down there she was dead.

Some of the crowd, mostly men, came into the shop out of curiosity; it made a diversion after the passing of the King. Later Master Spence was to miss two salt-fats and a ewer. One of the men said they all knew hereabouts who she was. "She would wait at night by the shop-doors, asking for custom." She had a keeper, he added, who beat her if she brought home no money from the night's doings; one of them knew of someone who could give his direction. Richard Sawtrey took note of it; he could do no more.

Presently, in none too good a humour, Master Spence bustled down, followed by his lady. The latter was affronted at the presence of a harlot's corpse in the shop; what were things coming to? It was all of it a reward for showing hospitality to Mr. and Mrs. Sawtrey, who were gentlefolk, or said to be.

Honor raised her ravaged face. "Have no fear, madam," she said clearly. "When we can get us a coffin we will have this poor soul's body out of here, and convey it back with us." She stood up and looked down at what had been Barbary, the blood dripping steadily from her own soaked skirts to the floor. In the distance, the shouts still sounded for the King's progress, and all the bells of London rang their peals.

4

SIR RALPH FARMILOE had attended the King at Breda, but after the voyage had not followed him to London though his son Lionel, always eager to see all things new, had chosen to ride on to Court. After parting with the boy Sir Ralph procured himself a good horse and, without delay, galloped north to Biding along the summer ways. After many years' absence it did his heart good to see the hedgerows white with blossom, the dog-rose blooming, the late may and Queen's-lace of his childhood blending together in sight and smell to make up England.

England! To be home again, to see trees again, after Dutch flatness! He rode on, and those who saw him pass would remember the tall handsome man, who had a look of the late King though he was longer in the leg and fiercer in the eye, and his hair and beard were less dark, turning grey. He laid spurs to his horse, causing it to leave the hedgerows behind, the fields, the villages; soon now there would be the fantastic carved chimneys of Biding coming upon one's sight from their hollow. There would be the remembered shining river, with the ford and Thwaite beyond; and soon after that the avenue, with two stone greyhounds flanking the entrance-gate that had been put there in the time of James I. Then, at last, there would be Maud waiting for him with the children about her, one of whom he reminded himself he had never seen; and the sun would shine on the fair gold of her hair.

She had written to him: all these years, despite privations at home, she had somehow managed to send him money. Ralph had hesitated to take it; but after the first he had found no employment for the sword he knew so well how to wield, and after the fight for Condé at Lens he would have become like so many others, penniless and rotting for lack of occupation among the scornful French and cautious Hollanders. Thirty years of war had ended in Europe too soon for such as Farmiloe. There had been many as he was, exiled on pain of death from England for having fought for the dead King. Most had their wives with them. But Maud had never agreed to come out to him, saying always that Biding needed its mistress and the children their mother. That this was true Ralph knew, but thinking of it now as he had thought for many years, he wondered afresh about the wounds his wife had received after Naseby fight. He had not seen her since; he himself had fled with the scattered remnants of Langdale's left, and by the time they obtained news from the supply-lines where the women were, the thing had been done. Many were mutilated; so savage a thing that one did not believe it could have been thought of as being carried out in the name of God, even the stern avenging God of the Roundhead army.

Maud. She had sent a note to him, from the place of safety where others than himself had conveyed her, until the boy should be born. *They have Cutt me somewhat about the Face and Necke, but now it is mending.* He had not dared dwell on it overmuch in his years of exile or let himself think of her as other than she had always been, cool and elegant and lovely with her white hands stitching at some embroidery, perhaps a child's cap, on the terrace at Biding that last summer before the world had plunged and changed, as day changes swiftly into night. Yet now surely, with the peace and the King's homecoming, things could go back to their old pleasant, harmless round? He and Maud, to be sure, were older, and he had had to take comfort sometimes from foreign women for lack of her; but there had been no unfaithfulness in his heart, which was hers always.

Biding. He stayed his horse for instants to stare at the chimneys. Always when he had been a small boy, first on his pony and then, as he grew, more manfully mounted, he had stopped at this place; it was as though one must take a breath before hastening down to so much beauty of mellow brick and stucco and glass, with the green lawns stretching beneath their stately chestnuts and oaks. He went on slowly now, in order to miss nothing; and soon descended to where the gateposts were. Here he found changes. The greyhounds had been broken, one with its delicate muzzle smashed, while the other lacked both head and rump. This angered Ralph and made him afraid within his heart. What other changes would he find at Biding? He knew from Maud's letters that the house itself had survived the onslaught of Cromwell's soldiery, the looting and burning. Maud had made little of it, while she had had to endure it, and he had been overseas, his skin safe. Yet what could he have done for her had he stayed, save die? Those who had kept their houses, goods and lives intact had been only such as Sawtrey, who took part neither from one side nor the other. Sawtrey would have few friends now the King's men rode home. Ralph had passed by Daneclere today without so much as a glance. But Biding. ...

It had not burned. There were no scars of fire on timber beams and brick front. Possibly what had been set on fire were the outhouses where hay was kept for the horses; some such thing. The grass on the lawns was overlong; there were no cattle grazing. For moments his mind saw it as a house of the dead, with none to welcome him. Yet he had written to say that he was coming home, and by now they must surely have heard his horse's hooves.

A child appeared at the top of the steps leading to the great hall; a boy with fair hair. He looked over at Ralph and then ducked shyly inside, like a young animal. This must be the lad who had been born after Naseby. He was not close enough for Ralph to have seen his face. "I will make him love me, and not run from me, now I am home," the father thought.

He alighted. A groom came to take his horse, less a boy than a man, whom Ralph did not know. He had a sullen look, and might well be one of the spies the major-generals had placed about great houses to report on their doings during the late Commonwealth. That being so, he should go. Ralph swept off his hat and entered the house, to find the boys, his sons, arrayed there in welcome; they were in shabby finery, with clean collars, and Edgar held young Gregory by the hand. By now he could see that the lad's head lolled and that his eyes were not like the others'   But it did not matter at this moment; Maud, Maud—

She was standing there, a little way back out of the light. She wore a gown of a dark colour, which made her seem smaller and slighter then he remembered. On her face was a mask. He saw locks of grey in her hair, but it curled as softly about her face as ever, and he went to her and she lifted her face for his kiss. She had not moved.

"Maud ... my heart."

"Ralph. Ralph, it has been so long." She spoke, he thought, while still in his arms, as to a stranger; what was

behind the damned mask? He had to know, and soon; they
could not go on together as man and wife with a barrier
between them of black taffeta. The notion almost made him
laugh aloud, and then he stopped his laughter on a breath.
She had suffered, more horribly than he had dreamed. He
should have known, when she would not come out to him,
what it really meant.

He made himself turn to his sons, and chaff them, asking if
they recalled him or not. Only the elder two tried to say they
did. Gregory, the scant-witted product of Naseby, came at
last and fingered his sword. Ralph made much of his son,
putting his arm about him as if he were a little child.
Presently Gregory was at ease with him, as were the others.
Ralph drew them into talk, using the charm for which he was
famous. He did not look again at their mother.

He has seen me, and guessed, thought Maud; and I repel
him.

Later, when they were alone, he could still feel the uncertainty, the misery, stabbing between them like a knife. He
watched her from where he himself stood by the casement;
behind him, the bed-curtains were of fustian because the old,
gracious embroideries of his Jacobean grandmother had been
looted long since with the silver and such other things as
could be carried away from Biding. Their supper tonight had
been eaten off wooden platters, like the poor.

He heard her speak presently, as if she knew his thoughts.
"You are saying to yourself that the places you have left
abroad are richer now than your home. There is little here to
bid you welcome, save the boys."

"And my wife."

She smiled bitterly beneath the mask's edge. "Your
mutilated wife, that you must not look on lest you remember
too much of what I was formerly, and hate me now."

She had not turned away, or moved, while she spoke.
When he went to her she raised her hands, as though in
defence against what she knew and feared he might do. He
heard her breathe "Ah, no," as he slid his fingers round the
shape of her small skull beneath the hair, coming to rest
against the scar where there had once been an ear. That could
be hidden; none knew of it. But the rest—

She had begun to sob and whimper, trying to evade his
prying, searching hands. He said gently "Do you not see that

I must know the truth, otherwise we are not one flesh?" and so saying he prised the mask gently away, looking down at the noseless face. He held her away from him that he might look, imprisoning her hands in both his own so that she might not fling them upwards to conceal signs of the brutality there had been. Then he drew her to him, cradling her face against his breast. He heard himself speak aloud.

"They claimed they were the chosen of God, those men. God himself urges us to forgive our enemies and bless them that despitefully use us. Can He know of this, and still exact forgiveness?"

She was weeping, partly with the relief that he had not after all spurned her, partly because, since that time at Naseby, none save herself had gazed even on the reflection of her ruined face; she had wound and washed her own bandages, made her own mask out of a scrap of stuff, kept the exposed nasal nassages clean and covered. Now—

"We are one," he said. He took her head between his hands and kissed her between the eyes, then let his lips travel round to the scar of the ear. Then he lifted her and carried her to their bed. "Are we not one," he whispered, "my heart?"

5

RICHARD SAWTREY had a sickness of the mind that might have dated from his brother's murder; he would be invaded with black melancholy and become capable of nothing. After Barbary's death it came upon him again; he was both torpid and sleepless. He said nothing to Honor, but she guessed some of it, and imagined it to be less due to any grief for Barbary's death—Barbary had in fact meant little to Richard—than to the coldness manifested to Sawtrey nowadays by the county. He had relied, more than he knew, on friendliness from his neighbours, and during his mother's lifetime had been protected from the lack of it by having Anna to whom to turn. Also, it had hitherto been unsafe to declare Royalist principles, and most of his enemies were abroad. Now they had come home or were at Court, and the tables were turned; it was inadvisable not to have been on the King's side openly. This was the case despite the new King's edict that there should be an amnesty for all past political crimes, though there was a clique at Court who were trying to make an exception of the persons of those, living or dead, who had signed Charles I's death-warrant in 1649. But Richard was far from concerned with such intrigues; he continued to pass his days as he had always done, showing neither joy or lightness of heart. Had that early death of his brother blighted his life? Would he have been different if the first Edwin Sawtrey had lived? It was possible.

He stayed within the house, and could seldom be persuaded to ride out. Honor would come into the hall to find him always the same, hunched over the fire, his face a yellowish tinge. He had little to say to her or to anyone. He would no longer attend church because former acquaintances markedly turned their backs when he rose from his pew after the service, and did not come to speak with him at the lychgate, moving away instead in groups of their own.

Honor tried to take his mind from such things. Would not he, she suggested, write to the King to remind him of the mercy due to Ned? "If you could see Ned again, it would cheer you." But Sawtrey turned away, and muttered "The King will read no letter writ by me; I may as well save ink and paper."

She began to give some thought to the matter on her own part; it was after all for Ned's release that Barbary had died. Till now there had been no sign or word that the King had so much as heard her, or understood her request at the time. Honor heard disquieting stories of how Charles was surrounded at Court by all those to whom he owed his safety, money, bastard sons; he put off from day to day, doing nothing for any of them, except for Lucy Walter's boy, James Crofts, whom he loved well. It was even whispered already that he would make the boy, whom he intended creating Duke of Monmouth, his heir. But there was talk also of a Portuguese marriage for Charles, by which he might get legitimate children.

None of this helped Sawtrey. For some time—she was shy of going to him—Honor had been wondering if Sir Ralph Farmiloe, who had a son at Court, would ask him to speak there for Ned. "It is not that he wants any reward, only freedom to return," she thought. They had heard twice from

Ned over the years: he was in service with a gentleman planter in Virginia. It might be that he was as happy there as at home now, and looked in the end to make his fortune: Honor had written to tell him of the death of Barbary. Knowing her dead, he might not wish to come home. "But he must be given the chance," she decided. At length she went to Sawtrey to ask if, as he would not visit Sir Ralph, she might do so.

"Do as you will; they have nothing against you, only myself," he muttered, and so Honor put on her hooded cloak and went to give orders to saddle the mare. Riding slowly, followed by a mounted groom, over the path and bridge that joined Daneclere lands to those of Biding across the river, she tried to think of words to use to Sir Ralph; then ended by admitting that these were best thought of on the spur of the moment. There was at least no untruth or doubtfulness in the tale.

As it chanced, halfway across the bridge she saw three riders come; one was tall and sat his horse well, the others were boys. She recognised Sir Ralph and his two sons.

He bared his head; the two boys, at a glance from him, did likewise. "A good day to you, Mrs. Sawtrey," he called. Honor reined in her mare.

"I had hoped for a word with you, sir. Is it permitted that we talk together?"

His brows flew up, but he made a courteous answer, and waved his two sons on while Honor's groom remained nearby. Sir Ralph came down from the saddle and came to assist Honor to descend; the groom took the reins of all three horses, while Honor and Sir Ralph walked, her hand on his arm, for some distance in silence. When they were out of earshot, she turned and looked full into his handsome face.

"Sir," she said, "I know you have little reason to love my husband. It is not for his sake I come, but for his son's." In a few words she told Sir Ralph the tale of Ned's aiding of the Black Boy, his imprisonment and banishment, and Barbary's sad fate and death. "There is none now who will bear the tale to Court, my husband being sick, and in any case he would not be welcome there. Can you aid us?"

He was silent, and she took his silence to mean that he was unwilling. She flushed a little. "I know it is to ask you to take some trouble, which there is no reason why you should do for us. But the young man himself is guilty only of helping the King; surely that will earn your support?"

Sir Ralph looked down at this comely woman who was herself going to some trouble for her husband's bastard. He smiled. "I was not silent for any reason but that I was thinking of the best way," he said. "My son Lionel is at Court, he did not ride home. If Sawtrey, or you yourself, were to write a letter, I would see that Lionel presented it, when there is a chance to do so, to the King. That may take some little time, I fear; as you will know, he is surrounded by those who ask for favours less well deserved than your own, and humours them."

Honor held out her hand. "It is kind in you," she said. She felt great liking for this handsome, greying man who had himself suffered banishment abroad for many years. He bowed over her fingers, she asked for Lady Farmiloe, was helped back into the saddle and returned to Daneclere. Perhaps some little, perhaps even much, had been accomplished in the matter of Ned's release. She made haste to take the news to Sawtrey.

Nothing was heard from Ned for five months, though Sir Ralph sent word to say that Lionel Farmiloe had presented the letter to the King. At length, when they had well-nigh given up hope, there came a scrawled letter from Ned, saying he had received his pardon and would take ship for England. At once Honor wrote to Sir Ralph and his lady, thanking them for their son's efforts on Ned's behalf and for their own. "For without you nothing would have been accomplished," she ended, and wished Lady Farmiloe well, for she was with child. Honor did not add that Sawtrey was now so sick he kept his bed. Perhaps it was true that diseases of the mind could in the end affect the body, or the one the other. He was more than ever yellow, and could keep down only milk. He had smiled a little on hearing that Ned was to come home.

Like Sawtrey, Uthred Jansen had been troubled in his mind; but for a different cause. It was not that company avoided him at Cambridge or that others of his age would not have sought him out; but he avoided them. Where he was, in Cromwell's very college, there could be small rejoicing over the return of the King. In former days there had been a puritan triumph, a kind of long-faced self-sufficiency; now, men looked furtively over their shoulders. Uthred, above all honest, disliked the air of the place. He would refuse to drink with no man, but he made close friends with none. He had been solitary all his youth, and it made small odds to him. As for his degree, he had gained it, thus pleasing old Hawkin at Thwaite.

Other matters would please Hawkin less. Uthred stared across the sparsely furnished room of his lodging to where, in a box which served for cradle, his year-old son Arnulf lay asleep. He slept there of nights since the time, some months ago, when his mother, Morwenna, went back to her own people. The child had a deformed foot. For this reason and because he believed him to be part of his own flesh, Uthred loved the boy and had called him after his father.

He rose now and went to look at the child asleep. Arnulf looked like his mother; he had her straight, lank dark hair and narrow almond eyes, and his skin, like hers, was sallow. Cornish folk boasted Spanish blood from the time of the Armada, and before that had always been different from the English, different from the Danes. It might have been that very difference which had briefly attracted Uthred to Morwenna; by now, he seldom thought of her.

Rather than difference it might have been loneliness. They had first met one evening above the river, where Uthred was leaning with his elbows on the parapet of Magdalen Bridge. As it happened, he had been thinking of Robin, whom he would not be following to the Inns of Court. Now that he had finished with Cambridge, or nearly so, he would return to Thwaite. He knew old Hawkin's obstinacy; the old man had banished both Honor and Robin from his company because he wanted to see them rise in life. For himself, Uthred desired no further advancement. He would refuse, he thought, even at the risk of the old farmer's anger, if Hawkin planned further studies for him. He had his own money and was his own master, and he would return to Thwaite.

She had spoken to him then, the young woman. Uthred had turned from gazing at the water to survey her as she stood there, swinging her narrow hips in a red skirt. Her hair hung lank to her shoulders, no further. She was not a pretty girl, but her voice was cozening, and for some reason a mole on her left cheek attracted him. He had let himself be drawn into talk and some banter with her, then to a tavern. After that they had spent the night together, and other nights. It could not have happened before the King came home; now there was no let to enjoyment of women, song or wine.

He knew that he had not been the first man to sleep with Morwenna. If asked of it, she would have laughed and tossed her hair and walked away. But she had not been pregnant when she came to him, and he did not think she kept company with other men while she was with him. His landlady, who was the widow of a fishmonger, thought differently and said outright that Morwenna was a harlot, which might be true. "They came up here out of Cornwall to start a fish business in my John's day, but it never prospered; they were lazy and their wares had journeyed too far to be fresh." She would have added that Morwenna was not fresh either, but hesitated to offend her lodger; he was a quiet young gentleman, and hadn't given trouble before. So by the end, when the bundle was left on Mrs. Platt's table because the door had been open for the summer heat, she showed less disapproval than Uthred would have expected of her; she even changed the child's linen and found it a wet-nurse. After Arnulf was weaned his father kept him by him, and diverted himself with him at the end of the day when his studies were over. Later he would take him to Thwaite.

The rub was to tell old Hawkin. Uthred had already written one letter which, when he read it through, sounded cringing and humble. "I am not ashamed of my son," he thought. He burned the letter in the fire and in the end, wrote another. *I am bringing my son home with me. He is a bastard, a year old. He hath one foot not as it should be, but otherwise is strong. I have called him for my father.*

He had done no worse than Robin, in the end; and except for the matter of the foot, had acquitted himself as well. He had not meant to copy Robin in anything; matters were as they had fallen out, no more. In due time he took the child, well wrapped against the cold, in front of him in the saddle, with his gear behind, and thus rode home with Arnulf to Thwaite. When he was older, he would make a playmate for young Hawkin.

Three

I

FRANCIS WOLFFE lay on the bed in his Holborn lodging, fully clad against the bitter cold of late January. It was past midnight, and the fire his landlady had grudgingly lit the previous day had almost died. It cast flickering patterns on that part of the timbered ceiling which could be seen above the closely drawn bed-curtains.

He was weary of the lodging, and weary also of waiting for the Earl of Albemarle, until lately plain George Monk, to make up his mind whether or not to employ Wolffe as a secretary. Wolffe's luck had not held in the capital, despite his assiduous place-seeking. In fact—he admitted it readily enough in these self-revealing hours when there were no witnesses—it had not held since losing Barbary. She had made him a pretty penny at first when she was decked out in finery and set up in rooms he had taken near Fenchurch Street, but after the pox had claimed her he could not, for his own reputation, keep her there. As it was, he had himself regularly examined by a physician to make sure he had not caught the disease from her. So far he was clear, at any rate of that; but his debts were mounting now, enough to keep him awake of nights.

The fire was dying. It gave a fitful burst, reflected itself in one last ray of splendour on the ceiling, then sputtered out. Presently, there came other patterns made by torch-bearers for roysterers going late home. They came and passed and were gone, leaving him alone in his darkness. In the dark, growing now towards dawn, thoughts still claimed him that he would not have taken leisure to endure by day. By day he was busy, bustling Frank Wolffe, elbowing his way after patrons at Whitehall, bowing low when the King or the Duke of York passed by; even, for it might be as profitable, bowing when the King's mistress, Barbara Palmer, Lady Castlemaine, passed by. It was only lately that her husband had earned a title for her labours; why should others not do as well from her? He himself was adept at many things which could be of use to such a lady; could write a good letter, keep accounts, keep secrets, cut a figure in company. So could a hundred others, his mind told him; he should never have left Daneclere.

It was useless to regret it now; Mrs. Honor would never have him back. He had seen Richard Sawtrey in London, his wife on his arm. He had not then heard of Barbary's death, and despite everything had gone up to them and made his bow. Mrs. Honor's eyes had stared through him with freezing distaste; she had drawn her husband away. He had not encountered them again, which surprised him: he had thought they would make some ado about Ned Sawtrey's banishment.

Lately he had heard what became of Barbary. He had for long thought she must be dead, or, pox or not, she would have loitered about his doorway to pester him. "Frank, ah sweet Frank, do not cast me off; Frank, ah sweet Frank, sweet Frank. ..." The sound came to his mind, like the crying of a sea-bird.

Why could he not sleep? It must be near dawn. He lay listening for the watch to pass; two o'clock, three o'clock, and a fine dry morning.

He should have slept through what was to happen then.

He heard them come, as he had known he would do if he were still awake; the hurdles, dragging with a rough sound over the cobbles, shaking the tied burden they held. It was inert, and would not win free. The street outside would be grey now, grey with dawn, which was why they had chosen the hour; as yet there would be few folk about, none to shout or pelt filth, none either to cry out for shame at the dishonouring of the mighty dead. Dragged past, they were, the bodies of Cromwell, Bradshaw, Ireton; the late King's executioners twelve years back, dug from their graves after a year or more, and condemned this day to swing on Tyburn gallows and then be cut down and beheaded. Dead men, all of them; why fear them? Why tremble, as he was trembling now, as the heavy sound rumbled and then passed, and died away?

He was not afraid, he told himself; later in the morning he would laugh at his night's megrims. Later in the morning, he would stroll along to see them, with all the fashionable world except the King; Cromwell, Bradshaw and Ireton dangling in their winding-sheets from Tyburn tree. They would be scarce seen as men; there was no power left in any of them; why shiver? What did he fear? Perhaps death itself, when it came, would find him in such terror. Barbary was fortunate: she had had no time for fear of death. Death, trundling past; death, thrusting its skeleton head in at the door, in at the window. He dared not go to the window now, and look at the clear street. The sweat broke out on his face and body, and grew cold.

They had dragged them far off now, the corpses. Yesterday there had been a mass reburial; they had tumbled all the late Protector's kin into a common grave, even the body of a little child, his grandchild. A common grave was where whores lay.

Whores. Barbary, dead, her warm flesh chilled, corruption upon her. But Barbary's body lay at Daneclere.

It was growing colder than ever, he thought, the early day. He would get up himself and light the fire.

2

THE MORNINGS were the worst time of day for Jeremy Whyteleaf, because he had not had leisure to sustain his flagging self-opinion with wine and ale at the tavern, where he went daily before dinner. Sabbath mornings were the worst of all, because then he must go to church, and sit in the Daneclere pew by Mrs Honor and the children, while the servants sat behind; and nowadays there was no longer the nonconformist ranter they had had in former days, but a genteel scion of the Establishment, whose sermons caused Jeremy to fall asleep in his place, with his hat tilted forward over his eyes. Yesterday, also, had come news which for some reason had made him sit up late by himself and weep; my lady Farmiloe, who for some time now had been big with child, had died giving birth to a daughter at Biding manor. She had been a brave lady and her lord must feel very sorrowful, for his homecoming had got her pregnant. The baby was a first girl, and Whyteleaf told himself he knew how Sir Ralph must feel, like himself at the birth of Sophia. Then he searched his mind and admitted honestly that he knew full well Barbary had never borne him a child. No woman ever had. He had known the truth for years; known

that she merely endured his thumbing of her, his inept
fumbling, for one cause; that she might bear children to the
bailiff and give them Whyteleaf's name. The thought of
Frank Wolffe in his very bed, penetrating his wife and
getting her with child, aroused in Whyteleaf sudden bursts of
self-pity, and when he remembered how Barbary had at last
gone off with Wolffe, and her sorry end, and the closed coffin
that had come back to Daneclere and lay now in the church
vault by Mrs. Anna, he knew anger. But there was nothing
he could do; in all the happenings of his life it seemed he
could do nothing, nothing, nothing. Even when he wandered
into the schoolroom to see the three children said to be
his—little Sophia had run far ahead of her brothers, she
would be clever as well as pretty, the little minx—having
their lessons at one table while Dick and Edwin construed
Latin at another, everyone, including the tutor, looked at
Whyteleaf with amused contempt and made him feel an
intruder. An intruder among his own children; an intruder at
Daneclere. Honor had fed him and borne with him all these
years, but even she would grow weary, he felt certain. At least
her own sons had been fathered by Richard Sawtrey; the man
had that to his credit.

He retired to his room one day to brood on all of it, and as
it so happened it was the hour when Gwenllian, who helped
in the tower household still, was making his bed. She had just
leant over to firm the coverlet on the far side, and her plump
backside and thighs—she had gained in girth with the
years—were outlined beneath her skirt. Whyteleaf made a
great oath to himself, locked the door, and plunged at her.

He could not afterwards recall much of it; only the time
when, fearful lest her crying be heard, he had stuffed her
skirt in her mouth. The brown eyes had looked up at him,
frightened and beseeching, but he had not heeded them; he
had his oath to keep. He had done what he would; it had not
lasted long, and before leaving he had turned her over again
in bluff fashion and slapped her bare buttocks and said
cheerfully "That will do, my wench; now get about your
duties," and had fastened up his breeches and gone out. He
felt the better, more his own man, for the encounter. Perhaps
from time to time he would take her again. A man needed a
woman. He had endured his humiliation for too long.

Honor was shortly afterwards emerging from Sawtrey's

room, where she had been giving him his milk gruel though he could hardly keep it down. She did not know how long he would live—the physicians could not tell her—and she grieved at the fact that, despite all their remedies, he was now in great pain. By this time he was her child rather than her husband; a sad child like Dick, whom she could regard with affection. If only further news of Ned would come, it would cheer Sawtrey more than anything; but they had been timely in asking, for folk were beginning to say that the King, though blithe of promises, had done little enough in fact for those who had helped him win safe freedom, and he was more greatly busied with his mistresses and with his marriage to the Papist infanta from Portugal. Such things seemed far from Daneclere, and for Honor herself the thought of London would always be coloured by that sad journey home they had made with Barbary's coffin, and the horror of the unforeseen meeting with Wolffe in the street. She had been glad to come home, to the children and to her duties. Here, there was no feverish seeking after place, no heartlessness such as had abandoned Barbary at the last to the alleys and doorways. The new bailiff was a harmless fellow, with a wife and children. He deferred to her, Honor, for her least wish. Indeed she was mistress of Daneclere more than Richard was its master now, though she would not let him know it. Matters had grown pleasanter with the neighbouring county, who had nothing against Sawtrey's wife; since Honor had begun to go to church supported only by the children and Whyteleaf, smiles and bows were frequent and genuine, and when poor Maud Farmiloe died she had felt able to write to her lord without constraint.

It was while thinking of all this that she encountered Gwenllian, face running with tears and bodice loose.

"Why, child, what has happened?" When she heard, she was filled with resentful anger against Whyteleaf. He must leave the house, and go back to his own. The children, whom she knew long since to be none of his, could stay on here; Whyteleaf was no more fit to care for them than he had been to beget them.

"Go to your room, Gwenllian, and lie down for a little; come to me when you are rested." But Gwenllian was already pouring out another tale, sordid and unheard, about how it must have been Whyteleaf and not Ned who ravished her years since. "A woman can tell, madam; it was the same touch, and the wine on his breath, and the—the useless feeling of it, as if he could not do all he would. I had rather even so it had been Mr. Whyteleaf, madam; when I thought ill of Mr. Ned it was more than I could bear."

Then it all came out, or Honor guessed the rest; Whyteleaf had himself been used by Wolffe to bring about the marriage, and had never known it. Disgust filled Honor, almost including poor Gwenllian who had been the double victim; it did not matter now to anyone else. "Go to your room," she repeated; Gwenllian had a part of the attic where she slept alone, apart from the other servants who were three and four to a loft-chamber. But the young woman would not go and clung to Honor's skirts like a child.

"Madam, I cannot stay; I must leave here, or it will happen again. He won't keep his hands off me now, when he has done it once and more."

It was true, Honor thought. She regretted losing the girl; but there were enough maids in the house, and more could be found; conditions of service were known to be good at Daneclere. She had kept Gwenllian for the sake of Barbary, but now—"I will send a letter with you when you go, to procure you some other place," she said. "Fear nothing; go and rest, and wash your face; it is stained with tears."

Later, when the girl had washed and rested, she came and said she had a grandmother in Pembrokeshire. "If I go there, I may get me a place at the great house; but 'twill not be like this," she said shyly. Honor was relieved; she had latterly had the thought that perhaps Biding manor could use a good servant now the poor lady was gone, but Sir Ralph was best left to decide his own concerns. She would see him at church on Sunday, in the Biding pew, while among others in that of Thwaite sat the young man she had never met, Uthred Jansen.

Gwenllian had taken the path which led to the coach-road. Her bundle of gear was light, and she walked steadily, not looking back at Daneclere on its rise lest she weep again at losing her home. For home it had been, and she would never find such another. She knew she had a friend in Mrs. Honor; if times grew hard, she would send word somehow. Mrs. Honor had given her a month's wages and also her fare into Pembroke, but Gwenllian thought that she would walk and save the fare. No one knew she was coming, and so no one would fret, she told herself; she did not know or greatly care what became of her, despite Mrs. Honor's letter she carried, which would get her a good place. The sun travelled towards the west; if she followed it, sooner or later she would come to a part she knew, and maybe now and again she would ask for a lift in a farmcart. She plodded on, not letting her thoughts drift backward; of what use was that?

She had walked for two hours when a rider appeared on the road. He travelled in haste, and was mounted on a bay. As he drew near a gust of wind tugged Gwenllian's hood from her head, and she was left with hair blowing about her, lips parted and eyes wide. She knew the rider, even if he did not know her. It was Mr. Ned. He had come home.

She went on, saddened that she would see him no more; if only Whyteleaf had let her alone, she would have been at Daneclere with the rest to welcome him. As it was, not having set eyes on him for many a day, she felt he was the same. "That tilt of the head I'd know anywhere," she thought. But his face had been lean and sunburnt and bitter, no longer a boy's.

Thinking of it, she knew how greatly cheered poor Mr. Richard on his sick-bed would be, more than them all; he had known, she was aware, that the King had remembered his promise and that Mr. Ned was to return to England. But time had gone on and it seemed as if he would never come. Now—

There were hoofbeats on the road, growing nearer. He had wheeled his horse about at the gallop, and had returned to her; why? A great joy filled her heart. Whatever the reason, she would see him again; would have the memory of speech with him, and could take it with her wherever she went.

What did he want of her? She saw him smile from the saddle, and at that the whole of his face lit up and he was the Mr. Ned she knew.

"It is the maid Gwenllian, is it not?" he asked. "You attended Mistress Barbary."

Ay, and the worms are eating at her, thought Gwenllian; how terrible a thing if he did not know, and she must tell him! She curtseyed and said in a low voice "She died, sir," and suddenly the tears were welling out of her eyes again and spilling down her face. She heard rather than saw him alight. Presently his arm was about her shoulders.

"I know it," he said. "I mourned her in a far land. Tell me

of her death." He remembered, none better, Honor's news which had come, sending him to the brandy-bottle till all the world was a retching vomiting ruin. But Honor had written little enough. It was because he would know more that he had returned to the small plump Welshwoman, knowing she had attended Barbary. She must have loved her mistress, to weep so. "I remember Bab saying she loved the maid," he thought. He listened to the low voice, with its odd Welsh syllables, telling him what he had not known before.

At the end, he found himself pressing a coin into her hands. He had stiffened and the day had grown grey. "I will to the house, then, to see my father," he told her. "Wait for me at—" He named an inn not far distant.

"Ay, sir." She did not know why he would have her wait, but she would do anything in the world for Mr. Ned; she thought she would die for him, if he asked it of her.

"Buy yourself food, and wait till I come."

He was gone, and she was left clutching the coin in her hand. It was a sovereign. Gwenllian drew a breath; she had never had as much money. It was far more than would be needed to buy a meal. Mr. Ned must have fallen on fortune. "And so he deserved, the dear gentleman," she thought. Mr. Sawtrey would surely grow well now he had his favourite son again. But if Mr. Ned was returning by way of the inn, perhaps he did not mean to stay at Daneclere? Many things had changed.

Ned also saw change, as he entered Daneclere. The house was the same, with the great tapestry he remembered still in the hall; but there was no one about the hearth, though a fire blazed there. A servant went scurrying to fetch Mrs. Honor; when she came, not at first knowing who he was, she halted, then hurried forward, both hands outstretched.

"Ned! It cannot be, at last, at last! How glad your father will be!"

He kissed the hands and then surveyed her, as he would not have done when the raw boy he had been had left Daneclere. He had known something of women on his sojourn abroad; and except for Barbary herself he could not recall seeing so handsome a woman. It was not only that Honor's looks had blossomed and ripened, like fair fruit; she had changed subtly, and was no longer, he could tell, the discreetly silent, low-born bride who had come to Daneclere in Mrs. Anna's day. That she had knowledge, poise, and certainty beyond the common he could tell: she wore a dress of a dark-blue colour which set off the brightness of her hair. His father was fortunate indeed, he thought, in this wife who could genuinely welcome home his bastard. He asked for his father. "Take me to him," he said. "He is well, I hope?"

Her face changed. "Not so, Ned, I fear. I would have written again when he began to ail, but knew you to have left by then. He has not been himself for many a day; it is a kind of yellow wasting. He lies in bed." She smiled. "The sight of you will work wonders, if anything can. Have you eaten, or will I have them set down meat before you go to your father?"

"I have not eaten, good madam, nor will I. I do but visit here, to see my father and yourself."

"You will not stay?" she said incredulously. "But your chamber is ready, with the sheets aired; I have kept it for you since I heard the King had signed the pardon."

"Then I must beg your own. I am for London, and came here first because I have a task there which may mean that you do not see me more. I met the maid Gwenllian on my way; I am taking her with me."

"But, Ned, how— "

"I met her on the way."

"Did she tell you— "

"Gwellian told me much," he said grimly. "I would hear it from your own lips also; but first I must see father." He still saw bewilderment in her gaze, and suddenly said, in a fierce voice, "Do you not see it? She is all I have left of Barbary."

In Richard's room the windows were darkened because he said the daylight hurt his eyes. Honor drew back one of the hangings and the light fell on Ned, standing hatless in the doorway. "Look who is with you," said Honor softly.

The sick man on the bed tried to raise himself, and held out his arms. "Ned! Ned! It does my heart good to see you. I had begun to fear I never should do so again."

"Father!"

They embraced, awkwardly as men do who are unaccustomed to it. Honor could see that Richard's appearance shocked his son despite her warning. She said "I will leave you together, and, Ned, you will surely take some wine? If you do not, I will fear that you are offended with us for some matter."

"You will not stay?" asked Sawtrey with the quick perception of the invalid. "You are leaving us again, after so long a time away?" Tears came to his eyes and his mouth trembled. Ned's face hardened.

"I have a task to do, father. Need you ask what it may be? I will tell you. I must to London, to meet with Wolffe where I may, and settle the reckoning."

He stayed with them an hour, then went.

Gwenllian had waited as she was bidden, having sustained herself with a dish of eggs, some ham, and a drink of small-ale. There were few in the inn, and such as there were took no heed of her, humbly clad as she was and with her cloak pulled well over her, not thrown back as a whore's would be who invited custom. They came and went, and the landlord bustled in and out; then at last, when it was growing dark, she saw Mr. Ned stride in, having left his horse with the ostler. She could tell nothing of how he had fared from the set expression of his face.

He caught sight of her, nodded, and came over to sit by her and to order more small-ale for them both. He wanted no food, he said. He cast his broad hat down by them on the bench, and when the ale came quaffed it as though he were parched, and ordered more. "Will you not drink?" he said when he saw her barely tasted noggin.

"I have little need of more," she answered shyly.

"Then I have need of it." His eyes raked her as if she were indeed a whore, but her own were cast down and she did not see him. Ned stretched out a hand, lean and dark with the sun, and laid it over her small fist. The red-brown eyes she remembered searched her face, no longer as if she might be any woman; they had a gentler light in them. Before he left Daneclere Honor had told him the whole of why Gwenllian had left.

Gwenllian herself knew a great urge to comfort him; he must have heard more of Mrs. Barbary, she knew. It was as though some force were driving her she had not known was within her; when she heard him bespeak a room, she made no outcry. She was no maid, and had been ravished twice; far rather Mr. Ned than Whyteleaf or any man, and if this was what he wanted of her she would give it him.

She left him still swilling ale, and followed the inn-maid upstairs to the room which had been hired for the night. She undressed, folding her clothes neatly as she had been used, and got into bed. The sheets were damp and she began to shiver a little, but it was not with fear. It seemed a long time before Mr. Ned came up.

When he came, he was drunk. He flung off his clothes with uncertain fingers, ripping buttons and tapes; turned to make water in the privy corner, then came to bed. She could tell from the way he touched her that he had already forgotten who she might be, except that she was a young woman with plump desirable flesh. He took her forcefully, using her in a harder way than Whyteleaf had done; she was not sure whether it gave her pleasure or pain. She felt the tears run down her cheeks and heard herself sobbing. It seemed as though he heard also, for he began to comfort her afterwads in a rough way, when it was she who in the beginning had wanted to comfort him. She cried out at the injustice of it.

"I am Gwenllian, sir, Gwenllian!"

She felt him smile against her. "And a good wench. You will come with me to London, Gwen ... Gwenllian. We have neither of us a roof of our own, but we'll find one, a humble one. I have a little silver, enough to last till ... to last till. ...

Till when? It was not for her to question him. She would keep what was left of the money he'd given her, lest he need it himself. London was a grand and fearsome place, very different from going to her grandmother in Pembroke. She did not care. She would follow Mr. Ned anywhere in the world, and see that he had food and clean linen.

3

IT WAS four months since Lady Farmiloe had died, and the stone which marked the vault where she lay had been replaced by now, bearing her name. By it Sir Ralph stood, bare-headed. He often came here, the more so in that his own house had become alien to him; since Maud's death he had almost resented Biding. He would live the time over again—he had done it often—when his wife lay in labour in the upstairs room, with the stir of women about her, then the waiting and the silence; and suddenly a great cry, and the women wailing. He knew then what they came later to tell him: that Maud was dead.

"I killed you," he said aloud. It had been, he knew, his own fierce desire that things should again be as they had always been between them that had caused her frail body to conceive when she was past the age for bearing. At first he had hated the tiny, living creature in the cradle, his only daughter, whose coming into the world had taken her mother's life. He had hardly borne to look at the small lint-white head, covered with fine curls that would soon darken to gold; so like the heads of all the other children, Nigel, Lionel, Ralph, Edgar, Gregory. They all had Maud's hair. Now, as the months passed, he began to see a likeness in the baby to Maud herself. How could he hate it? It was furthermore in his nature to love, not hate; and to have a reminder of Maud again as she had been in youth should be all he could desire, lacking her. Even this seemed heartless; it was part of the reason why he had come here today, to be near Maud in silence, to hear, with an inner hearing, any word she might send from where she was with God. "Help me, aid me, you who never did harm to a creature," he begged her. "Help me in the name of our love." The clergymen said there would be no carnal love in heaven; his own for Maud transcended the body, the impermanent body lying in the tomb. He had loved her more during this past year than ever before in life, when her beauty was lost, when they were both growing older. Would she grudge him the reawakening of feeling after sorrow, the capacity to love all of life, the children, his dogs and horses, even Biding itself in the end, lacking her? He could learn to love Biding again, he knew, even while she who had been its heart and his lay here among the dead.

He recalled her body as it had lain in the coffin before they closed it, early by his order; he would not have gaping servants and tenants know the secret Maud herself had kept so well hidden from all eyes except his own. Now it was still hers and his only; the savaged face was shielded by a flat oaken lid while the candles still burned round it. Folk might murmur, had no doubt done so, that there had been no viewing of the dead. Let them talk; he cared nothing. He had rendered Maud that last service.

He had wept for her, and now was beyond tears. He stared at the tomb, round which the grass already grew high. Come high summer, the children would pull at the pallid flower-heads and suck the white juicy ends of the stalks, as he himself had done when a boy. Things changed little, in such ways; they would be the same when he lay by Maud beneath this stone. Love lived; and so he had come to love this child named after her. Would she forgive him, or know there was no need for forgiveness? Perhaps both; she had been wise. Did she foresee the future, in which it would become clear to him that this daughter, the only one among so many sons, would grow dearer to him than anything on earth? Already he was promising himself that she should never know the lack of a mother or, of less importance, the lack of such things as toys, a pony, fine clothes, cherishing. Her mother over again, without the tragedy of a mask, she might become. The way to achieve it had occurred to him.

He thought of that, wondering whether the elder Maud would herself approve the plan he had. He had not yet ridden to speak with Honor Sawtrey: it would not be convenient to broach the matter whilst her husband lay sick. But after—

"Is it not the best we can contrive, lacking you to guide her?" he said to the stone. He stood in the silence for moments, his hat with its black plume held still, against his thigh. He murmured a prayer, looked down at the tomb once more, then turned away.

4

NED had set Gwenllian up in lodgings in Friday Street, where the fish smelt in the market when it was summer. She seldom opened the windows, accordingly, but often stood by them when Ned was out, watching, unseen, the coming and going of buyers below. Some of these wore shabby clothes, some fine; some were servants in the pay of a rich master, carrying away the best of the crabs and eels; others were citizens' wives doing their own marketing. Gwenllian told herself she had known nothing of fashion before coming to London, for Mrs. Honor had not cared to follow it and some of the other county folk wore gear from the days of Queen Bess. Here everything was made or altered to be of the latest; neck-lines of women's gowns were cut wantonly low, to show bosoms often white-leaded to hide moles or blemishes. The women's faces would be painted red and white, and if they had a spot on their face they put a black patch on it; their hair was frizzed out sideways to look shorter than it was. The men were no less fine, though seldom stopping to buy fish; their shoes had great bows and their small-clothes were looped with coloured ribbons. "If it were not that this is London I could laugh at them," Gwenllian thought. But Ned had told her that the fashions came in any case from Paris, where the young King Louis XIV and his ladies set all that was new.

Ned was out for much of the time and she did not ask where he went. It was enough that late at night he came home to her, emptied his pockets of money to buy their food, and for a time, when he was doing well, even paid a cookmaid. "I do not like you to slave over pots and pans at a fire," he told Gwenllian. But the cookmaid was lazy and it was easier without her, and Gwenllian liked to cook meals and do everything else for Ned. It passed the day for her, she told him. He looked at her oddly.

"Do you never want to walk abroad in finery when I am not here, as other young women do?"

Gwenllian shook her head, not troubling him by saying she had no finery but the gown she stood up in, and her life was happy enough. But he must have given thought to the matter, because one day shortly after that he bade her get her cloak and, instead of leaving her alone, escorted her on his arm to a dressmaker's and milliner's, and bought her two gowns, four shifts, a pair of shoes with green ribbons, and a great half-beaver hat dyed black. He laughed at the last when he saw it on her head.

"Now you look like a Welsh witch, with your little round face half hidden," he teased her. "We must buy you curling-papers." But Gwenllian shook her head. She did not want to lie with him in their bed with knotted papers jabbing at her and making her head ache. "I do not mind that my hair is straight, if you do not," she said. He pretended to frown, and disapprove of her.

"Then we must cut it all off, and buy you a periwig. That is how the King's Castlemaine and other fine ladies deck themselves." If he had known, he was doing an injustice to

Barbara Castlemaine, who still wore the glorious red-gold hair which was the most famous of her charms except her bosom. "Who is that?" Gwenllian asked innocently. "I expect she is a great lady."

"She is a great whore. Some day I will take you to see her, walking in the King's pleasure-gardens he is having weeded and cleared from Noll's time. She has a little black boy in a turban who goes behind her and carries her train."

When the new clothes were ready he took Gwenllian to the gardens. He himself was dressed more finely than usual, but wore by habit nowadays a black periwig which Gwenllian thought made him look older. She would never say so, however, and clung shyly to his arm and eyed the fine world passing back and forth across the grass, with newly planted bushes and the great palace of Whitehall rearing beyond.

"Look," said Ned, "here is the King."

A tall dark man, two others on either side as tall as he, was approaching, with a multitude of courtiers about him begging for favours: he strode so fast that none save his two companions could keep up with him unless they broke into a run. Gwenllian laughed; the King saw her and laughed also, his teeth flashing white in his swarthy face. He was tossing food to the fowls in the pond, as he liked to do daily. Gwenllian was uncertain whether or not his thick black curling hair were a wig; the Black Boy might have such hair of his own. She whispered to Ned concerning it, but he paid no heed to her and she realised he was making a way for them through the press towards the King. Gwenllian knew panic for a moment; who was she to curtsy to the King of England? But he had laughed, and it had been when he had heard her laughter; herself, a servant girl who would never be different, but Ned could talk with the highest in the land. When the time came she picked up her skirts as she had seen Mrs. Honor do at Daneclere when company came, and bobbed a curtsy to the tall King, who was already talking languidly to Ned and using his name.

"You granted me a favour, sire. I thank you for my freedom."

"Would I could grant more with such ease," murmured Charles. His languid eyes raked Gwenllian; she blushed as red as a rose, and he put out a hand and pinched her cheek. The tall fair man on his left side, and the tall white-faced, hawk-nosed man with bitter eyes on his right, paid no heed;

they were waiting for King Charles to continue his walk. "You have a good wench there, Ned," she heard the King say. "We see few wild flowers in London."

Then they were gone, and Gwenllian in some confusion asked Ned timidly if she had done well, for she greatly feared shaming him before all these fine folk. He smiled. "Very well, as to the manner born, and I was proud of you. Those two were the Duke of York, the King's brother, who only likes ugly women, and Prince Rupert of the Rhine, the great cavalier, who hardly likes women at all except for his needs."

"He hath a disappointed look," said Gwenllian. Ned gave a shout of laughter. "Would proud Rupert could hear that! Nay, but he has known his sorrows; his favourite brother was drowned in far seas where they set sail together, and before that he had fought for the King's father and loved him well."

He was in a merry mood, she thought; presently he pointed out to her the great hoops the King had caused to be set up on a part of the grass for the new game of pell-mell, and said that presently they might see him play. Then he stiffened, suddenly, and stared through the press of people to where a lean man in a brown wig, plainly dressed, was making his way back alone in the direction of the river. Something about his back and the set of his shoulders was familiar to Gwenllian. She exclaimed "It is the bailiff, it is Frank Wolffe, oh, I am sure of it," and trembled when Ned did not answer and began to take such long purposeful strides of his own that she could only keep up with him by running, as the courtiers had done. It was as though he would not lose sight of Wolffe for all the world. Gwenllian began to be jostled by the crowd, some of whom called back offensively at having been thrust aside in their hurry. Gwenllian's grand new half-beaver was pushed awry, and she felt close to tears, for not only was Ned no longer thinking of her, she was a hindrance to him. "Hasten," he said once, and she knew that had she not been with him he would have made up on Wolffe by now and finished whatever business he would with him. She said nothing more, keeping tight hold on her small purse of money in one hand and clutching Ned's arm with the other, for without him she was lost. She would never find her way home alone among all these strange people, and she would be accosted by fine gentlemen who thought a woman walking alone was fair game. Tears started to her eyes as they struggled on. Wolffe was gaining distance, as though he knew they were following; Ned's face was white and drawn, as though life held no other purpose than to catch the man he sought. He said nothing more; then a voice hailed them. It was the friendliest she had heard since speaking with the King.

"Ned! Gwenllian!" It was Tom Street, the young lawyer's clerk who like themselves had lodgings near the fish market. He was a short, jolly youth, who all his life would look more butcher than lawyer.

"A good day to you," said Ned, and then "Tom, I'd ask a favour of you. Will you look to Gwenllian for me? I have caught sight of a man I have sought this past half-year, and I would fain speak with him, but he presses on."

Tom was willing, and Gwenllian found herself on his arm instead of Ned's, while Ned's back rapidly disappeared into the throng as Wolffe's had done. Gwenllian felt a prickling of fear, which she told herself was nothing. It was easy to talk to Tom. He was poor like themselves, and had to do his own marketing; that was how she had met him, and later made him known to Ned. Together at last they reached home.

Ned followed Wolffe out of the park and eastwards, to where instead of palaces there were hovels in alleys, their upper floors crowding across the intervening space so that one could not see the sky. Urchins played among the filth in the gutters; at one point they fished in the mud of a small stream running down to the Thames. The air here was no longer clear, but fouled with smoke from many chimneys and with the odour from the refuse thrown out and left to rot. Wolffe's figure would be seen and then would vanish as the ground rose and fell; once Ned thought he had lost him, and would have made ready to search the intervening passages and doorways; but he saw him again, at the end of a street; then Wolffe turned left, and Ned followed. He came to an entry as dark as the rest. When he went in, Wolffe waited there, a hand on his sword.

"Why have you followed me?" his voice asked. At the sound of it, heard again after so many years, Ned's gorge rose; but he answered quietly, standing in the entry with his back against the light.

"I have word from someone who is of importance to your affairs, Mr. Wolffe. I would have a private word with you, if I may."

He had altered his voice to the affected drawl of a Court

gallant; that and the black wig, and the years since they had last seen one another, had, he saw, made Wolffe forget him, or rather not think of him; for all he knew, Ned Sawtrey was safe in Virginia.

Wolffe's eyes gleamed and he saw that he had struck the right note. "The Earl has sent word?" The voice hissed with eagerness. Ned bowed, keeping his back to the light.

"If there was a place where we might talk privily, with none to hear— "

"My landlady is out at this time of the day. Come to my lodging. It is but a step from here."

They walked on, Ned jubilant—it was what he had hoped for—but watchful lest, in their desultory talk, the other might suddenly recognise him. A great sense of loathing filled him at the man's closeness and he contemplated the wisdom of murdering him here, in the street. "But I want him to know why he must die," he told himself. They walked on, and presently came to a shabby doorway where a bracket waited for a torch. Wolffe bowed and Ned preceded him up a flight of stairs. Now he can murder me if he chooses, by stabbing me in the back, he thought; perhaps he has intended it all along. If that were so, he would give Wolffe a reckoning before he died. But nothing of the kind befell; Wolffe ushered him into a moderately sized upper room, in which the grate was empty and littered with papers.

"Now, sir, your word," said Wolffe, entering and latching the door behind him.

Ned turned slowly. He saw the narrow dark eyes, the sallow skin and lank hair, greying somewhat now at the temples, but other change was small. "My word is this," he said, and lunged forwards, catching Wolffe full under the chin. The man fell back, and Ned thrust him down to the ground, pinning him there with the weight of his own body. The other would have cried out, but Ned was ready for him; he gripped Wolffe's throat with both hands, squeezed, and said softly "If you call, or move, you shall hear nothing before I despatch you to hell. Otherwise you may know why you are about to die."

Wolffe gasped and gurgled like a fish; the black eyes were full of hate. He must feel a fool, Ned thought clearly; then he himself began to speak. "For what you did to Barbary Mountchurch, for what you made her become, for her death; for sending me, Ned Sawtrey, whom you knew not till now, to far places, that you might work your will; for all this, and a hundred damned meannesses and crimes, I will cut your throat, you felon; and if time is given me I will hang your body from that beam." He jerked his head upwards to where the timber crossed the ceiling; he had seen it as he came in, and had thought of such a use for it. He brought out a sharp-honed knife, such as all Virginians carry; at sight of it Wolffe struggled convulsively. Ned cut the man's throat slowly, watching the blood well out and sweep to the ground. He used his other hand to stop Wolffe's mouth.

When Wolffe was dead, or nigh enough, he dragged the limp body across the floor and took off the man's belt, and hanged him with it below the beam, where there were several great hooks. They must once have been used for smoking ham and drying herbs. The thought came to him as he wiped his knife, returned it to its place, opened the door, and went. He did not look back at the dead body dangling from the ceiling, no longer jerking now even in the dance of death.

Gwenllian knew her fear had been real; night had fallen, and Ned had not yet come home. She made herself a meal and made pretence to eat it, then put coals on the fire to keep it high for his return; though it was summer, the nights could be cold. Lying alone in bed later, she found herself asking questions of her own mind that it could not possibly answer. Had Ned found Wolffe as he desired to do? Had he gone to Wolffe's lodging? Had they gone to an inn together? Were they still talking, far into the night?

But Ned's face had not worn the expression of a man eager to talk.

At last, in the silence and loneliness, with no sound except that of the watch in the streets, she faced the cause of her fear. Ned's look had been that of a man resolved to kill. She was uncertain how she knew of it, but she knew.

"By now, one or the other of them will be dead," she thought. She fell into a cold sweat of fear, waiting. Had they arrested Ned? Was he in hiding? Would he perhaps never dare come here any more? Would the watch come here if they found a dead body? If they asked, she must say that she did not know what had happened. Or would it be best to lie, and say Ned had been with her all of the evening, and had only lately gone out? She would get good Tom Street to lie also and say he had been in his company.

124   *Daneclere*

Someone was coming upstairs. Gwenllian tensed herself, seeing, as she heard the mounting footsteps draw nearer, the small squares of the window grow grey in the coming dawn. She clenched her small fists against the bed-sheets, almost tearing them. The fire still glowed in the hearth.

The door opened. It was Ned, moving slowly like a man who is very tired. She could see his head without the periwig; it seemed like a stranger's; why had he taken it off? He latched the door and came slowly into the room.

"Are you awake, Gwenllian?"

"Yes." She would say nothing, ask nothing until he told her, not trouble him.

He began to undress. He had not looked at her. She saw him at last kneel down, naked, and thrust his bundled shirt into the fire. A small flame spurted up, catching at the linen. Presently there was a small of burning horsehair. Gwenllian drew a breath.

"That is your new shirt you are burning, and your periwig. Why do you not let me wash the shirt?" Her voice died away. The silence faced them; then he began to laugh. He stood up, naked and white as a god, still laughing, "You know, do you not?" he said. "Blood will not wash away easily, and I hid till it was dark. It is safer to burn it, and they will be looking for a man in a black wig, and not for me."

She took refuge in ordinary, everyday things. "Your other clothes, are they clean?" she said. It seemed a pity to burn such fine clothes. It came to her that there was much she did not know about Ned; where he had got the money for the clothes, what they lived on.

"They will serve," he said, adding "Tomorrow we must leave town." His voice was flat and weary and a swift compassion came to her. "Have you eaten?" she asked him. It did not matter about leaving London, she had never never greatly liked it, except for meeting the King. As always, she would follow Ned wherever he might take her.

He came and stood over her, so that she smelled sweat and blood. "You do not ask how I killed him," he said.

Then he fell on his knees and laid his head on the bed's edge and began to sob. She moved in the bed and cast her arms about him, cradling him against her bare breast as though it were his mother's. Her mouth was on his neck; now and again, as his mother might have done, she kissed him.

Presently he raised his face, wet with tears in the growing light.

"They will not think it strange if we are gone," he said. "Many leave the city when they have lost at gaming, rather than pay. I have not won lately. I never told you, did I, where the silver came from? Sometimes I was fortunate. I was fortunate in you."

"I will tell no one anything," she said, holding him.

"Gwenllian, Gwenllian—"

Afterwards, before they went, she herself raked the ashes to make sure no bloodstains remained. She heard Ned moving about the room gathering and crumpling papers, packing their few belongings. Presently he came over and shoved the papers in the fire. "That is all," he said and kissed her neck. "You have been a gambler's wench, Gwenllian. Now—"

What would he do now? "Surely your father would give you money," she said timidly. He was angry at once.

"I would not owe it to him. He is dying, and I have not stayed by him. I had this thing to do."

He turned away. "It is the open road for us," he said. "You shall live like a fine lady, but with small company. I have enough money left to buy a good horse, and weapons. We will lie up a little way from the coach-roads, in some house where they ask no questions."

Later, she went with him out of town. It was a relief to her when the air grew clear, leaving the foul smoke behind. Perhaps all those who were searching for Wolffe's killer would not look beyond the smoke. By now, someone, perhaps the serving-maid, or the landlady, would have given the alarm. Gwenllian found herself thinking of it coldly. The man had deserved to die. She herself would not find it difficult to keep silence. She had never talked much. Nothing mattered except that he had come back to her and was taking her with him, despite having little money. Nothing mattered but that.

Two days later, a messenger rode in from Daneclere, searching for Ned Sawtrey. He brought word that Richard Sawtrey was dying at Daneclere and would fain see his favourite son before he went. No success greeted his questioning as to which way Mr. Ned had gone, but he heard the news of Wolffe's murder. Nobody knew who had done away with him, except that he had been seen in speech with a man in a black periwig, some time before the death. It might have been anyone in the honeycombed city. Wolffe had had secret ways and few friends, and would soon be forgotten.

5

RICHARD SAWTREY'S funeral was well attended, though few present would have called him friend and it was tacitly assumed that the county had come for the sake of his widow. Honor had made herself liked and respected. Also, it was an occasion of solidarity, an admission that all, gentle and simple, would come to such an end, and so they honoured his. A few, a very few, had come out of curiosity.

Richard had died as other men go to sleep. His death had been after the manner in which he had lived, quiet and unremarkable. Except for Ned, he had wanted to see no one to be reconciled to them; he had had no enemies any more than he had had friends. Now, such of Meg's tall broad-shouldered sons as were here would bear the light weight of the coffin as it passed out of the great hall where it had lain. Only Ned was missing; and only she herself, of anyone left alive, Honor was thinking, now knew what had been said to prove the identity of Wolffe's murderer. Richard had known, and he was dead. It was unlikely Ned had confided in anyone else.

She stood and watched the coffin go by at last, unable to rid herself of the feeling that a stranger lay in it. What had she known of Richard Sawtrey other than that he had fathered her two children and had always been courteous to her? He had never loved her, nor she him. They had borne with one another, shown patience that they might not have done had they been younger; that was all. She had nursed him to the end, and he had been grateful; now it was over. She looked across to where young Dick, as heir, stood two paces forward from herself and his younger brother. How puny he seemed by contrast to Edwin's red-gold height! Dick was his father's son, already showing the apologetic stoop of the shoulders Sawtrey had always had. In time, no doubt, he would grow up into a furtive, harmless, perhaps lecherous man like his father. If only Edwin had been the first-born!

She grasped at Edwin's hand, for he could be unruly, and on her other side stood poor young Gregory Farmiloe, not knowing where he was or why he had come. It had surprised and pleased Honor that Sir Ralph was here, with all his sons. The Whyteleaf children, who would not give open trouble, stood in a group behind; Sophia, with the dark curls pulled well forward to advantage under her cap, would miss nothing and nobody. Despite her love of children Honor found it hard to like Sophia; knowing this, she was more indulgent with the child than she need have been. Sophia's brothers seemed unremarkable; dark, narrow-eyed, quiet, and sly. Honor had been glad when the tutor came to take charge of the Whyteleaf children, with Dick and Edwin. She herself, and the nursemaid who had at first looked after their needs, had found it a burden.

Jeremy Whyteleaf himself, having kept on good enough terms with Honor since she had expelled him from Daneclere, was in the hall, drunk, and straddling his feet to keep his balance. He shed tears for Sawtrey, for he was an affectionate soul. Sir Ralph Farmiloe aided him with an arm in following the coffin and as he did so, turned to make Honor a bow.

"I would have speech with you later," he murmured. "May this be?"

Honor inclined her head, its aureole of hair half hidden by the veil, like the sun in the midst of rain-clouds. Beside her the child Sophia had already noted the talk, and lowered her lashes, gazing through them at the Farmiloe boys as they filed out. She was already much aware of the Farmiloe family. Perhaps what Sir Ralph wanted, she thought, his own lady being dead and aunt Sawtrey now a widow, was to propose marriage. It would certainly be something to call oneself Lady Farmiloe. If only she herself were older! She could divert and entertain, she knew, far better than dull aunt Sawtrey, who only did and said the proper things for fear anyone would remember she was only a farmer's daughter. If she, Sophia, could choose a bridegroom from among the Farmiloes, which would she have? Not Gregory, he was soft in the head. Lionel was the eldest and would inherit the title, and he was very handsome, but he never looked at her. Neither did Ralph, but Edgar sometimes did. Sophia saw them every Sunday in church, and knew their bent fair necks intimately, but little more. Perhaps after all it would be best, though he had a lined face and threads of grey in his hair and beard, to marry Sir Ralph himself, and become my lady; that was if aunt Sawtrey did not snap up the offer.

The coffin by now had been carried out of Daneclere and down the steps. All of the company began to move, and a shuffling of feet and hushing of skirts drowned the prosing of the clergyman, who was reading aloud from the Prayer Book. *Man that is born of woman hath but a short time to live.* Honor raised her head and stared at the crowd: women did not go to the graveside. Among those passing was Uthred Jansen. Her glance dwelt on his dark head, and his eyes, the colour of the sea as they were, raised themselves and met hers with a kind of shock of recognition, as though a thread joined them that would not break. She had often seen him in church and he her, but that was all. If only Hawkin would tolerate her visiting Thwaite again, she would have known Uthred long ago. It was absurd that such near neighbours should remain strangers.

Where was Ned Sawtrey? folk were asking, in hushed voices now the reading was over and out of respect to the dead. Why had he not come to be with his father at the end, and take his place with his brothers in shouldering the coffin? A messenger had been sent to London, everyone knew. Maybe young Ned was in prison again. Of all the bastard Sawtreys, Ned had been the only one permitted to have an exalted idea of his own station, brought up at Daneclere as if he were the heir. Much harm had been done by that; there was the banishment to far parts lately ended, by His Majesty's clemency; but even the King might not be lenient twice. Odd things befell concerning Daneclere; that man who had been their bailiff, whom no one liked, had been found hanged, they said, and with his throat cut. As for Barbary Whyteleaf, she had gone off, leaving her children to be brought up by good Mrs. Honor, and now was dead. They would lay Richard by her in the vault, near his mother. And she—

The trail of gossip faded, slowly, as the procession passed on its way.

Sir Ralph Farmiloe rode back again to Daneclere after the burial. What his errand might mean Honor had not taken time to think, as the remaining company from the funeral, the women, had stayed some little time. When the house was clear of them, she got out her embroidery and sent for Sophia to sit by her with her sampler. It was a new sensation not to have to toil constantly back and forth from the sick-room, with possets and aids. She tried to pray for Sawtrey and found that she could hardly remember his face. The work she now held had occupied her during many of his hours of illness, when she could sit by him and progress with it without having to make talk. If they had spoken, it would have been of Ned; and both he and she had kept their own counsel.

Sophia came with her sampler and sat demurely on a footstool, setting stitches. She spoke little and had none of a child's prattle. Honor could not know that she had a lively curiosity about Sir Ralph's visit, and had been gleeful at being sent for with the prospect, if she remained quiet, of being forgotten and allowed to stay.

Sophia's hopes were not sustained, however. When the sound of Sir Ralph's arrival came, Honor rose to greet the guest, sweeping forward with one hand holding her heavy skirts and the other, large, white, and capable in its frail cuff of linen and lace, outstretched to the visitor. Sir Ralph swept a bow, his plumed hat in his hand, and kissed his hostess's fingers.

"Sophia, you may run upstairs to join the others," Honor told her. Sophia, inwardly mutinous, could do nothing but seem to obey; she bobbed a curtsy, as she had been taught, and gave Sir Ralph leisure to see her pretty manners and pretty face; then she made as slow a task as possible of ascending the stairs; inwardly craning to hear whatever it might be they had to talk about, those two in the hall. But nothing of importance was exchanged while she was still in sight, merely condolences, and an apology from Sir Ralph to Honor for troubling her so soon.

Sophia reached the top step and, knowing exactly where she was going, turned not towards the schoolroom but to the musicians' gallery, which held various unused pieces of furniture including a discarded ingle. One side of this was missing, and it was possible for Sophia to insinuate her small person in beneath what had once been the hinged seat. She grimaced, for the ingle was dusty with neglect on the inside, and Sophia disliked getting grime on her clothes. But there was no help for it, and it was a good vantage-point used both by herself and her brother Lewis; Jem had already grown too big. One could hear without being seen, and perhaps use the knowledge and again, perhaps, merely hoard it for future use. Jem and Lew had already learnt that, and she had not been slow in picking it up for herself. She listened; and presently was glad to hear that she had learned something which would divert Jem, Lew, and perhaps Edwin, perhaps not. Dick she would not tell, because he would go straight to his mother. In fact, perhaps she would not tell anyone; the more she listened, the more interesting it seemed to have sole knowledge of this proposal to marry Dick to a chit not yet out of the cradle. So Sir Ralph did not wish to wed aunt Sawtrey after all! It had been worth cramping oneself in the dirty ingle to find out. Sophia listened, and made notes in her mind.

"It is not as though her mother were alive, or could ever be replaced by another," Ralph Farmiloe said, standing with the flagon Honor had brought him and staring out at the afternoon sky. He looked older of late, Honor thought. She herself was not small-minded enough to resent the overt neglect of her own charms, or even to have thought of what had immediately occurred to Sophia. A man would not choose another's funeral day to propose to the widow. And this man was bereaved, would never cease to mourn his wife or blame himself for her death. She knew all this, and said gently,

"Surely the child would be happier in her own home at Biding than here? She would have your love and care, and—and good servants can be found."

"No servant could give her what you may. All speak well of you for what you have done, are doing, for Whyteleaf's children. They would be destitute and neglected now but for your kindness."

He set down the flagon and smiled shyly. "You are like the good woman in the Scriptures," he said, "who sees to her house, her children and her soul. Could Maud but grow up in your care I'd have no fear for her. I'd give her a fine dowry; she and young Dick would grow up not as strangers, but as friends in daily company. That is not a bad start to a marriage, or would you say otherwise? I was married to her mother when we were both very young."

Honor nodded slowly. At first the notion had surprised her, but now she saw its advantages. Dick would never get himself a better-born wife; the dowry did not matter for happiness, but it would be welcome enough. Already she felt glad of the thought of caring for the motherless baby.

"I ask that it should be soon, if at all," said Sir Ralph. "At one time I thought I never could part with little Maud even for her own sake. As it is, there will be much coming and going between us, and I hope you will allow me to see her often here, and bring her to Biding."

He glanced at the staircase. "That child who went upstairs just now—a pretty little wench—is perhaps not too old to become Maud's playmate when she is grown. They would bear one another company among all the men." His smile widened. When he was gay he was irresistible. Yet Honor still felt caution.

"You must give me a little time to think upon it," she said, looking down at her own white fingers. "I confess I see no great matter in the way, if you do not—unless maybe Dick should be older before he seeks a bride."

Sir Ralph laughed. "Let them grow up together as I have said, and it will rid the matter of its strangeness for Dick, who seems a shy lad."

"He is like his father," said Honor. Sir Ralph nodded.

"Over many young folk are stangers when they meet at the altar, however wise and provident their kin have been," he said. "It would please me well to think that they knew one another."

Honor said again that she would think of the matter, and let him know by a note: and he rode off, refusing to stay and dine so soon after the burial. That now seemed to have taken second place in the day. Before Sir Ralph was out of sight Honor knew that she would accept his suggestion of Maud Farmiloe as a bride for her son Dick. There was everything in favour, and nothing against. What could happen ill? And Sophia was too smug, it would be good for her to have a rival.

Four

I

—"AND IF THE FRENCH can sail as far without mishap, why not we? Why not, I say?" demanded Robin Thwaite, seated at his sister Honor's fire with a tankard of mulled ale between his hands and his bastard, Young Hawkin, sitting silently by. Hawkin said little, but his dark, shrewd eyes assessed his father's every word and movement. At the end of the speech he had nodded briefly, as if to let the company know he had made up his mind that this was no idle fancy, but truth. Hawkin was younger than he looked; he had a man's air about him and broad shoulders.

Robin looked his age nowadays, perhaps more; there had come lines of irritation about his eyes and mouth, for he had spent the past years in an occupation which was not congenial to him, in a solicitor's office in Liverpool. Having justified his father's training of him at Cambridge and the Inns of Court, he had saved some money, given in his warning, and left; and now would seek adventure. None grudged it to him except Old Hawkin, who grumbled that his younger son was a ne'er-do-well. Robin had come to Honor for solace; and his fixed notion was to go to sea, to find the country still known as New France, and gather its riches.

Honor let the men talk, continuing gently to rub her fingers with a clean linen cloth dipped in rose-water; she had been greasing eggs against the winter and the grease clung. By her, playing quietly with her spaniel, was young Maud from Biding, who took no heed of the adult talk. Her silver-gilt hair fell in ringlets, growing back from a peak on her brow in a way that showed the heart-shape of the exquisite little face. Her eyes were a clear grey, fringed surprisingly with fine dark lashes. She gave no one trouble and seemed happy. Dick, her bridegroom, stood about nearby in the feckless way he had, doing nothing, not joining in the talk: his thoughts were elsewhere and his narrow face withdrawn. Beside him Edwin, the younger brother, seemed all eagerness and fire. He had taken up his uncle on his last saying. "Where would we get a ship?" he asked, and Robin, the weary lines lifting, grinned over at him.

"So I am to number you already among the crew, eh?"

"Not unless you can find a boat."

"No," began Honor, but Robin had begun to speak again and went on, not heeding her. "Two of the Biding men, when I spoke to them in the tavern, were sharp-set to join us, I can tell you. You ask where I can find a ship? Why did I spend many a weary year in Liverpool port if 'twere not to find out men and places where I can beg or hire gear and a crew? If there are enough of us in this, a ship will be found. That I doubt not."

"They say," said Edwin, forgetting to tease his uncle, "that there are fortunes to be made in those far parts, but it's a case of devil take the hindmost."

"The Indians may not be friendly," said Dick quietly. Everyone listened, as he so seldom spoke; then the talk broke out again. There were friendly and unfriendly Indians; which a man met was his good or ill fortune. "If we offer to trade with them, they will surely leave us our scalps," said Edwin.

Honor's heart turned over, knowing that her darling was set on Robin's venture and would in all probability want to go with him. Yet how could he bide forever in Daneclere, living the life of a younger brother only? At the first hint of deeds or danger, Edwin would be off; and she could not stop it if she would. He had not a mind that would be satisfied with bookish things, like Dick: she knew Dick would never give her a moment's anxiety in such ways, but Dick had not her love.

She set aside her finger-cloth, and said, looking down at her spread, newly fragrant hands, "It is so long a voyage that you would not soon come home. There would be many a mishap before meeting an Indian; storms, snow and ice. You are not a boy, Robin, to indulge in idle dreams. Think it over well, I pray."

"Do you not suppose that I have done so?" answered her brother impatiently. He shrugged aside his ill-temper. "Woman, you would have us all stay at home and grow old over dice and cards. Why, it might happen that we found the North West Passage, then we would be rich indeed." He set down the tankard and smiled at her, saying "That was good ale."

"It has gone to your head."

He ignored her. "So you, nephew, will come if your mother gives you leave; and I myself, and Young Hawkin here. I do not want the Whyteleaf tribe." He looked over his shoulder, but they were out riding. "It is a ploy for honest men, who are not afraid," said Robin squarely. His blue eyes met his sister's, and there was still some doubt in hers. "It is maybe not a ploy for very young men," she said softly.

Edwin snorted a denial, tossing back his bright hair. "Hawkin goes, and he is scarce older than I. What befell your hand, lad?" A brief movement had shown Hawkin's square brown fist red with the marks of teeth, like an animal's. He gave his rare, grim smile. "Arnulf, Uthred Jansen's son, bit me," he said. "He wants to come on the voyage and if his father goes, he will take him. They are never apart since the limping little devil grew out of piddle-clouts. I like him not."

"And what did you do to him when he bit you?" asked Edwin innocently. He liked his uncle's natural son; they often rode or played chess together. "I thrashed him," said Hawkin squarely, and everyone laughed. The sound rose to the high rafters and was lost there. Honor thought with pity of her father, whose great age would not permit him to go on this far voyage after beaver, deep into a part-known continent peopled by savages. The wild seas between, the icebergs and fearsome storms, would not have deterred the old man, she knew, had he been younger. As it was, he was prepared to lose Uthred Jansen for the time and make do, no doubt, with David and the farm-hands. "I will steal down and see him, angry though he may be," she thought, and remembered how, as Robin showed no taste for farming, the farm at Thwaite rested now between David and Uthred, whom Honor had heard worked as knowledgeably with the land and the beasts as if he had been born to it. As if to answer her thoughts Robin spoke again. "Our father is willing to let Uthred go, for he says the man has worked well now for many a year and deserves his chance to sail the sea. Anyone would think Uthred was in thrall to our father, whereas he may go where he pleases."

"At any rate, there is a gathering of us, with the Farmiloe men if they should come," put in Edwin eagerly.

"I can see that there will be naught left on either side the river but the old and the young, women and children," said Honor. Robin stood up, stretching his lean limbs.

"Never fear, Honor lass; our father and David between them will break a pike if war should come—with whom? It is because all the wars are over that men are weary of the peace. Nothing remains for a fellow to do now but hope to make his fortune, then lose it again gaming at Whitehall." Robin's eyes had a faraway expression: she knew he still thought of ships and Indians. But his next proposal had meat to it.

"We have thought, Uthred and I—it was he who suggested it," he added honestly, "that it would be well for some among us to go to London to wait on Prince Rupert, and tell him of our plans, as the Frenchmen did on their return. The Prince in his youth sailed those seas, and lost his brother in a shipwreck among the islands. They say he still hopes to hear news of him, even now; no doubt he asked the Frenchmen of any rumours. But after so long a time, it is not likely he lives still."

"If we brought home Prince Maurice, our reward would be very great," said Edwin.

"Hawkin will ride by us now, at any rate: he has never seen the city. And one or more Farmiloes may come; they are used to Court ways, and may smooth our rough tongues for us."

"I would lief see the city also, and the Prince," burst in Edwin. His uncle frowned.

"We cannot wait on the Prince with a rabble of boys. His temper is known to be short."

Edwin looked downcast, but Young Hawkin put in reasonably, "I care naught for princes and fine ways, so long as the voyage goes forward. Do you take my place, cousin, and I will stay at Thwaite and see to the winter saltings." Robin thumped his shoulders, and said "Well spoken, my bumpkin! There is another thing, Honor; we must make haste with the voyage this spring, while Uthred can still leave Thwaite. At any minute David's wife's father may die, and Dave himself will be off to Bents, which is richer by far, and leave Thwaite without a main arm."

"Then you are all of you mad to be talking of the enterprise at all," said Honor, "but I suppose you will go."

Robin regarded her. "You do not speak from your heart, unwilling as you are to part with Edwin here. The sea is in our blood, Honor, your own as well as ours. You would take no pride in us if we settled down as farm-folk before we grew old, having known no other life. This is a God-given chance, while we have money and leisure; do not stint us of't."

"I can prevent no single one of you from doing as he will, nor ever could," said Honor, but despite herself she was prouder of Edwin than of Dick, who some time since had sidled from the room lest he be asked to join the voyage. "But go to see the Prince, and take such advice as he is surely able to offer; at least he knows the dangers—"

"Rupert of the Rhine knows danger better than any man living," cried Edwin, his eyes shining. "Glad I shall be to see him in the flesh, for he has been a legend all my youth! Why, when they killed the King's father it was Rupert alone, among all the craven folk and nations, who would not make peace with Cromwell, but carried on the war in himself; he sailed out the Protectorate in a rotten old hulk off Ireland and off Portugal, with mutiny and I know not what all, and old Noll trying to stir up trouble for him wherever he might be, but they never caught Rupert, and he has lived to come back to London to be with the King again."

"Well, you will see this famous man, since Hawkin has given his place to you," soothed his mother. She still hoped, against hope, that sober advice would prevent them all from making this voyage.

After they had gone she went to where Maud sat and smiled down at her. "Time for bed, my child. Yes, you may take dog Tray with you." The fair curls dropped against her shoulder as they ascended the stairs. They had talked overlong, and it was growing late, and Maud was half asleep.

Honor saw the men ride off, dressed in the best they had; it was not to be a long stay and they took little baggage. All through the ensuing days her mind was with Edwin and Robin, though she talked as usual with Sophia and her brothers and Maud and Dick, and directed the servants and saw to the purveying of household meals. "I must beware of tying Edwin to my apron-strings, lest he grow weary of me," she told herself. Nevertheless she hoped with all her heart that the visit to Prince Rupert would in some way disillusion them.

They did not write; there was scant leisure, for within four days they were back again, brimming with news. Robin tossed his hat on the bench like a boy; his eyes beamed with mirth and pleasure, and the lines of boredom and weariness seemed to have gone, as though he had shed the dull years and were young again. As for Edwin, he wore the expression of one who has looked upon the sun. Honor realised with a pang how dull life at Daneclere must have seemed to him of late. "Perhaps I should have sent him to Cambridge like Dick, but his tutors said he had no aptitude," she thought. Edwin's joys had always been riding, shooting, anything which exercised his splendid young body. He looked like a god, she thought, or a prince himself; and knew pleasure when he strode forward to kiss her on the cheek.

" How fared you?" she asked, and tried to keep her voice from trembling; it was plain they had fared well.

Both of them began to talk at once. "Peace, braggart, and let your elders speak," said Robin. "Peace, uncle, and let one who kept his wits about him tell the tale," retorted Edwin. "Such ale as he drank in a riverside tavern you never imagined, mother, and then we— "

"What of the Prince?" said Honor. "I make no doubt you both played the fool in London, but what did *he* say?"

"Give me ale," said Robin, "ay, again. Well, when we first waited on the Prince in Spring Gardens it did not seem as if he regarded us with favour. He is very tall, with a haughty look, and he stared us down as though we had come out of the earth; he was wearing a leather tunic for his chemical experiments. Then by God's grace, it was borne in on him that three of our company were called Farmiloe, and he knew Nigel who fell at Edgehill. Thereafter nothing would do but that we must stay, and talk and talk, while a boy stoked wood and coal in the stove with a great retort bubbling on it, full of stinking matter. I thought they would never be done talking of battles while we held our noses, but by the end we had come round to what he wanted to know."

"Mother, there are great things in prospect for fur-trappers and explorers; the Prince is giving his favour to the launching of a company situated in Hudson's Bay, for trading, and shipping skins home. There will be auctions, and— "

"Boy, you speak too fast of what has not happened yet. To be sure such a company is mooted— "

"Well, with Rupert, when a matter is mooted 'tis as good as done. The company will have the rights of buying and selling through all the lands about the coast— "

"To hear you speak, good nephew, a man would think you

and Rupert were in a corner by yourselves, whereas it was
Lionel and Ralph— "

"So all three Farmiloes rode with you," said Honor.

"All the brothers rode, with their father's blessing; except
for Gregory, on account of his wits. But they are all to sail.
We are to sail, with a word from the Prince to the officials of
the Company that we are his privileged friends, and— "

"It will maybe not extend to the selling of beaver," put in
Edwin soberly. "Nobody except the Company will have the
right to buy and sell over the territory, which is very large.
You will see I have looked at the map."

"Maybe we can go further inland and find territory which
is not theirs."

"Then it will be a question of finding a port to take it out.
I tell you, they have the whole seaboard to the east, unless one
goes down country through the places where the Indian tribes
are, past the lakes."

"Hark at the boy! He has a good head on his shoulders
after all. Whatever befalls, we sail, and under the Prince's
protection. We will not be treated like pirate trappers. See
how Honor blanches at that! Fear not, sister, we will be
looked after very well. The Indians nearby are friendly, and
will be more so if they have a trading-place to exchange their
beaver for whatever it is they crave."

"Tobacco and whisky," said Edwin.

2

THEIR SHIP sailed on 11th April, 1672; not from Liverpool
despite all Robin's friendships, but from the Pool of London.
They had left Daneclere four days previously.

Honor watched them go and, as soon as the sounds of their
going had died in the distance, made herself—she was near
tears—go and write a letter to her father at Thwaite, asking
if she might come and visit him. This done and sealed, she
sent for the Whyteleaf boys. "Take horse," she said, "and
give my father this. You may bring back word by mouth
whether or not he would that I should come. He may be
solitary."

She stared at the dark, silent boys as they went to do her bidding. She had tried to love Barbary's children, but could not. Now, with Edwin gone, it might be for years, she must fill her heart somehow. But they had said nothing, merely gone to carry out her commands, showing no pleasure in it.

He blurred eyes took in a hesitant figure in the hall; it was Dick, nearing the end of his Easter vacation.

"Mother—"

"What is it?" she said, more sharply than she had intended. It would have been better had he ridden out of her life, she thought, and the other stayed; but in the nature of things that would not happen.

Dick Sawtrey swallowed; he was intensely shy and he knew well enough that his mother cared little for him. "I would like, mother," he said, "to offer you some solace, if I may."

Honor laid her hand on his arm. "Why, Dick, you cause me no trouble. For that alone I should be thankful. Forgive me if at this time my mind is filled with thoughts of Edwin, and what may befall him. But I am glad of your support and company."

"I would give you all you desire," he said, almost eagerly. "I did not want to go on the voyage; such things are not for me. I had sooner be a scholar."

That was true, she thought; he had a mind filled with matter she herself could never understand, and never would. "Whatever you would make of your life, I will not hinder you," she said gently, and for almost the first time in her life leaned towards him to kiss him on the cheek. Dick flushed with pleasure. They parted soon, for he had to go on his way.

Jem and Lewis Whyteleaf rode into Thwaite yard at such speed that they sent the hens and geese flurrying and squawking and injured one, which limped away on a hurt foot. A young woman, one of David's daughters, looked out of the stack-yard in surprise; she carried a bowl, with collected eggs in it. Jem slid out of the saddle and threw the reins to his younger brother. "Here, wench," he called, holding out Honor's letter.

She came slowly, not used to be so addressed. She took the letter, but could not read or write. "It is for your grandfather, I believe," said Jem, and being nearby her he pinched her on the buttocks. She squealed, and dropped the bowl of eggs; the mess fouled the swept yard. "You are not a civil gentleman," she said, "whoever you may be."

"You know me well enough from church, my wench. Come, give us a kiss." Jem was growing old enough now to have ado with women, and they were seldom out of his thoughts. He thrust his sallow, lean face towards her, so closely that she could see the sparse dark hairs which grew on his lip and chin. She evaded him, and ran off, crying indignantly "I'll tell grandfer of the eggs and all else, be sure I will."

Jem laughed. "I care not what you tell him," he called but she had gone into the house. Within moments an old, grizzle-browed man appeared, shaking his stick. "Be off with ye for misbegotten rubbish," he called to them. "Be off out o' Thwaite yard."

"We are come from your daughter, old one; what am I to say to her? She writes that she would see you; would you so?"

"Tell her what I told her when she was wed; unless for grievous harm, she is not to cross Thwaite ford. You yourselves had best be gone; I like ye not."

"He likes us not, he likes us not," Jem and Lewis chanted, between bursts of laughter. Old Hawkin almost made to pursue them in his anger, mounted though they were. They galloped off, and soon the young woman came out again to see to the injured hen, and to clean up the mess of egg-shells and throw it into the straw to the waiting birds. "Don't do 'em no harm to eat the shells, they'll allus do it," she muttered. "Yon were a thievish pair."

So Honor did not visit her father, for she knew him well enough to be certain that thwarting of his wishes would mean no welcome. She stayed on at Daneclere, sad and alone, for Dick had by now gone back to college. There was nothing to do but wait for news from the adventurers, when they should have time to write.

Fort Rupert, 3rd May, 1673.

My dear Sister,

Mine is a Slovenly Hand as you will have told yourself, else should I have written long since. Truth to tell the sights here are so strange, even the Birds and Beasts being none I ever saw the Lyke of before, and the Weather Changeable, that I have had scant leisure through Gaping and riding into the Country for what I might see. Your Son is well, and in better shape with the Trading Company than what I am; he seems not to mind the Task of being a Clerk provided he may please them, and stay here. He is forever out hunting, or following the Indians who show him where to find Beaver. These Creatures are Cunning in the way they construct their Houses, and can swim like Fish; but they have great thick Pelts, in particular in the winter, which folk pay for. The Snow cometh here of a Sudden, and covers everything; then again it is Summer for a short while, and nothing but the Heat and the Flies.

Hawkin is well. We have already been, all of us, on one Expedition into the Interior, when we saw many marvels, and met the Tribes who dwell further from the Sea. They Grease themselves against the Cold and stink greatly. They Scrape the skins they have gained with a Sharp Sliver of Ice, this being done in their dwellings which are not Tents, as in the south. I hear talk of a Second Journey Inland which I hope to join: as you will know, It has never been my Nature to sit with my Backside on a Stool or Bench, though here there is no such Luxury and we sit on Boxes covered with spoiled Skins, which is comfort enough. But after all of it I will come Home, though what I shall doe there remains to be seen as I will not goe back to a Lawyer's Profession. The Farmiloe brothers talk of setting sail, except Edgar who will remain with the traders,

I will leave Edwin to write to you when he will, but he is an Idle Young Hound when it comes to Pen on Paper.

Your Brother,
Robin Thwaite.

Fort Rupert, November 3rd, 1673.

My Dear Mother,

I fear I send Sad News, which I hope you will Bear: my poor Uncle is Noe More. He went out with four of them to Explore a Second Time (we had all been once) and of a Sudden as happens here the Snow began to fall very thick, and he was caught out of Shelter, having gone some Miles on to look for Moose whose Horns are fantastick. I fear me we did not even find his Body, nor will we doe so until the Thaw. I think that if it comforts you, mother, he would Sooner have Died than goe back to what he had been in England, and he had noe Patience to be a Clerk for the

Company here although the Prince's Name would have stood him well.

As for me, they have offered me a Post here which I have taken. I know not well what Other Thing to Doe with myself, and Edgar Farmiloe is of a Like Mind and will stay with me. When we come Home, I will ride straight to Daneclere.

Hawkin is sad, as would be expected for having lost his Father, and will goe Home on the next Ship as he would return to his Grandfather and the Farm, which he likes well. Uthred and his little Wretch of an Arnulf will goe too, I thank God, for that is a Snivelling Urchin and one who never should have come here, for he setts everything at Odds.

I hope that God will comfort you, mother, and that Dick will not be long till he is Home, and to his Wyfe.

Your sonne,
Edwin Sawtrey.

3

SOPHIA adjusted the curled feather which hung down to her shoulder from her riding-hat. She was more interested in this pursuit than in the welfare of Maud, whom she was supposedly escorting to Biding to see Sir Ralph. It has become important to Sophia to look her best when Sir Ralph was present; and as aunt Honor was too dull or too stupid to make the most of her own chances regarding this eligible widower, Sophia had some time ago determined to fill her place. After all he was not so old; the title would be hers; and with his three sons still away and only the slow-witted Gregory to keep him company, he must be lonely.

She herself knew how she looked, and the picture was pleasing. Her riding-clothes were of dark-grey stuff with red frogging, and fitted her like a glove; the feather, curling down from her great beaver hat, was of the same red, and set off her dark curls and clear complexion. Had there been more eligible men in the county, by now, Sophia knew, she would have been married; but the toll of the Civil Wars had killed many a county-family's heir beside Nigel Farmiloe. Sophia had tried her best, before they all sailed to Canada years since, to fix her interest with any one of the Farmiloe brothers, Lionel especially, but Ralph or even Edgar would have been better than nothing. But they had regarded her as a little girl, which at that time she had still been; and now that her breasts were full beneath her bodice, they were far away, and in any event she had no dowry.

But Sir Ralph was at home, and Sir Ralph was rich.

Sophia cast a glance at Maud, who was mounted on her pony, riding it like the hoyden she still was, with no thought for her fair tangled curls, which the wind had blown loose beneath her hood. Surveying her coldly, Sophia decided that there was no doubt Maud would turn into a beauty; to have married her to Dick Sawtrey was to have mated a dove to a sparrow. The marriage would not be consummated for a year or two yet; and there Sophia left it. She had plans of her own which were to a degree more interesting, and profitable, than any speculation concerning young Maud Sawtrey.

They cantered into the courtyard at Biding and then drew rein. Within moments the grooms were about them, aiding them to dismount, leading the horses off to be watered and rubbed down, though this was hardly necessary after the short journey on which they had come. Sophia picked up her dark-grey skirts in one hand, shepherded Maud with the other—no harm in being seen to take a motherly interest in Maud—and by her side entered the great hall, with its banners hanging from the roof-beams to commemorate Edgehill and Marston Moor and Naseby.

Sir Ralph came bowing and kissing her hands, then kissed Maud warmly and held her back to look at her. "How is my sweetheart?" The girl smiled.

"Well, thank you, father. Are you well also?" She was repeating the words taught her by aunt Honor, and one must wait till they had been said; must watch Sir Ralph indulging in his doting fondling; take part in vapid talk about Maud's tutors, her health, her prowess at embroidery and dancing, other such things; and then at last Maud was permitted to go and see her brother Gregory, who was the only one she recalled clearly and who was too shy to come into the hall. Sophia was left alone with Sir Ralph, who hastened to pour her wine.

Their talk always ran on the same lines. "It is good of you to come here with Maud, Mrs. Sophia."

"It is a pleasure, sir. Maud is a sweet child." (Feed the old fool with talk about his girl; take a lingering glance at the portrait of her mother, wearing a high lace collar of the kind made fashionable by Queen Henrietta Maria, long ago.)

Sir Ralph's eyes would follow her own to the portrait, and then he would look down at the floor, and say, in the courteous voice he used to any guest, "Mrs. Sawtrey has been more than a mother to her. And you, my dear, you have aided them both. Maud herself tells me of how you have taken her riding, and violet-picking, and the like. It is good of you; but young people keep one another company. I," and he would sigh, "am growing old."

"Sir, you are not an old man!" The answer at this point was always the same. Make him feel young, and perhaps one day he will imitate youth, and make a marriage. "In any event—" pouting pretty lips, turning one's bosom, ever so gradually, towards where his glance rests, so that his eyes cannot help but dwell on it and assess its curves—"in any event, I mislike very young men. They know so little, and they are rough in their ways." (A glance upwards here, through thick eyelashes.) Sir Ralph bridles; this is what was hoped for.

"Has any young man used you roughly? Give me his name, and I will horse-whip him."

"No, sir." Sophia cast her eyelashes down. "I meet few; life at Daneclere is gracious and orderly, but there is little company. I often wonder if my own life will ever change and hold more than it does at present; embroidery, dancing, household tasks, walks with Maud. She bears me company, as you have said, otherwise I should be lonely, as my brothers have their own concerns and are often from home."

Sir Ralph's mind dwelt briefly on what he had heard of Sophia's two brothers. They were wild and rough, frequented the taverns and would have been better of a man's restraining hand; but all the grown men about Daneclere, except Dick, were still away in Canada, and showed no sign of ever coming home; likewise—he sighed—his own sons were there, and each night he would eat his dinner and drink his wine alone, except for poor Gregory who had nothing to say.

"My child—" He did not know what he had intended to say to her; it ended on a sigh. She was a pretty creature, and kind to Maud. Could a man be blamed if, after so many years alone, he let his glance, his thoughts, wander a trifle?

Her father was Jeremy Whyteleaf; an abject drunkard, beset by creditors' bills, alone in his house these many years. He would not object to an offer for his daughter which demanded no dowry.

An offer ... and himself no longer lonely, with this pretty creature by him, to warm his bed and beguile his days. Was it sinful in him, ungrateful of him, to know such thoughts? It was long now, very long, since Maud's mother had died.

4

ON A BITTER DAY in early spring, a woman and two children were walking the two miles from the mail-coach road to Daneclere. The woman wore a faded unfashionable hat with a high crown, which made her look taller. The children—they were aged ten and eleven, with the boy the younger—held each one a handle of the hampers she carried on either side of her; these were heavy, and contained all their gear as well as certain things which must be guarded carefully. The little party staggered, for the children were growing tired, and presently the woman said, in a flat voice which had lost all hope and youth, "There are the chimneys of Daneclere."

The two children stared. They were thin and pale-faced, with straight hair of a light brown colour. Presently Gwenllian set down the hampers and said "We will rest here for a little," and sat down beneath the sparse shelter of a hawthorn scarcely in bud. Beyond, the fields were already tilled and brown, with a glint of frost still showing on the furrows, and not far off ran the river. Gwellian looked about her with a sick longing; if only things might be as they had once been, and she coming back to show her children to Mrs. Honor with pride!

As it was, they had escaped the law. Ned had not.

She closed her eyes and thought of Ned, while the children, who were tired and hungry, moved up against her for warmth. There would be food for them at Danceclere; they had finished all they had with them on the journey, which had had to be put together in haste, like everything else they had brought.

Everything they had brought ... she had obeyed Ned's instructions gasped out before they had come and carried him off, dying, to prison. "He'll not live to feed the gallows," Gwenllian had heard one of them saying. The shot had passed through his body and left a pulsating piece of lung exposed, and in the brief space of time she had had with him she had tried to cover it. The law-officers had come next day, following the trail of dried blood Ned had left along the coach-road. Perhaps if he had hidden himself instead of coming home, leaving his horse to come back by itself, they might not have found him. But she was glad he had come to her, if only to say farewell.

It had been Lord Newey's coach this time. Over the years he had earned a precarious living on the highways; sometimes there were rich pickings from the increasing number of coaches, sometimes not. They either fed well or went hungry. This loot of Lord Newey's would fetch plenty of silver once the matter had been forgotten and she could safely sell it. There were my lady's jewels in a box, some loose coins, my lord's bloodstone ring.

Blood! She could still see it welling up out of Ned's wounds; she thought she would see it all her life. The coachman had fired the shot from where he lay, Ned having wounded him first. It had been the kind of risk Ned always had to take, working alone. She had grown callous over the years, hearing the stories; once it would have horrified her to be carrying stolen jewellery. But looting was their bread and meat, not only hers but the children's; and Ned must hide himself always because of that killing of Wolffe, years back, in London; then there had been the other things he had done. The highways by night, in the dark of the moon, were the only place to earn money, he said. He had been good to her, never stinting a share of what he had made to her, for the children.

This time, when he rode home wounded, he had said to her "Turn out my pockets and hide the stuff in the straw." And she had done so, anxious to get him into the house and to bed to mend himself, and had stuffed the jewel-box and the ring and other things beneath the straw in the horse's stable. They might not think of looking there. Even then Ned must have known that they would come to search for him; it had happened before, but he had always eluded them.

After they had taken him away and she was left desolate, she had gone down and grubbed up the stuff from where it lay, and put it at the bottom of the hampers, unable to see for tears. It was there now, safely brought here beneath the pile of poor thin clothes and the wrappings for the food. The children did not ask why the hampers were so heavy. They had in the nature of things learned not to ask questions.

The sound of horses' hooves approached. Honor had been visiting a neighbour, and had taken Maud with her. They drew rein as they saw the weary little procession in the long drive. Gwenllian looked round over her shoulder, with the furtive expression of those who are accustomed to guilt. Her heartbeats pounded, and then were still again; she thought it had been the officers of the law.

"Why, Gwenllian! It is, is it not? And the children—they are your own?"

Mrs. Honor had come down out of the saddle, leaving Maud on her pony. For instants Honor's beauty drove all other thoughts from Gwenllian's mind. Mrs. Honor wore a full beaver hat with a broad brim shading her face, and a great curled feather falling down to the shoulder and setting off her rich hair; her riding-gown was of black stuff, well cut, and she had a complexion like a girl's. Gwenllian began to sniff and sob, so overcome was she at the meeting; Honor put one arm about her, while Maud stared in silence. She did not know who the travellers might be, except that they looked tired and poor.

Honor turned presently, asking her to take up the little boy and one hamper; she herself would take the girl and another. "What are their names?" she asked. "The girl is like you."

"They are Gwenllian and Alun, madam. We call the girl Gwenny. Their father taught them to read and write. He—ah, madam, Ned is dead, my Ned is dead." The tears flowed down.

Honor said gently "So is Mr. Sawtrey; you may not have heard of it even yet." She wanted to divert Gwenllian's mind and stop her sobbing; she would hear later of how Ned had died.

"I had not heard. We heard nothing where we were. A kind gentleman he was always, madam. I grieve to hear of't."

Gwenllian's face, pallid and tear-stained, looked up at her two children in the saddle; pray God no one would ask why the hampers were so heavy. It was almost worth losing the stuff to be sure of Daneclere, and a welcome. Her voice had taken on the whining note of the suppliant; she followed Honor with praises of the two children.

"Gwenny can sew and iron, madam, and she'd make a right little lady's maid. And Alun is willing, though he is young." She could think of no talents for Alun. Honor, once more in the saddle with Gwenny up before her, turned.

"We will see what can be done for the children." Perhaps there would be work at Thwaite for the boy if there was none from the grooms here. "As for yourself, I am sorry you will have to walk; but there will be food waiting." Before riding off she turned once more and said, almost shyly,

"Gwenllian, Mr. Whyteleaf no longer lives with us at Daneclere. His three children stay with me." Then she whipped up the mount and was off. Gwenllian trudged on in the dust the horses made, glad to be relieved of her heavy burdens. She had been right to obey Ned in coming back. The last thing he'd said, when they had carried him out of the house to prison to die, had been,

"Go back, Gwenllian. Go back to Daneclere; they'll care for you and the children there."

And she had come back.

They slept well that night. Next day Gwenllian beckoned her daughter to her and put on the child's cloak. She carried a bundle under her own; it was the jewel-box, and rags to wrap it.

They walked beyond the house itself to where there was a wood of oak and beech. In the green places under the trees one might hide anything, almost be lost oneself if searchers came. Gwenny stared at the shadowed places and the great grey-brown fissured trunks of the oaks; they were so old that they must have been part of the ancient forest that once covered the whole of Britain.

Gwenllian found a hollowed place by a tree's roots, took a knife she had brought and scooped away the moss and earth. When the hole was deep enough she wrapped the box in the linen scraps and placed it in the scooped-out hollow, smoothing back the earth and leaves and moss so that it looked as if no one had disturbed the place. Then she looked at her daughter.

"I want you to remember this tree, this place," she said. "If aught becomes of me, 'tis your fortune and Alun's. 'Tis all we have in the world. Tell no one."

Gwenny promised. She had already learned to keep a still tongue in her head. She would not even tell Alun.

5

IT TOOK eight days for the sheriff's men to find Gwenllian.

They rode into Daneclere, shouting when they saw a dark-haired lad idling among the stabled horses. It was Lewis Whyteleaf. He looked at them incuriously.

"We seek a Mrs. Sawtrey," they called.

Lewis shrugged. "It is Mrs. Sawtrey's house," he said. They frowned, puzzled.

"The Mrs. Sawtrey we seek is a common person, who travelled on the coach; she speaks with a Welsh accent."

"There is such a person here; she answers to the name," said Lew contemptuously. Had Honor herself been there, she might have hidden Gwenllian's whereabouts; as it was, they had already found one item, a jewelled brooch, in the straw at the house the small family had left. It would be enough to damn Gwenllian, Ned himself having escaped them by death. They followed Lew's pointing finger in the direction of the kitchens.

Alun and Gwenny saw their mother taken away. They had never been parted with her in all their lives and it was as if the world had ended. Alun shed tears, but Gwenny stood dry-eyed. She saw the men lift her mother up to the saddle, her hands bound by the wrist; an officer rode on the horse with her. Before Gwenllian left she looked at her daughter, and Gwenny knew what the look meant. She nodded once, her eyes wise like an old woman's. The place in the forest should be unknown to anyone; they would never make her tell of it. What would they do to mother now that she no longer had the jewels? She could deny everything; that would

avail her little. They would carry her off to prison. There she
would be put to the question, which might mean thumbscrews
or worse.

Honor Sawtrey, who had been in the still-room bottling
wine, came down in her apron when she heard the horses
move off. It was too late to stop them or to save Gwenllian.
She would go to visit her in gaol.

She went, and found her, lying on stinking straw. Above, a
small window with a grid looked out on to the level of the
street. When rain came, water would seep into the cells.
There were others there, both men and women. All were
filthy, some half naked; they had exchanged their clothes for
food. Honor had brought a clean shift for Gwenllian,
blankets and bread and meat and wine. The air of the place
was foetid. She wondered how long she herself could endure
to be here; some stayed for months, but not longer; for light
crimes there was branding and release, for heavier crimes
hanging. Gwenllian would hang. My Lord Newey was an
important personage, and he had been robbed.

She sat apart from the rest against the wall, looking almost
childlike with her pale face and long straight hair. She made
no complaint and did not weep. Honor took her in her arms.

"I do not trouble for myself," said Gwenllian against her.
"It is the children. They have no one, neither father nor
mother, now."

"I will look after them," Honor said. "I promise you that."

Some days later she saw the hanging; it was one of seven. A
crowd had gathered in the market-place and were ready to
throw stones and filth if it suited them and if the men and
woman about to die angered them or did not divert them.
Gwenllian stood, hands tied, with the others in a cart. The
rope was put about their necks and then the cart was pulled
away. A preacher read words of comfort, his voice drowned
by the murmuring of the crowd. The victims hung and
twitched, and then were still.

Honor found her eyes full of tears. Gwenllian had stolen
nothing, it had been Ned, and he had evaded justice and
justice must have its due. She turned away from the dangling
corpses and went to where her horses stood with one of the
grooms by them. Riding home, she felt inadequate and guilty.
She had been able to do nothing to save Gwenllian, nothing,

despite the fact that Richard Sawtrey had been a man whose word should have carried weight. The dead were worth nothing.

On arriving home, Honor sent for the two children. In gentle and quiet words she told them that their mother would not come back. Alun wept aloud, but Gwenny said nothing. She knows, Honor thought; her childhood is ended.

"Why," demanded Alun, "has mother gone away without us? She always took us, and the hampers."

"No, it was only once," said Gwenny. "Before that we never went anywhere."

"Now you will stay here, this is your home," said Honor, "and though I am not your mother you are to act as if I were, and if you are in any trouble come to me with it, and I will try to help you. Alun, you are to be a man and look after your sister," For he was still rubbing his fists in his eyes.

It will be Gwenny who will always look after him, Honor was thinking; and he will be first to forget.

She did not know, was perhaps never to know, that from the time of their mother's going the children, each of them, were separately exposed to evil.

The seduction of Alun came about in this way. He had begun to stand down in the stable-yard, sometimes with a broom to help to sweep the straw which blew about the cobbles in a high wind. He had seen the riders come and go, least of all Mrs. Honor who seldom in fact rode out on her bay palfrey; often Mrs. Sophia, with young Maud, in the saddle on their way to or from Biding. Also, there were the Whyteleaf brothers, Jeremy and Lewis. Lewis rode a grey pony and Jeremy another bay. Alun had admired them, perhaps a little envied them, when they rode off on their business, which might be visiting or fishing; he had often longed to make a fish rise to his hook, but there had been no opportunity. Then, one magical day, Mr. Lewis spoke to him, and asked him if he would like to be taken up in the saddle. Alun put down his broom—the head groom would not mind, he himself was of no importance and it did not signify whether he were there or not, as he was paid no wages—and let himself be taken up by Lewis's strong arms, and be settled at the crupper, tossing his fair hair out of his eyes as they rode. They came soon to a green place where there were trees and, beyond, a river which purled among stones; in the end it would merge with the great ford between Thwaite and Daneclere, three miles south.

Alun was lifted down, and was given the tackle to hold while Mr. Jeremy secured the horses. The other brother, Mr. Lewis, turned away, and found a pool for them to try in the green shadows; gnats danced above it in the summer sunlight. Alun was enchanted, and set himself to watch while the brothers cast a line; but to his delight Mr. Jeremy took him, and set the fishing-rod in his small hand, and guided it over the pool. In time there came a pull, and Alun could not disguise his squeak of excitement; Mr. Jeremy put his finger to his lips, and Alun was silent and still. The fish pulled again, and they played it, letting it have enough length of line, then drawing in; presently they hauled it out of the water, a brown trout, the sun glinting on its wet body, tail thrashing in anguish, mouth agape, eyes flat. Jeremy took the trout at last and killed it by smashing its head against a stone, then said "Let us try again, and if we catch more there will be plenty for breakfast." They tried again, but without fortune. Then Mr. Jeremy told Alun to fetch wood and they would make a fire, and cook the fish; Alun saw the gleam of his knife preparing to gut it, and ran off eagerly on his errand. He came back with twigs of willow and branches of dried furze, and they made a fire and roasted the trout by wrapping it in clay. It tasted delicious. When he was filled, Alun lay back, feeling sleepy. He was aware then of Mr. Jeremy standing above him.

"Have you had a good morning, Alun? Have you enjoyed yourself?" Alun said he had; he had never in fact enjoyed a day so much in his life. Hitherto there had always been his mother, crying, and Gwenny telling him to do this and that. So when Mr. Jeremy said that perhaps now Alun would do something for him in his turn, the boy agreed gladly. What would it be? To clear away the ashes of their fire? To clean the tackle and wind it tidy again about the reel? He would do all of that gladly. But what Mr. Jeremy Whyteleaf wanted was something different. "Take down your breeches," he commanded.

Alun flushed and tears came into his eyes. To have to do such a thing had always been the preliminary to a whipping, and he knew of no other reason why he should be asked to do it. He saw Mr. Jeremy laughing.

"It is not a punishment, Alun," he said. "For what should I punish you? It is to do something which will bring us pleasure; would you refuse to do that for me, after what I have done for you"

Alun said "No," while obediently unfastening his breeches. He lay presently on the green turf, his buttocks stripped bare.

"I promise you it will bring pleasure to you also, Alun," said Jeremy again, kneeling down. Lewis was still fishing in the river. He did not turn his head.

Afterwards, Alun knew that what had happened had indeed brought him pleasure, of a kind he had not expected. He knew that he would ride out often with Mr. Jeremy to catch fish, and let him use him so again. He would not mind it, he decided. He would not mind it at all.

It was not to happen all at once; such changes take time; but as Alun grew towards young manhood it would begin to show; the stigmata of pouting lips, long lashes, the languid airs of a girl. That day by the river Jeremy Whyteleaf had begun the fashioning of his Ganymede.

6

GWENNY knelt down by the oak tree. It was almost two months since she had been. There among the grass and moss was the line of lifted earth mother had left, though no one would see it who didn't know it was there. She lifted the earth carefully. There was more underneath, dry and fibrous with the shelter of the tree, and then when one scraped with a stone, there was a solid object underneath again: presently it showed white; linen wrappings, that mother had carefully folded about the box to keep it from damp and mould. Gwenny felt the tears rise. She dashed the back of her hand across her eyes, then went on digging; it wasn't any use to weep for mother, which Gwenny had heard from the servants; nothing would bring her back, or alter the way she had died. Better keep thinking of the present, of now, and finding the box again; unwrapping the linen, till it sat there like a tiny trunk, of gilded leather, with little studs made of brass or gold on its arched lid. She turned the key; it opened. Inside was a hoard that made her draw her breath in wonder; shining rings, pendants, earrings; she did not know the names of all the stones, but they were green and red, clear water shining like fire, and a milky colour. There was a long string of beads of this, and Gwenny drew it out and marvelled at it; unthinking, she put it over her head and let it hang over her flat child's breast. She stroked it with her fingers. It was beautiful, more beautiful than anything she had ever seen. Would it be wicked to keep it, to hide it somewhere and wear it in secret? She felt like a beautiful lady, a town lady going to Court. Her plain stuff gown was changed to satin and her hair, her lank straight hair, frizzed out in curls. She could be beautiful if only she might wear such stones. She—

"Little girls shouldn't pry."

The voice made the scared blood rush to her heart, causing her to turn a white face in the direction whence it had come. Mr. Jem Whyteleaf was leaning against a tree, idly watching her; his brother stood by him. They must have stolen up while she was unaware; they must have followed her.

There was nothing at all she could say, nothing; there was the jewel-box lying open, and there were the beads about her neck. Jem strode forward, and Lewis followed. She shrank back from them, her mind empty of anything except terror. It wasn't a secret any longer, the place where the box was hidden; it wasn't a secret, and she had broken faith with mother.

Jem said in his dry drawl "Those are the Newey jewels, little thief. Do you know that you could hang, like your mother?"

She began to sob, stuffing her fists in her eyes. Jem came forward and jerked her to her feet by one arm. His eyes raked her; the small tear-streaked face, the lank hair, the servant's gown, the body innocent of any single curve of womanhood.

"Do you want to hang, little wench?" he said softly.

"No," Gwenny whispered. She could still hardly think for fear. If it had been anyone else who found her, a servant, Mrs. Sophia, Mrs. Honor herself, or even the Farmiloes from the manor, it would have been different; they would have had mercy on her. But these Whyteleaf boys were cruel. She had seen them twisting the wings off butterflies, turning out young birds from the nest before they could fly.

Jem had turned and winked at his brother. "If you do as we bid you, you will not hang. Will you do it—Gwenny, that's your name, eh? Will you do whatever we tell you, and swear to tell no one? If you do tell, we will see to it that you hang. They'll take our word; there are two of us and only one of you, and there are the jewels for us to show, if we wish to."

She began to cry again; they would take away the jewels. "Please, of your kindness, leave a little for me and for my brother. We have not anything in the world, and our mother promised—"

"Your mother promised too much, and she died at a rope's end. Come, give me these." He laid hands on Gwenny and pulled the necklace over her head. In the struggle the string broke, and the pearls scattered like drops of milk over the ground. Jem slapped her face.

"Careless bitch. Lew, you gather them while I see to this. Come, wench, lie down."

"No," she whispered; something, not knowledge, told her that far worse would happen to her than the slap, if she did so; something that made the thought of dying, terrible as it must be, almost indifferent by comparison; but she had not enough knowledge fully to compare. Jem's hands were busy at her dress. Lewis, kneeling on the ground to collect the pearls, looked up and laughed. He was a swarthy, thick-set lad with the same growth of coarse single hairs about the mouth and chin as Jem. The bodice was loosened now and Jem was undoing Gwenny's shift.

"The wench hath no tits yet," sniggered Lewis. Jem smiled calmly, pinioning Gwenny's arms by pulling down her sleeves from the shoulder. Her child's body was revealed naked to the waist. She looked away and sobbed. Jem clapped one of his hands over her mouth; the other held her by her bundled clothes.

"If we do it to her often enough, they will grow," he said lightly. Lewis listened, storing the information away in his mind. He was aware of rising excitement; unlike Jem, who was free with tavern-wenches, he had never had a woman. This child was good enough for a start.

"Lie down and pull your skirts up."

She suddenly ducked and made to run. Jem caught her, turned up her skirts and smacked her twice across the buttocks, then flung her down on the ground. "Bide quiet there, or by God you'll hang."

He was already unfastening his breeches. Lewis, the pearls safe in the jewel-box, had meantime sidled up. He looked enquiringly, somewhat jealously, at his brother. "The eldest first', said Jem smoothly, "it's tricky with a maidenhead."

Still smiling, he knelt down over Gwenny, forced her legs apart and bundled up her clothes still further; there must be no tell-tale blood on the linen. "One screech out of you, and we tell," he said.

He went into her, deflowering her swiftly with the second thrust. Despite her terror, she cried out. Lewis stood aside, waiting his turn, and kept watch part of the time for strangers walking nearby. He watched Jem's jerking buttocks with interest. Jem didn't care whether he took women or boys. He himself would have liked to try the maidenhead; from what one heard, there weren't many to be had nowadays. The girl was green; tears streamed silently down her face, and her white splayed legs remained passive, lying as Jem had forced them, taking no share in the rhythm of the act. Presently its jerking stopped, and Jem and the girl lay still together. In a short while he rose, and began pulling up his breeches.

"There, she's warmed now," he said, "you can go in."

Lewis had undone himself, to be ready. He lay down and went into the girl forcefully, in the way he had seen Jem do. The sensation was unlike anything he had ever known. He thrust happily, feeling his breathing shorten, panting at last like a dog's.

Jem had gone over to where the Newey gems lay and was wrapping them again in their linen. There was a man he knew of who would buy them, perhaps singly, and would ask no questions. In the meantime they could hold the little fool of a wench to ransom over it until they had tired of her. Jem sat down to await Lewis's pleasure, watching his brother's prowess with some amusement. By the time the boy came out, he himself might be ready again. It was seldom such a stroke of luck came, without Mrs. Honor to pry. They would have to let Sophia into the secret; from now on, they could go and take the wench in her room.

They raped her till she bled. They raped her until, with the repeated driving of their thick parts in her body, a kind of unripe willingness was forced from her, and she began to jerk and respond, hearing her own sobbing and their jeering laughter. A thing was happening to her of which she had no understanding, for as she had not reached puberty no one had

told her of it. This was her education. They left her at last
lying dishevelled in the wood, while they went off together.
With difficulty and pain Gwenny rose, adjusted her dress and
looked across to where the jewels had been. There was
nothing now but bare clawed earth, and a throbbing hurt
deep in her own body. What was it Mr. Jem had said before
they left? Tomorrow night ... in nothing but her shift. ...

Tomorrow night; or she would hang. They had the jewels
to show. Tomorrow night.

Sophia turned luxuriously on her feather mattress, savouring
the comfort of the clean linen newly unfolded from lavender.
Certainly Gwenny made a good lady's maid; such leisure as
she had left from household tasks was given, by Mrs.
Sawtrey's order, to dressing Sophia and mending her gowns,
arranging her hair, darning her hose, changing her bed-linen.
Honor had intended it to benefit the girl, as the more she
knew of such things the better she would fare when she went
out into service beyond Daneclere. For Sophia it was more
than satisfactory, and that young lady had her reasons for
feeling at ease with the world in any case. It was almost
certain, by now, that Sir Ralph Farmiloe would make her an
offer of marriage.

She spared a brief thought for him, less aware of that than
of the cool feel of the linen against her smooth skin. She
stretched her bare legs down the full length of the short bed
and felt in every limb, down to her pointing separate toes,
that she was desirable. It had been a challenge to bring the
old man to the point, but she'd done it, or almost, and with
lessons from no one. She smiled. Prudence had dictated that
Sir Ralph should make the proposal by way of her father,
Whyteleaf, rather than Mrs. Sawtrey or Dick. Those two
would prate of the difference in ages, and make what
difficulties they might. "But they will not have the chance,"
she thought, "it will all be arranged without them."

A moment's regret, a suspicion of true feeling, crossed her
mind for Edwin, overseas. Edwin was so handsome that once,
when Sophia was younger, she had imagined herself in love
with him. But he was after all only a younger son, with no
prospects beyond the Hudson's Bay Company. "Fancy
waiting for a husband who could not come home but every
few years, or going out with him to those savage parts," she
thought, slightly mollifying the blow to her vanity in that no

one had ever suggested she should. Perhaps, later, she decided, Edwin could become her lover, when he came home. As a married woman she would have more freedom.

She yawned and stretched, showing her white kitten's teeth. Soon now she would sleep, despite what went on—she sniggered—almost nightly in the adjoining closet. How shocked aunt Sawtrey had been the first time she came in and found Gwenny's pallet, which had used to lie at the foot of Sophia's bed, removed to the small, stuffy place one reached from this room only! "What is the reason for it?" Honor had asked with horror; an animal could hardly sleep in so small a space, with no window: it was little more than a cupboard. Honor always, Sophia had told herself at the time, paid over-much attention to the feelings of servants, being of low birth herself.

Sophia had tried to look concerned. "She is restless at night, and disturbs me," she said, for God knew that was true, but aunt Sawtrey's face if she knew the whole truth would be worth seeing. Gwenny had been sent for and asked if she minded sleeping in the closet, and having learned her lessons well had said "No, madam," to everything, even the offer of a shared garret with two other servants. So things had been left as they were. Sophia was becoming indifferent in any case; at first she had grown weary of the thuddings and pantings beyond her own bed-curtains when Jem and Lew, singly or together, would visit the little fool to lie with her. It had been a sensible notion to put the pallet where it was now; she could still hear the sounds, but there was more privacy for herself. Sounds, in fact, from Gwenny by now were few; she had been reduced to sullen acquiescence long since. "There is your love-nest," Sophia had told the boys, pointing, next time they came. To Gwenny herself she never said a single word that would indicate her knowledge of anything irregular, or remarked on the girl's reddened eyes next day. It was more often Lewis alone who came nowadays, as Jem had Gwenny's brother for his minion. "The family earn their keep, though my aunt knows it not," thought Sophia.

Presently, in the dark, a shaded candle glided past beyond the curtain. That would be Lew, going in to Gwenny. Sophia listened idly to what followed. There was no greeting of one another, only, soon, a creaking of the floor, and Lew's familiar grunting and panting as he had his way. Would old Sir Ralph prove vigorous as a lover? Sophia doubted it; she had no illusions about the marriage bed. When all was said, she was taking Sir Ralph better things than a dowry; wit, a comely body and face, and her virginity. The last was an inconvenience, and better lost. Sophia's eyes half-closed in the darkness. When would Edwin come home, and how could she inveigle him to Biding? Later they could meet, on horseback, in the woods; Sir Ralph did little riding abroad these days.

It was dawn before Lewis emerged from the closet, furtively setting his clothes to rights; he had pulled on a pair of breeches and a shirt lest anyone met with him and asked where he was going at such an hour. "To the privy," he would reply. It was as seasonable a time for that as any other. He passed his tongue over his lips, savouring his recent experience. He had forgotten his candle; the girl would bring it back to his room later today. Between them, he and Jem had schooled her well.

Sophia did not wake, nor did her brother glance towards the curtained bed. Soon the bitch would be gone, he was thinking, if her hopes bore fruit. Lewis slipped out as silently as he had come, replacing the door on its latch. Presently the servants would begin to stir, including Gwenny; he'd given her little sleep. He smiled, going softly along the passages. Shortly he reached his own room unobserved, undressed again and lay down, and was soon asleep. Jem's place beside him was still empty.

The county had much gossip to sustain it during the coming months. Sir Ralph Farmiloe of Biding to wed again, and to none other than that young chit with the bold manners, who lived by courtesy at Daneclere! And Sir Ralph had not gone to Mrs. Sawtrey with his offer, nor to Mr. Dick who to be sure would have had little to say, but to the young wench's own father, Whyteleaf the drunkard, who of course gave the matter his blessing with hardly a moment to spare. The marriage would be a godsend to him, with his pockets to let. Few had to do with him nowadays, except in the ale-houses. Honor Sawtrey had her own troubles, to be sure. It had been a sad business about her brother Robin, killed in far parts.

They did not know of a letter Honor had had from her father.

Daughter,
Doe not grieve for me, and doe not try to come here. I am as
well able to sustain Goddes blows as I have done all my life.
We can only pray that Robin meeting his Death in soe
Heathen a Place had Recourse to God. There are folk and
doings here enough to comfort me; Joan her Father is Dead
at last, soe I am glad Uthred will soon be home. As for the
Farmiloes, I know not; you will hear more of that than I.
They say they have grown rich beyond the common.
I pray nightly that matters speed well with you, daughter,
and that your Sons continue safe in the ways they have
Chosen. Young Hawkin is well, I had a letter. He will come
home with Uthred, but of Arnulf they say nothing. That is a
useless Lad. I had as soon not have him here.

Your father,

Hawkin Thwaite.

7

"THAT GWENNY, she'm wi' child. That isn't one day she's
puked at her breakfast, that's four days in a week. I'd not
have spoke otherwise; who the man is, don't ask."

Honor stared, horrified, at Meg Sawtrey, one of Richard's
daughters who helped in the house. Physically she bore a
great resemblance to Ned, and Honor had to remember that
she was, after all, Gwenny's aunt and would not have carried
the tale out of spite. But Gwenny with child! "She is no more
than a child herself," Honor said. Who could have done so
shameful a thing?

Gwenny was brought. When she stood before Honor, the
latter chided herself at not having noticed the change in the
girl's appearance. Her face was ashen, partly with fear at the
interview; her eyes were red, and her nipples, not yet full
breasts, thrust out beneath her bodice in a swollen fashion, as
if the stuff chafed them.

"Gwenny, is it true you are in some trouble?" began

Honor gently. The girl shook her head, and mumbled something; she seemed almost bereft of her wits. Honor spoke more sternly. "Have you been with a man, Gwenny? Do not be afraid to say who he is; whatever happens we will do the best for you." Marriage, she was thinking, might not be the best in the event; the child was too young for it, and if she had been mishandled must not be tied to a brute. "Do not be afraid," she said again; and Gwenny broke down into sobbing.

She didn't know if she were with child, she said, she didn't know; she had never had any courses. Yes, she had been sick, mostly in the mornings lately, and didn't fancy her food. How long? For some weeks now.

Honor thought of the miserable pallet, shoved into the closet off Sophia's room. To ask Sophia anything would implicate her, and now that the marriage had taken place might offend Sir Ralph. Who could have done evil of such a kind as this would be? She asked again, taking Gwenny's hand, if any man had been familiar with her. The small damp grasp tightened against her fingers.

"A man came at me. 'Twas in the wood, a while back; no, I do not know who he was. It was dark."

"What were you doing in a wood in the dark?"

"I was walking." The eyes shifted. Honor wondered if the child herself were devious or cunning; after all, she herself knew little of her except that like her mother she made a good servant. She thought for some moments; the best thing to do was to have Gwenny where an older woman could keep an eye on her. "You shall sleep in Meg's bed with her," she told the girl. The whites of Gwenny's eyes showed in fear.

"I dare not—I dare not—please, madam, leave me where I am—" The sobs deepened, and with every choking breath Honor was sure that some other matter than a man in a wood troubled Gwenny, but could not come at the truth. She repeated her edict that Gwenny must sleep with Meg. "Now go, and if there is to be a child we will see that you are both taken care of. And no more walking by night in the woods."

"We'll tell if you don't come. You know we can tell." Jem twisted Gwenny's thin white arm against her back; she bit her lip in pain. It was seldom, as he knew, that she cried out. "You'll come to us, instead of our coming to you," he repeated. "Old Meg falls fast asleep; it takes a curfew to waken her. You'll come to us when she once drops over; up the back staircase, and then on to third left. You know the way well enough." She had often returned candles.

She spoke in a low flat voice, her eyes on the ground. "If so be as I can't come, I can't. If she doesn't sleep, I dursn't come."

"She'll sleep, If she wakes while you are gone, you've been to the privy. They can't stop that, can they?" He went on to make an offensive jest. "You come to us, Gwenny, or you know what we can do."

Her slow mind groped round it; it was a long time, she forgot how long, since they'd taken the jewels. But the law had a long memory; sometimes they hanged a thief years after the event, and old Noll Cromwell had been hung up on a gallows after he was dead, for killing the King a dozen or more years back; her mother had said so. She looked at her tormentors, seeing them as they were; Jem with his refinements of cruelty, Lewis with his coarse unheeding lusts. They would both of them be in the room, if she went up. And she'd have to go; she'd known that from the beginning. Whatever they bade her do, she must do it. She'd have to go, or feel a rope about her thin neck in the end. She wouldn't tell them about the child, if there was one, it hadn't begun to show yet. She knew what happened because during the year, one of the maids named Janey Sawtrey had had a baby to the cattleman; she had bulged thicker and thicker until they had married her to him and it was born. They wouldn't marry *her* to one of the Whyteleaf boys. That would be worse than hanging. Anyway, she'd have to come tonight, somehow. She nodded, again looking at the ground.

"I'll come."

It was Honor who came upon her, huddled halfway along the corridor where a window jutted out and made a place to hide. The moon was bright and Honor had seen the flitting whiteness of Gwenny's shift through her open door; she had not yet gone to bed although it was late. Gwenny must have known that she had been seen and when Honor found her, she was like a little ghost of fear, her eyes enormous and dark in her head, her lank hair blanched by the moon. Honor laid hands on her and took her back to her own room. She was angry; perhaps the child was a wanton after all, going by night—it could be to no other place, for they slept at the end of the wing—to the Whyteleaf boys' room. It had maybe happened often enough, while Gwenny slept with Sophia; after Sophia was abed and asleep, the little wanton would slip out, like a cat, to her doings.

"I should whip you, Gwenny." She was slow to chastise any of the women; it had always been her way to right matters with words, hard ones if they had to be so: but looking at the frail waif she knew in any case she could not touch her. It must all be settled in the morning. "What of Meg?" she said.

Meg had been asleep. It had all seemed quite easy. Then—

Gwenny began her sobbing again, and a long tale in which Honor could distinguish a fear that she might hang. "*What?* You have done nothing that they could punish in such a way. Your mother, poor soul, paid for the theft."

"Then they'd not hang me after?"

If it was true—and what Mrs. Honor said would be true—she need have listened to none of their lies, nor let them mishandle her. She set her lips. 'Twasn't no good crying over it, the thing was done.

"The crime is paid for, Gwenny. Think no more of the sad past. You have your life to live, but do not spoil it by wantoning. One day you will meet a man who will be your husband, and you would do better to have been chaste; men do not respect a wanton."

A wanton! Something gave way in Gwenny's mind. She heard herself speaking, rapidly, evilly, using words she had not known she knew. Mrs. Honor turned white and red; she would never have heard the like, poor lady. Gwenny felt pity for Mrs. Honor, and some for herself. Presently the tale stopped.

"This is—true?"

"As true as I stand here, madam. Wherefore should I make up such a tale? And I shall never marry."

Honor had no answer. She had almost heard the story with unbelief. The Whyteleaf brothers were about her daily, ate at her table, seemed quiet and inoffensive, and yet Gwenny said they had done this thing. What was she to do? If it were true, they should be banished the house, as their father had been. She must see them, speak to them.

She talked to Gwenny gently. "Go and lie on the pallet in my room till you are rested. You need have no other duties today." She would see to the matter in Gwenny's absence; the sad little pale face with its red eyes unnerved her.

Later she found she could not go to Barbary's sons and repeat the whole of the monstrous tale. Perhaps the child was simple, crazed in the head; her mother's death might have warped her. She would ask the boys if they had handled the little maid, no more; if they lied, she would surely know of it.

She turned to Gwenny. "From tonight you may sleep in my room; I will tell Meg. So there will be no more wandering in the night, do you promise?"

"I promise, madam," said Gwenny.

Honor sent for Jem and Lewis separately and asked them about the affair. They said they knew Gwenny by sight, no more; their statements and behaviour were the same. Surely Barbary's sons could not be monsters? "We will see what is to become of you," she said coldly, knowing they had defeated her with their easy gait, lacking in blushing or evasion. "Remember that you are here at my will, and that I can have you sent from the house to your father's; you will find it less easy living there than at Daneclere; mark what I say."

She did no more then. The best thing, she thought, was to keep close watch on Gwenny until her child—if there was a child—should be born, and perhaps by then there would be some word of the father and she would know what to do. Not for the first time she wished for a strong master at Daneclere who would take some of the decisions from her shoulders. Dick, when he was at home, was worse than useless.

8

SOME DAYS before their sister's marriage Jem and Lewis had been riding back from a visit to old Jeremy at his dilapidated house. For once they were unaccompanied by Alun. They reined in just where, between the thin branches of winter trees, the chimneys of Daneclere could be seen.

"Now we may talk, I believe," said Jem. "In that place there is eternal watching," His dark eyes narrowed almost to slits as he watched the great house, but when he spoke it concerned old Jeremy.

"He did not look so well today, did you think so? He is drinking more than ever, and I doubt if that sloven he calls his housekeeper gives him a farthing's worth more than he asks for."

"When he dies, maybe we will come into some estate," said Lewis prosaically. His brother turned a cynical gaze on him, and laughed.

"The estate is in debt to the hilt. Moreover why should we inherit?"

Lewis looked puzzled. "Why? Why should we not? He is our father, when all's said and done, and has given us little enough since we were born." His mouth dropped agape; Jem was indulging in one of his rare, bitter fits of laughter.

"Whyteleaf is not our father."

"Eh?"

"You are simple, Lewis; or else you do not listen to enough tavern-gossip, which often has truth at the back of't. Our father, as is well known to all the countryside except yourself, was Frank Wolffe the Daneclere bailiff, and they married our mother in haste to Whyteleaf to give her children a name. They say Wolffe continued her lover in Whyteleaf's very bed."

"I never heard of that," said Lewis, and started his mount again, shaking his head slowly. "I never yet heard of't."

"'Tis true enough. Moreover with our Sophia to be nobly wed and our Gwenny in the family way—that was your doing, I swear, never mine—"

"How was I to know the wench could conceive? She had no tits."

"Leave that. We must think of ourselves now. It is like enough, at the beginning, that we can get money from Sir Ralph Farmiloe at Biding; but when his sons come home all that will stop."

"When do they come?"

"When they will. It is time we went to seek our fortunes, Lew; there will be short commons for us at Daneclere, maybe, when the wench's child is born and looks like you or me, or when precious Edwin comes home." Edwin had never liked the brothers, nor they him.

"Is Edwin to come home? I had thought him bound to the Company."

"Maybe, and maybe not; but we will not always be young. We can safely take the rest of the jewels to London and sell 'em by now; the hue and cry hath died down. We can set up in a small way there after that, and make our living by chance, as others. You may be grateful now that I did not let you part with the pearls for a song, to spend on wine and tavern-women."

"If we can buy us a woman with flesh on her bones in London, I'll not grumble. Jem, what became of our mother?"

"She died. That is all I know." The taverns had not been permitted to lay hold on what had happened to Barbary Mountchurch. Lewis shrugged.

"Then I for one will follow where you lead. You'll take Alun?"

"I had thought to. He costs less than a servant hired in the town, and works better."

"He works well in more ways than one," sniggered Lewis. The brothers smiled as they rode on. Jem thought of Lewis's last saying, and it was in accordance with his own thoughts; male prostitutes might be expensive and scandalous to hire in London, and Alun had his uses in this way and as a body-servant. They would certainly take him.

They went to confront Mrs. Honor with their plan. Both had washed themselves for the occasion and put on clean linen, and combed their hair. They looked like honest country-bred lads eager to learn the ways of the world.

"We would fain ride to London, madam," said Jem. "We have been a burden on you for long, and though we did not relish the voyage with the rest to Canada, this is nearer; we hope to find fortune there."

"Then you will not, I hope, be strangers to Daneclere," replied Honor courteously. Gwenny, who was seated sewing on a little stool at her foot, stitched on and never raised her head. Her body was thickening and it was evident now that she was with child.

They made a speech of thanks to Honor, prepared while they were changing their clothes; each kissed her hand. Then Jem asked, humbly, if he might take Alun with him as his servant. At this Gwenny's eyes closed for instants, and she paused between one stitch and the next. She did not know what it was Jem Whyteleaf had done to Alun, except that it was evil. Alun now looked on Jem as his god, who could do no wrong. They would hurt him, thought Gwenny, in London.

She heard Mrs. Honor say that it was to be Alun's choice. How soft and innocent she is, thought Gwenny, and her a widow-woman and a great lady! Of course Alun will choose to go; it will break his heart if he does not.

Alun went. The three rode out early on a winter's morning, the new sun hardly showing over the horizon, so that a lantern had been lit in the stables for the preparing and saddling of their horses. Alun wore plain clothes, as befitted a servant, and a broad hat which half hid his girlish features. His mouth, already red and full, smiled beneath. He had grown long of limb and could meet the stirrups without having them shortened, and he let his mount break into a trot behind the brothers, who rode very fine, with great hats of beaver and collars edged with lace. Honor and Gwenny and the servants stood in the doorway to bid them farewell. Sophia was at Biding, and cared nothing. The sound of the riders grew fainter as they left the cobbles and made for the muddy road. Soon they were out of sight. The watchers turned back out of the cold and the great door of Daneclere was closed. Pray God they never return, thought Gwenny; pray God they never return.

9

SOPHIA'S BROTHERS had been still in the house at the time of her wedding. This had been quiet, as befitted the remarriage of a widower to a portionless bride. Present were Jeremy Whyteleaf, who gave the bride away; the Daneclere household, with Mrs. Honor in a cape of beaver skins Edwin had sent her, and a matching muff to keep the January cold from her white hands; and those of Biding, with the one son remaining, Gregory, standing bridesman to his father, and having been well schooled beforehand he acquitted himself well enough, though he was not called upon to speak afterwards, at the great feast which took place at Daneclere.

Honor had done her best for Sophia's bridal. The girl

herself she had dressed, at her own expense, in palest blue silk with a collar of fine Valenciennes, over which Sophia's dark hair fell curling. Seen thus she had, for the first and last time, a look of Barbary; several remarked on it as she made her way later up the short aisle of the church, on old Jeremy's arm. She was not shy or awkward and made her responses clearly. The bridegroom, on the other hand, showed little joy; his hair and the beard he still wore had grown very grey, and it was whispered that he felt himself unfaithful to the memory of his first wife, who had suffered so greatly. But he was courteous to Sophia and the kiss he gave her after their vows were exchanged was warm enough.

Among those watching the ceremony stood young Maud, in white satin, her hand laid lightly on Dick Sawtrey's arm. Soon it would be time for their marriage, made some years ago, to be consummated, and many glanced at Maud's fair loveliness and her long neck and slim body and breasts, and asked themselves why Dick was laggard. He looked as ever, hangdog and narrowfaced, and did not lift his eyes either to Sophia or to his own bride. The whisperers decided that it had been a pity to mate a white doe to an unwilling stag. But Dick Sawtrey's father had after all had the self-same look, and he had fathered many children. No doubt it would come right in the end.

The feast took place, with great roasted sides of beef saved from the saltings, and syllabubs, and every delicacy that could be concocted out of eggs, bottled fruit, and fish from the river. The wine was good; among the late Richard Sawtrey's more praiseworthy achievements had been to maintain his father's cellar, and his lukewarm position in the Civil Wars had ensured that this was not raided by the soldiery. All that was long past, and the King reigned safe in Whitehall with his succession of mistresses and his barren Queen. His health was drunk, and that of the bride and bridegroom. There was music for dancing, but only the younger folk danced; Sir Ralph watched his new wife led out on the arm of one of the men, and sat by Honor, talking throughout the evening. When it was time to bed the bride and groom, he slipped away. There was to be no public showing, and Sophia was made a wife by him in privacy and darkness, though the bed was wreathed with evergreens; there were no flowers because it was winter.

Next day, Sir Ralph returned with his bride to Biding.

Now she was my Lady Farmiloe, in truth. She remembered
the time long ago, at Richard Sawtrey's funeral, when she
had eyed all of the Farmiloe men and decided that whoever
should wed Sir Ralph would after all be my lady. She did not
regret her marriage with an old man; he had used her gently,
and now she was in possession of the great manor and would
exploit her position to the full; no more quiet evenings
stitching by Mrs. Honor's side at Daneclere! There should be
suppers and feastings, cards and dancing and wagers made
and kept, at Biding now; she would invite all of the county,
except—she frowned—Jem and Lew, whom she had warned
already to stay away; they were not gentlemanly in their
manners and would try to filch gold from Sir Ralph. Her
origins were to be forgotten in her new graciousness: folk
should not say any longer that she was in truth a bailiff's
bastard and had come to Sir Ralph with only a half-dozen
shifts. She would order more from London, even Paris; the
nuns there embroidered exquisitely; every Court lady had her
underwear from French convents. And there would be such
gowns, fashioned of satin and velvet and silk and lace, with
great feathered hats and gloves and slippers, that she could
not show them off solely to the country-folk here; sooner or
later Sir Ralph must take her to Court, to see the King (they
said he had an eye for a pretty woman) and to make her
curtsy to the poor little Portuguese Queen who could not bear
him a child.

Children of her own, she decided, must be lacking. The
bearing of them spoilt one's figure, and Sir Ralph had enough
heirs already. Now that she was married she would be free to
find out about herbs to prevent conception; perhaps also—she
gave a little smile—other herbs to spur a laggard lover. There
was no foretelling when Edwin Sawtrey would ride home, or
the four handsome men who were her husband's sons. Life
opened out like a fan before her, full of flirtatious opportunity. She had always got what she wanted, by keeping her
own counsel and doing as her mind bade her; and so it would
continue, at Biding as at Daneclere, except that by now she
wanted more, much, much more.

10

"SHE'M TOO BIG for her time, unless by hap 'tis twins. 'Twill not be easy for her, and she so narrow. 'Twere maybe best to burst the bag, and bring it on."

Meg Sawtrey stood before her mistress, hands screwing together in her apron. Honor was aware that the woman knew how to bring about such things, and had much knowledge of midwifery; but she herself could not endure the thought of hurting Gwenny more than she need be hurt. She looked up from the letter she had been writing, one of refusal to attend yet another banquet at Biding. Gwenny needed quiet and her own constant presence; the girl clung to her. Sophia might mock if she would at the thought—the guests would hear of it—of the lady of Daneclere rejecting the lady of Biding's hospitality to attend upon the birthing of a serving-maid.

One thing was certain: Gwenny did not look as she should, for the time of pregnancy. Her body was grossly distended and her limbs thin as sticks, and she did not eat her food. She still stumbled on about her household tasks, though Honor long ago would have had her stop them and take some rest. "You've been good to me, madam," Gwenny had replied. "Let me do what I may while I can." It had been the answer of a little old woman rather than a child.

The days passed, with no birth or any sign of labour. Finally Honor made up her mind to send for a physician. They might mock at her—even the women would mock, who ever heard of such a thing for a serving-wench?—but they could do as they would. The physician came, bent his ponderous wig over Gwenny and prodded and poked at her stomach and parts. When he straightened again his face was grave.

"Madam, I would have a private word." He spoke in a low voice. When they were alone he said to Honor "It is not a twin-birth. I was feeling for the heads, which I did not find. You have some notion of her dates?"

"It is difficult to say. She was attacked by a man in a wood, she said, and then told another story; it may have been at any time, and I have refrained from troubling her overmuch on the matter." Honor felt ashamed, for she had not borne to think of the part Barbary's sons might have played. They had written civilly enough, and had given her their direction in London; they had already been to Court. Sophia also had visited them when, at her entreaty, Sir Ralph had taken her on a visit to the capital to see the sights. Sophia said Jem was courting a rich widow. Of Lewis there was less news. Why had her mind flown to them at this moment? She should think of nothing but Gwenny.

The physician had been silent, as though he sought for words. When they came it was with difficulty. "I have seen only one other such birth in my time, but I know what is to be done. We must end the pregnancy; the child in any case will not live long, and we must save the mother."

Honor had cried out in distress; they were in the passage, away from where Gwenny lay in Honor's room. "Is there no way to save both?" she begged. "I had hoped the child would be a comfort to her."

"Such a child will comfort no one," said the doctor curtly. He asked permission to proceed. Honor gave it; she could not well refuse it. Such a man knew his professional duty, even if the proceeding was no more than Meg had already advised.

He went back into the room, after assuring Honor once more that there was nothing else to be done. The birth-pangs, he said, would now begin within minutes, or at the least within the hour. "They will be the easier in that we have not delayed," he promised, averting his eyes. What shameful thing did he hide, she wondered? What more had Gwenny to endure than other young women? A great sadness rose in Honor for the girl. She had shown great patience, great humility, during the pregnancy; she was grateful for the least favour or thoughtfulness. It would have been pleasant to see her happy, with her child in her arms.

The physician emerged presently. "It is done," he said. "Leave a woman with her." Meg was in the room; she would stay "and so will I," Honor thought. "There was no cry from her," she said to the physician.

"It did not hurt her. The birth may, but not unduly; there is that to be thankful for." He said he would stay for the birth. There would be gossip, Honor knew, rife throughout Daneclere; the old women of the village would be sour because they had not been called in. But Gwenny should have all that money could buy, Honor had decided; she had already been left too much alone, to endure what she might.

There was more.

The birth-pangs themselves started almost at once. Gwenny was weeping; she had a humiliating memory of a probe inserted into her, and something had broken with a great flooding of waters. She felt distaste and guilt at soiling Mrs. Sawtrey's fine polished floor. "Never heed, it is clean now," said Meg Sawtrey gently; she had fetched a cloth and bucket and swabbed the floor clean.

Still the pains came. At the first they had not seemed so very bad; they were quick and sharp, felt in the small of the back, and Gwenny clenched her fists and endured them without outcry. Meg told her walking up and down the room might hasten it, and this she did; trying to keep her attention fixed on the beautiful and gracious things in Mrs. Sawtrey's bedchamber, which she had so wondrously been permitted to share; the copper warming-pan, which she herself kept bright and polished on its hook nearby the fire; the shining fire-irons themselves; the heavily embroidered curtains about Mrs. Honor's bed, and the fair linen sheet turned down within. Gwenny returned to her pallet; it was better, Meg said, not to lie on a soft bed as this slowed the pains. In any case she would have felt shy of giving birth to her child in Mrs. Sawtrey's own bed.

Would it be a girl or a boy? She tried to take an interest in this. Up till now, she knew, her mind had been full of her own hurts, her mother's death, Alun's departure with the Whyteleaf brothers. Now there would be someone of her own to care for, and she must forget the child's begetting and think of its life. When all was said she was fortunate to be here and well looked after and well fed and ...

"Cry out if you will," said Meg. But Gwenny would not cry out until she had to. She hadn't cried, save once, at her ravishing, and she wouldn't let this make her cry if she could help it; but the pains grew worse, and presently she was gasping rather than crying; desperate, repeated gasps, as the agony grew in her body and a creature with a force of its own pressed down. She was passive, tormented, in anguish, while the child struggled to be born. Meg made her lie down again;

time passed and the pains came and went, strong at first, then less so, while Gwenny lay and clawed at her pallet and shift.

"Bear down." Meg's voice was terse, not from unkindness; she knew there was something wrong, the physician wouldn't have done what he did if this were to be a healthful baby, and the pains had been going on long enough; the head should be showing by now. "Bear down, love," she said again, and thought of the sad luck of this poor little creature; too young, she'd been, for all that had happened to her. But Gwenny didn't look young now. Her face was livid, with the congested veins standing out at temples and neck; she bore down again and again. "It won't come," she moaned.

Meg went to call the physician. When they returned, Honor with them, there was an arm limply dangling where the head should have been. The physician bent over the pallet and did something that hurt Gwenny, for she cried out loudly and he spoke to her in a soothing voice, but did not straighten himself. He was holding the part of the child that had come down; whether arm or shoulder now, no one could tell.

"God in His heaven, he's thrusting it back inside her again," breathed Meg, and then saw the obstetrician's trick of twisting a difficult birth so that it changed its direction and emerged from the mother's body at length with aid. He hadn't used forceps. Presently they saw why. Meg clapped her hand to her mouth to prevent a scream; there was no sound in the room but the mother's harsh breaths.

"Fetch a little wine for her, and lay the child aside," said the doctor. He tried to hand the baby to Meg, who would not touch it; impatiently, he laid it down himself and returned to the patient. Gwenny was slumbrous now, and the wine they brought to moisten her lips put her finally to sleep. Honor went over to look at the child. Unlike Meg, she had felt no urge to scream. Instead she knew an immense horror and pity.

The child had no brain. Its head was a flat, almost oblong shape composed mainly of the face and features, and covered with slimy dark hair. It had no neck, and its body was squat and limp, acknowledging the fact that such a thing could not live long; whether left alone or not, it would die. Honor covered it with a cloth, dismissing an urge to press this over the face and finish the life in it quickly. But instead she brought herself for a moment to stare at the face again, wondering if any except herself saw the truth. Gwenny had told her no less, and she had doubted her word.

The face was that of Francis Wolffe the bailiff.

The room stank of evil. There had been evil done to Gwenny, Honor knew now by whom. There had been evil done to Barbary, by the man who by this evidence was her children's father, and had destroyed her. Over the years the evil had borne flower and fruit and continued to flourish; where and how?

Gwenny must never see her child. When she awoke and asked for it, she must be told that it had been born dead. Honor looked away as she saw Meg Sawtrey, her digust overcome, go across to the place where the child lay and place a piece of flannel over its nose and mouth, and hold it there. "She is braver than I," Honor thought.

Gwenny slept on, her ordeal ended. The physician bowed, and went out.

I I

SOPHIA sat in the upper room at Biding, surveying her fashionably shod foot as it swung back and forth, less in time to the melody young Maud was playing on the spinet than to the tuneless rhythm of her own thoughts. First of all she thought of the shoe itself, and its neighbour; this year coloured bows were huge, and so were hers, of a cherry colour. She had taken off—it was uncomfortable when one sat—the lace pinner that stood behind her curls when she went out, but she had not washed the rouge from her cheeks. She knew it became her, as her gown became her, and the way she did her hair; she was the perfect picture of a modish young married woman, but what was the use of that if no one saw her except young Maud, intent on her music? Sophia, somewhat spitefully, stared at the long white arms, the bent white neck, of her husband's daughter. The fair curls were smoothly parted to hang over the girl's narrow shoulders; put Maud in a grey gown and veil, and she'd make a nun, Sophia was thinking. "As far as Dick Sawtrey is concerned she might as well be one."

Dick was in London, on some business of his own; Sir
Ralph was away on county affairs in his capacity of Justice of
the Peace. It was all very dull. There was no other company—everyone here was too old to stir from home unless
goaded—no party or supper in prospect, other than an
invitation, which she had refused, to go and stay at
Daneclere. Who would want to go back to that tomb of a
place, where servants were of the first importance?

She returned her thoughts to London. It had been in a
turmoil because of the late accusations against Papists made
by a Doctor Titus Oates, whom Sophia had briefly seen
leaving Whitehall while her husband, in turn, had been in
talk with the King. Oates' long-jawed face under the great
black horsehair wig was scarcely human, more like that of
some gigantic pallid fish; they said his speech was unaccoun-
tably drawling and foppish. Whatever he had drawled to the
King that day, there was trouble about; a number of Papists
were later arrested, they said the Queen—Oates had accused
her of plotting to kill her husband—was confined to her
rooms. As for the Duke of York, lately converted to Papistry,
it was probable he would have to leave England for a time.
Sophia had found the situation diverting, and would have
liked to stay in town to see and hear more; but Sir Ralph,
who loathed being away from the country, would come home.

She yawned. It was deadly dull at Biding, with only slow
Gregory left to creep about the passages. She had sent to ask
Honor if Maud might come and bear her company for a few
days, and the request had been granted, with the proviso that
if Sophia cared to come to Daneclere instead, she might.
Maud was hardly a diversion of the kind Sophia required;
certainly the girl was good-natured enough and had duly
admired the gowns Sophia had bought in London. "But she
has no real interest in fashions; look at her gown," Sophia
thought incredulously. To herself there were two absorbing
subjects, fashion and gentlemen. She had not yet forgotten her
own chagrin at not having caught the particular eye of His
Majesty King Charles II, who was enamoured of a French-
woman far less pretty and talented, Sophia thought, than
herself. She had however come away from Court with a
useful secret; the direction of an apothecary patronised by no
less a person than Barbara Palmer, Duchess of Cleveland.
Although that lady was no longer the King's mistress and, it
was whispered, had received the title in compensation, she

was still influential, and of necessity knew much about potions. Sophia had visited the shop and had come away with a store of powders recommended by Barbara, with whom she had actually talked once or twice. (Brief talks they had been, because Sir Ralph kept a tiresome eye on her.) But the powders were safely hidden, and when Sophia needed to use them she would. She hugged the knowledge to herself. They were not all to prevent conception and birth; some were love-potions. What could such a concoction do for Maud, tinkling at her spinet? Sophia hid a smile behind her hand; it would be amusing to turn Chastity into an itching nymph.

In any event, Sir Ralph had not got her with child; and she could ensure he would not.

Maud had finished playing and rose from the spinet. Returning to where Sophia sat, her skirts made a quiet hushing sound. Her gown was trimmed with Holland lace at the neck and wrists; its laundering had been done by Gwenny, Sophia surmised; *she* couldn't get a maid who would launder lace as it should be done, and although she had asked Honor particularly, and offered Gwenny a good wage if she would come to Biding, the foolish wench would not leave Daneclere. Sophia's eyes narrowed. There had been a curious incident about three years ago, after Jem and Lewis left for town. She recalled it while at the same time watching Maud, who had sat down and picked up some sewing she was at. Sophia continued to watch the girl through discreetly lowered lashes while recalling the strange return of Alun, Gwenny's brother, to Daneclere. It had been shortly after Jem's marriage (to a pock-marked widow fifteen years his senior, and not of the upper classes, but it kept him in money). It had been a wild night and the boy, evidently, had stumbled in out of it, soaked and almost exhausted; Lewis had dismissed him and had given him his fare home. Alun said it had been stolen by a pickpocket and he had walked. *That* was as good a story as any; however it befell, Alun took to the stable-loft and hid himself there, and would not come out for some days; when he did it was to go back to London. "As far as I know, they have heard nothing more from him; he must have found his own way of earning a living. Certainly Jem could not keep him on with convenience in his wife's house," thought Sophia.

She turned to Maud. "Have you heard from Dick, child?

He is a laggard husband to be sure; why did you not pester him to take you with him to London?" She watched, with amusement, the girl grow confused. *That* was no marriage; likely enough the fault lay with Dick, who had never been known to have ado with a woman.

"I do not like the town so well as here," said Maud, flushing. She did not answer the criticism about Dick, and Sophia was about to tease her further. But below there was commotion, and an arrival. Presently Dick himself was shown into the room, wet with rain from his ride. Sophia jumped to her feet, glad of another presence. Maud stood also and made a little curtsey. Her husband, his sallow cheeks redder than usual with the ride, saluted Sophia's hand and then Maud's cheek. "I fear I discompose you both," he said. "My mother is low in spirits, and asks that Maud may go back a few days early. She hopes you will forgive her, Sophia. I have a note." He handed it over and Sophia broke the seal.

"God knows, I daresay we are all of us in low spirits, with all the men away—except yourself, Dick," she added, smiling. "Will you drink wine before going? You must hardly have had time to draw breath from London when my cousin sent you across here." But he declined, and would not even seat himself, walking restlessly over to the window and looking out at the drizzling rain. "What is new from town?" said Sophia's voice behind him.

News from town are fearful tidings, his mind answered; and in memory he saw the recent scaffolds, the men executed with all the grisly detail of a mediaeval sentence carried out to the full. The smell of blood was in his nostrils; the revolting nature of the injustice done stayed with him. These men had done no harm; they had been betrayed; the King was helpless. Whatever happened now—and truth would prevail sooner or later—they were dead, and had died bravely and terribly. "Papists?" he could hear his mother saying. Yes, but a Papist feels pain like any other. A Papist lives, breathes, has feeling, knows right from wrong, can fear the rope and knife.

A thing had happened in the crowd, wolfish and yelling for blood as it had been. During one of the bouts of yelling, a man had been stabbed. The crowd were so close-packed that he had not fallen for some time, and whoever stabbed him had eased his way out before it was known who he might be. Dick, intent on the executions, had seen nothing of it and only recalled one other thing as he turned away, sick at heart, from the sight. A tall figure with girlish features had walked away, rapidly, from the fringe of the crowd. He thought it might have been Gwenny the maid's brother Alun, but he did not follow him.

He himself had left then, and knew no more.

He turned to Sophia. "There is little from town that is new." His tone was absent, his eyes hardly seeing her.

What a dull fellow he is, she was thinking. If only Edwin would come home! He should have come three years ago, when Uthred Jansen and that grim young Hawkin, whose father had been killed, had returned to Thwaite: she had heard that somewhere. Everything would be livelier once Edwin was at home.

Maud came with her cloak and gear and they went off, Dick escorting his wife as carefully as if she were made of glass. Precious Maud had never in her life been permitted to ride between Biding and Daneclere without an escort, Sophia thought scornfully. Maud, the copybook bride! It would be a jest to overturn her, as Dick would not.

There would be nobody but herself and Gregory for supper, after all. Boredom mounted in Sophia. The whole evening, with herself at one end of the board and Gregory at the other, saying nothing because he had nothing to say; his fair head shining in the candlelight, his angel's face intent on mutton chops, his wit God knew where! And the three others, all full men, far away in Canada with still no word of returning. ...

It was dull. The devil entered Sophia.

12

MY SON Edwin,

Yesterday I was Low in Spirits, so much so that I sent Dick on his Return to bring Maud back from Biding. She is a Sweet Girl and brings me Much Comfort, though it left Sophia without Company. I would greatly that you were Home, and if the Time is drawing near I am glad of it.

Had I known the News that would come, I had felt the Worse maybe. Soon after Maud returned and we were all of

us at *Supper, a Letter came from Jem Whyteleaf in London,
written in Haste. It bore Grave News, apart from the Rioting
against the Papists which there has been all year. Lewis
Whyteleaf was found Stabbed to Death in the Crowd which
watched the Papist Killings for the death of a Magistrate in
October, and it is said they also would have Killed the King,
if they had been Let. Certainly Lewis was Killed. They do
not know who did it, for the Man got away Safely with the
Great Press of People and the Noise of Shouting.*

*My Son, I have Prayed for Lewis but I cannot feel Grief.
You know, for I have told you, what they Did Here. It is one
of the Reasons for my Lowness, which is unlike me and I
would I had your Company.*

*Dick and Maud go on as is usual with them. I cannot
conceive why. It is still No Marriage, and a lovelier Girl one
would not Find. He is Fond of her, but as a Brother. If his
Father were alive, or if you Yourself were here, some One of
you might speak to him, for I as a Woman cannot easily do
so. He will not see a Physician.*

*I fear I show little Care over Lewis. I have written to his
Brother and have sent a Note to Sophia. She continues very
Grand as the Lady of Biding but I fear it is small Solace to
her as there is little Company, every one in the County
having their Own Concerns, and Sir Ralph is away.*

*God be with you, my Dear, and may we meet soon. I trust
there are Big Beaver.*

Your mother,
Honor Sawtrey.

In her room by Honor's, where she had slept since her child's
birth, Gwenny knelt and prayed for Alun. She had guessed as
soon as the news came. She had always known that,
somehow, it would happen; he had promised it. He had
promised it that time he had come home tired and broken-
hearted from London, because his god Mr. Jem had cast him
off. He had lain in the straw of the stable-loft and cried like a
little child, cried till his heart would break again, and then
she had told him the truth. She had told him how Jem and
his brother had ravished her repeatedly and brutally, had
stolen the jewels, had by the end got her with child, and since
the child's birth she could not walk except with a limp. At the
same time as Jem was daily caressing Alun he had been
coming nightly to her, and that more than anything else had

changed Alun and had made him sit up with a white face and bloodshot eyes and said "They have ruined us both. I will avenge us, Gwenny. I will do it, I promise."

He had gone then back to London, with money she had given him. It was a long time, three years back. But Alun had patience. He would have waited till the opportunity came, till he stood behind Mr. Lewis in a noisy crowd. A knife slipped between the ribs could kill with a single cry, drowned as it would be in the shouting. A dead man could not fall between the packed bodies of the people. Mr. Lewis was dead, and would never torment her more.

She must pray for Alun, and for Mr. Lewis also, as the Papists did. She should pray also for Mr. Jem, because sooner or later Alun would also kill him.

1 3

SHE HALF-SAT, half-reclined in a place in the attic which was clear of lumber, cobwebs and dust. There was little of value left hidden at Biding since the Civil War. Only a broken chair full of worm, an Irish harp with frayed strings, a child's doll lacking an arm and an eye, other such things were left up here forgotten. The rest was mounded under dust-sheets, themselves smelling of age and moth. She herself, the only living, breathing thing in the place, was on the contrary filled with physical satisfaction: her lover had just left her.

She stretched, at ease in her loose wrapper; and laughed and yawned. This was the second time they'd done it; the first had been on her own bed, the night she first tried the herbal drug on—Gregory. Yes, the slow-wit, who never yet spoke, who could neither read nor write nor, it had been assumed, readily understand, had understood; and acted, without experience but with a kind of boyish wonder, which endeared him the more to her. He had the makings of a good lover: she'd turn him into a better. At the beginning it had been for a diversion, that night they had all gone back to Daneclere and she was bored. Now ... with Sir Ralph shortly to return, they'd have to find a better place than the attic; she, the mistress of Biding, had every right to be up here, looking through the things, and no servant dared question her. But if her husband came upon them together among the dust sheets and the harp, it would be a different matter.

Where else could they go? She had already half thought of a place; it would be cold enough at this time of year, but better in the summer, screened as they would be then by hawthorn and elder. The ruined chapel, where Cromwell's men had stabled their horses before setting it alight on leaving, had not all burned; part of the roof was left. There were stone pews where, to be sure, the lying would be hard enough; she might take cushions for her comfort.

She began to laugh with a quiet self-satisfied chuckling: the difficulties themselves challenged her. One couldn't leave Biding armed with cushions, to meet with Gregory sidling later through the wood. It would be expected of my Lady Farmiloe that she take a servant to bear the burden. Certainly there were drawbacks to rank. In the days when she'd been Sophia Whyteleaf she could have carried armfuls of cushions and pillows wherever she chose and no one would have questioned her.

Sir Ralph was expected home tonight.

Sophia sat up, ran her fingers through her tousled ringlets, and got to her feet. She was still deliciously unsteady with the force of their love-making. Who would have thought it of Gregory? She must not be made to part with him. No one must know or guess, not even the servants. Sir Ralph's lady, and his son, would in any case cause gossip together, but when the son was a lackwit they would scream her out of Biding, if ... if they were to find out. So they must not; it must be left to her discretion, as Gregory himself had none. Poor Gregory.

Sir Ralph returned home that evening, his business concluded. He sighed a little; it would have been of interest to talk over it with his sons, particularly Lionel: he wished that they were home. Gregory would understand nothing of it, and his young wife little; Sophy, he had long since noted, was chiefly concerned with the notions and desires of women, such as fashion, outrivalling the rest in church, resulting in dressmakers' bills to make him grimace. He did not admit to himself that he regretted his marriage; after all it had been undertaken with his own full consent and understanding, and he had pondered it for long after first concluding that such an alliance might be a trifle ridiculous, given his age and hers. But she was a pretty creature, and seemed fond of him. Yet a companion such as his first wife would have been ... never.

He diverted himself with a sad little fantasy, on seeing Biding rise from among its containing trees, that not Sophy but Maud would be waiting, fair as in her youth, and that she would run out to welcome him with the little boys at her skirts. But at the door, no one met him; he handed his horse to the groom and went inside to where Sophia sat waiting, and kissed her dutifully. "Have you been idle while I was away?" he teased her.

She smiled, and fluttered her eyelashes. "No, not idle; bored, a little. But I found ways of diverting myself. Have you had supper, sir?"

Over the supper-table they sat as always, with himself in his place at the head of the table, the servant standing behind him; Sophia at the opposite end, with the candles' sconces between them so that they appeared to one another in a golden haze; and Gregory between, his vacuous blue eyes fixed steadfastly on his stepmother. After some time his father noted it, and spoke to him sharply. The young man turned, and stared at Sir Ralph for a few moments; then he was back to looking at Sophia again. She wore a gown of wine-red satin, cut low to show a loose chemise such as they wore at Court; it fell back at the sleeve-ends to show her white forearms to advantage. Suddenly, as they were still at meat, Gregory reached out his hand and lovingly, curiously stroked the exposed flesh of Sophia's breast.

She sat still, her expression unchanging; the episode might not have occurred. Sir Ralph stood up angrily, clouted his son across the ear, and bade him begone from the table. "And do not return till you can use the manners of gentlefolk," he shouted, scarcely knowing his own voice; he was as a rule soft-spoken and gentle, and had hardly struck one of his sons in all their lifetime.

He stared at his wife. She sat now with downcast eyes, daintily crumbling the bread on her plate. "Have you been encouraging him in this?" he asked, and was again surprised to hear his voice so soon level. Sophia shook her head, with an air of detached amusement. "He pesters me some little, that is all," she said indulgently. "He is, after all, a young man." Her tone might have indicated that he himself was an old fool.

"By God, he shall spend his youth elsewhere," swore Sir Ralph, and rose and left the table. He went to their room, but when she joined him later said no word to her; he was in bed, his shoulder turned from her, and feigned sleep: which suited Sophia well enough. She had not intended such a thing to happen: but as it had, how else should she have acted? It was not possible to explain to Gregory that he must be passionate in private, while continuing discreet in public. There were many men in full possession of their wits who would have found such a distinction difficult.

Next day Sir Ralph stated that he would ride over to see his old friend Sir Nigel Brysson at Newhall, who was his son Nigel's godfather; his wife also was dear to Sir Ralph, as it had been she who brought Maud Farmiloe safely home to Biding after Gregory's birth. Of all people in the world, he thought, those two would aid him; also, though he said nothing of it, he wanted a word with Mrs. Honor at Daneclere.

"Am I to come with you?" asked Sophia. Anxious as she was that her husband should be out of the house, she was also concerned that old Lady Brysson—the hook-nosed old Royalist had given her a set-down at supper once, and was a notable dowd—should be forced to admire her new riding-habit and feathered hat. But Sir Ralph said he wished no company; and at that Sophia displayed pretty manners and asked when he would come back to her again. Below the arched grey brows his eyes regarded her with an expression hard to read.

"I may stay the night," he answered curtly, and mounted his horse within the hour. She heard him canter off, and went then to the window. It looked like being a clear fine day. The new excitement pulsing in her veins would not be suppressed; she sent for Gregory, stroked his cheek and scolded him as if he could understand her. "My bold lad, did your father hurt you very much? I am sorry for it. Let us go out together, you on Toby, I on Meg; it is a sunny day and there are few such." And she gave orders to the servants to saddle his mount and her own, after dinner, which was at three o'clock.

Sir Ralph rode away from his visit to Newhall in a happier frame of mind: there had been no difficulty made over his suggestion that Gregory might, for a little time, stay with them there. Lady Brysson had soothed his fears; it was natural, she said, for a young man to act so, and Gregory could not tell right from wrong or, possibly, even know that he handled his father's wife though he had been groomsman at the wedding. "It is better that he be here with us meantime," she had said, and Sir Ralph kissed her worn fine hands. Newhall, like Biding, had endured a visit from Cromwell's men in the late wars: such things bound their owners forever to aid one another in any fresh disaster or danger. This might be neither. Gregory's father rode back to Daneclere with the fresh wind cheering him and making his cheeks flush as they had done when he was a young man. Also, he had great liking and respect for Honor Sawtrey and looked forward to drawing on her wisdom. Mrs. Honor would know Sophia better than anyone, and also what was best to be done. The day was not so far spent as he had thought; he had made good speed, the wind with him.

Honor greeted him in the hall. As he sat himself opposite her he marvelled, as he always did, at how little she had changed with the years. When she had first come as Sawtrey's bride from Thwaite she had seemed, perhaps, mature for her age, like many young women who have already shouldered responsibility. Now she was like a goddess—Ceres, he thought—her hair darkened only a trifle, admitting a few strands of grey. Her face was placid and unlined although, as he knew, she had had her share of disasters. Her brother's death must have saddened her. It flashed across his mind that had he not been besotted, it would have been better to ask Mrs. Honor to be his wife than Sophia. "But the child will surely gain wisdom with the years," he told himself charitably. Already his young wife seemed remote. He brought her name into their talk almost with reluctance: Mrs. Honor had been telling him what pleasure she had in looking forward to the return of Edwin, who had written to say he had put an end to his term with the Company and would voyage home as soon as there was a ship, having meantime cleared up his affairs there.

"He has served them well, and need not feel ashamed of leaving," she said. "But I look to see my own boy, not a grown man; what fools we mothers make of ourselves! I would not hinder him in anything he wants to do; but truth to tell I miss his company." She flushed, bit her lip, then told

Maud's father outright about the state of affairs concerning Maud's marriage.. Sir Ralph frowned a little.

"I had feared it," he said. "I too think of my girl as a child, not a grown woman, else had I made enquiry ere this. Time is the only cure, I doubt me."

"I have them sleep in the same bed, so that it may come by nature, given time as you say. She is so lovely and so good that he—"

Her voice tailed off unhappily. She had for some time now thrust Maud and Dick to the back of her mind, delighting instead in thoughts of Edwin's return. Now here was Sir Ralph with his troubles over Sophia. I could have warned him they were coming, she thought; and perhaps should have done so. But it had been an advantageous marriage for the penniless girl.

She said gently "Sophia is a young woman, and lonely when you are away."

"You by your kindness invited her to stay here, and she would not come. She prefers—I cannot but say it—to sit in Biding hall making much of her state there, or planning some extravagant occasion to which she can invite the county and receive them in a new gown. I have tried to interest her in grave matters, but—"

Honor smiled. "Dear sir, Sophia will never be grave. Your own Maud would make her a better companion than any; I regret taking her away this time. I was lonely also, and perhaps selfish. Maud is fond of Sophia, and withal somewhat grave, and as you know they were together while the child grew up. Many a time Sophia has ridden with her to Biding to cheer you."

Ay, thought Sir Ralph; and to cozen me too.

"Would it not now cheer you both," said Honor, "if Maud were to return to her home for a little? You would see more of your daughter; Dick may miss her absence, which will be good for him; and as for Sophia, to—to have other than frivolous company would aid matters." She had almost said Sophia ought to be watched.

Sir Ralph nodded. "You have spoken well. It will suit me, and it shall suit Sophia; and maybe Dick, lacking his wife for a time, may become less of a laggard husband, eh?"

They smiled, drank wine and parted. The sun still shone outside. Honor walked round afterwards to look at her knot-garden, where green shoots were fat and a few early flowers were already out. She had heard Sir Ralph ride off with compassion. It was a sorry marriage; she knew now that she should not have fostered it; and Maud's was hardly better. "I must give up matchmaking," she thought.

But Edwin was coming home; and her heart felt light again. She bent and touched the flowers, yellow against the brown earth. By the time he came, they would be in full bloom. She prayed that he might have an easy voyage; it was a better time of year than when he had gone. He would be a full man, hardened to danger, now; she must remember not to treat him as a child, as she feared she still at times treated Dick. Perhaps Edwin's company would make a man of his brother.

Sir Ralph cantered leisurely home by the bridge, the river, the woods. Before he came to Biding he saw two horses tethered, a black and a bay. They were from his own stable. He checked an oath, and dismounted, casting the reins over a branch, and strode forward on foot. The walls of the chapel, which he had hardly visited since its burning, reared before him. There was a great empty place where the stones had fallen down and one could look inside. Through this space, beneath the remains of the roof, on a stone bench, Sophia lay half-naked under Gregory. Her eyes were closed; on hearing a twig break under Ralph's feet, they opened and she sat up abruptly, her lips parted as if to speak. Gregory did not turn round; his head lolled on her bare breast, like a child with its mother.

A choking sensation overcame Sir Ralph. Then it was as if the world spun from him; the chapel, its walls, the trees, the sky, all merged into one whirling dizzy sensation of loss. He fell on his side among last year's bracken, breathing harshly, and lay still.

14

THE NEWS of Sir Ralph's seizure was received with dismay at Daneclere. Honor at once prepared to ride to Biding, and would have gone, but Maud prevented her.

"Who should help nurse my father if not I? Of course I will go," she said. Honor looked at the girl, marvelling as always at her grave beauty and dignity; the latter was beyond her years, and set at naught the figure she might have cut as the wife on whom Dick Sawtrey would not get a child. As a nurse, especially with aid, she would be competent; Honor herself had instructed her in the use of herbs and potions, and cupping when there was a physician. Moreover, she was loving as well as lovely; her presence would, Honor reflected, do the sick man more good than anything, as much as—though that was half forgotten now—making company for Sophia. So she kissed the girl and bade her get her cloak, and ordered a horse to be saddled and some baggage packed, the last to be taken over by a servant who would return to Daneclere. Honor wrote a letter to Sophia, to be sent with Maud; in it she offered to come herself, if it would do any good; but in her heart she knew that it was not necessary. Sir Ralph's daughter would tend him well. Honor sighed a little, thinking of her pallid elder son; what ailed Dick that he would not love such a wife? Fondness there was, like that of a brother for a sister; but that would not make heirs to Daneclere. "Yet now is not the time to think of it," she admitted, and watched Maud ride off, followed by the servant. Maud's slim hands on the reins were light, and she guided her mare to perfection; in a short time they were out of sight.

Maud herself, on the ride, was able to assemble her thoughts; this had not been easy in the hot, shameful nights she spent with Dick. He had tried, on more than one occasion, to make her his wife, and had failed; she had remained always sweet and courteous to him, but knew he blamed himself, and that this blame, which everyone in Daneclere must know of, made him wretched. It would be a relief to lie alone in a cool bed on the nights when she was not sitting up with her father. Poor father! She wanted to reach him quickly; they said one seizure often led to another. Maud remembered her childhood visits and the way Sir Ralph had always been kind to her, kissing her and tossing her up in his arms as though she were a doll, asking her how her reading was progressing, and her horn-book, and her sampler. All the time she had known that behind his cheerful, loving air there had been great loneliness, and together they had often stood before her mother's portrait in the great hall and he would talk to her of that other Maud, who had died when she was born. Once she had cried, saying "You cannot love me if I killed her"—that had been later, when she was older—but Sir Ralph had bent to kiss her again and said "I did not think at first that I could love you, let alone look at you; but I looked, and then I loved you both for her sake and your own."

He had been handsome and kind, her father; and the brothers she could well remember had been as handsome and, in their separate ways, kind. Perhaps, if word was sent to them of their father's state, they would come home.

She rode into Biding courtyard and dismounted, and was shown inside and straight up to Sir Ralph's room. Sophia was absent. "That is strange," thought Maud. "Had I been his wife I would not leave him," but no doubt Sophia had reasons one knew nothing of. She must not judge her.

The room was dark after the outside sunlight, and Maud had to adjust her eyes to the great bed, and the pale bearded figure lying on the pillows. Her father had altered a great deal; one side of his face drooped, and he could not speak. She was to find later that an arm and a leg were helpless also, but now she went straight to his side.

"Father, 'tis Maud. You know me?"

His eyes shone, but he said nothing; he could not. She laid her smooth cheek against his on the pillow and said softly "Father, I have come to be with you, to help nurse you till you are well." Then she rose and took off her cloak and laid it on the bed-chest, and went and sat down where he could see her. She would sit like this for as long as he wanted, many hours, day or night. The physician had been already, and had cupped him; they had told her that in the hall. There was no more to do now but comfort him and make him feel that he was not alone.

The following day the Bryssons, who had had the news, drove over in their new-fangled coach, my lady's pride, to take Gregory back with them to Newhall. Sophia tried to stop it, but, to her mortification and rage, the servants accepted Lady Brysson's orders and ignored her own, as though they knew Sir Ralph's wishes. Sophia flung herself on her bed afterwards in a fit of sullens, and did not come down for dinner.

15

EDWIN gathered his mount's reins slackly into one hand, shaded his eyes against the sun with the other, and stopped to stare at Daneclere, rising above the bright river and the green summer growth of trees and grass.

Anyone passing—there were not many at that hour—would have taken a second glance at the tall, big-boned, bright-haired young man on horseback, clad in a fashion more casual than was seen here nowadays even in country places. He wore a leather tunic thonged and fringed in the Indian manner, and his high boots were made of the same.

Staring at his home again after so many years, he found that his thoughts were not concerned with Daneclere. They went back rather to the time he had left it; to the rough voyage, the landing at last in the unknown country with its dangers and hazards, and its winters which were long, dark, and bitterly cold, then suddenly its spring and short, lovable summer, then swift snows again. That was a land where the mountains and plains, the great rivers and deep valleys and awesome glaciers, were of a dimension undreamed of here, so that this seemed by comparison to be a child's country of toy farms. But Edwin was light of heart, pleased enough to be home for a while, and would stay as long as his mother needed him. "After that, I will return," he thought. There was no finer life for a man than in the land of big beaver; always provided one did not allow oneself to run to too much drink and too many Indian women. Edwin had as good a head as any man for the former, but he knew when to stop; and as for the women, he had not indulged in them overmuch because he had been warned early that they carried syphilis. He had given his chief interest, all his application, to his work at the Fort; his employers there thought highly of him and had regretted his going. Wider in travel and experience by far than when he had first come to the Bay, he had at last journeyed home on the first ship taking bales of pelts; leaving Edgar Farmiloe in his place at the trading-post. He must ride over to Biding soon, and give Sir Ralph news of his sons.

He had seen the Farmiloe brothers now and again, except for Edgar, separately; once, when he had visited the great rival fur auctions at Montreal, they had all met together. The Farmiloes had preferred to make a living as free trappers further south to acknowledging the yoke of Hudson's Bay, even with its sure market in London. Edwin himself had no complaints about the Company; he had found the other men friendly and the work congenial and not over hard. He had in fact, despite his haste to reach his mother, spared half a day to wait on Prince Rupert at Spring Gardens; but the Prince was out at Hammersmith, where he kept a pretty mistress, a former play-actress who had borne him a little daughter he adored. Edwin had not taken time to follow him; he would see him on a subsequent visit. Meantime he had hastened on to Daneclere.

He started the horse again to a canter, hearing its hooves hit the soft summer dust, and was soon in the courtyard. A groom ran out, a lad too young to know him. Edwin smiled, and asked for his mother. He was told that she was in her garden; and walked quickly round. The young groom looked after him wistfully, admiring his easy stride and travel-stained clothes. There was a man who had seen far places! He was soon informed who Edwin was.

Honor was weeding her garden, her hands in old gloves. She wore no hat and the sun shone down on her hair. Edwin saw the grey in it; he knew a sudden fear that when she turned round, she would be an old woman. He addressed her.

"Mother!"

And she turned. "Edwin, Edwin!" and flew into his arms like a girl. The joy in her face touched him; she had missed him, he saw, more than he had known, more even than the contents of her letter to him had conveyed. He was doubly glad that he had made haste to come home on receiving it. Her face was hardly changed from that he remembered; the same firm, soft mouth, clear skin lacking wrinkles or sagging, and honest eyes which looked at him, now, as if she would read his very thoughts. Yet she spoke little; she had never been a voluble woman. "I did not expect you yet," she said almost shyly. "Had I known, I'd have had them kill a fat lamb; as it is, we have only cold meat from yesterday, but I will have them make you a pasty. Did you breakfast on the way? No? Then we will go in, and drink wine to refresh you, and talk while they prepare the food."

"Where is Dick?" he asked, and her face clouded. She bent her head and began to peel off her gloves.

"Ridden to London, as he often does nowadays. You might have passed him on the road. I know not for what reason he goes, and I never ask him. Maud is at Bidling. You would not hear, I think, of Sir Ralph's seizure. He is confined to bed and Maud and Sophia are with him."

They walked on, mother and son striding together, tall folk at ease. Edwin frowned over the news of Dick. From all he had both heard and guessed, there was enough amiss with his brother to cause their mother heartbreak. Maud herself he dismissed as the child he remembered her. Yet it was true—time had passed so quickly—that she would be ripe for marriage. He found he could not picture her at all. Maybe—the thought caused him to grin ruefully—he himself could talk to Dick, the younger to the elder. It was time his brother took the responsibility of Daneclere and let their mother have more leisure: not that she would take it.

They went into the hall, and soon Edwin found himself with a filled wine-cup before the empty hearth. The summer sun streamed through the open doorway. He found he was weary after his ride, and the wine refreshed him. They talked of many things, and Edwin felt renewed sadness over the tidings of Sir Ralph. Tomorrow, he would ride over and give him news of his sons. But today was Honor's own. He let her talk as she would, ridding herself, he doubted not, of the lonely worries over days and nights these past years. At the end he rose; the savoury smell of the meat pasty began to reach them from the kitchens, and two servants came quietly in to set the table and put out the salt.

"I am glad that we have talked, mother," said Edwin quietly. "I can see that I have stayed away overlong."

"I have asked you little of your own life; and it is to remain your own, Edwin. I will not hinder you if you do not choose to stay with us at Daneclere for ever. But if you will, you are welcome; that you know."

"Perhaps Dick would not make me welcome," he told her.

Honor frowned. "He has no decision," she said. "If there are problems, the folk here come to me, for he cannot satisfy them. He has no interest in his inheritance."

They sat down to meat.

16

EDWIN had nerver greatly liked Sophia, and on seeing her again after so many years, and notwithstanding her marriage, she still seemed to him to have the makings of a whore. She could not have expected him—he had sent no warning of his arrival, simply riding over from Daneclere after dinner—but she was painted and dressed as if to receive a company of courtiers, he thought; to his eyes, used as they were to women simply dressed in homespun, or in Indian dyed wool and soft leather, she was grandly and somewhat shamefully clad in a low-cut gown with tight lacing down the bodice, so that her breasts showed pouting above. On her head was a lace confection such as he had briefly noted on other fashionable women when riding through London; it was stiffened with starch, and stood up at the back of Sophia's head, making her older than her years; and she was rouged and wore patches. He made his condolences about Sir Ralph, and asked to see him; he was aware that his own manner was curt and that Sophia would have preferred him to stay downstairs talking pleasantries, and no doubt admiring her appearance.

He was correct as to that last; Sophia, weary of her life again now that Gregory had been taken from her, had been ecstatic at the sudden arrival of a personable man. Many years since, she reminded herself, when she was quite a child, she had thought herself in love with Edwin Sawtrey, but as Sir Ralph could give her a title and a fortune had settled for pursuit of the latter, though he was so much older. Now, a solitary young wife (almost a widow, she told herself; Ralph would never walk nor speak again), it was delightful to be able to set her cap, and her glances, at Edwin. But his abrupt manner discouraged her swiftly. She decided that he was after all very rude; no doubt the years of living in a rough far-off country had coarsened him. She thrust out her painted underlip, but offered herself to take him to Sir Ralph's chamber. "Maud sits with him," she said. "You will remember her, I doubt not." *For he has hardly*, she told herself as they ascended the stairs, *shown that he remembers me.*

There was sunlight in the room; the wind had dropped, and the curtains at the opened casement hung motionless in the still air. Edwin could see, from the doorway, the figure in the bed, which showed Sir Ralph greatly aged and changed. But the sun fell and shone on the fair hair of a young girl, who rose as they entered, and stood waiting uncertainly; when Sophia had performed the introductions, she curtsied, and Edwin bowed. That was all; but he would remember the moment, he thought, for the rest of his life.

She was still slim, almost childish; she wore no paint. She was all of the things that Sophia was not, and he would have liked to take her aside and tell her so; he would like to tell her many other things; but he must pay his respects to the invalid, and sit down by the bed, and talk to Sir Ralph, while the two young women waited for a while, and then withdrew after Sophia had pressed Edwin to stay and take supper with them, and he had refused. Why? He did not know; yet, thinking of it later, he told himself he knew very well. He must not sit yet across a board from his brother Dick's wife, lest his very glance tell watchers that he loved her, had loved her at sight, when the sun shone in on her hair.

One watcher knew already; had known from the first encounter. So he fancied that nun! Well, it was unlikely he would pierce her virtue without help, and it might make a diversion to have him try. Such was the caprice of Sophia, whose rejection by Edwin, though brief, had angered her so much that she was ready for a revenge on him before they mounted the stairs. After, it was all of it much simpler: she knew what she might do. Moreover, she had found out where to write to the Farmiloe sons; if needed, as Edwin had told her father in her hearing, Edgar was to be found at the post in Hudson's Bay. To bring the sons home would at least rid the house of its boredom; and the Bryssons could not—she smiled sourly—come with their coach and carry off three able-bodied and quick-witted young men.

Meantime she turned to Maud, who sat nearby, hands clasped in her lap. She looked tired and there were shadows under her eyes. She had sat with Sir Ralph night and day sometimes, relieved by the servants when it was necessary for her to obtain a little sleep. "Perhaps I myself may sit by him, to relieve her, now," thought Sophia, and being a lady of foresight said so, sweetly, to her sister-in-law. Maud smiled.

"That is good of you, Sophia," she said. "But I will still take my turn; he likes to see me. How glad he was to see Edwin! He can understand, you know, even though he cannot speak; and it is good for him to hear about my brothers."

"We must bid Edwin come often," said Sophia, smoothly.

Maud had been glad of Edwin's visit. She liked him—she could recall having done so as a child, when little as they knew one another he had always been kind to her—and felt none of her accustomed shyness in the honest wish to see him again. Nevertheless she would not have sought him out of her own accord; her manners were modest, and she had been carefully reared both by Honor at Daneclere, and by her father at Biding. It was not for nothing that Sophia had once noted that Maud was always escorted on the ride between one great house and the other. Nothing in her upbringing had encouraged her to be a tomboy or to risk scandal by her behaviour, and she was shielded so carefully that in fact, she had made few friends of her own age. She was so much younger than her own brothers, the Whyteleafs and the Sawtreys that she had grown accustomed to defer to them in everything, even the way in which she might spend her leisure. It was for this reason that, two days after Edwin's visit, she went to Sophia to ask permission to ride out, while a servant sat with her father. Sophia gave it readily and with a shrug; why not? "Only I cannot spare anyone to go with you," she said, and this was true; the nursing of Sir Ralph meant that all of the servants were fully occupied at Biding.

"Then I will go alone," said Maud, with a curious sense of relief; she wanted for some reason to be alone with her thoughts, and it would be easier if no one followed. Sophia nodded, looking openly into Maud's pale face.

"The air will do you good," she said. "You are too much indoors."

So Maud rode out, on her own bay mare she had brought from Daneclere. She would not, she had decided, ride far; she would not even take the time to visit them at Daneclere, because Sophia needed her help with Sir Ralph and he himself, she knew, would want her that evening to play chess with him. This had been her own suggestion, and passed the time for him, for he could make the moves with his good arm and his mind was clear. So Maud cantered pleasantly along the dusty lanes between quickset hedges, and found her thoughts dwelling on Edwin Sawtrey; so much so that when she came upon him, likewise mounted and riding the opposite way, she flushed, and this and the wind-tangled hair beneath her hat heightened her usually pale beauty.

He greeted her somewhat curtly; he had been riding alone to drive out the devil that had plagued him since he saw her at Biding. How could he tell her, without eternal damnation, that the sight of her, so like a wild rose today, disturbed and weakened him to an extent that would make him glad to betray his brother? If Dick had shown that he valued her—if that had been so, then she would not have been at Biding, he would not have come upon her two days since, as he had, and again now, alone. She would have been at Daneclere, loved and cherished, the mother of Dick's children, occupied with her duties, housekeeping, brewing. He found that the thought of it made him savage, and bent his head so that Maud thought he was adjusting the reins; then he looked up.

"May I come with you?" he said. She assented gladly; she had been abashed, thinking by his manner of greeting that he had no wish to be with her, and she had been about to ride on alone. But now he turned his mount's head, and presently they were side by side in full gallop, while the hedges flew past.

"Let us to go the Bye Field; 'tis fallow," she called presently, and they went in, he dismounting and holding the gate for her, and then they let the horses have their heads and galloped delightfully over the great lush field, with tansy and daisy underfoot and Daneclere hidden beyond the rise. The sun was warm again today and by the end they and the horses were all of them flushed and sweating, happy in one another's company and as free as if all the world were their own, to be ridden over. They drew rein at last, and Edwin said "You ride well," and the look in his eyes as he spoke to her confused Maud, she did not know why. She smoothed Bessy's neck and said, in a low voice, "I must go back; already I have stayed away longer than I meant. Sophia will be waiting, and I—"

He cut in suddenly, brutally. "What right has Sophia over you? You do her untold good by being there at all, as a favour; she is your father's wife, and should wear herself out in the nursing of him, not you."

She was dismayed; no one in all of her life had spoken to

her as roughly. "'I am glad to do it," was all she could think of to say. "Will you open the gate?"

"I will do more; I will ride home with you, and persuade Sophia that she has no reason to blame you for staying. It was I who detained you, and I shall tell her so."

He spoke with determination, and she was too shy to deter him; so they rode back to Biding together, and he cast his horse's reins to the groom with a word that he would be back, while Maud was dismounted by another. She watched Edwin stride into the house, and when she came in he was standing by Sophia. His mouth was set in a hard line and she feared there might have been words between them; but Sophia was smiling.

"Edwin assures me that you must have more fresh air and exercise," she said. "Why do you not call for her each afternoon, Edwin, and afterwards stay and sup with us? I can sit with my poor husband while you are both away; I could even—" she grimaced—"make an attempt with him at chess, though I'm not as good as Maud; I have no patience, and my queens and castles tumble too soon by reason of haste."

"Edwin has other business," put in Maud hurriedly. He must not be made to think that he was tied to visit here each day, she was thinking; it encroached too greatly on his time. But she saw him give a little, ironic bow, as though to an adversary partly vanquished.

"I could have none which would give me greater pleasure," he said, and turned on his heel and went out; presently they heard him ride off.

Maud turned to Sophia, her cheeks suffused with crimson. "Sophia, you should not have—"

But Sophia was still smiling.

17

A LETTER reached Edgar Farmiloe at Fort Rupert some weeks later. As sometimes happened in summer, his brothers were with him; they passed the time in smoking, drinking and dicing, for summer pelts fetch little money.

My dear Sonne, the letter ran,
*I feel that you are this in truth although I did not give you
Birth. Your father, Sir Ralph Farmiloe, has had a Grievous
Stroke and keeps his Bed. I myself am worn out with
watching him and there is little the Physicians can Do. If you
would see your Father Alive, and can send some Word to
your Brothers concerning it (but I doe not know their
Direction) and can come Home, it would be well.*
*Maud is with me. There are Other Matters which I would
fain speak of with you all, but sufficient until the Tyme when
you come Home.*

Your father's Wyfe,
Sophia Farmiloe.

The other matters of which she wrote had been proceeding
now for some weeks. They had been helped, of course, by
Sophia's doctoring the wine; it had been an easy matter, now
Edwin was accustomed to stay and drink with them, to slip
the powders into each wine-cup, and thereafter proceed to
supper, by which time the drug was already doing its work.
Maud had sat, suffused with blushes, the chaos of her
thoughts strange to her, for she had never been thus before;
she stared at Edwin hungrily, with parted lips, and he could
not keep his eyes from her; it was as though their two bodies
joined already in the act of love. After supper Sophia had
suggested that they should all go to the upper chamber, and
saw to it that they were close to one another as they followed
her upstairs; after they were all seated, she made some
excuse, rose and slipped out. "You will entertain one another,
I know," she told them, and closed the door. For a moment
she leant with her back against it, listening, but there was no
sound. "They will not use words," she thought.

She made her way down to the room beneath, which was
where she kept her household accounts. Sir Ralph had always
insisted that she be punctilious about these, and since his
illness the books needed looking into; but although she stared
at the paper Sophia did nothing yet with her quill. Presently
she was rewarded for her wait, and pricked her ears for the
sound she thought she heard; then she was certain. It was the
rhythmic, regular creaking of the bed upstairs. Sophia
dropped the quill and clapped her hands over her mouth to
stifle her laughter. When she drew them away, there was red
paint on the palms. She took up her quill again and made

pretence to look through the books. After all, there was little else to do.

Next day Maud had been in an agony of shyness and guilt. She did not understand what could have happened to make her act so; she had been unfaithful to Dick; she was a harlot, an abandoned woman, worse than anyone; she could never face aunt Honor again. She could not even face the Biding servants; supposing they knew? She sent word by her maid that she felt unwell, and would not come downstairs; the morning passed as she lay and stared at the ceiling between her bed-curtains. Surely Edwin would not come today? If he came, what was she to do? She could never, never behave again as they had done last night; she must stop riding out; she must see no one. Her duty to her father must come first; it had made her leave Daneclere, and now she could never go back. Her eyes, dry and tearless, focussed at last on the bed-curtains; she would never forget the pattern there of doves on a grey ground. She must devote her life to Sir Ralph, and live like a nun. What did even Sophia think of her, if Sophia knew? She had been gone long enough last night to let them do what they did, then Edwin had gone out alone. For Sophia to know was in some way the worst thing of all. Maud felt soiled. She could never hold up her head, on its proud little neck, again. She—

At midday Sophia came up herself and wrenched aside the curtains. "You are going out riding with Edwin," she said. Maud stared at the pillows, fingered the sheet, said she could not ride out today, and burst into tears. Sophia opened the curtains further. "You should go out more," she told the girl ruthlessly. "Did not Edwin say so? He told me I was selfish to keep you indoors so much. You owe it to me to go out, do you not? Come, get dressed in your riding-clothes, and let me send for water to wash your face." She bustled about the room, opening chest-lids, lifting ewers. Maud, her heart beating rapidly like that of a bird, got out of bed, and went to do as she was bid, washing her face when the water came. The sobs still racked her, but she tried to down them. She must obey Sophia.

Edwin came within the hour and Maud, mounted on her mare, rode out with him through the gate. They had greeted one another as usual before the grooms, as though the thing that had happened last night had not. Maud stared ahead between the mare's ears. Edwin stared at Maud. Her confusion touched and diverted him; for himself, he was filled with triumph. However it had come about—he suspected that little minx Sophia—it had come, and Maud was his. He was filled with physical well-being, some pity for Maud, and determination. It should happen again, today; he needed no more powders, and presently neither would she.

He made them stop in the wood. Dismounting, he went to lift Maud out of the saddle. "No," she breathed, "please, no." He was laughing. He took the two sets of reins and fastened them to one branch. "See," he said, "how they are joined, as we shall be."

"No, no—I must not—I must not—"

"That you must," he said. His eyes were shining, like those of a god. She began to tremble. Oh, if only it were not so wrong, if only—

"It is wrong," she wept. "It is wickedness—I should not have stopped here—I—we—"

He had seized her in his arms and began kissing her roughly, till her pleas turned to gasping and then even that ceased. He laid her gently down on the ground in the shade of a large oak. Its huge ancient branches towered above them and when she opned her eyes, it was to see the sky between the leaves, and Edwin above her. His weight crushed her; she sobbed as he thrust; then presently was filled with a sweetness she had not thought possible, like last night, last night. ... Would it always be thus? How could she resist? Her body responded to his as though he thrust magic within her. She grew wanton, clinging to him with arms and legs; she cried out in ecstasy. He was still laughing. He was laughing at her, she knew, and was filled with delicious confusion.

"Maud, my little nun, my little Maud; so you like it, eh? You like it well."

"Ah. ..."

Presently he kissed her again, gently this time, on her mouth, her throat, her breasts where he had opened her bodice. Each time his lips touched her flesh a little thrill went through her. Who and what was she? No longer Maud, good dutiful Maud, who sat by her father and played chess. Father ... she had not seen him this day.

"Again," said Edwin, demandingly as though he knew she

had half forgotten him; and he made her remember him, while the oak boughs watched in silence and the horses cropped their grass.

As the summer passed and the days grew shorter they would return early to Biding, and instead of making love in the open they would go to bed. It could not be possible by now that Sophia did not know, Maud was aware; but she herself was caught fast in a net of passion and delight. Nothing mattered but that she and Edwin should share the bed, naked; he would come to her and undo her bodice, slip off her gown and shift and shoes and hose, carry her to the bed; then he would undress himself and she would watch his body in a dream. God had made a magnificent man. If she was sinful she would pay for it, but now, now. ... She would hear herself crying out, presently, and wonder if the servants heard. She was still in a state to remember that, if little else.

Sometimes, during the mornings, she would sit with her father. He had not changed; he was no better and no worse. Sophia went to him in the afternoons, and at nights a servant would sit by him. One day Sophia came to Maud, a key in her hand. She said "I like you to feel free at Biding, Maud; it is your home. This opens the postern in the west wing, below your bedchamber, when the great door is fast. I have a second key, never fear."

Maud did as Sophia had known she would do and gave the key to Edwin. Now they need no longer borrow a bed in the afternoons and lie together with the whole house knowing; Edwin could come to her by night, and sleep with her in her bed. They made love till the cocks crowed in the morning, then he would slip downstairs and out at the postern, and back to Daneclere.

Maud would not go to Daneclere, though Honor had sent to bid her come and sup. Did aunt Honor never wonder where Edwin went? She was, she knew, ashamed of meeting Honor, and perhaps meeting Dick. Dick never rode over here; he seemed to have forgotten her. She did not care. So the weeks passed; and Sophia said nothing about the Farmiloe men, who she knew were voyaging home.

In the fields about Thwaite, Young Hawkin would pause in his task of autumn harrowing if, as often happened, Maud and Edwin Sawtrey rode by. He spared no glances for the man, whom he knew well enough as the younger son, without claim to Daneclere or claim to Maud. If it were Hawkin's own good fortune, he himself would ride by her; would have her, at the day's end, in his own bed: but not at the farm. Some day, by some means, he would be more than a farmworker, the bastard son of dead Robin Thwaite. He felt the strength in himself both of body and mind. No, he hadn't been to Cambridge, as his father had; but he could cipher and spell. He knew what he wanted, and that was to have a great house, like Daneclere across the water, and at the table's head a fair highborn lady, like Maud Sawtrey, who would be the mother of his sons. He would go back at the day's end to his taciturn farm supper and meantime think of Maud, but not with any sentiment; one day, in whatever manner, it would come about that she should be his. For the present, he got on with the work, and pleased his grandfather.

18

HONOR KNEW, or rather had been led to guess, the state of affairs between Edwin and Maud. At first she had noticed nothing wrong, merely that, as any young man would, her son was attentive to her in the mornings and went off by himself in the afternoons, generally, as she at first assumed, to Biding to call on Sir Ralph. Then she began to wonder at his assiduity in attending, daily, an elderly invalid with whom he had never been closely acquainted. Presently she discovered, through the maids, that his bed was not slept in of nights.

It must, she knew then, be a woman; that also was natural; but at Biding who could it be? A maidservant? Sophia? While she thought it must be Sophia, Honor's heart was wrung; such as Edwin should not be made a prey to her like. Then one day Honor happened to ask for Sir Ralph, as she often did; she and Edwin were walking together over the grass paddock beyond the yard, where the horses were put out to graze in fine weather. These stood about now; one cantered over presently and nuzzled Edwin's hand. It was the bay he commonly rode to Biding.

"He knows," said Honor, "that you will take him to see Sophia today. She used to ride him."

As she spoke she acknowledged the falseness of her own words, words with which any mother would attempt to trap any erring son; and reproached herself. But Edwin threw back his head and laughed.

"Sophia?" he said. "I would not ride three yards to see her; she married the old man for his title, and now, when he is ill, neglects him; and they say she was unfaithful to him with his own son. It is all over the countryside."

"But—" Honor's eyes widened, part with relief and part with shock. "Gregory Farmiloe hath not all his wits, and Lady Brysson took him to Newhall with her months since, and he stays with them."

"For that reason, that though he lacketh wit he hath other parts, as Sophia was quick to discover, if all they say be true."

Honor was horrified, so greatly so that it was only later, when she was alone in her room that she made herself face the truth; if Edwin did not ride to Biding for Sophia, then it must be for Maud. A great sadness took her; how was it possible that Maud, if Edwin loved her, should not love him in return? "I should have told Sir Ralph that he would make the better husband," she chided herself uselessly. But how could she have foreseen the way Edwin and Dick would grow apart, and grow differently? And Maud had been a little baby.

Dick rode home sometimes. He was always taciturn, though never uncivil. She summoned courage to speak to him regarding his marriage. "Will you not go to Maud at Biding?" she said. "She is solitary," and asked herself that she might be forgiven; solitary, yes, except for Edwin.

But Dick shook his head, looking at the ground in the way he had, and said courteously that he would not go. "Maud is in her own home, with her father; how should she be solitary?" he asked, and there they left it. Honor had no heart to meddle more.

She was more than ever troubled about Dick's absences. Apart from whatever business it was that drew him to London, she learned, by an unguarded remark he let slip, that he had been on at least two occasions across the Channel to France.

The Farmiloe men rode into Biding on a night of thick mist.

It swirled whitely about their horses' fetlocks and made the party seem like an assembly of ghosts, suddenly manifesting itself out of nothing. They entered the stable-yard and put up their horses themselves, as the grooms were abed. Groping back through the baffling mist, they saw a lantern-light and a woman's figure holding it up in the great doorway; it was Sophia, in a wrapper with her hair loose about her shoulders. Only she in all the house had known that they would come. Their letter to Sir Ralph had been intercepted and read by her, and she had not told the news to him or anyone. Nevertheless she had food and drink ready, and after they had entered Biding served them herself till their hunger was satisfied. A servant appeared, having heard the sound of arrival; she bade him go back to bed, and bid any of the rest who stirred to do likewise.

The brothers were shy with her, she noted, despite their gratitude for the meal and for the fire which still glowed, by her orders, in the hearth. The notion of their father's second marriage could not have seemed real to them in Canada; now, they were confronted with it. Sophia wasted no time over what she had to say.

"You think of me as a stranger, I doubt not. But you shall see your father tomorrow and satisfy yourselves that he is well cared for. Before then, I have a matter of great urgency which I must lay before you, for I wot not what to do."

She turned to Lionel, the eldest of the brothers, and addressed him as by right. In a few words she told him and the rest that Maud had a lover, that he was Edwin Sawtrey, and that he lay with her in her bed this moment. She was certain Edwin was in Biding as she had watched him come and enter at the postern, leaving his horse in the grounds as he always did. It was seldom he left before dawn.

"Maud?" They sounded bewildered; they still thought of their sister as a little child. Suddenly Lionel stood up and began to speak, his face flushed with anger and wine.

"Is this certainly true, and no tale?" he ended. Sophia said they could go and see for themselves; the pair lay in the south wing, and would have heard no sounds of arrival or talk. "Then our only sister is a harlot," said Lionel. Edgar stood up.

"Edwin Sawtrey was my friend in Canada, and found me my preferment at Hudson's Bay."

"That matters nothing," said Lionel. Sophia watched them

without expression, but with growing certainty; they had responded as she had known they would do. "Take us to where they lie," said Ralph. He, the middle brother, was the most silent, and prone to action rather than talk. But they were all of them full of wine, and ready for trouble. She led them upstairs and along the passageway towards the room. She herself went downstairs quickly then and locked the postern door. It would not be necessary for her to show herself in the bedchamber except afterwards, to tend Maud.

The three men stood in the doorway of their sister's room. There was a candle still burning, ringed by the mist. Round the bed the curtains were not drawn and the lovers lay there asleep, in one another's arms.

"'Tis time we were home," said Lionel grimly. Edgar still hesitated.

"That marriage to Dick," he said in a low voice. "It may not be happy. They do no one harm."

"They foul our name," said Lionel, and followed by Ralph he strode forward to the bed. The two struck swiftly with their short knives and pierced Edwin's body between back and side. He gave a little groan, turned partly and then lay still. The blood began to seep from him.

Sophia was already in the doorway, bearing a cloak. "Wrap him in this, and take him to the river, she murmured. "He might have been set upon by thieves. Do it quickly, before she wakes."

It had all been easier than she thought. She moved about the room, gathering up Edwin's strewn garments, and when she had everything, even the riding-boots of soft Indian leather, she took them downstairs and burned them in the grate. Presently she heard the sound of the body being brought down; they must have tried the postern and found it locked.

"Quick, out the other way," she said, "I have the key." She went with them. The three men, carrying their burden, went out into the night, with the lantern she had given them to guide them on their way.

When they returned, she was still waiting; it was towards morning. Ralph bore the bloodstained cloak. She took it from him.

"What of Maud?" asked Edgar, who was weeping.

"Leave her to me. Have you turned his mount loose? It will find its own way home."

She became aware of the blue eyes of all three men, turned upon her. No single one held liking.

Sophia had already dealt with Maud. The bed was soaked with blood. She went to the girl and shook her awake, saying "Maud, are you ill? I heard you cry out." Then she touched the sheets with her fingers, and drew them away with a cry of her own. "Child, you have had a bleeding; fear nothing; you must come to my bed, while I soak these in cold water."

Maud was drugged with sleep, and knew little. She went unprotestingly to Sophia's bed, guided by her stepmother's arm. Sophia gave her a posset and afterwards returned to the room with water and cloths, and cleansed the floor and removed the sheets. She would not wash them; she would burn them. The fire in the hall had its uses.

By the morning, Lionel was resolute that Maud should leave Biding.

"We are here to tend our father now," he said. "Her proper place is in her husband's house; she hath been overlong away."

Sophia protested; the longer the drugged creature slept, the less likely it was that she would recall anything, or ask questions. That it was her own blood in the bed she had never doubted; she had not looked at it. It could be her courses, or a miscarriage. There were plenty of tales to tell her. Sophia cozened Lionel.

"Give her a little time, and me also, to prepare her," she said. "Remember that we must not seem to know of anything which has taken place. It would be better to wait till the body is found, and then she may in nature be sent to comfort his mother."

But Lionel was adamant, in the way, she knew, that stupid men can be so. "She may bid farewell to our father, then she leaves today," he said. "I for one will not remain under the same roof with her."

Sophia shrugged; if they would bring trouble on themselves, she was not to blame. There was no single thing left to connect her with the killing.

She went up to her own room, where Maud lay abed, still drowsy with her syrup. The shining hair fell about her face;

her lips wer parted, as if after a kiss. Sophia suddenly knew furious jealousy; when had *she* ever known true passion? "Had he loved *me*, not this whey-pale creature, he'd be alive today," she thought. She leant forward and began to shake Maud's shoulder. The fool knew nothing but that Edwin had gone, as was customary, while she slept. "No matter how often she asks, it is all she will know, till he is found in the river," thought Sophia. "She dare not say at Daneclere that Edwin was with her. It is maybe as well to let her go."

Maud awoke, with a little murmur of unwillingness. "Ay, you dream of lovemaking," thought Sophia. She spoke briskly and made Maud sit up. "You are to greet your brothers today, and return to Daneclere," she said. Maud's eyes blinked open.

"My father—"

"They and I together will tend your father."

Maud slowly brought her hands up to cover her face then wipe the sleep from her eyes. Something was hammering in her mind, some dread thing. Had she had a dream? And now Sophia was talking of sending her to Daneclere. Edwin cannot come to me as readily there, she thought, and began to cry.

Sophia got her dressed within the quarter-hour, and had the maid bring her strong coffee, which she drank. Afterwards she was taken to Sir Ralph's room. The sick man lay there, surrounded by his sons. They rose as the two women entered. Sir Ralph's eyes shone with joy. I have them all with me again, he seemed to be saying; all with me again, except for Nigel and their mother.

Sophia spoke quickly. "Now that you have so many to tend you, sir, Maud will make her way back to her husband, whom she has neglected for your sake these many weeks. Is not that so, my dear? Kiss your father; and you will soon maybe ride over on a visit, to see that he is well."

Now they will blame me for the parting, she told herself, but it could not be helped; those three great men had stood silent as stones. And Maud would not be riding over on any visit; were she to do so, Lionel would forbid her the house.

So it was farewell. They kissed, and Maud shed tears on her father's shoulder, and then bade him goodbye. Her mare was saddled presently and she rode to Daneclere, followed by a servant with some of her baggage. The rest would follow later. Sophia watched her go, and also watched for a messenger to come riding, to say Edwin's body had been found in the water. But no news came.

The mist muffled Daneclere thickly, making the view from the window seem like the edge of the world. Honor stood looking out, but she saw nothing of the mist and did not think of the house, standing with its foundations wrapped in white wreaths, unsubstantial above the river. She was reproaching herself. The house, with every curtain brushed and every floor swept, its larders full, its stables clean, its bedchambers ready for occupants who never came, was hers; even the little office below stairs held her account-books, neatly made up to the last day. It should not be so; it should be Dick's house and Maud's. Had she become a possessive, grasping woman like Mrs. Anna in her own early days here?

"If they would come back, I would hand the rent-books to Dick and the keys to Maud, and live in my own part, if they wanted that," she thought. But neither Dick nor Maud had come near for many a day. Was it truly her fault that this was so? Maud's father, it was true, had needed his daughter's attention. But Dick—

"I never loved him, any more than I ever loved his father," Honor told herself. If she admitted it, she did not even love Daneclere; it had been a duty that must be undertaken, and being as she was she could not see it badly done. Her love, the only thing she loved in all the world except Maud, was Edwin, her second son.

Where was he? Why had he not come to see her that morning?

A servant came. Mr. Edwin's horse, he said, had been found loose in the yard with its reins still on it. They had not seen it for some time because of the mist. Would madam have him go out and see if any accident had befallen Mr. Edwin?

She gave the order. "Take the rest with you, and search all ways." But she knew that, had ill befallen him, it would have been at Biding. Yet she dared not say to them "Look first towards the bridge." It would be to admit that her thoughts were reality, and could have the worst possible end.

Later in the day, when the mist was clearing, a pair of riders came into the yard. She did not know them and it was not till Gwenny, face radiant, came limping to her that she was aware that Maud had returned to Daneclere.

" 'Tis the young mistress, madam!" Gwenny had loved

Maud from a child. Honor went down. Maud was helped out of the saddle and, pushing back her hood, came into the hall. Her hair was beaded with drops of moisture from the mist and her face had a waxy, unreal quality. Her eyes glistened with unshed tears. Honor went to her and kissed her. The girl's hand sought hers and then dropped, as if contact were distasteful.

"My brothers have cast me out of Biding," she said calmly. "They say it is time I was back with my husband."

Suddenly she gave vent to a burst of silvery, heartless laughter. It sounded through the hall and rang in the rafters and then was still. Honor knew great fear. The Farmiloe brothers home ... Edwin missing. There might be no more in it than coincidence; but it made her afraid.

"Do you know where my husband is?" said Maud. "Can he be here? It is not likely."

Honor took her hand. It resisted, then lay passively in her grasp. "Child," she heard herself saying, "I am glad that you are home." She had not answered Maud's bitter question. Sooner or later, God knew, it would answer itself; and on Edwin's account also.

She began to speak, as if silence were to be dreaded. "Maud, only this morning I thought of you and that I had never given you your rights over Daneclere." She unfastened her belt and took from it the twelve great keys of the household: great door, postern, spice chest, dairy, still-room, larder, silver-closets, linen-closets, cellars. She hung them about Maud's slim waist. "They are yours," she said, "as they should have been this many a day. Order the house as you will."

"Madam, madam—" the girl had begun to cry. Honor beckoned Gwenny, who waited still in the recesses of the hall, and said to her "Put fresh sheets on Mrs. Sawtrey's bed, and light a fire in her room." Then she put her arm about Maud and led her to the settle nearby the great hearth.

"You are home," she said. "Remember that, whatever today and tomorrow, the rest of the days of our lives, may bring. Daneclere is your home while you wish it to be, and you have returned to it and I am glad." Thus she thrust away, for a little time, the dread in her own heart. It was too soon to have the certainty she had that she would not see Edwin alive again.

19

THE FARMILOE BROTHERS waited on their father next morning. Of the three of them Lionel was grave, Ralph truculent, and Edgar hung his head. A servant was feeding the sick man from a cup: Lionel bade him begone. When they were alone he began to speak at once.

"This will grieve you sir: but it is right that you should know of it. Maud our sister had a lover who visited her nightly here over the past months. We found them together. We have killed him, and covered our tracks—no one knows of it except you and ourselves, and one other—and we have forbidden Maud the house. She knows nothing of how her lover died. She is returned to Daneclere, to her husband. You will know in your heart that we acted rightly."

The tears filled Sir Ralph's eyes and rolled down his cheeks. He made a protesting motion with his good hand; he seemed to be trying to speak. "We have avenged your name and honour," repeated Lionel. "Had you yourself known of it, you would have acted in no other fashion."

It was not possible for the father to ask more concerning his daughter. That his sons' arrival home had taken him by surprise they were not to know; they assumed that he had had their letter. Presently Sophia came in. She had shed whatever guilt she felt at facing her husband after the Gregory affair; the old man was helpless, and she came and went freely. Lionel turned now and spoke to her, not with courtesy.

"You, madam, may take yourself elsewhere than this chamber, in which you have small right to be. I and my brothers will sit in turn by our father, night and day." Later, when he had ascertained more, he informed Sophia that Gregory would be brought back to Biding. "And, by God's word, you will have a taste of this belt I wear if aught happens that once did," he told her roundly. He had by then talked with the Bryssons at Newhall and otherwise made himself familiar with most things that had happened since Sophia came to Biding as a bride. A bride! he thought; their father should never have married her. "Not a one of us shall leave to go abroad again while our father lives," he swore.

Sophia had bridled, and pled that she was Sir Ralph's wife and their stepmother, and deserved better treatment. In fact she would have enjoyed a beating from this tall and handsome, though evidently cold, young man. Despite attempts, she made no progress in winning over any of the brothers; presently it appeared that Ralph, the silent, had brought an Indian woman home with him and left her at an inn. Shortly he fetched her to Biding to act both as mistress—for all anyone knew he shared her with his brothers—and servant. Sophia was horrified when the copper-skinned creature, whose name was Laughing Tree, stood in her woven blanket and headdress behind Ralph at meals, and served him as she had been used. At times she would cook food such as the brothers had liked in Canada; these were tasty enough to everyone but Sophia, who said she could not bear to eat anything the creature's hands had touched, or in fact eat at all under Laughing Tree's eyes, which were, she said, like currants. She received short shrift from Lionel and the rest, and shortly began to take her meals in her own room.

Gregory was brought home. At first Sophia submitted to Lionel's order that she must not meet him, but, gaining boldness as she grew bored, she went despite the fiat to Gregory's room. It availed her nothing. She was stopped in her progress by a burly, heavy, not very tall man whose nose had long ago been broken. He was in fact an ex-pugilist, eager for employment in the dearth of country fairs at which he had been used, in his younger days, to draw numbers of the fighting fancy. Lionel had hired him to have charge of Gregory, see to his needs, and prevent Sophia's access.

It did not need a wit so sharp as Sophia's to guess that what Lionel meant to do by the end was have her out of Biding. Sophia pouted, wept a little—the good days were gone—and in the solitary hours she spent in her own room gave herself to thinking of the future. It was tiresome that Jem had a wife in London, or she might have gone to keep house for him. Perhaps she could make a visit there later on; but meantime there was only Daneclere to go to; should she go? They had constantly pressed her to do so; at least she would be welcome there, for as long as she cared to stay. Perhaps it would be as well to wait till there was some word of Edwin.

They did not find Edwin's body for four days. By then fish had eaten away the face and it was only by the hair, darkened with water and tangled in green weed, that they knew him.

He was brought home. Honor received his body and stood alone, after the bearers had gone, looking down at the son who had been her hope and her love. She would wash him herself, prepare him for the coffin.

Going out of the hall she met Maud. Tears were streaming down the younger woman's face. She said "I would see him," but Honor barred the way.

"Do not," she said. "It is for you to remember him as he was; warm, alive and loving." She laid both hands on Maud's shoulders and kissed her mouth.

"You know, then?" said Maud, and fell to weeping again. Honor comforted her.

"Yes, I known; I have known for long. Do not go to him now, I pray; remember him, and your happiness together."

"If you can say that ... it comforts me."

Dick did not ride home for his brother's funeral. None of the Farmiloe men were there, although Honor knew Sir Ralph would have sent word had he been able. She accepted their absence as she had accepted, had known, everything concerning the love and death of Edwin. She owed it to him, and to Maud, to be calm; and there was nothing to be done, it would not bring Edwin back were she to bring in officers of the law against the sons of her old friend, Maud's brothers, to hang them. An eye for an eye, a tooth for a tooth ... it did not signify. At the same time she knew herself to be frozen in her own grief: when the thaw came, she would perhaps run mad.

It was a ghost of a service. Maud kept her room; only Honor and the Thwaite men were present, and the Bryssons from Newhall, and old Jeremy Whyteleaf who came alone. He stumbled across afterwards and took Honor's hand, kissing it wordlessly. No talk passed between them or between anyone; she had the sensation that everything about her was unreal, that the mauled water-rotted body in the coffin could not be that of Edwin, her son. Where was his warmth now, his love and his life? What was to become of her own?

After they had all gone she went upstairs to Maud. She found the girl lying on her bed, pale with weeping. "Sophia has written," she said to her.

"Sophia? What does she want?" It might have been anyone, someone known in another life.

"She asks that she may visit you here for a little. It will be company for you. I am going away."

"Away? But what shall I—"

"The house is yours," said Honor, "and Dick's if he should care to come home. I cannot stay longer at Daneclere. I am going back to my own."

Now she was crossing the ford. She had no fear, for it was shallow, and already a lantern bobbed on the far side: they would have known of her coming. As she pressed her horse forwards to take the bank, a light blinded her and a hand reached out to hers. It was a man's hand, with the forearm bare below the rolled shirt-sleeve; she could see the fine down of hair upon the flesh.

"You have come home, Honor Thwaite."

She knew it was he, Uthred Jansen. Their eyes met, as they had met before. It no longer seemed strange that he should have known her intention. Each of them, in their separate ways, had long been aware of the other and of what that other might do. She returned his handclasp and let him help her from her horse at the top of the rise; for instants, in the gathering dark, they stood again surveying one another. Honor thought absently "He is less tall than I," and then that it did not matter. From now on, her life would be bound up with his.

They found old Hawkin lying in his downstairs chamber, where he had slept since a seizure took him, a year back. It had left him without power in one arm, but he had not let them tell Honor. His sound arm reached out to embrace her; he showed neither surprise nor anger at her coming. "Ye have come home," he said, as Uthred had done. Honor felt tears prick her eyes for the first time.

"Yes, father, I'm home," she said, as if it were yesterday that she had left it. Thwaite was much the same; the hearth bright and well made up, the great beams hanging with hams and herbs, and Hawkin's great wooden chair, in which he never sat now, by the fire, where a kettle steamed. She sat down by it, knowing she was weary.

"Ye crossed alone?" said her father. "Ye brought no gear?"

Uthred answered. "I met her on the way."

The grizzled brows surveyed them both, then Hawkin smiled. "It had to come," he said. "Ye'll suit."

Five

I

GOSSIP was rife far beyond the shire borders concerning Honor's second marriage to Uthred Jansen. In the first place her age was noted; she must be, they calculated, fifteen to twenty years older than her bridegroom. Such a difference was hardly proper; of course, as everyone agreed, he would have married her for her position and goods, which as Richard Sawtrey's widow she had now in her own hands, for Dick was never at home. This absence also gave rise to speculation; and the death of poor young Edwin would be remembered, and the short time which had elapsed between it and the marriage. It was unanimously decided not to call on the newlyweds at Thwaite; if one met them one might be civil, but Honor had lost her position as the lady of Daneclere by marrying back into the farming community from whence she had sprung. As for the rumour—no one knew how it started—that old Hawkin Thwaite intended leaving the farm to Uthred and away from his own son, that too was unjust; David Thwaite, though no one greatly liked him, had worked hard enough over the years at Thwaite acres before succeeding to Bents through his wife.

All of this affected neither of the principals at all. Never in her whole life had Honor been so gently happy.

Uthred was a considerate, almost a diffident lover. She might have been a queen whom he handled with such reverence; yet she knew he loved her. Between them was a feeling of unity in all they thought, said and planned; it was a sensation she had never known in the years of her marriage to Sawtrey.

Often when after their passion he slept, she would lie awake for a while, watching the moonlight as it made streaks of light between the drawn curtains; and she would think of love, in all its guises. She had loved Edwin better than herself; the thought of his death still harried her. She had loved her brother Robin, who was dead. She had a tender protectiveness for Maud, almost her own child, left behind at Daneclere, managing as best she might; Sophia was with her.

But all of this bore no relation, and little likeness, to Honor's feeling for Uthred. They were one flesh, and now she understood the saying; he was a part of her, she of him. "All these years we have lived one on one side of the ford, the other on the other," she thought, without regret for the lost years; when they had come together at last, it had been the time for it, as it would not have been earlier. Honor would look across at his sleeping face; it bore lines which made him seem older than his age; his dark greying hair was tousled on the pillow, and his eyes, so blue by day, were closed, his mouth relaxed in sleep. It was not the face of a physically strong man; she had fears that the farm-work was too much for his strength, and made great bustle about feeding him. "You have neglected yourself for years, shovelling down what came first to hand, and not taking time to rest after, but going straight to the plough," she would scold him. Work was his life; and work he still did, while old Hawkin lay useless on his bed. Uthred and young Hawkin, and Uthred's sullen bastard Arnulf, would go out at sunrise, till the fields, mind the cattle, mend the tools and harness. Hawkin helped willingly and well, Arnulf less so, but his father excused him much on account of his club-foot, which left him able to do little in the way of striding over the fields to visit lambs or cut the hay. His tasks were mainly in the cattle-sheds. Honor never in her life heard Uthred speak other than patiently to Arnulf, though the young man was idle and slow of purpose. It was as though his father must shower affection on this son to atone for his deformity and for having forgotten his mother long ago.

As to that, Honor had presently another cause for happiness; at the age of almost fifty years, she had conceived again. It set the seal on their joy.

It rained hard for the next few weeks; there seemed no end to the flooding. The river overflowed the ford and no messengers could come or go from Daneclere. One day a man struggled through by way of Biding; he bore a letter. "It hath been in the house these few days, madam, but none could bring it here," he said.

Honor, her figure already thickening, sent orders to rub down the man's horse—it would be soaked again on the return journey, but they could give it warmth and rest—poured him ale, and heard his small-talk. Mrs. Maud

and Mrs. Sophia were well, he said; there was small other
news. Uthred came in then for his dinner and it was not till
an hour later that Honor took leisure to open the letter. The
careful, crabbed writing was Dick's.

My Dear Mother, it read,
*This news will not please you, I fear, but a man must live
out his Life as God wills.* (That has always been his plea and
his father's, Honor thought; if none of us strove, where would
we be?) *You will not know, for I did not write it, that I have
been back and forth to France on the Duke of York's
Business. It was better than None should Know it, as his
Affairs here are Suspect. I did not tell you either, for I knew
that you were in Grief over Edwin's Death, that I have for
some Time embraced the Romish Faith, which to me and to
many here is the Only Truth. Do not Chide yourself, or
weep; it could not have Fallen Out otherwise, and any Blame
is mine and not yours; you were ever a good Mother.*

*I did not for this Reason come to Edwin's Burial. I had a
Priest here say a Mass for him, and I pray daily that he may
find Peace and that Eternal Light may shine upon him.*

The worst Part for you is to come. (What now? thought
Honor; he was never happy among us, never a full man; I
pray on my own account that that at least may be righted.)
*When I was in France earlier I was taken by a Friend, who
knoweth the Duke and his Household well, to St. Omer to
the Jesuits there. It hath become my Earnest Plea to join
them and to be Ordained Priest. It is a Hard Path, twelve
years long, and I may not have the Wit or Learning to do all;
but God will Aid me. If they take me, mother, it means that I
must not be a Married Man with my Wife living. As you
Well Know, my Marriage to Maud was None in Truth. I
must now set about to Annul it, as these Things are done; it
will not hurt Maud or anyone, and it is what I must Doe. If
Evidence is Wanted, I pray you prevail upon Maud to give it.
I doe not look forward to any Difficulty in the Matter. I say
only again that it Grieves me to grieve you, and I wish rather
that you might Rejoice with me. In myself I am happy as I
have never been in all my Lyfe. I was never made to be a
Lord of Acres and Father of Sons; as for Women they have
meant little to me except you, my Mother.*

I will make you a Gift of the House, for they will not in

England let the Value of it goe to those where I will be. I will
sign all before a Lawyer, and keep you Informed.

If I ask your Blessing, despite all of the above, it is with the
earnest Intent in any case that I shall pray for your
Happiness and health for the rest of my Lyfe. Commend me
to your Husband.

Your sonne,
Richard Sawtrey.

She felt her senses swim a little; presently, when taking the
broth-pot off the fire, she handled it clumsily and a drop or
two of the boiling stuff fell on her foot. She winced, but made
no sound. Uthred had noticed nothing, he was slowly reading
the letter, which she had handed him in silence. Presently he
looked up and said "And what of Mrs. Maud?"

It was like him, she thought, to see straight to the heart of a
problem. She made herself laugh a little. "Maud had a
lover," she said. "They will not find her virgin." It sounded
as though she spoke of those known long ago. Uthred's brows
drew together in a frown.

"And what of you?" he asked her then. "In your state you
must have a care to yourself; there must be no riding up and
down to see lawyers, and the like. They may come here, or
else to Daneclere." He spoke the name of the great house
slowly, almost unwillingly. Honor's mind cleared and she
forgot the throbbing in her foot.

"I must go to Daneclere," she said. "I must be with Maud,
if they come." The thought of a possible physician's
examination, embarrassment, denial, was strong in her mind.
Uthred rose and came to stand where she was, by the fire.

"It was for you to say it, not for me," he said simply. "But
if you go to Daneclere, I ride by you. You have borne enough
alone."

"And Thwaite? In rain such as there has been?" The rain
now had slackened a little; they could see the runnels on the
small panes of the casement, reaching the frame and
dripping, dripping down. Beyond, the farmyard ran with
water.

"Young Hawkin is well enough able to tend Thwaite, and
keep your father agog with news of the day's doings. The old
man hath a love for him. Arnulf can stay also, and make
himself of use. I will ride back and forth when it may be
done. I have often thought that, were you to agree from your

side, we could build a causeway atop the present ford. Then there would be no fear of rough weather or high water." As he looked at her she knew that, like herself, he was remembering Edwin's body drowned in that same river. Once again, as ever, their thoughts were one.

She smiled through her pain and made her voice gay. "I to agree from my side! We are of the same side, Uthred, did you not know it? The great house is not mine, but yours. I can love it for your sake, if never for my own."

"You never loved Daneclere," he said thoughtfully. "All through the years of your marriage to Sawtrey you did a duty bravely borne, without love such as most women feel for goods and chattels."

"That is true, and in any case I'm no longer the lady of the manor; the county hath cast me off. A farmer's wife I am, no more."

"Do you regret it?" he said quietly.

"Never for as long as I shall live."

They embraced, and then he said to her, his hands on her shoulders, "Who will tell your father of it? Would you that I do so?"

"No, that is for me to do," she said, and went to tell old Hawkin.

It turned out to be a matter of signing, oaths, proofs and agreements drawn out by reason of the fact that Dick was already in France. By the end, however, Maud was freed without scandal, except for the shire tongues, eager for titbits such as Dick's defection to Rome. Daneclere by the elder Richard's will reverted to Honor notwithstanding Dick's gift, both her sons being dead in law.

By now she had another son. His birth had been easier than she and Uthred had feared, because of her age. He was a small baby, a Thwaite, with red hair; he grew fat quickly by reason of his amazing greed for milk. He made her laugh, and brought happiness to what would otherwise have been a sad time. She named him for Uthred.

By then, the new causeway stood clear above the tide, and it was possible to come and go with ease from Daneclere.

2

SOPHIA leant over the side of the bed and vomited into her
ewer. As she had for some time suspected, Fyfield, the
ex-pugilist who looked after Gregory at Biding, had got her
with child, and no herbal draught would shift it. Rage filled
her; she should never have let him come to her bed; he had
done this of purpose, she was convinced, on orders from
Lionel. Lionel had been determined to have her out of Biding
by any means; and now that she had perforce gone, would
make it difficult for her to return.

Here at Daneclere she had shelter for as long as she chose;
Maud in her solitude had welcomed her; but it was deadly
dull. She might stay till the child's birth; Maud, when all was
said, was in no position to carp at a woman for taking a virile
lover. If Maud told anyone of her state, she could retort with
tales of Edwin. But so far such matters had not been spoken
of between them. On second thoughts—Sophia had had a
great many thoughts lately—it might be possible to convince
Maud that the child was Sir Ralph's. She was not to know
how her father was guarded by his sons night and day, not
permitting Sophia access to her own husband; the memory
came now as an injury, though she had cared nothing at the
time. She had not even troubled to try to bid Ralph farewell
when she came to Daneclere; he cared nothing for her now
since finding her with Gregory last summer.

How did Maud feel about her own brothers? She must
scarcely be able to remember them; all her childhood they had
been in Canada, and Maud herself at Daneclere. She could
surely nourish no affection for Lionel, Edgar and Ralph.
"The way they treated her at Edwin's death was scurvy
enough, bundling her out of the house before others found his
body," said Sophia to herself. A further bout of sickness came
and occupied her thoughts for the next few moments. Betty
Sawtrey, her maid, would have spread it about already that
my Lady Farmiloe had morning-sickness.

Leaving Biding she had paused at the gallery and looked

down into the hall, at the place where she had so often sat in state to receive county-visitors. The three brothers had been together, by the fire; they must have left Sir Ralph to Fyfield. Lionel pulled at his Dutch pipe which he affected, and the other two were idly casting dice. Sophia, in her hooded cloak over her pinner, giving the impression of an immensely tall woman (but that was the fashion in London) had a premonition of a kind that seldom came to her, occupied as she generally was with herself. This is the way they will go on into old age, she thought; they will never marry, no woman will be allowed to break the company, not even Laughing Tree.

She had descended the stairs, making her way out towards where the carriage waited; Maud had sent it from Daneclere. At the hush of her skirts all three brothers rose punctiliously, and bowed her to the door. We will never meet again, she had thought, these county gentlemen and I.

Afterwards she regretted not having bidden farewell to Sir Ralph; she could have told him she was going to his daughter. Well, she would write. But the weeks had passed and she had not written. How dull it was at Daneclere! Maud, at this hour, would be out riding.

Maud was spurring her mare across the flat fields. She was in a mood composed of bitterness and melancholy and it was impossible to stay in the house. The fierce wind whipped at her cheeks and tugged her hair from beneath the broad hat, tugged also at the mare's mane and made it fly after. There was nothing in all the landscape that would relieve despair; a greyness was over everything, and she knew now, had known for some time, that despite her frantic prayers she would not bear Edwin's child. If she could even have had such a memory of him her life would not have been lived in vain. Now, she was the rejected wife of one brother—she had no right even to Daneclere but for Honor's generosity—and the mourning mistress of the other, and she would mourn Edwin while she lived. The night of his death baffled her. All that she could recall was their passion and falling asleep in one another's arms, and then there had been a brief dream of horror she could not name, then Sophia shaking her awake and saying she had had an issue of blood, and holding a cup to her lips that she might drink. Then, next day, she had wakened in Sophia's bed, and everything in her own room had been again white and clean, as if it belonged to no one, as if no one had ever made love in it as love had never been made before.

Then they had found Edwin. On that day her heart had died.

She reined in now and looked at the flooded fields, at the river where they had found him drowned, after being set upon by thieves. It did not matter that these had never been brought to justice; in any case, Edwin would not come back. He had not even visited her in dreams, and her sleep was black and empty, only her youth failing to ensure that she lay awake, hour after hour, on a solitary pillow. Even tears dried after a time.

"I cannot continue in solitude," she thought, "I shall run mad." She did not trouble to keep Daneclere as Honor had kept it; the servants did as they would there, and she had not the heart to chide them or to see to anything.

Honor. If she might see Honor again she might be given some of her calm and power, her fearless judgments, her truth, her honesty. "She was well named," Maud thought. Would they be inconvenienced if she were to ride over and visit them at Thwaite? Through all of her childhood Thwaite had been barred, because Honor's old father would not permit visiting between the houses. Maud had accepted this as children do, but now questioned it; why might Honor never visit the farm?

Today, she herself would ride over, come what might. It gave purpose to her empty existence, hope to her solitude. She turned the mare's head and rode on into the wind, blinded by her hair.

Thwaite was silent and mud-splashed, the mud in the yard having blown with the rain athwart cow-sheds, steadings, huts. The house itself was clear. Maud rode into the open yard and looked for a place to leave her mare. From nowhere, a stocky dark-haired man came out. His eyes regarded her unblinkingly. This must be Hawkin or Arnulf, she was uncertain which; she had little interest in the Thwaite folk or their appearance. Whoever he was, he disturbed her for no reason that she could name; using the way of thought to which she was accustomed, she deemed him impudent. He came and took the mare's rein. Maud thanked him haughtily. "I may be an hour, or less," she said. The dark eyes followed her as she made towards the house, and she dismissed him from her mind. Why complain about one unmannerly herdsman when she had come here without invitation?

But her welcome was unmistakeable. The door was opened by Honor herself, clad in homespun.

"Maud, my dear, my dear!" And she gathered the girl to her. Maud felt the tears come; why did love make one weep?

"Come in," said Honor, and led her into the homely kitchen, with its bright hearth, its steaming kettle, and the smell of baking bread and cured hams, herbs and humanity and small-beer. She stayed; she stayed to see Honor's baby, and to hear the news that shortly they would return to Daneclere. Gently, Honor broke the news she had had from Dick. Maud felt bewildered; it was as though she heard news of someone met long since, and as long forgotten. Dick and she had been nothing to one another. "It was not so much that he could not make me his wife in truth, as that he would not," she thought. The letter she was shown explained his reluctance. She wished him Godspeed.

Thwaite was a happy place; and she could feel it, and wished that she might come again, and again. She herself, shut out from happiness, had found an hour's kindness. It would be good to have Honor and Uthred again at Daneclere.

When she was ready to go back, the man with dark eyes led out her mare and spoke to her. "Place your foot on my hand," he said. Maud, who could mount unaided, did so, placing her small arched foot in his broad palm. He kissed it before lifting her up to the saddle; she drew her breath at such effrontery. A farm-hand to act so! But she would not offend Honor and Uthred by making complaint.

She rode home, still upset by what had happened; it was more in her mind than any news of Dick, Jesuits, or the new ownership of Daneclere. When she went into the hall, Sophia was seated on the settle, her face somewhat yellow beneath the paint.

"I must talk to you," she said fretfully. Maud, still in her hat and cloak, sat down by her. She heard then Sophia's tale of how her poor husband, Maud's father, last time they were able to be alone, had got her with child. "He is not incapable in such ways," said Sophia. But then the cruel brothers had come and separated Sophia from her husband, as they had already done with Maud and her father. "Will you that I stay here till the child is born? I would be afraid to go back to Biding."

"You may stay for me," said Maud warmly. But she told Sophia that Honor and Uthred were coming to the house, and at once Sophia's wish to stay became naught; she feared Mrs. Honor's clear eyes and honest ways, for it was more difficult to lie to her than to Maud, who believed everything.

Maud had from the beginning tried to do her best to make her young stepmother feel welcome at Daneclere, and the news of the coming child made no difference. At first her ladyship had been all gushing gratitude and easy satisfaction. Maud decided that in kindness to her visitor, she would direct Gwenny to wait on her as her lady's maid, and sleep in her chamber on a pallet. To her anger, Gwenny refused. It was not the first time Maud had met with disobedience from a servant, and she knew many of her orders were flouted or improperly carried out behind her back. She had not the knack of managing, as Mrs. Honor had had; she was relieved for this reason also to think that Honor would soon be back at Daneclere. Meantime Gwenny stood her ground, glance fixed humbly enough on the floor where she stood. Maud tried to persuade her after her own manner; generally Gwenny was a pillar of obedience.

"Do I hear aright? Do you tell me you will not carry out an order of mine, your mistress here?"

"Any except that, madam." The woman's tone was not impudent, nor were her manners. Maud looked at the colourless little face and tried, with rare imagination, to picture such a life as Gwenny's must be; surely nothing notable had ever happened in it. But she herself was weary of struggling with a great house which after all was empty, empty. Was she to spend the rest of her existence here where Edwin had lived as a boy, lacking him? Was she forever to gaze out beyond the windows at the river where they had found his dead body? She tried, each day, to forget and think of other things; but he could not be forgotten.

She turned to Gwenny again. "As I have told you, do. I shall not speak of your unmannerly ways to Lady Farmiloe. Fetch your pallet, see that it is put in her room, and that the water you fetch her is hot."

"Madam, no, no, if it please you; I—I cannot." Before Maud could say more the creature had fled, down the many passages to her own place; when Maud sent another servant after her, Gwenny was gone and so was her cloak. Why should she have such an objection, having served here for many years, to obey an order which concerned a guest at Daneclere whom she already knew well?

Maud could not understand it, nor think what to do with the woman when she returned. She ought to be beaten, but she was lame and looked frail. In any case she did not come back.

Gwenny herself could not have begun to explain to Mrs. Maud her terror at again lying on a pallet at the foot of Sophia's bed, let alone describe what had long ago taken place there of nights. Mrs. Maud was so untouched by the world that she seemed a nun, strict and cold. Gwenny had never known a nun, but she had heard of them, and rightly imagined that pale waxen face under a dark veil, the slim figure in a black habit, the hands telling beads. There was no warmth nor humanity about Maud any more, though Gwenny could not have said as much to Mrs. Honor, to whom she was going; to whom she was running, with her breath coming in short gasps, splashing her skirts as she lifted them across the new causeway that led to Thwaite. Mrs. Honor wouldn't need telling why she wouldn't sleep in Lady Farmiloe's room. Mrs. Honor had had her in her own, had helped through all the time before her child was born, and then when it came had held her in her arms. Mrs. Honor wouldn't treat her like a runaway servant, and send her back.

She arrived breathless outside Thwaite door, which was opened by Uthred himself, with Honor behind him. "She's happy," Gwenny's thoughts told her. "If I could have done for her what she did for me, I would have; though thank God it was a live and healthy birth, with her age and all." Aloud she said, respectfully, as though they had been strangers,

"Would you be wanting other help, madam? I've left my late place," and Honor laid a hand on her husband's arm and laughed and said "Gwenny, you have such a long face I thought you brought bad news from Daneclere! Come into the house and tell me all that is wrong; you have been in your late place, as you call it, for so many years that we cannot have you abandon it now."

"Please, madam—"

Honor saw that Gwenny was crying. She put an arm about

her as she had been used to do in the days of her great
trouble, and said gently "Come in and dry yourself, and have
some food, then we will speak of it. Have no fear that we will
see you wronged, if that is so."

The end of it was that Gwenny stayed on at Thwaite with
them till they should move, and Honor sent one of the
farm-men across with word to Maud, and the offer of one of
her own dairymaids meantime if Gwenny's place left the help
short. There was no question of any contract, any hiring-
time, for Gwenny. She had been in service with them since
her childhood and should stay as long as she wished.

At the month's end they moved to Daneclere, followed by the
horses with baggage and bed-furnishings. Gwenny rode by
them in the saddle with one of the farm-men. From now on
she would serve at Daneclere when she was wanted, and
Thwaite when she was not. This arrangement suited
everyone well enough, for Honor did not want to have to
reproach herself with neglect of the men left at Thwaite, or
lack of a woman to prepare their meals for them. She herself,
her child in her arms, laughed at her own situation; was she a
farm-wife, or one of the county again? Was Uthred a squire?

It did not matter.

3

WINTER came, bringing frost and snow; the causeway grew
treacherous with ice, and Honor no longer rode across to see
her father. One day the old man sent for his grandson, Young
Hawkin. The frost had made fern-patterns on the windows,
thick even at this hour of the afternoon. Inside, it made the
house dark.

Young Hawkin came, carrying a candle in its holder. The
yellow light shone upwards on his determined jaw and chin,
the stubble of the day's beard, and the shrewd dark eyes
above. The old man on the bed turned his head, not saying
what pleasure it gave him to watch this grandson. None of
David's brood could touch him for sound sense, hard work,
and determination.

Yet his speech when it came was testy. "Set it down, lest it burn the bed-curtains; set it down, I say."

Young Hawkin obeyed, with the air of having done no one a favour. The sick old man laughed suddenly, showing yellowed teeth.

"Ye do not ask why I sent for ye."

"I am waiting for you to tell me, if you will."

"And if I will not? Wilt go away again? Ye are a thrawn beggar, I say."

"Maybe. I am what I am."

"I need tell ye nothing, then, for ye know't already behind that hatchet face. Ye are my heir, none other."

Hawkin the younger shook his head. "Uthred is that, sir. Recollect you have left him the farm." Hawkin knew of this, because there had been neighbours called in to sign as witnesses to the old man's will, and from this source the gossip had spread about the countryside. His grandfather looked at him sardonically.

"I am near death and I see clearly. Uthred will inherit, 'tis true; I owed Honor no less, and I value him. But in the end, in the end. ..." He began to waver."

"We spoke of Uthred," said the young man. Old Hawkin's eyes slewed round to where his grandson sat.

"All he does will come to naught, I say," he predicted. "He is no kin of mine, save far out. I love him for his father, whom I knew; and he hath worked well, this many a year, at Thwaite, and you also. In the end it is yourself, my own blood, who will own both Thwaite and Daneclere."

"Not Daneclere, grandfather; that will go to young Uthred." The old man was becoming confused.

"Hear what I say, but tell it to none. The certainty is in my bones. You and your son will inherit."

Young Hawkin smiled, the rare gesture breaking up his forbidding face into something lovable and human. "This is no weather for inheritance," he said. "Let me draw up the blanket over your bones, sir, and they will feel the less certain for warmth."

He ministered to the old man, leaving him with the covers drawn up to his chin. Old Hawkin's eyes, their whites long discoloured, followed him. They held devotion.

" 'Tis time ye took a wife, Hawkin, lad," the voice followed him. The younger man flushed, blood swiftly suffusing his face and neck. Old Hawkin gave a cackle of laughter. "I see ye," he said, "blushing like a maid. Who is't to be, Polly, Sal or Jane?" All these young women had worn ribbons in their bodices for Hawkin at the fair, but he would none of them. Old Hawkin heard of everything. Young Hawkin spoke up for himself, eyes fixed on the floor. "I will take the wife I want, or none," he said.

"Then I'll not live long enough to see a son of your loins. Yon haughty piece from Biding won't come when ye whistle. How do I know of't? They tell me ye kissed her foot when she rode off, and moon about her like a lovesick calf."

Young Hawkin said "The time will come when she hearkens to me."

"Maybe, maybe. But I'd sooner see ye wed here at Thwaite, and a son within the year."

"I shall have sons of her."

"Maybe one, but no more. 'Tis flighty stock. They say all four brethren sit night after night alone, playing with cards, the devil's books, and never a one of them takes a wife, but they fornicate with the Injun woman. And your Maud had neither chick nor child to her husband, nor to Edwin either."

"Sir, you speak of what you know not." Hawkin's mouth had tightened with anger; there were things the old man might say to him, and other things he might not.

"None will turn your mind," groaned the old man. "Pour me ale and leave me be."

As he was drinking the stuff, he choked. Young Hawkin raised him on his pillows and tried to make him lean forward, to let the choking cease. But the thin old frame coughed on, and after some time Hawkin laid him gently back in his place. The eyes stared at him, dark with blood from the late coughing. Suddenly they had the look of no longer seeing anything.

Hawkin bent over the dead man and closed the staring eyes. In his mind was neither fear of death, which all had known would take the old man soon, nor thoughts of inheritance. He still thought, as he did each waking hour, of Maud Sawtrey, the lodestar of his life, solitary even yet at Daneclere among them all.

At the great house, Sophia was weary of her life; there was no diversion now Honor had come back again, for she mourned her father. As for Maud, she was a whey-faced ghost of the radiant girl Sophia had known at Biding, and had no talk when they met, moping as she still did for Edwin. Altogether it was a weary place; but she could not leave it with convenience, having meantime nowhere else to go. Biding was closed to her and she had not enough ready money to live in town. She chafed at her situation; surely it was Lionel's duty to see that she be sent an allowance, as would have been done if she was a widow? Pray God that would happen soon; it was small pleasure to any woman to have a palsied wreck, no more, to call husband. Meantime, everything was at sixes and sevens; all she could do was pass the long days here by whatever means, and wait to see what befell her in her condition.

As fortune had it, her difficulty was already solved, had she known it; one day a man rode over from Biding with a letter for her which, he said, had lain there some days. "Why the devil did you not come with it earlier?" said Sophia, and broke the seal. Then the news it contained banished all her ill-temper, and short of silver as she was she sent the man away with a sixpence for his trouble.

Jem had written from London to say that his wife had died. Would Sophia come to him and keep house for a time, till matters arranged themselves? "He means my own matters as well as his, but hasn't put it on paper; he has overmuch wit," thought Sophia, who had kept her brother informed of late happenings since Sir Ralph's seizure and the coming home of his sons. It would be a relief to be with Jem, with whom she had never had to pretend to be other than she was. She stood up, stretched her arms above her head and yawned; what a blessing to be rid of Daneclere!

4

SOPHIA suffered from malaise on the journey, and was thankful when a hired chair set her down at last before Jem's house in Holborn. The servant who answered the door was a young man who seemed vaguely familiar, but Sophia took little heed of him or of the house and its furnishings, which were of good quality but ugly. No doubt they had all of them

belonged to the dead woman; Jem had had nothing of his own
to bring.

He came to greet her, and her first thought was of how ill
he looked. His colour was almost yellow, with a hectic flush
on the cheekbones; he had grown very thin. He bowed over
her hand and led her in to take wine till the food should be
ready. The young man, who was evidently valet as well as
house-servant, had disappeared with her baggage.

They talked of their affairs, then Jem said "Alun will
show you your chamber and the closet, and when you will,
supper shall be served down here." Sophia would rather have
had food brought to her in bed, but decided to be civil; all
things said, this was a providential chance and she must mind
her ways till she was established here. Jem did not seem short
of money, though to date she had noted only the one servant;
no doubt her brother was as mean as ever, and would not
keep others in the house.

A thing he had said to her remained in her mind as the
servant showed her upstairs. Alun; where had she heard the
name before? She remembered, presently, the pair of pale
children who had come to Daneclere many years since, and
whose mother had been hanged. This must be Gwenny's
brother; how had he found Jem again? She asked the man of
it, while he poured water for her into the ewer. He did not
turn his head, and when he answered her kept his eyes on the
ground; he seemed a furtive creature.

"Mr. Whyteleaf asked me to come here, madam, on Mrs.
Whyteleaf's death. I was employed nearby."

And do him many favours besides those of house-servant, I
wager, she thought. She dismissed the man and set about
making her toilet. Already the sickness she felt in the coach
was receding, and she could begin to look forward to a meal;
she had eaten none since morning, at an inn.

The food was set out when she descended, and Alun, who
waited on them, showed her into her place. He is ever-
present, she thought; I must alter that. He cut her a portion
of meat pie, steaming from the kitchen. "It has oysters in it,"
Jem told her. Perhaps it was the oysters that made it a shade
over-sweet. The meat tasted as if it were tainted. Sophia
made play to eat hers, then ate the pastry and thrust most of
the meat away. "Oysters are not kind to me," she smiled. "I
could never keep 'em from turning my bowels to water." She
drank some wine.

Soon after the meal was over, she excused herself and said that she was weary. The child she carried had disappointed her in not voiding itself with the roughness of the coach-journey; perhaps it would oblige her tonight. She had said the correct things concerning Jem's wife's death; evidently that lady had succumbed to a sudden fever. Such deaths were common in London, especially in warm weather. Jem did not seem to mourn greatly. If she knew him, it would be a relief to him not to have to lie with any woman.

"I do not like his looks," she told herself. Perhaps it was the London water. Had Jem made a will? If a fever took toll of him also, she herself might well benefit as next of kin, if he remembered it. But one could hardly press the point on first arrival.

Sophia felt thirsty: that pie at supper. ... There was a jug of water by her bed. She drank of it sparingly, and noted again the sweetish taste. She undressed, got into bed and put out her candle. The sheets were damp. There were few comforts in Jem's house despite his wife's wealth; it was time she herself was on the scene; things would change.

The sleep she fell into was uneasy despite her weariness. She woke to agony. Something was tearing at her bowels that was more, far more, than the oysters. She clutched her stomach and began to scream. None answered; was it her fancy that there were other cries echoing her own? Still clamouring with the unbearable pain she struggled out of bed and to the door. It was locked. Sophia beat on it with both hands and then collapsed on the floor, tearing at the floor-boards until her nails were broken. She began to vomit in the darkness; in the midst of it she felt something slide down within her, and wetness poured from her to the sullied floor. The child had obliged her, and had miscarried; but she was in no state to feel relief.

In the morning, when the daily maid came, she found locked doors in an empty house. She called in a neighbour, who broke the locks. Thus they found them, the dead man in his room, his sister in hers. There was no sign of the young manservant who had been taken into the household only a short time ago. The neighbour's wife, searching her memory, said she had known of him before; he had run errands for an apothecary.

Alun himself had left the house when he knew everything was certain. He had already penned a note to his sister. It had to be short; the neighbours might soon hear the crying. Hastening towards the river now his mind worked itself back over the past months, the past years. After the murder of Lewis he had been careful not to show himself in that part of London; he had found casual work here and there, not all of it savoury. Then he had a stroke of fortune. One late night when he was in a certain street he had heard muffled shouts a short distance off, and had come on an elderly man being beaten and robbed by two vagabonds. Alun, never physically strong, hit out as best he might, and the surprise of his arrival and the shouting he made scared them and they made off, Alun bent over the old man and helped him to his feet. "They have taken my purse," his voice whimpered, "or I would reward you." He had thin grey hair straggling down from a bald pate, for his hat had been knocked off in the affray; Alun found it and gave it back to him.

"They might have taken your life, sir. Where do you live that I may give you my arm?"

The old gentleman replied that it was not far off, and took Alun's arm. Once in the lit candlelight of his own house, he saw that his rescuer was not only of shabby appearance, but very thin and pale. "A good meal will go some way to reward you, if not all," he said; the thieves had cut his lip and the swelling made him lisp. Alun admitted that he would be glad of the meal. "I have had none since yesterday."

"What do you do to earn a living?"

"I am looking for work."

"Can you read and write?"

"Yes."

He had been taken on, first as errand-boy and then, when he had shown himself trustworthy, to help in mixing unguents and linctus at the back of the shop. It was the first step to his long-planned revenge on Jeremy Whyteleaf. In an apothecary's shop he could fairly soon, without its being discovered, possess himself of a quantity of white arsenic and corrosive sublimate. These he wrapped carefully and carried always inside his shirt, against his bosom.

He had seen Jem with his wife: it was possible sooner or later to find out where everyone lived in London. The woman was plain and pock-marked, but she would prove an obstacle to the plan Alun had worked out; to get himself, by some means, into Jem's house as his servant, and there destroy him. With that woman about there was no hope. Alun waited; he waited more than two years, during which time he pleased the old apothecary and worked well and carefully at any task he was given. But one day his chance came. He had already followed Jem's wife as she marketed and made her way home; he knew now where Jem lived. He did not see the woman for some time, and one day, there was a funeral from the house. Jem was chief mourner, his long face enhanced by sober clothes. Alun waited till his own tasks were completed at night. Then he washed himself, put on a clean shirt and combed his hair, went to the house and asked for Mr. Whyteleaf.

The rest had been easy.

He came to the river. There were figures, more like beasts than men and women, groping about in the mud of the ebb tide. These were the mudlarks, the poorest of God's creatures, who scavenged in the mud for any object of whatever value, even a rusty nail, and sold it for what they could get. They were never dry and never clean, nor did they live to old age. Alun approached them.

"Have you stones?" he asked.

They jeered, and came up to him hopefully, showing their bloodshot eyes in streaked faces. One was a child. "Get me stones, anything heavy," said Alun. "I will pay you well."

They brought him rusty iron, stones, hooks, anything that had weight, and he took them all and stuffed them into his pockets. Then he took all the money he had and flung it to them, and left them scrabbling and shouting in the mud. They will have a meal this day, he thought. He himself must wait for high tide.

He went to the bridge, and looked down at the water. For two hours he watched the boats and barges, while the tide rose. No one yet had come after him. He smiled at the thought of it. His coat weighed heavily; they would not find him yet. Knowing all of it, he cast himself over the parapet at last, and sank.

A short while later Gwenny received her letter. It was many years since their father had taught Alun and herself to read, and she was out of practice. She spelled out the letters of her name on the superscription and opened the missive. It read,

It is all of it done, Gwenny, as I promised. They have paid. You will not hear of me more. Pray for me if you can.

5

GWENNY kept her own counsel over the deaths in London; if her eyes were red, no one heeded it. The news itself finally reached Daneclere by reason of the social ambitions of a Holborn housewife, who cherished the remembrance of Jem Whyteleaf's aside to her, after his wife's death, to the effect that his sister, Lady Farmiloe of Biding, would be coming shortly on a visit. When Sophia's soiled corpse was found in the locked room, this woman had been able to gabble who she might be and whence she had come. Thus the news came to Biding, and from Biding Edgar Farmiloe rode over to break it to his sister at Daneclere.

He had not seen or written to Maud since the day she left Biding after Edwin's death; there had been no communication between the houses. He found Maud alone in the hall, which he had not expected. He went to her and kissed her; her cheek felt cold and she did not return the kiss. Was this pale, stern-faced woman his lovely and lovable sister? The memory of Edwin stood between them like a drawn sword.

Edgar blurted out the news of Sophia and Jem and said "They have been buried in London and the expense paid by the lawyers. Ought we not to arrange for their conveyance here?"

"It matters little; see what Honor says," replied Maud coldly. Her eyes looked through him in a way that made him cry out, protesting,

"I had no hand in the killing of Edwin. I would have you believe that."

"He is dead," was all she said, and slowly traced the pattern of the stuff of her gown with a finger. Presently she spoke again. "I always knew it was not thieves, as they said, who killed him. But I could not serve my brothers as they had served me. Yet I shall never cross the threshold of Biding again, not if Lionel were to beg me on his knees."

"Then let me, who am innocent of his blood, visit you here now and again. It is not good to be so much alone. Does Honor bear you no company?"

"Honor is happy," she said, "and I cannot bear to watch it. I was happy once."

"You are bitter for so young a woman," he said.

"I am no longer very young."

He looked round the deserted hall, at the fine polish on everything, the signs of a well-kept household. Nevertheless he had the feeling that a film of dust lay over Maud's heart and all about her; as if time had ceased to pass while outside the world went on. A fairy princess in an enchanted castle was the fancy of an earlier age. This was real. Maud must return to life though her prince was dead, and would never come again to receive her kiss.

"I am always glad to see Honor for herself," she said suddenly. "She is kind to me."

She showed him upstairs to see Honor, who was with her child in the nursery. The fat little boy waddled about, between his nurse and his mother; his mouth oozed milk. He was laughing. The likeness to Edwin saddened Edwin's friend. Honor had greeted him coldly: she could do no less in Maud's presence.

After he had left them he rode to Thwaite. Officially he was the bearer of news of Jem and Sophia, but he decided that he would also speak of Maud's solitude; Uthred would be at Thwaite by day. Perhaps he would invite a little company to Daneclere, wrapped up in his wife and child as he must be. Maud should meet other men who might marry her. His concern grew as he remembered her remote, cold air. Madness was not always clamorous; she had not the air of a sane woman; but the thing which had happened to her had been enough to rid her of her sanity, her laughter.

He spoke of it afterwards to Uthred. "She cannot return to Biding," he said, "for neither she nor my brother Lionel would agree on it, and she would not be happy there. She is no man's wife, and has no home of her own. Even while she jangled the Daneclere keys I wager she was not happy with them; she has none of the possession most women feel for property and household goods." He smiled at Uthred, who had greeted him courteously. What a coil it had been! "Had

Lionel and Ralph stayed their hand in the killing of Edwin, he would have married her ere now," he thought. Fate had dealt tragically with his fair sister, who had been the cause of so much hope and love to their father. Even Sir Ralph could not see her again.

"May I come to Daneclere?" he asked Honor's husband. Uthred stroked his chin with his hand.

"My wife—" he began. Edgar burst in "I know, I know; she thinks I am Edwin's murderer. I swear I am not."

They settled it in the end that Edgar should come when he might to take Maud out riding. That would not offend Honor, who might still object to having a Farmiloe brother in the house. The news of Jem's and Sophia's deaths had taken second place; nobody had greatly cared for them.

There was another death in that year; that of old Jeremy Whyteleaf. He was found dead in his bed after four days; the sluttish housekeeper had not troubled to open the curtains earlier, thinking he was drunk. In his will he left all his goods to Honor, who he said had always been kind to him. No record was left of what he thought of the deaths of the three he had called his children. In fact, Honor's legacy was of the stuff of dreams; old Jeremy's debts had to be settled out of the Daneclere estate, and the sale of his house just covered them. But she was glad to know that he had had an affection for her, even though she had cast him out of her house.

She thought again of old Hawkin's death. They had found his opened Bible in the place where he kept it. As they had been forewarned, the farm and all his goods went to Honor, which meant that Uthred, as her husband, received them. David, as the eldest Thwaite son, contested the will, saying Uthred had exerted undue influence over his father. But those who had known Old Hawkin best were aware that no one had ever influenced him. When it came to the court hearing, impressive witness was borne by the dead man's grandson, Young Hawkin Thwaite. He related the conversation he had had with his grandfather before he died, in which he had clearly stated that Uthred was to be the heir. Hawkin's determined gait, strong jaw, and uncompromising speech had their effect on the judges, and the verdict was for Honor and against David. Bad feeling was left between the families of Bents and Daneclere, who would not speak or visit for a generation or more.

Meantime life went on at Daneclere as it had done at Thwaite. Young Uthred grew, and from staggering about on his short legs learnt to ride a pony; he would never be tall, and preferred to be seen in the saddle. Honor was content, watching her husband cross the causeway daily to supervise matters at Thwaite, then return to her for dinner. News from the outside world was less pleasant; it said that the King was ailing, worn out by his debauches, and that the Duke of York, as heir, would cause trouble as he was a Papist. At Daneclere such things would have been remote had it not been that Dick wrote sometimes, with his view of the other world of his enclosed college. Honor read the letters and cherished them, but her own life occupied her so completely that any other seemed like a dream or a play. Her happiness was like a spring of clear water in her.

So passed the years of her marriage to Uthred.

The one flaw in the marriage was the boy Arnulf, grown now to young manhood. Honor hid her dislike of him from Uthred, who loved his son passionately, and Arnulf was cunning enough not to disturb that feeling; when his father was by he seemed docile and hard-working, as he had been on the ship when, long ago, they all sailed together to Canada. In Uthred's absence, however, Arnulf was not only lazy and a liar, but lecherous as well; the maids fled at sight of him. Honor's rare anger blazed out one day when she found him struggling with poor little Gwenny, who had been carrying linen sheets back from the wash. They lay scattered on the muddy ground, and Gwenny would have had the worst of it had not her mistress come upon them and given Arnulf a sound cuff on the ear. He fell back, snarling like a dog, but without the courage to defend himself before this tall beautiful woman whose cheeks were flushed and whose eyes sparkled with anger. He shrugged it off and limped away; why make such a pother for a serving-wench?

That night Honor told Uthred of it; the time had come when she could no longer keep silent. He heard her out, then said in his calm way,

"It is natural for a young man to seek women. I would not have it matter to him more than anything else, but did he take no interest in them it would perhaps be more cause for concern." He smiled, but Honor was still angry.

"Any other serving-maid could protect herself, or it would

perhaps not matter so greatly if she did not. But Gwenny
when she was no more than a child was raped by two cruel
boys till she fell pregnant of—of a monstrous birth." Even
now she could not recall without shuddering the brainless
creature which had been born. Uthred listened gravely.

"Can you send her elsewhere?" he said.

"I will not. Her mother, who is dead, asked me to protect
her children, and a sad business I've made of it. Gwenny
must stay by me, or else at Thwaite; she will never marry
now, or be like other women." She averted her eyes and
thought of the sad nunlike little creature, limping about like
an old woman on her tasks about Daneclere. Other events
had somewhat ousted Gwenny from her mind; she must not
forget again.

Uthred was silent for some time. Presently he said, quietly
and sadly, "Then Arnulf must go. I must send him out to see
the world for himself; I have kept him too much at my side,
and he knows little."

"But he means much to you; how will you part with
him?" She was conscious of her own relief at the thought of
parting with Arnulf, but must not let his father guess at it.

"He is as much my son as your child is, and I love them
both. But no boy can stay forever with his father. I believe
that if Arnulf saw foreign parts again he might find that such
a life contented him better than journeying forever between
Daneclere and Thwaite. His deformity would prevent his
being a member of any crew, but he could undertake book-
work, trading, the like."

And enjoy his wenches where he found them, she thought;
but kept silent on it.

Later, when they were in bed, Uthred returned to the
matter. "I believe that the Prince might find him a place
again with the Hudson's Bay Company, especially as he was
with us before. They say it fares well, and the directors grow
rich. It would be an opportunity for Arnulf."

She said, jestingly but with fear in her mind, "You would
not wish to sail with him?" She knew Uthred loved the sea,
and would have been a sailor.

He smiled in the darkness. "Were I a boy, maybe. But
there is much to be done here and at Thwaite, though I doubt
not you would contrive without me, as you did before."

"Do not speak of it," she said. "The thought makes me
afraid. I need you as you need me."

Before they set out for London he said to her, and she knew he remembered their talk, "Will you not ride with us to London, Honor? It is long since you have seen the sights, and you could meet the Prince."

She shook her head; she must not shackle him to her. "How could I leave this carrot-headed rascal you gave me? He is worth more to me than many princes."

The father and son set out alone, with Arnulf's gear on a packhorse. He never turned his dark head as he rode away from Daneclere.

Uthred returned from London within the week, elated because Arnulf had been found a place in the Company's employment. Otherwise he had, he said, no disposition to linger after the boy went off. The new city they were building for themselves after the Great Fire, though they wanted it in all respects like the old, was different and he did not know his way about. "There is not even to be a spire on St. Paul's," he told her.

Honor smiled as she listened; many husbands would have taken the chance of a few days' roystering in the capital. She asked about Prince Rupert.

"He has been ill, but is mending a little now," Uthred told her. "They performed a trepanning operation on his skull some years agone, and that has relieved his headaches; but he has an old wound in his leg which troubles him, and makes him short-tempered.

"Was he so with you?"

"No; he was courteous to us, especially when he knew we were old Company men."

"You found a place for Arnulf quickly. Has he left town already?"

"No; there was a signal honor for Arnulf. Until the next cargoship comes in, which will convey him to Canada, he is to help the Prince with his experiments. No, they do not always concern stinking smoke! He hath invented a new way of engraving copper-blocks in colours, and makes them himself; and improved gunpowder, and I know not what all. My head cannot take in all the notions that lie in his, but he is a great man as well as a fine general and sea-captain. It is fortunate that the King shares his interests; together they have founded a society for the pursuit of such knowledge."

He turned away, and at sight of his profile Honor knew a

moment's uneasiness. For all his informed talk about the King and the Prince, he seemed haggard and tired, though the whole distance he had covered was not more than three hundred miles. But she forbore to fuss over him; he might dislike it, and he had come home to her and she would see that he was well fed, better than at inns.

He showed his pleasure at being with her again; that night in their bed he belied any semblance of tiredness, becoming her lover in a way that would not have seemed possible except between a younger man, a younger woman. Afterwards, she lay fulfilled against him, feeling the great slow beating of his heart beside hers. How had she ever lived without Uthred? How had she endured all those years alone, when he was no further off than the opposite bank of the river?

"Then I crossed the ford, when it was time," she thought drowsily. Before she slept she thought he murmured words which might have troubled her and for a time did not, so contented was she, so certain now that their days together would be long.

"Arnulf has been much in my mind, the more so because I never loved his mother. Perhaps it was that I must copy Robin in all things; he had got himself a bastard, so I must needs do so. How foolish young men are! I should not grudge Arnulf his own youthful folly. When in town I made a will, Honor. I have left half my goods to you, the other half to him. You may settle it between yourselves when the time comes."

She soothed him with promises, downing the terror that rose again in her heart as he spoke of his own death.

6

ON A MARCH NIGHT in 1683, Sir Ralph Farmiloe slipped quietly out of life. He had known nothing of what befell England during the latter years; he had not heard even of the death of his sometime commander, Rupert of the Rhine. Unchanging things were all that remained to him; Biding itself, the curtains of the bed where he lay, the portrait of his first wife which they had hung where he could see it. He hardly thought of Sophia; she had never been a part of his life, and it is doubtful if he understood her death.

His will was read. In it, to his sons' anger, he had left a handsome portion to his daughter Maud. There was a sum of money also for Gregory, enough to keep him in comfort all his lifetime. Liferents for Sophia would revert to the main heirs after her death. The rest of the brothers had fared less well, for whatever reason; they were left only Biding itself without the means to keep it. At first Lionel murmured hotly of contesting the will, but as time passsed he did nothing; it had been made while their father was of sound mind.

They tried to sustain themselves. Over the years they would attempt farming the Biding land, breeding horses, other such things becoming to country bachelors on short commons. It never occurred to any of them to return to fur-trading, or to marry for money. Single they remained, grudging Maud her portion, thinking of her as a stranger, which indeed she had become, for after church she would walk past them without a good-day to any except Edgar. They had thrust down the memory of their crime; to the end they would remain as they had become, half-comic reminders of the Royalist days, dressed in fashions of the time of Marston Moor. The good years had gone; they entertained few visitors, and kept to themselves, playing cards or dice of an evening, while Lionel smoked his long pipe. They were waited on by Fyfield, the burly guardian of Gregory, who paid for their food though he knew it not. The county acknowledged them because their name was ancient and their manor noble, though ramshackle now. The turn of the century was to find them still the same.

At Daneclere, a letter came from Arnulf to say that he was being sent home from Hudson's Bay by reason of ill-health.

7

A PACKAGE arrived for Maud from France, and she paid the messenger and departed upstairs to her own room.

Some time later a servant came to Honor where she

worked in the still-room; would she spare the time for a word with Mrs. Maud?

Honor went at once, leaving the bottling of ale to the maids and cleaning her hands on her apron, then taking it off. It was not like Maud to send for her; she generally came herself for whatever reason. This must be something of moment, and Honor knew an instant's curiosity as she climbed the stairs.

When she came to Maud's door, she called out. "It is Honor; may I enter?" She had never used haughty manners with Maud as the mistress of Daneclere; "after all is said," she reminded herself, "she herself was mistress once; we are equals."

Maud called to her to come in, and she did so. The light from the window outlined Maud's fair head, and shone on a gleaming chain of beads she held between her hands. There was a silver crucifix attached, with the figure of Christ stretched upon it. Some of the beads were larger than others. It was the first time Honor had seen a rosary.

"Child—" She did not know what it meant; and then Maud told her.

"Dick sent it me. I wrote to him. I-I do not know how to use it yet."

"You wrote to Dick?" Of all things that were unlikely to happen, this was the strangest. She had not even suspected it. Maud slid her fingers over the gleaming rosary and laid it carefully aside.

"Honor, it is my wish to pray for Edwin's soul; I do not care if I spend all my life at it. Protestants do not pray for the dead in the way Catholics do. It is my desire to enter a convent and spend all of my remaining life in such prayer. I have not told you of it before because I did not wish to trouble you." Her voice had grown breathless; her eyes never left the rosary. Honor was practical.

"Maud, you cannot suddenly enter a convent knowing nothing of the Catholic faith but that they pray for the dead. You must find out more of it."

"I will take instruction. That is why I wrote to Dick; I knew that he would help me. He says there is nowhere nearer than London where I may easily do so. Now that I have father's money I can go, and when I enter the convent—Dick says there is a community of Carmelites in Paris—I may bring them a dowry. It is different from being penniless. I have thought of it ever since father died."

Honor felt the world spin about her. Maud a nun! It was true that she lived the life of one, had always done so but for that short interlude of brief happiness, of ecstasy, with Edwin. Pity came to Honor's aid. She said "Go and find a little gaiety at Court, Maud, while you take your instruction. I doubt not that, with the Queen and the Duke and Duchess of York all of them Papist, it will be a fashionable pursuit—I mean no harm—but you have never had any pleasure in the world; find it now, and try it against the thought of the convent. I confess I cannot see why you may not pray for Edwin, as you wish, and stay among us. I myself pray for him nightly."

"I should have remembered that," said Maud affectionately. "But I do not know who could take me to Court, and I cannot go alone; you yourself have not the time."

Honor was thoughtful. "Sir Nigel Brysson can fend for himself: his lady might be glad of the diversion. Shall I write to her to ask if she will go with you? Once you are known, and have made friends there, you would no longer be a tie on her."

"I shall not stay longer than I must," said Maud stubbornly. They discussed news of Dick, and Maud gave his mother the note to read that she had had with the rosary. He must have obtained permission from his superior to write to her.

Lady Brysson was amenable, and she and Maud set off for London in the Brysson coach. Maud had, under Honor's insistence, furnished herself with one or two gowns; she was not interested in the stuffs and laces, but Honor knew that she would look very beautiful in what had been chosen; perhaps despite everything she would meet a courtier who would make her a worthy husband. "I cannot think that she would be happy in a strict convent," Honor told herself repeatedly. It seemed an unnatural life for Maud.

Letters came bearing enough news to let them know at Daneclere that Maud had been to Court, and had been presented to both Queen and Duchess—*the last is very beautiful*, she wrote; and had followed them to the chapel in St. James's where they heard Mass, and had found there a priest who would instruct her. Maud had little to say about the rest of Court life, except that the King and Queen were on better terms than they had been for years. The Titus Oates plot had brought out Charles's loyalty to the Papist wife who could not bear him children; he could have put her away at that time, but had not.

Maud's going was not welcome to everyone. One day when he was at Thwaite, Uthred came on young Hawkin, as a rule so busy and taciturn, with his head on his arms, weeping because Maud was to be a nun. "She may not be so," said Uthred comfortingly. "It is a notion women take; life in London may rid her of it."

"Ay, and some fortune-hunting braggart may marry her."

"Take heart, Hawkin; it is not like you to be dismayed." But Hawkin had loved for years without reward; now he was losing heart.

8

FOR ARNULF to say, as he had done, that he had been discharged for reasons of ill-health was true. During his trip to the interior to watch the killing of beaver led by an Indian guide, he had fallen into the common error of white men, lain with too many Indian women and caught syphilis. This disease was common among the tribes and troubled them little, but in its time had killed white men like flies. Arnulf was not to die yet. On his return his superior found him with opened breeches, ruefully examining a chancre. "You witless fool," said the man, who disliked Arnulf and had done so from the first. "Do you know that you can end mad and palsied? You should see a physician." Certainly the rough-and-ready cures they had at the Fort would not cure Arnulf, and he began to think of his illness as an excuse to return home, see a physician, and end his contract with the Bay. Prince Rupert, who had sponsored him this second time, was lately dead; Arnulf himself had no liking for the hard life he had found, to his surprise, to be in no way improved from his last visit. As well be a damned grocer, trading goods over a counter, he told himself and his companions. With the latter he was not popular. After the failure of his first treatment the senior who had first found him took him aside and spoke with frankness.

"If as you say you would as soon go, Jansen, it is good enough for us and for London, when I write there. Most of us here would rather have your room than your company, and we can find better men to fill the place you despise, who will not cause ill-feeling whenever they speak. You are idle as well; by God, I shall write enough to London to shake them on their velvet chairs!" There were still no chairs at the Fort; he spoke with envy. As for Arnulf, he felt aggrieved, but was glad to be gone.

He reached London two months later, shaved of the beard he had grown against the cold. He did not report to the office of the Company—he desired never to hear of it again—but went to a physician whose direction he had been given by one of the men who were not unfriendly. The doctor examined Arnulf in silence, then shook his head.

"There is no cure which will make certain you never again have an attack," he said. "All I can do is prolong the time of its coming. We know little of this disease yet, only some of its results; and those can be terrible, less for a man himself than for his children."

"I have none," said Arnulf. He took the tinctures and mercury pills the physician gave him, all the time feeling vindictively that he, Arnulf Jansen, should have been singled out for this indignity by lying with an oily copper-coloured bitch in a wilderness of snow. He would choose his women more carefully in the future. As for his children, he could not imagine them. Had anyone told him his mind was set only on a picture of himself, he would have resented it.

He went home to Daneclere, where his father embraced him—how yellow the man looked!—and his stepmother kissed his cheek. Arnulf knew well enough that Honor disliked him and was sorry to see him return. It troubled him not at all. He would soon make way with Uthred which would put her out of the running, and he resolved to do so.

Uthred and Honor asked about his illness. He deluded at least the former with a tale of weak lungs, which had not withstood the Canadian winters.

"I am glad to see you again, for whatever reason," said Uthred gently. "Here you will soon grow well."

Arnulf set about devoting himself to his father. There were

many tasks which he could, gradually and without appearing to thrust his way in, take from Uthred, and he did so; the account-books, the payment of servants' wages and the rent from the tenant-roll by way of the bailiff. He was careful to be scrupulously honest; if Uthred, as still sometimes happened, chose to examine the books, they were in order. Arnulf began after that to see to tasks which were properly the bailiff's, but which that personage had no objection to leaving to him; the putting up of fences, the planting and cutting of quickthorn to keep the cattle from roaming into Biding fields; the killings for winter salting, and the salting itself, which occupied everyone in the house and over which there must be no delay, or the meat would go bad. Nothing seemed too humble for the once aloof and lazy bastard son, and even those who still disliked him—they were not few—said among themselves that the time in Canada had made a man of young Arnulf. As for Uthred, he was deeply pleased.

In the evenings, father and son would play chess together. It had begun on a night when, as often now, Uthred seemed tired and in pain. He would not admit enough weakness to take to his bed, and Arnulf smoothly suggested the game to pass the time and ease his father's mind. Soon it became a nightly habit after the day's work was done.

In such ways it became easier for Arnulf to watch his father than for his father's wife to do so. In the bustle of daily housekeeping and preparing for meals Honor had hardly leisure to gaze at her husband's face and see that it was growing thin and kept the yellowish tinge Arnulf had noted. Uthred would sometimes complain of pain in his right side, but said it was not sharp; when Honor offered to put a compress on the place he would not have it. He had always disliked drawing attention to himself when ill, and liked it no more now.

At Whitehall, there was another invalid; King Charles took a seizure. He was at first expected to live, but by the time the news reached Daneclere he was an unconscionable time a-dying. When he died, after the mourning came shock: most had been slow to realise that the next King, who had been James, Duke of York, was an honest man—more so than his brother—but lacking in humour and, worse, a Papist. "If he leaves folk free to worship as they will, it makes no odds," said Uthred to his wife.

Maud was still at Court; they had fewer letters from her nowadays, for she was much about the new Queen, who had stood sponsor for her when she was received into the Catholic Church at Warwick Street that summer. "They say King James hath the pox, though his brother never caught it," said Uthred. "Maybe that is why so great a number of his children have died, both by this wife and the last."

Arnulf said nothing, and moved a pawn. "There are the two daughters by the first wife," Honor put in. "Ay," said her husband, "and one married to a Dutchman and the other to a Dane, and neither with children living. Boy, you have put my bishop in sad stress."

"The Princess Anne of Denmark may bear a living child yet. At all events they are Protestant, and the King's heirs. That will please the extreme folk in the country."

"Folk both extreme and other must take what they are given," said Uthred. "Yet I do not think that since Mary Tudor's burnings they will be well pleased with a Papist. But the King is not young, and they will endure him for the space of his lifetime, with the Dutch pair to follow."

"Would they want the Dutchman?" Honor said. "His wife, maybe."

"She would not leave him behind in Holland."

"Maybe she will not be asked to. There were burnings in Elizabeth's reign as well as in her sister's. For folk to tolerate one another is the main thing, if we learned the art of't in nigh on a century."

Arnulf had waited, watched, listened, assessed. He won the game.

A letter came from Maud, describing James II's magnificent coronation; even the Queen's shoes had been made of cloth of gold. *She had all her black hair hanging loose to her waist, under a very rich crown,* Maud wrote. Lady Brysson, long returned, who had been to Daneclere to gossip, said that the Queen was in poor health and not expected to live. " 'Tis pity she hath borne no living heir," she concluded. Perhaps the King would take a third wife. But Maud seemed happy in attendance on Mary of Modena and would grieve if such prophecies were fulfilled.

9

THOSE at Daneclere would have heard little of the Monmouth rebellion —it took place mainly in the West Country—if it had not been for Maud. Soon after Monmouth's capture and execution she came down to visit them, and told them of the hundreds hanged, transported abroad as slaves under the new sentence only twenty years old, and of the end of Monmouth Jemmy himself, which had been pitiful, as the executioner had bungled his task. "The judge had the face of an angel—I saw him being driven away from court—but they call him Hanging Jeffreys," she said. "Yet the King had no choice but to execute Monmouth. Had he put him in the Tower there would have been more risings." It was hard and pathetic to think of King Charles's beloved bastard son crawling on his knees to beg his uncle in vain for his life.

They ceased talking of the sad matter and turned to admire Maud. She was dressed fashionably, in a tall-crowned hat with a jewel in it, and an elegant jacket cut like a man's and frogged with red braid. For the coach-journey she had brought a fur muff, to keep her hands warm. She glowed with beauty and, Honor was glad to see, love of life. Perhaps her devotion to the Queen was one cause; she spoke of it, laughingly saying that all her gewgaws were paid for as the royal household, differently from the late King's day, had its salaries regularly met.

"The Queen loves the King dearly," she said. "It is a pity he is unfaithful." King Charles had loved beautiful women and had got himself a plain wife; King James preferred ugly ones, and his wife was very beautiful, with magnificent Italian dark eyes and the long hair which had held watchers spellbound at the coronation.

"She speaks of going to take the cure at Bath, and I go with her," said Maud. Honor noted nothing of her former wish to enter a convent, but she must have guessed the older woman's thoughts. "The Queen says the Carmelites would be too strict for me," she told her. "She says there are other orders I can join, when the time comes. But while she needs me by her, I will stay. I like the Court life well nowadays."

While she was talking she had in fact been looking at Honor with compassion. The latter's hair was now nearly white, with narrow strands of auburn combed back from the forehead and neck. Uthred's illness must trouble her; and Maud, like Honor herself, felt only loathing for Arnulf. Maud made herself speak of gay matters; they must hear them seldom nowadays. When she prepared to return to London after a fortnight's stay, it was to meet Hawkin Thwaite lingering in the hall; he had come to give Uthred the news of a cow in labour.

" 'Tis a bull-calf, delivered safe enough, but only fit for slaughter," he said. Maud made a little grimace, and raised her fan. "Lord, how near the earth you are here!" she exclaimed, and Hawkin regarded her steadily.

"We all return to the earth," he said.

"Doubtless: but I hope not yet."

The Queen made the journey to the medicinal springs at Bath, and the townspeople turned out to give her a rare welcome; they would love her memory all through the troubles that were to come. Maud wrote amusingly of how they had gone to the baths, which had been built by the Romans, and bobbed up and down in the water wearing bathing-dresses of saffron linen which ballooned out as they dipped.

The visit to Bath was to have one notable effect. Nothing was said in public, but Maud, swearing everyone to secrecy at Daneclere, sent them the news, a few weeks later, that the Queen was pregnant. *Maybe the Waters have done some good*, the letter ran. *She is so retiring and shy that she will not that it be Known, but in the end it must be. I would they might have a living Child.*

Meanwhile there was discontent in the capital over the King's high-handedness in issuing a Declaration of Indulgence.

Uthred seemed a little better; he attributed this to the burdens lifted from him by Arnulf, and became increasingly grateful to and dependent on his son. He was still loving and affectionate to Honor and she could not know of the things his mind held, for he gave her no notion that anything was amiss.

The Queen gave birth to a prince. There was much ill-feeling in the country; some said that at thirty-one she was too old for childbearing and that it must be a plot. Subsequently a fertile invention was put about to the effect that they had smuggled in the child in a warming-pan. The nation disliked the thought of a Papist heir; in the meantime, the doctors did all they could to kill the poor little baby, and ruined his digestion, by feeding him with concoctions made of black-currant juice and stranger substances. When they said he was dying the King was called in. "Have you tried giving him milk?" said the child's father sensibly.

Whether or not James saved his son's life, the child lived. By now seven bishops had been arrested and put in the Tower; men waited for the Protestant wind which would waft William the Dutchman to English shores.

It was November, and bitterly cold. One night, in this weather, the Queen escaped, with her child in her arms, and took refuge in France. A letter came to Honor from Maud. *I am coming home to you.*

Honor was glad of her.

Uthred's respite had not lasted. By now the bones showed through his skin and his body was emaciated; the yellow colour persisted, even staining the whites of his eyes. Honor nursed him as best she might, no longer resenting the amount of time Arnulf spent in his father's room. Anything or anyone which would make Uthred content for even an hour was welcome. She had begun to realise that this beloved husband, who was so much younger than herself, would not outlive her.

"I did not go with her," said Maud. "Her fate—all their fates are uncertain, and hangers-on—there will be many—are an expense they can no longer afford. The convent? Yes, I could have crossed with the Queen, secret as her going was, and entered it, and they would have received me. But I did not. I thought of you, and of how you will soon be lonely here." She spoke without fear of Uthred's coming death. "You need me, I believe," she said. "*They* do not, or not yet."

Honor was moved, too greatly to speak of it. Instead, she asked concerning matters in London.

"They will have the Dutchman's wife at present, but not the Dutchman; and he says he will not be his wife's

gentleman usher. It may end with the pair of them side by
side on equal thrones. I am done with all of it. I did not stay
to see him; they say he is small and ugly, but a gallant
commander. It may be that he and the King will meet on
either side a battle one day soon. I could not say who will
win. The King was a fine admiral, but less of a soldier."

"What has become of the Queen in France?"

"Why, she is at King Louis' court at present. She knows it
of old, for she spoke of it to me once; she passed through
France on her way here to her wedding, when she was a girl
of fifteen. She says the French court is stiff, and full of
etiquette. They will not be very happy there. The Queen
would herself have been a nun, as you may know." Maud
smiled. "She was unwilling to marry, but they arranged it
despite her wishes; and now she loves the King devotedly. I
pray that all may turn out safely for them, if not happily."

Honor watched Maud, and thought how the years at Court
had improved her; she was animated, certain of herself, and
no longer shut away in her own mind. "I do not need to ask if
she prays for Edwin," Honor thought. "I know she does; but
she has seen other things, and is no longer a prisoner of the
past."

She sighed; it was a sad house to which Maud had
returned. Even young Uthred, with his jolly ways, could not
dispel the air of sadness which hung over Daneclere.

A month after William of Orange and his wife Mary had
jointly ascended the throne, Uthred died. His last visitor had
been Lady Brysson, who sat by his bedside three hours,
talking and tiring him. "Times are coming when no man
knows who rules him, or what to believe. There may be civil
war again, for the King's right will prevail." The dying man
saw an England rent with strife, where no lone woman could
be sure of the safety and protection of the law. After Lady
Brysson had gone he sent for his lawyer, who came post-
haste; he was closeted with Uthred for an hour, neither
Honor nor Arnulf being permitted to enter the room. Still
later, Uthred himself sent for the two of them, and made
them join hands.

"I have altered my will that I told you of," he said to
Honor. "It is for the best, as I believe." To Arnulf he said "I
know you will protect your stepmother." The young man

bowed his head and swore that he would do so, even with his life.

"I leave you in good hands," said Uthred to Honor, and then asked to see his younger son. The little boy was brought, with his carrot-mop of hair thrusting up like a brush, and his stomach full of food so that he belched and then laughed at it. Laughter was needed in that room. Uthred reached out his wasted hand and touched his namesake's cheek. "Do as you are bid, both by your mother and your brother here," he said. He watched the child being taken away, turned to Honor and gave her a long smiling look full of love; then turned his head and fell asleep. He was never to waken.

Uthred's will was read. The ownership of Daneclere and the farms, the land and all other possessions, went to Arnulf and his heirs. Honor herself received the liferents of half the farms and a wish was expressed that she and her son would continue to live at Daneclere and Hawkin at Thwaite. In the event of Arnulf's death without issue the remainder went to young Uthred, and if he died before his mother she was to inherit the whole.

Honor heard it with a sense of unreality. She did not question, still less would attempt to fight, the will. She had no feeling except a sense of irrevocable loss. "I do not love Daneclere," she had once said to Uthred. But it would be strange to live on there by charity of Arnulf: to have to be careful not to offend him, defer to his wishes, make oneself useful, unobtrusive, of secondary importance in this place where she had always, save for a brief interval, reigned as mistress.

There was nothing to be done. After the reading was over and the lawyer had departed, she went to the nursery and dismissed the maid who was with young Uthred, and gathered the boy to her with a sudden hard embrace which made him cry. He was all she had left now. He and Maud were all she had left.

Six

I

ARNULF made few friends, despite the fact that he was rich;
Uthred had carefully garnered the farm-rents and other
sources of money so that, at his death, the coffers of
Daneclere were full. But when the new heir rode out, it was
alone or with servants; even the tavern-company, such as had
welcomed old Whyteleaf, avoided him. The reason was
difficult to describe; apart from his club-foot Arnulf was not
physically repulsive, but there seemed to be some quality
about him that made others turn away. As for women, they
interested him little except as sources of brief satisfaction. He
had never yet kept a mistress, although he was beginning to
realise it might well be cheaper than casual encounters were
he to do so. He had no notion of taking a wife.

Except that he allowed himself full licence to spend the
inheritance as he chose, he was mean with money. He would
haggle over a purchase like a huckster, and he sacked his
bailiff, thinking to save the man's salary. Thereafter no
tenant ever had fair treatment. The thatch on the cottages
could rot, the broken windows let in rain, the blocked
chimneys continue to belch smoke down into the rooms;
Arnulf did nothing. If a tenant were ill he would die without
succour, and if he owed rent would have been put out in the
cold, dying or living. On one occasion Honor herself paid
Arnulf what was owing until a poor old woman should die.

Honor and Maud had short shrift. After Uthred's death
they had removed themselves and their personal gear into the
nursery wing to be near young Uthred; but Arnulf constantly
pestered Maud. She was still beautiful, and it was a challenge
to his manhood, evidently, that he should gain her. After a
time she would not move from her rooms without Honor by
her, and when the latter was forced to leave her alone Maud
locked the door, opening it only when she was certain Honor
had returned. It was no life for a woman who was still young
and had known gentler ways. Honor sometimes wearied for
Thwaite, even for its memories of happiness, but she thought
the rough living there would hardly suit Maud. Also, she felt

it her duty to stay on at Daneclere; for one thing, there would be nobody to defend the servants and hear their tale if Arnulf took one of his vicious fits and dismissed or raped them. She herself could at least see from day to day that they were given enough food and paid punctually, even though it might mean approaching their master on the latter head. She did not fear Arnulf, and she knew he respected her; and without her he would have to pay a housekeeper. But she often wished that Uthred, so wise and provident in every other way, had been less deceived in his bastard son.

One day Arnulf rode out followed by two menservants. They took the road north, which wound at last into by-ways and lanes where some of the tenants' cottages were. Arnulf rode swiftly to clear his head of a late night's drinking, and only slowed to a canter when a small holding was reached, beyond which lay a green. On this a dozen geese straggled, squawking and scattering as the party approached. Arnulf's horse reared, and he cursed the birds and drew up, the men reining in behind him.

The house they saw was shabby, and everything about it seemed starved and dark; a near-skeleton of a cat licked itself in the sunlight beyond the door, and the mean little slope of a dairy adjoined a field of thin cows. Arnulf realised he was thirsty; no doubt there would be a drink of milk to be had in the dairy for the landlord. He dismounted, tossed the reins to one of the men and lowered his head to enter, then stopped in his tracks. Inside, with plump bare arms working the churn and comely buttocks clad in homespun bending over it, was a young woman. The curve of her breasts was ample and showed from where he stood, but he had not seen her face. She turned then and stared at Arnulf. She was a handsome young wench, with rosy cheeks and smooth brown-gold hair under a cap. Her round blue eyes widened at sight of him.

Arnulf assessed her, letting his eyes travel up and down her plump young body. It was no longer the drink of milk he wanted. He asked her for that, but she shook her head.

"My father would beat me. He uses the milk for cheese and the like, that he takes to market. Keeps count of everything, he does." Her face had flushed at the expression in his gaze, which was fixed now on the cleft between her breasts. Arnulf asked her name.

"My name is Molly, sir. Mary Dilke." She wiped her hands on her apron, clearly ill at ease with this man who wore fine clothes and rode a fine horse, and had no respect for young maids about their concerns. Arnulf remembered a Dilke in the tenant-roll. "Does your father pay rent to Daneclere?" he asked, knowing the man did; but she did not reply and glanced nervously over her shoulder.

"Best ask him y'self, sir; I mustn't stop my work; butter has to be ready for him to take, and it an't turned yet; it is maybe the heat of the day." She went back again to her churn, but Arnulf had not done with her.

"Why are you not wed, Molly? A fine wench like you should have no lack of suitors." But she did not reply. Arnulf limped out of the dairy and over to the door of the house. It was ajar and a woman who might have been fifty, with hardly any flesh on her bones, came out. The thin cat fled. Inside the room—he peered past her shoulder—was a ragged curtain dividing the room in two. A low fire burned in the hearth, with a pot of herbs on it; he could smell the fragrant steam. "Tell your husband I would have a word with him," he said to the woman. "I am your landlord from Daneclere."

She went away, and presently a man came back with her whom Arnulf had seen bringing rents. He was older than the woman, seventy if a day, an age seldom reached by cottagers; meanness seemed to have rimmed his close-set eyes with red and drawn his mouth into a hard line among his stubble of a beard. Arnulf marvelled that such a pair between them could have got the pleasant wench in the dairy. The reckless mood which took him when he knew what he wanted came now; he held out two sovereigns.

"Know you these?"

"Seldom, sir." Greed shone in the eyes of the man; the woman was listless. No doubt she would never handle the money, Arnulf reflected; the old devil would hide it wherever he kept his store.

"This shall be yours, and a month's free rent, if I have your daughter."

The man's jaw dropped, revealing broken teeth; the woman raised a hand to her scraggy bosom, and murmured "Moll? Ah, no," and her husband rounded on her. "Hold your peace," he said, and turning to Arnulf again, "Maybe for three o' those," he said. "She'm a maid, and a good worker."

Arnulf knew pleasure. There was a saying that if a man lay with a virgin, it would rid him of the pox. In any case he

wanted her. "Two only, and it must be now," he said, and
jerked his head towards the curtain. A stirring was in his
loins as he thought of the girl. He still held up the gleaming
sovereigns, between thumb and fingers. Sooner or later, he
knew, the gleam of them would make the man yield.

This was so. Presently the man called "Moll! Moll! Haste
ye," and the girl came running out of the dairy, big breasts
bouncing beneath her bodice. She stopped and tucked back
her hair under the cap, abashed when her father said to her
"This gentleman would have ye. Go and make ready."

"Your landlord," smiled Arnulf again, seeing the woman
still grudged him of her daughter. She had begun to whine
about the ills of the house; it was damp, the roof leaked, the
rent was too high. Dilke turned on her and raised his lean
fist.

"Did I not tell ye, hold your peace? There's none better
will ask for her. Go ye in, sir, to the further place in a
moment; she'll be ready then."

Arnulf went in past the curtain presently and found the
girl, trembling and naked, lying ready on a bed of discoloured
straw. He was as prone to take her here as between fine linen
sheets. He went about the business vigorously. The father
had been right; a good firm maidenhead none had tampered
with. Afterwards he began to wonder at his luck. The folk
here had given way easily; too easily, he might have thought,
had he had all his wits. But her breasts were big and round;
he laid his hands on them and kneaded them, with his
member still lying hard within her, and said, for she was
sobbing, "Molly, don't cry. I'll buy you a new gown and a
new pair of shoes, and you shall live like a fine lady in a great
house. Will that not please you?"

Molly Dilke wept aloud. The breaking of her maidenhead
had hurt her. Also, she was afraid of this lame man with the
narrow face and secret eyes, almost as much so as she was of
her father.

Arnulf brought Molly back to Daneclere and set her up as his
mistress, buying her a gown, as he had promised, and shoes.
At nights she slept with him in the great bed which had seen
the Sawtrey sons born, but she would bear no child of his; he
saw to that. She was a good worker, as her father had said,
and did many tasks about the house as he ordered her. She
counted and mended the linen, made the beds, helped with

breadmaking and brewing; she would have made a good wife
and a good mother. Arnulf worked her well, taking his
pleasure on her most nights, generally after drinking late
alone. In the mornings he would waken to find Moll already
gone about her duties.

These fell to her the more readily in that, the day Arnulf
brought her home, Honor, with Maud and young Uthred and
the little servant Gwenny whom Arnulf had once pursued for
his sport, left Daneclere and went to live at Thwaite. Arnulf
was pleased enough with the arrangement, and pleased with
life; after a time he found that, since he had begun to lie with
Molly, he showed no further signs of the pox.

2

HAWKIN had lived on at Thwaite in the particular way of
many bachelors; everything was tidy and in its place, spick
and span. He had no housekeeper. When Honor sent word to
him that three suppliant women and a child would soon be at
his door, he readily moved from his comfortable house to the
room over the stables he had lived in as a boy. It was a deal
less warm than the farmhouse which he left vacant for Honor
and Maud.

Young Uthred was given an attic room. The stolid greedy
child minded nothing provided he was given enough to eat,
and leaving Daneclere, where he had lived all his knowing
life, did not disturb him. Hawkin let him raid the apple-loft
and saw him despatch the contents with great enjoyment, his
blue eyes sparkling with happiness at the gift. In all of
Uthred's life this capacity for joy was to come uppermost;
nothing was too small to cause it, no misery too great to
prevent it. He knew little of why his mother and Maud had
decided to leave Daneclere, only that he had been told to put
on his riding-clothes quickly, and had done so; then he had
found his favourite pony, Bet, saddled ready, and the two
women with Gwenny all mounted in grey cloaks, and they
had set off. The causeway had been wet and its stones
slippery, but Uthred knew his pony would guide him safe to
Thwaite. There was always someone, his mother or his nurse

or Maud, who would see that his wishes were met and that all went well for him. Now there was Hawkin also, and Hawkin's bold jaw and hard dark eyes would soften for the little boy and he would be allowed to watch while Hawkin sharpened a harrow-blade, or else would help carry winter hay for the horses and cattle in their stalls.

Honor and Maud fared well enough, except for one thing; Honor had told Hawkin why they had to leave Daneclere; she could do no other. It was the third or fourth day after their arrival, and Arnulf had sent no messenger after them although he knew where they had gone. Honor met Hawkin coming in for the supper she had cooked for him—it reminded her of the happy years here with young Uthred's father—and she told him of Arnulf's bringing in a mistress after his frequent sallies at Maud. "She could never be left in peace," she said, "and now there is this young woman, and we thought it proper, both of us, to come away and leave him to live as he will."

Hawkin's brow had lowered like a bull's when he heard of the troubling of Maud. He put a hand to his shirt-neck and said "There is a thing I would have spoken of this long time: if Mrs. Maud will wed me, none shall pester her more. I do not like to speak to her of it, she being a young lady I talk to but seldom; but I'd guard her well, and she'd not see hardship while I live, nor trouble neither."

She has nowhere to go but here, Honor thought; I must not embarrass her. She said aloud "I will tell her," and chose a moment when she thought Hawkin was out of the house. She had not mistaken the probable answer; Maud was angry.

"I—*I* to marry a low-born churl, a bastard to boot, to keep a roof over our heads! I'd as soon pay our way-bills at an inn. If my father but knew how it is grudged that I dwell anywhere in peace, even Biding, and now—and now *this*—"

"Nobody grudges you aught, Maud; and Hawkin has been good to us and has put himself out for our sakes."

"And I am to repay him so? Never!"

Honor saw a shadow move away behind the door. She was sorry Hawkin had heard. He said no more of it, even when, out of courtesy, she told him what he already knew. To have heard Maud say what she had must have been cruel. But he did not alter his manner towards them, which continued respectful and hospitable; nor was any difference made to their comfort at Thwaite.

Honor, Maud and young Uthred stayed on at Thwaite for three years. The women helped with the housework and the cooking of meals; Hawkin shot game and rabbits and there were cabbages grown for the winter. Young Uthred grew into a sturdy, short-legged little boy. He still ate prodigiously and was fat for his height. His blazing red hair became a familiar sight in the fields and woods, where he liked to shoot with Hawkin, though he was too lazy to do much work about the farm. Honor and Maud taught him to read and write. They did not draw attention to themselves by demanding a tutor, as the farm belonged by rights to Arnulf and if he chose, he could evict them all. But Arnulf seemed content enough with the way of life he had chosen at Daneclere, lurching between his mistress and his wine. There was little company. Arnulf never appeared in church and the popular opinion was that he had sold his soul to the devil. No one at Thwaite ever saw him.

One winter the snow drifted thickly against Thwaite door and they had to dig themselves out to go to tend the beasts. Hawkin generally did all such work but he was away, unusually, to attend to money-matters with the new lawyer, as the old was dead. Night came down early and the women built themselves a high wood fire. Its cheerful blaze made leaping shadows in the flagged kitchen and warmed the house. Honor and Maud sat by it, while Uthred crouched at their feet. He stared into the heart of the fire with his shallow blue eyes; a child of more imagination would have seen pictures there, but Uthred saw nothing.

Suddenly there was a scrabbling sound beyond the door, as of a stray dog.

"Who is there?" Honor called; in their lone state, if a thief came he might have what he willed, if he was armed. Honor herself went to the door and listened; a whisper came, hardly heard above the sighing of the wind that drifted the snow.

"It is Moll. Molly Dilke. I pray you let me in; I am ill."

Honor opened the door. There against the night stood Arnulf's mistress, wrapped in a man' cloak and great-eyed in her white face. Honor opened the door further. "Are you alone, on such a night?" she asked.

Moll fell rather than walked in; she was in a state of exhaustion, and when they removed her cloak they saw her once plump body bone-thin. Honor led her to the fire; what did it matter except that the poor creature was cold? "There is some broth," she said. "I will heat it for you."

"You are kind—kind—"

Suddenly she fell to weeping. They let her weep, seating themselves about her, while Honor signalled to the boy to go up to bed. He pouted; the bedchamber was cold, and it was warmer here by the fire. "Go when I bid you," said his mother, and as often when she was in a particular frame of mind Uthred feared her, and went, lighting a candle on the way. The weeping young woman drew her hands away from her face. "Forgive me," she said. "I should maybe not have come to such ladies, being a light woman as I am. But I dare not go home to my father, and if Mr. Arnulf finds out the way I am he'll forbid me the house; I have nowhere to go, and I am ill and will not grow better."

"You are very thin," said Honor, while Maud watched from her corner. "Is it the wasting sickness?" For she remembered the apple-cheeked, sturdy young woman Arnulf had brought home to Daneclere three years since; such high-coloured folk often had the sickness, which might not show for a long time.

"Ay. I am spitting blood. I dread that he will find out. But he thinks I've grown thin with working, and mocks me." Molly began to weep again. "He's as mean as my father. He beats me often because he says it makes me—makes me—" The starved cheeks flushed in the light of the fire. "I do not want to go back to him," said Molly Dilke flatly. "I will not live long, I think. Four brothers and two sisters I had, bonny they were, until all of 'em died of it. Our house was known as a plague-house and never a one of us was married, because of that. When Mr. Arnulf came for me, and gave my father gold, he said naught of't, and I was too much in fear. He let Mr. Arnulf take me away, knowing I had the sickness. It's a curse of young folk and animals. All the cows and the beasts on the farm had it, but not my mother or my father; they're old. I think, though, it was from my mother we took it; we drank it in with her milk."

"You must stay here with us," said Honor. She felt deep pity for the young woman. Maud said nothing, but sat motionless in her place. This is one time, thought Honor, when I will not consider Maud. But the sick woman must be kept away from young Uthred. She should have his attic chamber, and he should sleep with Hawkin in the stables. For tonight, they would make Molly a bed in the kitchen.

Four days after Molly had come to them, Arnulf himself rode over, swearing and blustering; by God, he'd hunted high and low, he'd have the wench out of there, and them all; she should not escape him thus, such a thing was never heard of! Honor met him, and said calmly,

"Your mistress hath the wasting sickness. It is not likely she will live. She spits blood, and I am nursing her. If you have any heart in you, let her be at peace."

"Peace?" he exclaimed. "Why, the damned bitch may have given me her sickness; why did none tell me sooner? Three years I've had her about me." His own cheeks were flushed with a hectic colour, and Honor hoped, against all charity, that he had indeed caught the sickness, and that it would finish him.

She did not ask Arnulf into the house. He departed, mouthing curses against herself and Molly Dilke. The latter lay in her attic chamber, weary and pale; she had offered to help in the kitchen, but Honor would not let her work. She went up now to tell the girl that Arnulf had come and gone. Tears ran down on to the sick woman's pillow, soaking the linen.

The first result of Arnulf's visit was one from the servant whom he employed cheaply now the bailiff had gone his ways. This man appeared with a demand that they all of them leave Thwaite within the week.

Hawkin was out at the fields. Honor met the servant, with Maud and young Uthred standing by her. She heard him out; his task was as a rule to put fear in poor tenants, folk like the Dilkes, and he was using methods on herself which were the only ones he knew. Having done, with no effect that he could see, he stared with dropped jaw at this tall handsome old woman who stood there calmly in her black gown, and did not weep or beg for time. Her voice was as always and she answered slowly.

"My father and his father's fathers have farmed Thwaite for longer than men can tell. Now your master's spite would have us out because he is angered. He will not succeed. Tell him though I loved my late husband dearly, I will contest the will that gave his bastard ownership of the estates that should be mine. While it is being contested under the law—and much silver wasted, which your master will not like—we cannot be forced out; any attempt so to force us will meet with the law also. Perhaps he would sooner leave us in peace."

She smiled a little; whether or not all she had said was true in law, she had put fear into him with the mention of it. As she finished speaking Hawkin came up, still in his rough working clothes, his black hair whipped by the wind.

"What is it?" He asked, and when she told him he went up to the fellow and threatened him with his fist.

"Would Arnulf Jansen have me leave my land here to lie fallow, with no seed sown? Who is to tend the beasts till he finds another tenant? Not he, I warrant; every bone in his body is idle and mean, and you may tell him from me that if the house is left empty I will bide in the stables, and get on with the task God meant me to do. It would be better for him had he some such, other than drink and women. Get you gone, and do not come and trouble us here again."

The man went, muttering in sullen fashion that he'd done as he was bid, and any trouble would be for themselves, not him. As soon as the sound of his going had died away, Honor turned to Maud and told her to get together her gear and the boy's.

"Go quickly to Newhall, where they will shelter you both," she said. "I will write a letter to Lady Brysson while you make ready." But Maud demurred.

"If there is to be trouble, surely it is better that we meet it together?" she said. Honor looked at her with affection. "No," she answered. "There is harm that can come to a young woman that will not to an old. Also, Hawkin will protect me and Molly. And the child must not be hurt in all this. Will you not go with him?"

"It may be for long," wailed Maud, who knew that Lady Brysson regarded her, though not openly, as a woman of doubtful virtue, the rejected wife of Dick Sawtrey, possibly his brother's mistress, and a Papist to boot. By some means her love for Edwin and his for her had become a legend in the neighbourhood, tnough it was still thought that he had been set upon by thieves at the end. And even her brother Edgar no longer came to see her now that she had changed her religion.

She rode off unwillingly, Uthred by her on Bet, and Hawkin had sent one of the farm-men to conduct the party

safely to Newhall. He would not, after Maud's refusal of
him, escort them himself.

So Honor and her nephew, with the sick Molly, were left
alone at Thwaite. Trouble did not come, however; either
Arnulf had repented of his vicious fit, or else Honor's
warning had prevented him from further action. So an old
woman had routed two men. She felt proud of herself, and
she knew Hawkin was proud of her.

Maud found the time at Newhall slow to pass, and despite its
grandeur wished herself back at Thwaite, in the room she
had shared with Honor where the sheets smelled of lavender
grown in the garden. At Newhall, she was put into a small
upstairs chamber, no doubt once a servant's, with a hard bed
and cracked ewer. Life was strict, for my lady Brysson rose
very early in the morning and those who stayed in her house
must do likewise and attend at chapel, except for Sir Nigel
who rode out to hunt: she frowned when Maud said she could
not do so.

"Then say your own prayers, with that heathenish rosary;
and do not pray for the Queen's soul, for it was a judgment
on her that she died after her treatment of her father." Queen
Mary II was lately dead, and her Dutch husband desolate.

Maud liked to ride; she asked my lady if she might go out
on her own mare in the mornings. Lady Brysson refused that,
but said that the afternoons were Maud's to do with as she
liked. So Maud cantered abroad then, and covered many
miles of the countryside. One day she had a great longing to
look on Daneclere and Thwaite, even though it were only
from a far distance; the slope of the woods about Newhall
inclined down to the valley where the river ran, and beyond it
there was the house and the farm, and Biding; she would not
look towards Biding. She turned the mare's head and slowed
her to a walk, and took one of the paths between the spring
trees. It was a fine day, and pencils of pale sunlight pointed
down between the branches with their veil of early green. On
such a day she might have ridden out long ago to meet Edwin
and make love: but foremost in her mind was the thought that
they would have done the sowing by now at Thwaite, and
that the small sharp spears of new growth would be showing
in the neat furrows of the ploughed fields, like rows of
soldiers.

Dreaming on, she walked her mare straight into Arnulf's

gelding; he had been standing still among the trees, watching her come. Maud's cheeks, which had had some colour with the ride, blanched; she tried to turn back, but he cantered over and seized her reins. His eyes devoured her. "Must we be enemies?" he said. She looked more beautiful, he was thinking, than ever; her bosom had grown fuller than when she was a girl, and the fair gold of her hair had darkened to honey-colour. Otherwise she was the same, cold yet desirable; he felt the stirring that always came when he wanted a woman. He would like to lie with her; here, now, and later on a bed. He would even marry her. One must proceed cautiously, however; this was not another Molly Dilke.

"If we are enemies it is your doing, not ours," she answered him. Arnulf made pretence to hang his head, so that the dark hair fell about it, and toyed with the reins before answering.

"Do not blame me for all my fellow does. He took certain instructions of mine too literally, and I have punished him for it. There has been no further molestation at Thwaite, surely?"

"I do not know," she answered coldly. "I do not dwell at Thwaite since the servant's visit. It was thought better that I and the boy should go elsewhere."

"Then I have incommoded you more than I thought. Ah, Maud, let us be friends! Dismount and walk with me a little way, and I will give you a message to take to Thwaite in order that they may not longer be afraid."

"They are not afraid, only ready," she said; but it was long since she had had speech with anyone from outside, and she allowed him to help her out of the saddle, and to tie their two mounts' reins to a branch. A shudder took her suddenly; when had this happened before? *See, they are joined, as we will be.* And he was dead.

But Arnulf gave her no immediate cause for unease. He offered her his arm, and together they strolled, as well as he could for his limp, among the trees and moss. He made her tell him of life at Newhall, and sympathised with her over it. He could be charming, she was thinking; no doubt this charm had been exercised on Uthred, his father. Perhaps he had got over his early wildness; after all for a man to take a mistress was no unknown thing.

They had reached a grassy place. Suddenly Arnulf turned and took her by the shoulders, planting a kiss on her lips. She struggled to be free, but he laughed, and ripped her bodice. "Why, Maud, not coy?" he said. "I warrant you were not so with Edwin, in this place. Am I to treat you as a maid when I know that you are none? Other men have enjoyed your favours; why not I? Think of all we could contrive together, were you to come to Daneclere as my—"

All the time he talked he made as if to undress her; he had pinioned her hands, and with his other free grasp had pulled the torn bodice and chemise down, so that her breasts came out; he kissed and bit then, relishing the struggle she made; it was the more exciting when a wench pretended unwillingness. Moll Dilke had been too easy; here was a challenge.

Maud began to scream. He put his mouth over hers, and tried to force her down into the grass; but she jerked her head aside and kept crying out for help, and help came, suddenly, from which quarter she could not know; Hawkin, who had been returning a scythe to a tenant at one of the farms, had been making the journey on foot, partly to work out the rage and pain he still felt; he had not forgotten Maud for all her absence, and still bore on his heart the scar of the cut she had dealt him. Suddenly he heard her voice, when he had been thinking of her; and ran to the place, and saw the pair struggling, Maud and Arnulf. Hawkin's fist crashed into Arnulf's cheek; he seized him and let Maud writhe free. Then he gave two more blows to Arnulf, one with each hand, and felled him to the ground, where he lay spitting blood and a broken tooth. Maud was scrabbling at the torn remains of her bodice and chemise. Without turning to look at her, Hawkin flung her his cloak.

"Get you back, and leave me to finish him," he said, and at last turned and looked at her, pale and large-eyed as she was, with her hair dishevelled and her body hidden beneath his heavy dark cloak. It flashed through his mind that he could take her now himself; the thought was no sooner with him than it was quelled. He returned to Arnulf, who lay quiet, his face turned into the ground, his breathing rapid.

"You will not kill him?" said Maud.

"There will be no trouble." The harshness of the reply surprised her.

"Can you get into the saddle unaided, or do you expect me to hand you up?" he said bitterly. Maud gave a sob and fled; he heard her horse, presently, break through the branches a little way off and ride away. He bent to lift Arnulf; he would put him across the saddle of his own horse and it should carry him home. The rain had begun to fall before Maud reached Newhall, and when she went into the house it was in a bedraggled condition, her hair in lank locks over her shoulders, her hat missing, and her body wrapped in a man's sodden cloak. My lady, who was there to greet her, regarded her with pursed lips.

"What has happened to you?" she said, and her eyes, which had a piercing quality, appeared to look through the cloak at Maud's torn and mishandled clothing underneath. "Did you meet with some accident? Your appearance is very singular." She did not offer comfort, or wine. Maud felt her knees tremble.

"I had a fall," she said.

"A fall? Where was that? Is the mare injured?"

"The mare is safe," said Maud wearily. She became aware of young Uthred's staring blue gaze at the further side of the ingle. He was quiet and obedient here, for he had been put to a tutor who birched him when he was lazy. I wish we were both of us back at Thwaite, Maud thought. Aloud she said "I would go up and change my clothes, if it please you."

She went up and, having taken off Hawkin's cloak—how thankful she had been for its protection, its soaked warmth, its smell of wool, the farmyard, humanity!—turned to see my lady in the doorway, observing her. Maud shrank, but the merciless gaze had noted her torn bodice, her naked breasts.

"You did not fall," said Lady Brysson. "You have lain with some man. I knew well enough you were wanton when I risked having you here. It was a risk I should not have taken."

Maud put a hand over her breasts: she was aware of cold anger. "I have lain with no man," she said, "but if you must know, one made to lie with me by force, and another came and rescued me, and lent me his cloak." She would have liked to have recourse to tears; she only wished that this hard-faced woman would go away and leave her alone, that she might change into dry clothing.

"Whose cloak is it?" asked my lady coldly.

"I will not say."

"If you were mine you would be whipped until you did so. Your poor brother Gregory was innocent as a lamb, and gave no trouble here; but you are a different matter. I would as soon you left here; we do not harbour light women."

"You insult me."

"I do not, and that is the truth of it; where you are, there trouble is. The child causes none now he is under a tutor, and he may stay if his mother wishes it. But you must go. I will write to Mrs. Jansen; you had best make ready your gear, and prepare to leave in the morning."

"I shall be glad to," said Maud.

All night it rained heavily, and by morning the ways were a sodden morass. Even my lady would have let Maud stay till they should harden; but it was Maud herself who insisted on going, and she set forth with her gear in a bundle on a following servant's horse, and her body wrapped defiantly in Hawkin's cloak; it was, she told herself, the easiest way to carry so heavy a thing.

The day was dark, and they saw a lantern bobbing ahead. As they drew nearer she heard the servant say from behind her "Those be the Thwaite men, madam; they have maybe come with some word." They drew rein, and waited for the men to come up. One was a farm-hand Maud knew, and he handed her a letter.

"There is another for my lady," he said, and Maud bade him ride on and give it to Lady Brysson. She opened her own letter, its ink turned to runnels by the rain.

The writing was Honor's. Arnulf was dead. *His body was carried home by his horse, and he was dead on arrival. None knows what befell,* Honor wrote. But I know, thought Maud; and I will never breathe a word to a soul. How thankful I am that I did not give Hawkin's name to that old woman when she would have had it from me!

The news meant something else, as she realised slowly, making her way back to Thwaite. With Arnulf dead, Uthred was now the heir, with his mother in her rightful place. They could all of them go back to live at Daneclere.

ARNULF'S BODY lay under a pall without candles; the coffin had been closed early because the face had begun to blacken.

Honor stood by it and thought how she, an old woman, stood here alive in the presence of dead youth: and, remembering that the Papists had it that one might pray for the dead, murmured a prayer that Arnulf's soul might rest in peace. Her own was disturbed; had she in some manner failed Uthred in her lack of affection for his son? She did not know of a single person who had ever loved Arnulf, except his father. Love was strange. At the back of her mind was a remembrance of the letter she had received some days ago from her priest son Dick; he had finished the long Jesuit training some time since and was now posted to Genoa, where he lectured in the college there. She must write and ask him to pray for Arnulf; it might be a prayer more readily heard than her own.

A touch on her arm started her; it was the clergyman, perturbed because the dead man had boasted that he would not be buried in consecrated ground. "We do not know what change of thought comes at the moment˝of death," Honor heard herself say. "Let him be buried by his father," for she knew Uthred, at least, would welcome the body of his son. If the unquiet spirit of Arnulf haunted a place where he did not wish to be, then they could uplift him. Such things had happened elsewhere. She did not know how such decisions came to her, clear-cut as if they were a man's; it was almost as if Uthred's mind spoke through her mouth, as if he had himself been here for the burial of his son.

The parson was still talking. "They say that when he rode in, all the blood in his body had run down on to the horse's flank," he said. "What evil can have befallen him?" and she heard herself saying that Arnulf had had weak lungs and that he had no doubt had a sudden issue of blood from them, and had somehow managed to climb back into the saddle to die.

What was the truth? Whatever it was, it were best to let it be buried with Arnulf. He had had many enemies, and a man riding alone was easy prey.

She looked round the house he had left. The hall and its furnishings were smeared and dusty, the floor foul. "Give orders that the house is to be cleaned before we come into it," she said to one of the men. He gaped and said there were no maidservants. "Then find them," said Honor sharply; no doubt every maid in the place had fled from Arnulf and his lusts. Now that she and young Uthred, Maud and poor Moll Dilke were to return to Daneclere, things would be different, the house made sweet and clean again, the kitchen seemly. She had already walked through room after room, finding dirt everywhere; it must go. It was almost as if she came here again as a bride.

When she reached Thwaite once more, Maud was in the kitchen; the younger woman ran to her and burst into tears on her shoulder. "You do not weep for Arnulf," said Honor drily.

"No—never that—they have sent me away from Newhall. I was journeying here when I had your letter."

She blurted out the tale, and halfway through it Honor looked about her to ensure that none heard, no servant, not even Gwenny, passing behind the door or outside the window. She put Maud from her and went to look. There was no one.

"Where is the cloak?" she said. Maud stared at her, slowly reckoning the meaning of what she had been asked. "I put it behind the stable door, where Hawkin always keeps it," she said. Her face was wan beneath the reddened eyelids, the mouth half-open in terror.

"That is good; you must know nothing of it," said Honor. "You told Lady Brysson what had befallen?"

"No more than I need, and no names. I do not like her."

"Nor she you, that is evident. But I think we are safe; they will bury him tomorrow, and had there been any questioning the funeral would have been prevented by the magistrate." She closed her eyes for an instant; in Uthred's later lifetime he had been a Justice of the Peace. So was Sir Nigel. Even now, how much depended on Maud's silence! She thanked God the younger woman had been discreet.

They heard Hawkin go by. "He will not come in because I am here," said Maud. Honor took a lantern and went out to the stables, where Hawkin was ladling mash for the horses. He had shared the house with her of late.

When Honor returned she said "I have told him what to say. Neither of you met in the wood, or elsewhere; he knows nothing of the death, and you know only what I have told you. If it should indeed be asked, say two men you did not know attacked and saved you. But I do not think it will be." She stopped, aware of her fear at the least sound; but it was only a horse stamping against the stables' cold.

"He did it for my sake," said Maud.

"Then never show you know it. That is the most you can do for him."

"I will do it," said Maud. She was staring down at her fingers. Honor took off her own cloak and set about preparing supper, and presently the younger woman, still dazed, came and helped her. Hawkin came in at last to the savoury smell of stew. Nothing was said, and not a look passed between him and Maud. They ate in silence, relishing the stew, and presently Hawkin let himself out to go to his old quarters in the place above the stables, carrying the warmed sheets Honor had got ready. Soon the women would be back at Daneclere, and he could come back again to live in the house at Thwaite.

4

"TELL Mr. Hawkin I must have lavender and dill, because the fish stinks."

She saw the servant ride off, and turned again to the endless task of freshening Daneclere, at the same time thinking how they could not, or not yet, have done without Hawkin in the matter of removing themselves from Thwaite. Hawkin had lent them men to bring the baggage and furnishings across; Hawkin had seen to it that the farmhouse was searched afterwards to see that they had left nothing behind; Hawkin had engaged more men to carry poor Moll, who by now could not walk, comfortably on an improvised litter over the causeway to the great house from which she had once fled. Hawkin even, though he had never tended any herb-garden, would know the names of the herbs and would send Honor what she asked for; as yet there had been neither time nor season to begin the task of freeing from choked weeds her old Daneclere plot, now a wilderness.

The house was as bad, or worse. Now that Arnulf was gone she had contrived to hire four young maids, but they were raw and needed training; Arnulf after the flight of Moll had given up all pretence of keeping the place as it should be kept, living on here alone with the few men he retained, dicing and drinking with them late into the night. Honor had found empty bottles everywhere, filled chamber-pots, stinking linen, dirty windows, tarnished pewter and silver, old wood stained with grease and ale. At first the sight had almost reduced her to despair, thinking she could never right it; then she had taken heart, and had begun as always, attacking a small part first, till by degrees she should have cleared the whole. She herself had cleaned the mullions till they sparkled like crystal; had set Maud and Gwenny to bring down all the linen to the kitchens, where they had soaked it in lye for three days before carrying it out to dry on the bushes in the clean open air. After it was dry Maud had mended and checked it; she had no objection to doing such tasks, but no doubt would not help in the garden for fear of spoiling her hands. That, as had been seen, would in any case have to wait: Honor still relied for her herbs on Hawkin.

She was, moreover, anxious that he should not cut himself off from them. Not only had his strong arm and iron will been of use to them in the past (he could discipline Uthred, who needed it), but Honor was fond of him. "He is my nephew, Robin's son, almost as my own," she thought, and wished that Maud were less high-flown in her notions and would, as he desired, take Hawkin for her husband. That he still loved Maud she knew: no one except herself could witness the glances he cast at Maud's back when he thought no one would see; he adored her "and Maud treats him as though he were made of dirt, or were not there, even after he saved her from Arnulf." But that was a matter mercifully overlooked and forgotten; most folk were glad enough to have Arnulf in his grave without asking how he came there so soon. There were other happenings, small in themselves but leading to greater matters. One day a small thin woman with gentle eyes and a mouth indrawn for lack of teeth, humbly clad in a homespun gown and linen cap, asked for Honor. When the latter came down from where she had been sorting sheets, the woman curtseyed and said "Oh, my lady, I am Molly Dilke's mother; how does she?"

"She is very ill, and will not get better, we fear. She will be glad to see you." Honor did not comment on the title given her by the woman; the word "madam" was still unknown to lowly folk. She turned to lead Moll's mother up to her room; she would do it herself rather than send a servant. "Molly and I have become good friends," she said. "She is a sweet girl; it troubles me that there is little hope for her."

"Oh, my lady, my lady, I would have come the sooner, but 'twas only two days since I heard of it, and of Mr. Arnulf's death; I'd thought her kept as a fine lady all this while, and Tom Dilke knew earlier, and did not tell me. I'd stay and help nurse her, my lady, if you will give me leave."

"But what will Tom say?" They had almost reached the upstairs room; sunlight slanted in on the upper passages of Daneclere, free now of their dust. Honor turned at the top step to look round at the little woman. The latter gazed back adoringly; already this tall lady seemed like a goddess, full of kindness and beauty; for any old enough to remember Papist days she would have seemed like Our Lady of Pity.

"He can say what he chooses, for many children I bore him, and they all died but Moll; then he sells Moll before my eyes to the first fine gentleman as asks for her, knowing she'd never be wed because of the sickness. A mean man he's been to me, and us all; he can look after hissen well enough."

They had reached the door, and Honor stood back to let the mother go in. She heard a faint cry of pleasure from the bed, smiled, and went back downstairs. When the time for the meal came, she sent a dish of food and a noggin of ale upstairs for Moll's mother as well as for Moll, who ate little now. Afterwards the old woman came down with the two empty platters and flagons.

"My mind is the lighter for seeing her, and hers the same; poor soul, she's changed, as they all did. My lady, will ye let me stay? I can help with tending her and with the housework, all number of things. I am not useless. I was housemaid once at Newhall, ere my Lady Brysson came to wed her lord." The toothless mouth closed on a snap; it was evident that even Tom Dilke had been preferable to Lady Brysson.

Honor let her stay, but sent a man to tell her husband. No word came; no doubt the mean fellow found it cheaper with no wife to feed, now she no longer gave him pleasure. Mistress Dilke—she asked them, surprisingly, to call her Rosemary—made herself useful from aptitude as well as gratitude. She could sew, mend, launder linen, and would help in the kitchens if one of the new maids was sick or had her courses. Poor Molly also was happy, because for that part of the day when she had had of necessity to be left alone, she

now had the company of her mother, diligently sewing young
Uthred's shirts or carrying water back and forth to wash the
sick girl, who sweated greatly because of her disease.
Rosemary would also empty chamber-pots and burn herbs in
a shovel afterwards to sweeten the air. The arrangement
suited everyone, and Dilke's wife stayed on.

Honor returned to the present. Stinking fish, rancid meat,
sour butter, these were the things Arnulf had latterly accepted
from the servants and tradesmen, being by then lost to
everything but the taste of wine. She must make it clear, once
for all time, that slovenly service was not for her. Daneclere
had once been a place of shining wood and clean food,
fragrant linen and comfortable dry beds; it should be so again.

Young Uthred needed a tutor. The suggestion had been made
that Mr. Poole, who had had charge of him while he was at
Newhall, should be brought to Daneclere. This had raised
such a yell of rage that Honor had hastily abandoned the
notion, especially as the boy seemed to have learned little
under that gentleman, despite the birchings. Meantime,
Maud supervised his reading and writing, and Mr. Southe,
the parson, spared time from his own duties to come and
teach Uthred his Latin. "He is not apt," he would say sadly,
afterwards. Uthred seemed apt at little except eating and
drinking, also riding his pony which he loved; he loved and
was friends with all the world, and would no doubt turn into
a pleasant country gentleman in due course. "But you must
learn the things gentlemen know, or they will think you a
savage," said Uthred's mother to him. The blue eyes sparkled
and the little boy gave his gap-toothed smile. He had a stocky
body and, still, short legs for his bulk. "I can cipher and
read," he said. "I can read a letter; I don't care for books.
When I am grown I shall hunt in the mornings and drink at
night, like Arnulf." She regretted that he remembered Arnulf,
and seemed to admire the latter's ways. There was no one
Uthred disliked, except Mr. Poole: he had been a favourite
even with Lady Brysson, who used to feed him marchpane, a
possibility which daunted anyone else who knew that lady.
He was beloved of all the servants and even of poor wasted
Moll, whom Honor would not let him visit often or long lest
he catch her sickness. But it was difficult to picture Uthred as
ill; since his birth he had enjoyed bouncing health, and no
doubt if he were not by the end a scholar, he would atone by

being a sportsman. Mr. Southe urged Honor to send him to school.

"He will meet other boys there, and become ashamed if he cannot compete with them," he said hopefully. But Uthred's progress was not such that any famous school would admit him. In the end Mr. Southe found an establishment which was run by two impoverished gentlemen who had returned with the late King, found his court not to their taste, and had taken up schoolmastering. But even for entry to this lowly place Uthred would require coaching, and Mr. Southe also found a young parson waiting for a benefice, who would be willing to come to Daneclere and din knowledge into Uthred's head.

The parson came, and proved to be a meek young man whose use of the birch could never be formidable. He was however an able scholar, and as Uthred liked him he learnt his declensions, the verbs, and a little French. Honor also asked if the new tutor might take family prayers at Daneclere, a habit which had been discontinued since she and Uthred had lived there. Each morning, therefore, the household assembled, the young maidservants in fresh linen caps and collars, with their hands and shoes clean; and the family, including Maud, who dressed in a way which was not of the latest fashion but which suited her; she wore dark gowns still, but had taken to adding a collar and deep cuffs of fragile lace: her honey-gold hair was caught up in a great knot at the back, with loose ringlets falling forwards at the sides over her cheeks. The new tutor fell heavily in love, and would cast despairing looks at Maud's bent head during prayers and the reading. But it was all of it useless, for she paid no heed to him.

Honor was concerned about Maud; she lived the life of a nun, or of a woman far older than her age; she had no diversions, except the knot-work she did in her leisure. If she were ever to marry it must surely be now; but Maud herself made her position clear, one evening, after the work of the day was done and supper over. They sat on the grass, for it was summer, and the cleaning and weeding had already made a pretty lawn. Maud might have been a dryad, with the evening sun bright on her hair; the young tutor was absent, and Uthred in bed. Honor said something of the matter which weighed on her mind, and which only made Maud answer bitterly.

"I know my state well; I am neither what I should be, not what folk say I am. My Lady Brysson thinks me wanton; had I been so it had been better for me. My mother died at my birth, so I killed her; you yourself have been more than a mother to me, and how have I repaid you? Your elder son put me away; then I had a lover who loved me, and my brothers killed him; ay, you know of it. Now I am past the age when women wed, yet I cannot ride out alone without some adventure befalling me which ends in death, and someone's blame for it, and all for me." She passed her hands wearily over her face. "I sometimes ask God why I was born," she said, "or why I could not die with my mother. How could I wed any man, only to bring evil to him?"

Honor answered carefully; her heart had turned over at the mention of Edwin's murderers. She had always known, as Maud had said; but it had not been spoken of between them.

"It is a joy for me to have you here," she said, "for otherwise I should be much alone. But there are others who love you; you know who they are. As long as one is loved, one is of use on God's earth. It is only when the heart itself dies that one is dead."

"Ah, madam, then I have been so these many years."

There was no shaking her out of her mood, and presently, as it was growing dark, they rose and went into the house.

5

MOLL DILKE died when Uthred was in his second term at school. After the fleshless body had been washed, laid out and coffined, Honor took time to write a letter to her son; he had loved Molly well.

The burial itself troubled the parson. He came to Honor with a furrowed brow, having no brethren to lean upon now the erstwhile tutor had departed to his benefice. The question of burying a whore in consecrated ground troubled the good man's conscience; and everyone knew the dead woman had been no less.

Honor blazed out at him. "I doubt your Master would have made another ruling. Do as you will with your graveyard for righteous souls which include, as God sees me, Arnulf Jansen. We will bury Moll ourselves where she will be watched over and loved. She was never a whore of her own free will, and a sweeter girl never breathed."

Mr. Southe quavered that he would write to take counsel of the Archbishop; but poor Moll's body would stink in its coffin long before word could come from Canterbury, and Honor had the body buried in a place in her own Daneclere garden, where Moll on days when she was well enough had used to look down on her from her window. Later Honor had a stone of red granite placed above the grave.

In this place lyeth MARY DILKE,
who dyed at Daneclere on the thirteenth
day of February 1696,
aged Twenty Foure Yeares.

Afterwards, Rosemary Dilke, her face set, had come to ask if she might stay on at Daneclere. "Indeed we should be hard put to it without you," said Honor truly, "but you must take some money." So Molly's mother and Gwenny for a time shared a bed, and Rosemary helped in the house as she had always done, but for a set wage. There was to be another place for Gwenny soon.

Honor had ridden over herself to tell Hawkin Thwaite of Molly's death; partly she knew that it would come best from herself, and partly it was a time, which had come now and again in her life, when she must be free of Daneclere. The little parson's uncharitable words had stung her; if Moll was a whore, who would gain the kingdom of heaven?

Hawkin soothed her, as he often did, not by any speech he made but by his very presence, hard as a rock and as unchanging. He seemed to have grown no older, though perhaps more solid, than he had been as a young man; his black hair was almost free of grey, his face of lines, showing only the strong planes and bones it had done since Hawkin was twenty. He must be solitary here, Honor thought; and wondered why, after so many years of despairing of Maud, he did not take a wife. At least some easier woman would bring him comfort. Honor spoke of it to him, pretending to tease lest he be angry.

"I can get myself comfort," Hawkin replied shortly. He had come in with a brace of rabbits, which he was making ready for the pot. "Come, eat rabbit-stew with me, Honor, and tell me if any of your grand fare at Daneclere can outdo it. I live well, I warrant you."

"With no one to wash your shirts and sheets, except yourself and some ignorant farm-lad! Why will you not let me send Gwenny to you? She is quiet, and would never trouble you, and I need her the less now Molly's mother stays with us at the house."

Hawkin rubbed his hands on a rough cloth to dry them. "If so be she will not set her cap at me, she can come," he admitted. "She can maybe sweep and clean somewhat while I am in the fields. Certainly Thwaite is not as it was while you lived here, Honor."

Honor promised that Gwenny would have no designs, as most women had, on Hawkin. Within two days, when the funeral was over, she brought Gwenny over with her gear, and saw her started in the kitchen at Thwaite, which she already knew well enough. At the least, now, Hawkin would have a hot meal waiting ready for him at night, without his having to cook it. And if Gwenny did—but this was not likely—set her cap, as he put it, at Hawkin, and win him, it served Maud right, Honor found herself thinking. But she knew in her heart that Gwenny had done with all men.

Some days later a reply came from Uthred, who had received her letter at his school.

My derre Mother,
I was werrie sad to have your News of poor Moll. Now she is Gone to where she will Suffer no more.
A boy here is Teaching me to Wressil.
                    Your sonne,
                    Uthred Jansen.
If it please you, may I have some more Rasens and Marchpane?

6

"KING JAMES is dead in France, and they say kept every tooth in his head sound to the end."

Honor, who had kept her own, listened indulgently to the spiced gossip of Lady Brysson, who now that she had grown old confused homely details with great events. She had come over, as she sometimes did after church, to drink tea with Honor and exchange the news of the day. Maud, who had never forgiven the old woman for her own dismissal, had retired to her room.

The tidings of James II's death meant less than they might once have done, for it was thirteen years now since he had fled from England at the time of the Protestant Revolution, leaving the throne vacant for his daughter and her husband. But Lady Brysson clung to the older dynasty, though she was no Papist. She was wearing mourning today for King James. Honor was not; she took little heed who sat on the throne, provided they did not interfere with her liberty; and she could say for Dutch William that he had never done that. She filled the delicate fluted tea-cup a second time; it was a pleasant habit, introduced to fashionable circles by Mary of Modena, when in Scotland.

Lady Brysson, despite the soothing tea, seemed ill at ease today; she fidgeted, and turned the handleless cup this way and that, then downed the contents as if it were physic. "We have a visitor at Newhall," she ventured, staring into the empty cup.

"Indeed? Yet he was not in church with you." Honor said it not in any carping or inquisitive way, merely as a means of sustaining their talk; but my lady sat bolt upright, and looked her between the eyes.

"You are a sharp woman, Honor, to be sure—a mighty sharp woman! Of all people, I know it will be safe with you. Sir Nigel takes the risk of it."

"I am sorry Sir Nigel is at risk."

"Ay; there are many curious matters afoot, and a man with a good conscience scarce knows what to do, and as for us women—suffice it that I came today to say this, apart from the pleasure of talking with you and drinking your tay; he would like to meet with you, here if it may be done. Sir Nigel will bring him."

"Sir Nigel will be welcome, and his visitor." Honor narrowed her eyes. "When will he bring him here?" she said. "If it is a risk, it had best not be to the hall; bring him to the accounts-office, through the little door. Then I can make pretence, if I have to, that his coming concerns the rents, and no one will look at him too closely."

"Did I not say you were a sharp woman?" observed my lady. "My husband will come with him tomorrow, about noon, and will take him straight to the office to see you alone."

Honor went down next day after the sound of riders had entered the yard, and found the visitor already established in his place. Sir Nigel Brysson stood by the casement, looking out, unwilling to spy on their reunion. From the chair, wearing a black wig which greatly altered his appearance, Father Richard Sawtrey, of the Society of Jesus, rose and held out his arms.

"Dick! I was certain of it. What do you here?"

"I will leave you now," smiled Sir Nigel. He kissed Honor's hand and then went out, for he bore none of his wife's ill-will, to walk in the garden with Maud. The mother and son sat down and talked of many things, and suddenly the priest said "Mother, I ask your forgiveness if in all this I have offended or hurt you. But you will know I could do no other."

"Are you still posted to Genoa?"

"No, I was there as a scholastic. Now I am a priest, ordained in France, to which I must shortly return."

"You cannot stay longer?" She could not tear her eyes from the face beneath the black wig. Dick, who had always had the indeterminate features, the uncertain air, of his father, had grown with hard concerted purpose and training into a narrow-faced, keen, subtle and clever man; she could feel the power in him as they talked. "He could persuade me, I believe, to change my very faith," she thought, knowing she would regret it as soon as he had gone. But Dick made no such attempt, only answering rather sadly,

"No, mother, I cannot stay longer. I had to obtain leave to take the time to see you at all; and as I would not stay under the same roof as Maud for her own sake, I took advantage of Sir Nigel's hospitality; he knew, for I wrote to him, that I was coming here."

"You had some other mission, then? Perhaps I must not ask."

"No, my dear, you must not ask." His face grew sad; in his

mind was a recollection of two ornate rooms, one in St. Germain and the other in England. In the first, a gentle, gallant, cherry-lipped, dark-eyed boy had still been quiet with grief for the loss of the father he had loved; in the second, at the Cockpit in London, a stout, ailing, obstinate woman would give Richard no hearing when he tried to speak to her of the boy. "If you come from my half-brother, I will not hear you," she said, and he had known then that the Princess Anne of Denmark had been won over already by her Whig favourite, Lady Marlborough, whose imperious red-gold elegance and tip-tilted nose he had observed in the anteroom. He had tried, with every nuance of that developed persuasiveness that had been the reason for sending him on this mission, to change the Princess, even make her listen to a point of view which was not her own; but all she would do was to repeat, like a parrot, the words that had been put into her mouth and convinced her, by now, that they came from her own mind.

"If you come from my half-brother, I will not hear you."

She had lost her only living son; the true and charming picture he had been ready to draw of the boy who might have consoled her, the good, devout, obedient, fatherless boy thirteen years old and in every way a Stuart, had never been drawn: they had bowed him out, his mission unfulfilled. He must return now and report his failure to the General of the Jesuits; to Louis XIV by way of the channels through which Louis, at King James's death, had unofficially reached him; to the boy's widowed mother; and to none else. James III would never rule England by the will of his half-sister, next in line, at William's death, to the Protestant throne. But they would try again to persuade her; they would try, while she lived.

Almost a year later further news was to come to Daneclere. William III had been out riding and had been thrown from his horse by a molehill, piercing a lung by a broken bone, and so died. Queen Anne reigned at Whitehall; but up and down the country there were toasts drunk to the little gentleman in black velvet, the mole who had made the mound which threw the Dutchman's horse. Honor heard of it, and a remark of Dick's which she had not understood at the time, became clear.

"Mother, do you have blackbirds in your garden?"

The Black Boy, saved after Worcester fight. The little
gentleman in black velvet; a black wig. The Blackbird, the
young boy with the dark eyes of his Italian mother, whom
Stuart supporters wanted to succeed Anne on the throne
despite the fact that young James Stuart was a Papist and
had been reared abroad. Black, the colour of mourning.

She said aloud to Maud, who was with her and knew of
Dick's visit, for he had left her the address of a priest who
would say Mass twenty miles off,

"My father was right. Old Noll Cromwell, whom they
hanged up at Tyburn Tree a twelvemonth after he died,
knew better how the heart of England beats than any Papist
prince, saving your presence! If James Stuart sets foot in
England after his rights there will be bloodshed; that I
know."

"Uthred is hardly old enough to fight yet," said Maud
comfortingly.

7

THE TIME came for Uthred to leave school, and he came
home, as pleased to be back at Daneclere as Honor was to
have him there: but he seemed to know very little more than
when he first left it. Cambridge was out of the question, and
he himself had only one ambition: to be master of the hunt.

In spite of herself, Honor had nursed hopes for him; now it
seemed he had inherited neither her will nor his father's wit.
It was purposeless to try any longer to turn him into
something other than he was; and at least he was honest, gay,
and loving; not vicious like Arnulf, nor devious like Dick. She
must make the best of it, and the best was not so bad.

His drinking troubled her. She was not to know that for a
year or more, the money she had innocently sent for
marchpane and raisins had been spent, as in course of nature,
at the Lamb and Flag tavern, which was convenient enough
to the school to let the older boys who had any money sample
its wines and ales, and also—this was never revealed to
Honor—the favours of the taproom maid, who would entertain any virile young gentleman in possession of a fourpenny

piece. The experience had in fact done Uthred no harm, and
satisfied his curiousity as to one aspect of the life a civilised
man should know. He was never to be greatly interested in
women. But, with the appetite for food and drink which
seemed to have been born in him and would never leave him,
Uthred could already put down more bottles in a day than
anyone Honor had known in all her life. She was horrified;
her last remaining child would turn himself into a toper, a
drunken hunting-squire if nothing worse. She mounted a
horse and rode over, a thing she seldom did, to ask counsel of
Sir Nigel Brysson at Newhall, for she felt incapable of
further decision over Uthred at his age.

Sir Nigel hummed and hawed; she had the impression he
hardly listened. Drinking in a young man was nothing new,
and he was vexed by the state of health of his lady, who at
last, in her old age, had persuaded herself that she was with
child, and bore a great belly proudly before her. It would be
the death of her, as he and the physicians knew though she
did not. In the face of this trouble, Honor's own problem
seemed to her paltry, and she made lighter of it than she had
intended. It had, in fact, she felt, been wise to get away from
Daneclere for some hours, to let the air clear her head; the
smell of wine was always in the hall now, and offended her.
Also, her thoughts had regained their balance. Young men
had their diversions, perhaps their vices; it was a part of
being a man. She prayed that Uthred would soon achieve his
heart's desire over the hunt; at least he was never too drunk to
swing his short legs into the saddle and ride off, coming home
at the end of the day mud-splashed and happy, roaring at the
servants, who loved him, to pull off his boots, put wood on the
fire, bring him a bottle and glass, and begone. She would see
to it that there was plenty of supper for him to eat; it helped
to do away with the effects of the wine.

The year passed. Throughout the country men were
talking—Honor learned this in the few moments she permitted herself to gossip with neighbours at the lych-gate after
the weekly morning service—of the Earl of Marlborough's
victories over the French. Never had there been so great a
general, and with his wife Sarah the power behind Queen
Anne's throne it could be said the couple ruled the land. Yet
somewhere conflict crept in; Sarah Marlborough was said to

be domineering and so sure of her position that she had
grown tactless, even insolent to the Queen.

Lady Brysson died of her tumour in the autumn. Honor
and young Uthred, the last-named sober enough to stand up,
attended the funeral service and Uthred followed with the
mourners to the grave. Honor tried to think of the dead
woman's more amiable qualities, and to ignore the three tall
men with grey hair who had ridden in from Biding. In all the
years since Edwin's death not so much as a glance had passed
between them except that time when, perforce, she had
received Edgar at Daneclere for Maud's sake. Someone had
told her that since his father's death Gregory Farmiloe was
even more subject to fits and must be kept under control. "So
they will have his money for their use," she thought, then
tried to turn her thinking.

Two months after his wife's death Sir Nigel Brysson came to
Honor to ask her to marry him. Being a gentleman of
punctilious habit, he had first asked Uthred's permission to
address his mother. He, diverted, raised his head, with its
complexion by now a curious plum-pink which made his hair
seem almost yellow by contrast, stared at his elders, and said
"By all means, go at her; no fence is too high," and relapsed
into silence.

Honor refused. Her love for Uthred's father had been so
complete in its knowledge of his for her that she could never
remarry. "Do not let this end our friendship," she begged.
"We have both enough years to regard such a matter with
humour, I believe."

"'Tis damned lonely at Newhall, that's the way of it,"
replied her suitor. "Never thought I'd see the day when I'd
miss Nancy! She wasn't an easy woman, as ye will know, but
I dare say we grew accustomed to one another. Now there's
no one to listen while I talk, except my damned bailiff, and
he's deaf of an ear."

"Come here and sup as often as you can," Honor begged
him. "There is no need for loneliness when you are nigh
Daneclere."

"Hospitable of ye, m'dear; maybe I will. When does this
young fellow marry?"

Uthred turned a glazed eye upon him. "M'mother 'ud have
me wed an heiress, a woman who looks like a horse. I'm fond
enough of the beasts, but in one's bed— "

Honor regarded her fingers. The heiress in question was Sir Nigel's niece and she hoped he would miss the allusion. His countenance still beamed good-nature, so she hoped for the best.

"Sound reason for marryin' a damned ugly woman is, she's bound to be good-natured; got to," said Sir Nigel. "Good wine of yours, this, my boy; ma'am. Pleasant to know I'm not unwelcome if I ride by. Honor, Honor, your servant."

When the time arrived for Uthred's coming-of-age Honor made great preparation. It was for the first time; Dick's had not been a temper to endure display, and with Edwin there had been no time. So she made every effort to show a board which would be remembered and talked of as long as anyone present lived. There was to be free ale for all the tenantry, a table on trestles on the grass if it were fine; sucking-pig, roast beef and sides of ham and mutton, fruit in great dishes, and lemon syllabub in glasses. Uthred had invited friends from all over the country; many had been with him at school. They came early; the house resounded to the clatter of their booted feet, and when they went to the hunt it was like an army riding out; besides horses they brought their body-servants, and the attics, where these must make shift beside Honor's men and maids, were full to overflowing. Hawkin, who had said he would come if he had time from the summer hay, lent Gwenny for as long as she was needed to help in the house. Rosemary and Honor had their hands full, and were glad of her; Honor spared a moment to remember the pale, lank-haired girl who had come to Daneclere long ago. Now her hair was white, under a servant's cap, but her face had changed little; the eyes peered out wistfully, like those of an old child. Perhaps great tragedy or violence froze the process of growing old, so that the victim stayed as he or she had been at the time, in mind and body. If that were so, Honor thought, she herself was no older than at Edwin's death, or at the elder Uthred's at Daneclere. But there was no time to dwell even on that, and there was also the need to hope that it would not rain, for that would spoil the feasting.

On the day itself there were clouds in the morning, but by the time of the feast these had cleared away. The tenants came in their best clothes; many of them were seeing Uthred for the first time. They marvelled at his bright hair, and remembered Mr. Edwin. He walked about among them,

toasting them and being toasted in ale; helped himself to
sucking-pig, then strolled indoors, where his friends waited to
drink his health in wine. The table was loaded here also, and
a smell of good cooking came from the kitchen. Honor was
nowhere to be seen; in fact she was basting a fowl, in a linen
apron among the servants. She could never be idle while there
were tasks to be done, and it was long now since she had
abandoned the pretence of becoming a fine lady after the
fashion of Mrs. Anna, born a Mountchurch.

The toasts went round. After a while they ceased to have
any propriety and became more and more ribald. Bursts of
laughter interrupted the wine-drinking, and what was being
said could hardly be heard as everyone was talking at once.
The young men, in their fashionable perrukes, frogged coats
after the manner of Marlborough, and steenkirks ironed to a
degree, sat or stood, depending on the room made for them;
Uthred himself stood on the table. Once Honor stopped her
basting and heard, in a matter of moments, from three or four
toastmasters,

"Uthred, damn him! May he live to be a hundred and we
will all of us come back here, quick or dead."

"The King over the water." There was a silver basin,
which had been set down with water in it; some passed their
glasses across it, others spat.

"Viceroy Sarah."

"The little gentleman in b—" "Ah, Harry, never say
you've joined the Jacks! That mole is dead and buried under
his own molehill; 'tis time for a better toast."

"The King over the water."

"The Blackbird, and may he never rule over us. D'ye hear
the news? They are sending us a damned German when the
Queen dies, and he can't speak our language."

"Long life to the Queen, God bless her."

"The King over the water."

"Uthred, damn him, and— "

Uthred stood among them, hair aflame, eyes blazing, face
plum-red. He raised his glass and drained it, as a thousand of
his Danish forebears had done during their raids from the
long ships. "To my mother," he yelled, "to the finest woman
that ever lived; to Daneclere, to— "

Among the noise and laughter, there was a crashing sound.
The laughter ceased and there was silence. A shuffling of feet
and a pushing back of chairs came, as though the company

had drawn away; then there were steps, slow, unwilling steps, to somewhere near at hand; then again silence.

It was Gwenny who came to Honor, her face white, her child's eyes full of tears. "Madam, madam, he has fallen; will you come to him?"

Honor went. She almost ran across the flagged kitchen and down the length of the hall. They saw her coming and fell back, respectfully, half drunk as they were, having been shocked back to their sober senses. Uthred lay half across the table, among smashed glasses and silver tumbled aside: wine dribbled from his mouth. Her first thought was one of disgust that he should make a show of himself here, on this day, before his friends, before them all. It was only when she went and tried to lift him in her arms that she knew he was dead.

8

IT WAS raining on the day they buried him. Afterwards Honor came back to the house and wandered aimlessly from attic to cellar to hall. She had the feeling less of grief—that, savage and bitter, was not yet past—than of hopelessness. All of her life had been lived in vain. There was no heir either to Daneclere or to Thwaite; after her own death both houses would pass into the hands of strangers. She had never loved Daneclere till now; she touched every piece of furniture, chests, cupboards, curtains, sideboards, beds. She ran her fingers over the embroidery she herself had done, with patience, through Richard Sawtrey's day, through Uthred's day. Doing so she saw her hand clearly; it was wrinkled and discoloured, the hand of an old woman. She caught sight of herself in a mirror and her hair, beneath the widow's veil, was white.

She sat down at last in her accustomed place in the hall. So would she sit, she was thinking, until one day death came and took her as it had taken her husbands, taken her sons.

"I have lived in vain," she said aloud. All about her was silence. In the kitchens, the servants went about their customary duties quietly, as befitted a household in mourning. One must eat, sleep, pass the days, then die. How old would she have grown before death came, or would God in His mercy let it come soon? Yet in herself she was still the bride who had come to Daneclere long ago to marry Richard Sawtrey without love; the same who, years later and for love, married Uthred Jansen; and had borne them both sons, only for this, in the end; this silence.

A shadow moved at the further side of the hall. It was Maud, coming towards her in her black dress. Maud had never aged. The sight of her was as the sight of frozen youth. pale face free of wrinkles, hair smooth and a trifle dulled. Nothing more could touch Maud now and Honor wondered why she herself should feel free of resentment for the younger woman. I myself, she thought, after all, have lived. She died years since.

"I wanted a word with you," said Maud. "May we speak now?" Her hands, pale waxen hands like a doll's, plucked at her dress. For whom is she mourning? Honor thought bitterly. It was not for Uthred but Edwin, dead long ago.

"Say what you will," she replied. Maud sat down at the further side of the settle and began to fumble nervously with her speech, unlike herself. She is over forty, Honor thought; yet one still thinks of her as a young girl.

Maud said "I grieve for you that you have no heir. Perhaps I— "

She flushed, and the colour flooded over her face and neck in the way it had used to do in her youth. "I am not yet past childbearing," she said. "If it would please you and make you less sad, I would marry Hawkin. If we had a child it would solace you, I believe. Do you think me unfeeling in that I speak of it so soon? Whenever I heard of Uthred's death I thought: this is what God wants me to do."

She flung up her hands suddenly in front of her face. "If it could have been Edwin's child, only Edwin's!" she cried aloud. She looks more of a living woman than for many a day, Honor thought with detachment; and stirred herself from her own hopelessness to think of Maud. It is true that we both loved Edwin, she told herself; she in her way, I in mine. She said gently,

"It is hard on you to have to marry and bear when you would not. Has your heart no direction in this?" A while back, she reminded herself, she was calling Hawkin Thwaite a low-born churl and bastard; he kissed her feet and saved her virtue, and she thought nothing of it, or of him. "Would a

child in your arms solace you also?" she asked Maud. "If
not— "

"Nothing will solace me," said Maud coldly. "If you wish
it, I will tell Hawkin that I am willing to wed him. If you do
not, matters can go on as they are."

"What of Hawkin?" Honor asked. He has waited many a
year, she was thinking, and has never loved any but Maud.
Will such a marriage console him? Will it matter that the
loving is all on his part, the endurance on hers? Will he
resent being bedded with a woman of marble?

Maud shrugged. Hawkin could have her body, as a part of
the bargain. Her heart was no longer hers to give.

Hawkin and Maud were married in the upper room at
Daneclere late on an October day. Outside the leaves were
whirling and falling, long free of their summer green. The
colour of the fields and woods had dulled and was not yet
bright. Hawkin had a strange look at the back of his eyes, a
red glow like that of an angry animal, contrasting strangely
with the grey streaks that showed now in his hair. He made
the responses quickly and without emotion and when the time
came for him to kiss his bride, embraced her hard and briefly
and left the imprint about her mouth in a swift red weal.
There were few guests because of the mourning. Maud's
brothers had not been bidden.

The couple were bedded and left alone at last. Hawkin had
uttered few words to Maud since their betrothal and spoke
none now. If she had hoped that he would be gentle with her,
having waited long, this was not so. He let it be felt that he
had not forgiven the long years of waiting, the hope deferred
or broken, the insult, the many unkindnesses. He took his
wife as if to force her to repay all of this four-fold, handling
even the fair globes of her breasts so that, next day, bruises
showed above her bodice. Maud bit her lips, and did not cry
out whatever he might do; throughout the night he used her
hard, without talk or acts of love. By the morning, when she
awoke, he was already gone to his work at Thwaite.

One thing Hawkin had done which would please both his
bride and Honor, to whom Maud spoke no word of the way
she had been treated. Later, it was proved that he had got her
pregnant from the wedding-night. Maud would fulfil her
promise. The rest she must endure.

The winter came and went, leaving traces of slush and snow well into February. They had not had much merrymaking at Christmas. The house stood silent, and Thwaite in its turn was grey and still, the frozen earth too hard to plough. No one lived there now except farm-hands and servants; Hawkin had taken his place at Daneclere.

He was no less taciturn, and Maud never spoke of how the marriage sped. She showed her pregnancy by now, the thickened body straining her gown; she seemed in good enough health. More than this, Honor saw, Hawkin had despite himself acquired a new gentleness, Maud a new contentment. Perhaps, with accustoming, they would find affection in one another; a man and a woman did not always know the height of passion she herself had experienced with Uthred. It was perhaps better to live as all of them did now, quietly, with no crisis or sudden anger to set the house in an uproar, as in times past. It was from here that Ned and, later, Edwin had ridden out to die, Gwenllian to be hanged, Wolffe to savour the knife, Barbary never to return while living. Old age was this; a quietness. She looked forward to holding Maud's child.

The birth was to be in summer. It seemed long in coming; the spears of green thrust presently through the hard earth, then it was sowing-time; Hawkin would be out from dawn till dust, striding across the causeway at Thwaite, then home again for his supper. By day Honor and Maud sewed baby-clothes. They talked a little. One day Maud said, out of silence, "If the child is a boy, I would like him to be called after Edwin."

Honor turned a shrewd, gentle gaze on her. "The child's father may well take it amiss, were it so; could not you call him Robert, after Hawkin's father, then maybe Edwin's name to come after?"

"As you wish," said Maud, and went on with her sewing.

The episode disturbed Honor; it seemed to argue a purpose in Maud not to live through the birth. She seemed already, in many ways, to be making ready to leave life; one day Honor found her burning letters, and she had given away much of her lighter clothing to servants, as if the summer, for her, would not come again. "She is too young to die," Honor told herself repeatedly. But if it was to be, it would be; she herself had lived long enough to know that.

The first wild roses came out, then the labour began. Maud lay in the bed where Honor herself had given birth to Dick, Edwin, the Daneclere sons; young Uthred had been born at Thwaite. The midwife had come; a physician awaited call. Hawkin had not gone to his work, but sprawled on a bench in the downstairs office, making pretence to see to the accounts, his strong jaw set. Honor sat by Maud.

At first all was well. The pains came regularly, and after some hours a child was born. He was a boy, and to Honor's great thankfulness he was a true Thwaite, with red-gold hair. The women dried him and held him presently for Maud to see. She smiled, and whispered "He is so like," but no more.

Honor held the child, having sent a servant downstairs to tell Hawkin of his son's birth. Word came shortly that he waited without, uncertain of being permitted to enter the room full of women and their concerns. There was no fire, as it was summer; the posset they heated for Maud had been made ready in the downstairs kitchen, and she turned her head away and would not drink it or any wine.

Hawkin knelt down by the bedside; his eyes were full of tears. "Maud," he said. "Maud." He had not looked at his son. His gaze dwelt on his wife's face. She looked at him, but as though she did not see him. Presently it seemed as if she would have spoken, but no words came.

"He is a true Thwaite," said Honor softly. "Daneclere and Thwaite and Biding have their heir." He resembled Robin more than Edwin, she was thinking. One could sometimes tell with a newborn child, rather than later.

Hawkin gave a sudden sound between a sob and a gasp. Maud's face on the pillow was smiling now, but as the dead smile.

The priest whose direction Dick had left came and, with a fair white cloth spread for the wine and water, gave Extreme Unction to the dead woman. One could not tell, he said, exactly when death came; hearing was the last sense to go; she might still hear, and he anointed her.

Afterwards, Honor came back to where the baby lay in his wood cradle, and lifted him out and hushed him, lest he cry. He had a lusty voice, a Thwaite voice; she had heard it at his birth. Birth and death, the beginning and the end to which all came, had visited Daneclere that day. Presently she would go down to where Maud's body, still and beautiful, lay under its black velvet pall between lit candles. Already Maud belonged to the past; the future was in this child. She herself would not see him grow to manhood. But not even death should alter her course now. Robin Edwin Thwaite should be the heir to Daneclere, to Thwaite and, if his uncles did not marry, no doubt to Biding in time.

The three houses who fortunes had been so strangely linked would come together under one owner. Old Hawkin, her father, would have been pleased. Was she herself so cold, so far-sighted a woman that she would let this joy she felt override mourning, sorrow, bereavement, regret? But this was Maud's promise. The boy had been made, and was the heir. Maud now was with God, or perhaps still in the strange purgatory they believed in in her religion; soon, in whatever fashion, she would be at peace.

Honor held the child against her, feeling the warm softness of his young flesh against her old bones. She had lived her life, after all, to the full. The inheritance was safe.

She laid the sleeping heir back in his cradle, and turned away from the window and its view of Thwaite beyond the causeway.